# THE YEAR'S
# FINEST FANTASY

# THE YEAR'S FINEST FANTASY

## EDITED BY
## TERRY CARR

Published by
BERKLEY PUBLISHING CORPORATION

●

Distributed by
G.P. PUTNAM'S SONS, New York

Also by Terry Carr:

CIRQUE

# Table of Contents

# THE YEAR'S
# FINEST FANTASY

# Introduction

THE OLDEST FORM of fiction in the world is fantasy. The very earliest literary tablets and papyri known to us record tales of myth and wonders, starting with the famous Babylonian *Epic of Gilgamesh*, a quest story about a powerful warrior who travels beyond the borders of the known world searching for the secret of immortality; his adventures include battles with ferocious monsters and an account of a flood that has surprising parallels to the story of Noah as set down in the Bible a thousand years later.

(The *Gilgamesh* was a codification of various Babylonian myths that had been passed down for centuries by word of mouth; an unknown poet wove them together about 2,000 B.C. There's another Mesopotamian epic, *Enmarkar and the Lord of Aratta,* that may be even older. It too is a fantasy.)

Egypt was a land that has also given us several tales written down about 2,000 B.C.: the *Tales of the Magicians* also embody stories which had been told aloud for generations before. W. M. Flinders Petrie, who translated these Egyptian papyri and others near the end of the Victorian era in a book called *Egyptian Tales,* made a very interesting observation:

> The earliest is purely a collection of marvels or fabulous incidents.... Then we advance to contrasts between town and country, between Egypt and foreign lands. Then personal adventure, and the interest in schemes and successes, becomes the staple material; while only in later periods does character come in as the groundwork. The same may be seen in English literature—first the tales of wonders and strange lands, then the novel of adventure, and lastly the novel of character.

It's obvious from this that fantasy has always held a paramount

1

position in the interest of those who liked stories, and that the pattern didn't change from primitive times to our somewhat more sophisticated recent centuries. Fantasy stories themselves have become much more subtle—social observations and the exploration of character have been added to today's fantasy rather than supplanting it—but human fascination with the strange and frightening remains basic to our nature.

It would be difficult to compile a list of important authors whose works haven't included fantasies. Kipling? Shakespeare? Henry James? Du Maurier? Nabokov? Hawthorne? Updike? No; they all wrote fantasies, and very good ones too.

Of course, fantasy stories today aren't much like the collections of "marvels or fabulous incidents" that made up the earliest stories in written literature: current writers employ fantasy as a means of delving directly to the roots of the human psyche, and their explorations are enriched by a Twentieth Century understanding of *why* these manifestations of dreams and nightmares that have become real can say such important things to us.

Put simply: we are creatures of fantasy ourselves. We live our humdrum day-to-day lives as taxpayers, secretaries, computer programmers, husbands and wives, but our deepest existence still lives in fantasy. We are warriors using numbers as weapons, magicians at the stove, beings from other realities caught in a world where we must shuffle bits of photocopied paper from one tray to another pausing only to make mystic marks on them. We are, deep within us, monsters and heroes, succubi and muses, magicians and peasants.

The range of fantasy is inexhaustible. That's why this anthology of the finest fantasy stories of 1977 doesn't confine itself to bloody adventure or dark encounters with the inexplicable—our fantasies are about *everything*. An exploration of contemporary fantasy tells us more truly of the nature of humanity than any collection of "realistic" stories could. There are dangers here, yes, and horrors too—but there's also joy and wonder, triumphs and puzzles.

Fantasy is the oldest form of fiction because it's about the most profound forms of reality. Isn't that fantastic?

—TERRY CARR

# Jeffty Is Five
## by Harlan Ellison

*Harlan Ellison's fame as a writer of fantasy has come
primarily through dark, often angry tales of the
horrors that lurk in people's psyches, such as* Pretty
Maggie Moneyeyes *and* Croatoan. *Here he turns to a
more gentle, wistful story of progress and loss in
today's world. There's a good deal of joy in this story—
it's enormously entertaining to anyone who
remembers Captain Midnight Decoder Rings and
other epiphenomena of yesterday's youth—but as he
evokes this inner life of a child who managed never to
grow older, Ellison also says disquieting things about
the price that must be paid for holding onto the past.*

When I was five years old, there was a little kid I played with: Jeffty.
His real name was Jeff Kinzer, and everyone who played with him
called him Jeffty. We were five years old together, and we had good
times playing together.

When I was five, a Clark Bar was as fat around as the gripping end
of a Louisville Slugger, and pretty nearly six inches long, and they
used real chocolate to coat it, and it crunched very nicely when you bit
into the center, and the paper it came wrapped in smelled fresh and
good when you peeled off one end to hold the bar so it wouldn't melt
onto your fingers. Today, a Clark Bar is as thin as a credit card, they
use something artificial and awful-tasting instead of pure chocolate,
the thing is soft and soggy, it costs fifteen or twenty cents instead of a
decent, correct nickel, and they wrap it so you think it's the same size
it was twenty years ago, only it isn't; it's slim and ugly and nasty

3

tasting and not worth a penny, much less fifteen or twenty cents.

When I was that age, five years old, I was sent away to my Aunt Patricia's home in Buffalo, New York for two years. My father was going through "bad times," and Aunt Patricia was very beautiful and had married a stockbroker. They took care of me for two years. When I was seven, I came back home and went to find Jeffty, so we could play together.

I was seven. Jeffty was still five. I didn't notice any difference. I didn't know: I was only seven.

When I was seven years old I used to lie on my stomach in front of our Atwater Kent radio and listen to swell stuff. I had tied the ground wire to the radiator, and I would lie there with my coloring books and my Crayolas (when there were only sixteen colors in the big box), and listen to the NBC red network: Jack Benny on the Jell-O Program, Amos 'n' Andy, Edgar Bergen and Charlie McCarthy on the Chase and Sanborn Program, One Man's Family, First Nighter; the NBC blue network: Easy Aces, the Jergens Program with Walter Winchell, Information Please, Death Valley Days; and best of all, the Mutual Network with The Green Hornet, The Lone Ranger, The Shadow and Quiet Please. Today, I turn on my car radio and go from one end of the dial to the other and all I get is 100 strings orchestras, banal housewives and insipid truckers discussing their kinky sex lives with arrogant talk show hosts, country and western drivel and rock music so loud it hurts my ears.

When I was ten, my grandfather died of old age and I was "a troublesome kid," and they sent me off to military school, so I could be "taken in hand."

I came back when I was fourteen. Jeffty was still five.

When I was fourteen years old, I used to go to the movies on Saturday afternoons and a matinee was ten cents and they used real butter on the popcorn and I could always be sure of seeing a western like Lash LaRue, or Wild Bill Elliott as Red Ryder with Bobby Blake as Little Beaver, or Roy Rogers, or Johnny Mack Brown; a scary picture like *House of Horrors* with Rondo Hatton as the Strangler, or *The Cat People,* or *The Mummy,* or *I Married a Witch* with Fredric March and Veronica Lake; plus an episode of a great serial like The Shadow with Victor Jory, or Dick Tracy or Flash Gordon; and three cartoons; a James Fitzpatrick Travel Talk; Movietone News; a singalong and, if I stayed on till evening, Bingo or Keno; and free dishes. Today, I go to movies and see Clint Eastwood blowing people's heads apart like ripe cantaloupes.

At eighteen, I went to college. Jeffty was still five. I came back during the summers, to work at my Uncle Joe's jewelry store. Jeffty hadn't changed. Now I knew there was something wrong, something weird. Jeffty was still five years old, not a day older.

At twenty-two I came home for keeps. To open a Sony television franchise in town, the first one. I saw Jeffty from time to time. He was five.

Things are better in a lot of ways. People don't die from some of the old diseases any more. Cars go faster and get you there more quickly on better roads. Shirts are softer and silkier. We have paperback books even though they cost as much as a good hardcover used to. When I'm running short in the bank I can live off credit cards till things even out. But I still think we've lost a lot of good stuff. Did you know you can't buy linoleum any more, only vinyl floor covering? There's no such thing as oilcloth any more; you'll never again smell that special, sweet smell from your grandmother's kitchen. Furniture isn't made to last thirty years or longer because they took a survey and found that young homemakers like to throw their furniture out and bring in all new color-coded borax every seven years. Records don't feel right; they're not thick and solid like the old ones, they're thin and you can bend them ... that doesn't seem right to me. Restaurants don't serve cream in pitchers any more, just that artificial glop in little plastic tubs, and one is never enough to get coffee the right color. Everywhere you go, all the towns look the same with Burger Kings and MacDonald's and 7-Elevens and motels and shopping centers. Things may be better, but why do I keep thinking about the past?

What I mean by five years old is not that Jeffty was retarded. I don't think that's what it was. Smart as a whip for five years old; very bright, quick, cute, a funny kid.

But he was three feet tall, small for his age, and perfectly formed, no big head, no strange jaw, none of that. A nice, normal-looking five-year-old kid. Except that he was the same age as I was: twenty-two.

When he spoke, it was with the squeaking, soprano voice of a five year old; when he walked it was with the little hops and shuffles of a five year old; when he talked to you, it was about the concerns of a five year old... comic books, playing soldier, using a clothes pin to attach a stiff piece of cardboard to the front fork of his bike so the sound it made when the spokes hit was like a motorboat, asking questions like *why does that thing do that like that,* how high is up, how old is old, why is grass green, what's an elephant look like? At twenty-two, he was five.

Jeffty's parents were a sad pair. Because I was still a friend of Jeffty's, still let him hang around with me in the store, sometimes took him to the county fair or to the miniature golf or the movies, I wound up spending time with *them.* Not that I much cared for them, because they were so awfully depressing. But then, I suppose one couldn't expect much more from the poor devils. They had an alien thing in their home, a child who had grown no older than five in twenty-two years, who provided the treasure of that special childlike state indefinitely, but who also denied them the joys of watching the child grow into a normal adult.

Five is a wonderful time of life for a little kid... or it *can* be, if the child is relatively free of the monstrous beastliness other children indulge in. It is a time when the eyes are wide open and the patterns are not yet set; a time when one has not yet been hammered into accepting everything as immutable and hopeless; a time when the hands can not do enough, the mind cannot learn enough, the world is infinite and colorful and filled with mysteries. Five is a special time before they take the questing, unquenchable, quixotic soul of the young dreamer and thrust it into dreary schoolroom boxes. A time before they take the trembling hands that want to hold everything, touch everything, figure everything out, and make them lie still on desktops. A time before people begin saying "act your age" and "grow up" or "you're behaving like a baby." It is a time when a child who acts adolescent is still cute and responsive and everyone's pet. A time of delight, of wonder, of innocence.

Jeffty had been stuck in that time, just five, just so.

But for his parents it was an ongoing nightmare from which no one—not social workers, not priests, not child psychologists, not teachers, not friends, not medical wizards, not psychiatrists, no one— could slap or shake them awake. For seventeen years their sorrow had grown through stages of parental dotage to concern, from concern to worry, from worry to fear, from fear to confusion, from confusion to anger, from anger to dislike, from dislike to naked hatred, and finally, from deepest loathing and revulsion to a stolid, depressive acceptance.

John Kinzer was a shift foreman at the Balder Tool & Die plant. He was a thirty year man. To everyone but the man living it, his was a spectacularly uneventful life. In no way was he remarkable... save that he had fathered a twenty-two-year old five year old.

John Kinzer was a small man, soft, with no sharp angles, with pale eyes that never seemed to hold mine for longer than a few seconds. He continually shifted in his chair during conversations, and seemed to see things in the upper corners of the room, things no one else could see... or wanted to see. I suppose the word that best suited him was *haunted*. What his life had become... well, *haunted* suited him.

Leona Kinzer tried valiantly to compensate. No matter what hour of the day I visited, she always tried to foist food on me. And when Jeffty was in the house she was always at *him* about eating: "Honey, would you like an orange? A nice orange? Or a tangerine? I have tangerines. I could peel a tangerine for you." But there was clearly such fear in her, fear of her own child, that the offers of sustenance always had a faintly ominous tone.

Leona Kinzer had been a tall woman, but the years had bent her. She seemed always to be seeking some area of wallpapered wall or storage niche into which she could fade, adopt some chintz or rose-patterned protective coloration and hide forever in plain sight of the child's big brown eyes, pass her a hundred times a day and never realize she was there, holding her breath, invisible. She always had an apron tied around her waist. And her hands were red from cleaning. As if by maintaining the environment immaculately she could pay off her imagined sin: having given birth to this strange creature.

Neither of them watched television very much. The house was usually dead silent, not even the sibilant whispering of water in the pipes, the creaking of timbers settling, the humming of the refrigerator. Awfully silent, as if time itself had taken a detour around that house.

As for Jeffty, he was inoffensive. He lived in that atmosphere of gentle dread and dulled loathing, and if he understood it, he never remarked in any way. He played, as a child plays, and seemed happy. But he must have sensed, in the way of a five year old, just how alien he was in their presence.

Alien. No, that wasn't right. He was *too* human, if anything. But out of phase, out of synch with the world around him, and resonating to a different vibration than his parents, God knows. Nor would other children play with him. As they grew past him, they found him at first childish, then uninteresting, then simply frightening as their perceptions of aging became clear and they could see he was not affected by time as they were. Even the little ones, his own age, who might wander into the neighborhood, quickly came to shie away from him like a dog in the street when a car backfires.

Thus, I remained his only friend. A friend of many years. Five years. Twenty-two years. I liked him; more than I can say. And never knew exactly why. But I did, without reserve.

But because we spent time together, I found I was also—polite society—spending time with John and Leona Kinzer. Dinner, Saturday afternoons sometimes, an hour or so when I'd bring Jeffty back from a movie. They were grateful: slavishly so. It relieved them of the embarrassing chore of going out with him, of having to pretend before the world that they were loving parents with a perfectly normal, happy, attractive child. And their gratitude extended to hosting me. Hideous, every moment of their depression, hideous.

I felt sorry for the poor devils, but I despised them for their inability to love Jeffty, who was eminently lovable.

I never let on, even during the evenings in their company that were awkward beyond belief.

We would sit there in the darkening living room—*always* dark or darkening, as if kept in shadow to hold back what the light might reveal to the world outside through the bright eyes of the house—we would sit and silently stare at one another. They never knew what to say to me.

"So how are things down at the plant," I'd say to John Kinzer.

He would shrug. Neither conversation nor life suited him with any ease or grace. "Fine, just fine," he would say, finally.

And we would sit in silence again.

"Would you like a nice piece of coffee cake?" Leona would say. "I made it fresh just this morning." Or deep dish green apple pie. Or milk and toll house cookies. Or a brown betty pudding.

"No, no, thank you, Mrs. Kinzer; Jeffty and I grabbed a couple of cheeseburgers on the way home." And again, silence.

Then, when the stillness and the awkwardness became too much even for them (and who knew how long that total silence reigned when they were alone, with that thing they never talked about any more, hanging between them), Leona Kinzer would say, "I think he's asleep."

John Kinzer would say, "I don't hear the radio playing."

Just so, it would go on like that, until I could politely find excuse to bolt away on some flimsy pretext. Yes, that was the way it would go on, every time, just the same... except once.

"I don't know what to do any more," Leona said. She began crying. "There's no change, not one day of peace."

Her husband managed to drag himself out of the old easy chair and went to her. He bent and tried to soothe her, but it was clear from the graceless way in which he touched her graying hair that the ability to be compassionate had been stunted in him. "Shhh, Leona, it's all right. Shhh." But she continued crying. Her hands scraped gently at the antimacassars on the arms of the chair.

Then she said, "Sometimes I wish he had been stillborn."

John looked up into the corners of the room. For the nameless shadows that were always watching him? Was it God he was seeking in those spaces? "You don't mean that," he said to her, softly, pathetically, urging her with body tension and trembling in his voice to recant before God took notice of the terrible thought. But she meant it; she meant it very much.

I managed to get away quickly that evening. They didn't want witnesses to their shame. I was glad to go.

And for a week I stayed away. From them, from Jeffty, from their street, even from that end of town.

I had my own life. The store, accounts, suppliers' conferences, poker with friends, pretty women I took to well-lit restaurants, my own parents, putting anti-freeze in the car, complaining to the laundry about too much starch in the collars and cuffs, working out at the gym, taxes, catching Jan or David (whichever one it was) stealing from the cash register. I had my own life.

But not even *that* evening could keep me from Jeffty. He called me at the store and asked me to take him to the rodeo. We chummed it up as best a twenty-two year old with other interests could . . . with a five year old. I never dwelled on what bound us together; I always thought it was simply the years. That, and affection for a kid who could have been the little brother I never had. (Except I *remembered* when we had played together, when we had both been the same age; I *remembered* that period, and Jeffty was still the same.)

And then, one Saturday afternoon, I came to take him to a double feature, and things I should have noticed so many times before, I first began to notice only that afternoon.

I came walking up to the Kinzer house, expecting Jeffty to be sitting on the front porch steps, or in the porch glider, waiting for me. But he was nowhere in sight.

Going inside, into that darkness and silence, in the midst of May sunshine, was unthinkable. I stood on the front walk for a few moments, then cupped my hands around my mouth and yelled, "Jeffty? Hey, Jeffty, come on out, let's go. We'll be late."

His voice came faintly, as if from under the ground.

"Here I am, Donny."

I could hear him, but I couldn't see him. It was Jeffty, no question about it: as Donald H. Horton, President and Sole Owner of The Horton TV & Sound Center, no one but Jeffty called me Donny. He had never called me anything else.

(Actually, it isn't a lie. I *am*, as far as the public is concerned, Sole Owner of the Center. The partnership with my Aunt Patricia is only to repay the loan she made me, to supplement the money I came into when I was twenty-one, left to me when I was ten by my grandfather. It wasn't a very big loan, only eighteen thousand, but I asked her to be a silent partner, because of when she had taken care of me as a child.)

"Where are you, Jeffty?"

"Under the porch in my secret place."

I walked around the side of the porch, and stooped down and pulled away the wicker grating. Back in there, on the pressed dirt, Jeffty had built himself a secret place. He had comics in orange crates, he had a little table and some pillows, it was lit by big fat candles, and we used to hide there when we were both...five.

"What'cha up to?" I asked, crawling in and pulling the grate closed behind me. It was cool under the porch, and the dirt smelled comfortable, the candles smelled clubby and familiar. Any kid would feel at home in such a secret place: there's never been a kid who didn't spend the happiest, most productive, most deliciously mysterious times of his life in such a secret place.

"Playin'," he said. He was holding something golden and round. It filled the palm of his little hand.

"You forget we were going to the movies?"

"Nope. I was just waitin' for you here."

"Your mom and dad home?"

"Momma."

I understood why he was waiting under the porch. I didn't push it any further. "What've you got there?"

"Captain Midnight Secret Decoder Badge," he said, showing it to me on his flattened palm.

I realized I was looking at it without comprehending what it was for a long time. Then it dawned on me what a miracle Jeffty had in his hand. A miracle that simply could *not* exist.

"Jeffty," I said softly, with wonder in my voice, "where'd you get that?"

"Came in the mail today. I sent away for it."

"It must have cost a lot of money."

"Not so much. Ten cents an' two inner wax seals from two jars of Ovaltine."

"May I see it?" My voice was trembling, and so was the hand I extended. He gave it to me and I held the miracle in the palm of my hand. It was *wonderful*.

You remember. *Captain Midnight* went on the radio nationwide in 1940. It was sponsored by Ovaltine. And every year they issued a Secret Squadron Decoder Badge. And every day at the end of the program, they would give you a clue to the next day's installment in a code that only kids with the official badge could decipher. They stopped making those wonderful Decoder Badges in 1949. ›I remember the one I had in 1945; it was beautiful. It had a magnifying glass in the center of the code dial. *Captain Midnight* went off the air in 1950, and though it was a short-lived television series in the mid-Fifties, and though they issued Decoder Badges in 1955 and 1956, as far as the *real* badges were concerned, they never made one after 1949.

The Captain Midnight Code-O-Graph I held in my hand, the one Jeffty said he had gotten in the mail for ten cents *(ten cents!!!)* and two Ovaltine labels, was brand new, shiny gold metal, not a dent or a spot of rust on it like the old ones you can find at exorbitant prices in collectible shoppes from time to time... it was a *new* Decoder. And the date on it was *this* year.

But *Captain Midnight* no longer existed. Nothing like it existed on the radio. I'd listened to the one or two weak imitations of old-time radio the networks were currently airing, and the stories were dull, the sound effects bland, the whole feel of it wrong, out of date, cornball. Yet I held a *new* Code-O-Graph.

"Jeffty, tell me about this," I said.

"Tell you what, Donny? It's my new Capt'n Midnight Secret Decoder Badge. I use it to figger out what's gonna happen tomorrow."

"Tomorrow how?"

"On the program."

"*What* program?!"

He stared at me as if I was being purposely stupid. "On Capt'n *Mid*night! Boy!" I was being dumb.

I still couldn't get it straight. It was right there, right out in the open, and I still didn't know what was happening. "You mean one of those records they made of the oldtime radio programs? Is that what you mean, Jeffty?"

"What records?" he asked. He didn't know what *I* meant.

We stared at each other, there under the porch. And then I said, very slowly, almost afraid of the answer, "Jeffty, how do you hear *Captain Midnight?*"

"Every day. On the radio. On my radio. Every day at five-thirty."

News. Music, dumb music, and news. That's what was on the radio every day at five-thirty. Not *Captain Midnight*. The Secret Squadron hadn't been on the air in twenty years.

"Can we hear it tonight?" I asked.

"Boy!" He said. I was being dumb. I knew it from the way he said it; but I didn't know *why*. Then it dawned on me: this was Saturday. *Captain Midnight* was on Monday through Friday. Not on Saturday or Sunday.

"We goin' to the movies?"

He had to repeat himself twice. My mind was somewhere else. Nothing definite. No conclusions. No wild assumptions leapt to. Just off somewhere trying to figure it out, and concluding— as *you* would have concluded, as *anyone* would have concluded rather than accepting the truth, the impossible and wonderful truth—just finally concluding there was a simple explanation I didn't yet perceive. Something mundane and dull, like the passage of time that steals all good, old things from us, packratting trinkets and plastic in exchange. And all in the name of progress.

"We goin' to the movies, Donny?"

"You bet your boots we are, kiddo," I said. And I smiled. And I handed him the Code-O-Graph. And he put it in his side pants pocket. And we crawled out from under the porch. And we went to the movies. And neither of us said anything about *Captain Midnight* all the rest of that day. And there wasn't a ten-minute stretch, all the rest of that day, that I didn't think about it.

It was inventory all that next week. I didn't see Jeffty till late Thursday. I confess I left the store in the hands of Jan and David, told them I had some errands to run, and left early. At 4:00. I got to the Kinzer's right around 4:45. Leona answered the door, looking exhausted and distant. "Is Jeffty around?" She said he was upstairs in his room...

... listening to the radio.

I climbed the stairs two at a time.

All right, I had finally made that impossible, illogical leap. Had the stretch of belief involved anyone but Jeffty, adult or child, I would have reasoned out more explicable answers. But it *was* Jeffty, clearly another kind of vessel of life, and what he might experience should not be expected to fit into the ordered scheme.

I admit it: I *wanted* to hear what I heard.

Even with the door closed, I recognized the program:

"*There he goes, Tennessee! Get him!*"

There was the heavy report of a rifle shot and the keening whine of the slug ricocheting, and then the same voice yelled triumphantly, *"Got him! D-e-a-a-a-a-d center!"*

He was listening to the American Broadcasting Company, 790 kilocycles, and he was hearing *Tennessee Jed,* one of my most favorite programs from the Forties, a western adventure I had not heard in twenty years, because it had not existed for twenty years.

I sat down on the top step of the stairs, there in the upstairs hall of the Kinzer home, and I listened to the show. It wasn't a return of an old program, because there were occasional references in the body of the drama to current cultural and technological developments, and phrases that had not existed in common usage in the Forties: aerosol spray cans, laseracing of tattoos, Tanzania, the word "uptight."

I could not ignore the fact. Jeffty was listening to a *new* segment of *Tennessee Jed.*

I ran downstairs and out the front door to my car. Leona must have been in the kitchen. I turned the key and punched on the radio and spun the dial to 790 kilocycles. The ABC station. Rock music.

I sat there for a few moments, then ran the dial slowly from one end to the other. Music, news, talk shows. No *Tennessee Jed.* And it was a Blaupunkt, the best radio I could get. I wasn't missing some perimeter station. It simply was not there!

After a few moments I turned off the radio and the ignition and went back upstairs quietly. I sat down on the top step and listened to the entire program. It was *wonderful.*

Exciting, imaginative, filled with everything I remembered as being most innovative about radio drama. But it was modern. It wasn't an antique, re-broadcast to assuage the need of that dwindling listenership who longed for the old days. It was a new show, with all the old voices, but still young and bright. Even the commercials were for currently available products, but they weren't as loud or as insulting as the screamer ads one heard on radio these days.

And when *Tennessee Jed* went off at 5:00, I heard Jeffty spin the dial on his radio till I heard the familiar voice of the announcer Glenn Riggs proclaim, *"Presenting Hop Harrigan! America's ace of the air waves!"* There was the sound of an airplane, *not* a jet! Not the sound kids today have grown up with, but the sound *I* grew up with, the *real* sound of an airplane, the growling, revving, throaty sound of the kind of airplanes G-8 and His Battle Aces flew, the kind Captain Midnight flew, the kind Hop Harrigan flew. And then I heard Hop say, *"CX-4 calling control tower. CX-4 calling control tower. Standing by!"* A pause, then, *"Okay, this is Hop Harrigan . . . coming in!"*

And Jeffty, who had the same problem all of us kids had in the Forties with programming that pitted equal favorites against one another on different stations, having paid his respects to Hop Harrigan and Tank Tinker, spun the dial and went back to ABC where I heard the stroke of a gong, the wild cacophany of nonsense Chinese chatter, and the announcer yelled, *"T-e-e-e-rry and the Pirates!"*

I sat there on the top step and listened to Terry and Connie and Flip Corkin and, so help me God, Agnes Moorehead as The Dragon Lady, all of them in a new adventure that took place in a Red China that had not existed in the days of Milton Caniff's 1937 version of the Orient, with river pirates and Chiang Kai-shek and warlords and the naive Imperialism of American gunboat diplomacy.

Sat, and listened to the whole show, and sat even longer to hear *Superman* and part of *Jack Armstrong, the All-American boy,* and part of *Captain Midnight,* and John Kinzer came home and neither he nor Leona came upstairs to find out what had happened to me, or where Jeffty was, and sat longer, and found I had started crying, and could not stop, just sat there with tears running down my face, into the corners of my mouth, sitting and crying until Jeffty heard me and opened his door and saw me and came out and looked at me in childish confusion as I heard the station break for the Mutual Network and they began the theme music of *Tom Mix,* "When it's Round-up Time in Texas and the Bloom is on the Sage," and Jeffty touched my shoulder and smiled at me and said, "Hi, Donny. Wanna come in an' listen to the radio with me?"

Hume denied the existence of an absolute space, in which each thing has its place; Borges denies the existence of one single time, in which all events are linked.

Jeffty received radio programs from a place that could not, in logic, in the natural scheme of the space-time universe as conceived by Einstein, exist. But that wasn't all he received. He got mail-order premiums that no one was manufacturing. He read comic books that had been defunct for three decades. He saw movies with actors who had been dead for twenty years. He was the receiving terminal for endless joys and pleasures of the past that the world had dropped along the way. On its headlong suicidal flight toward New Tomorrows, the world had razed its treasurehouse of simple happiness, had poured concrete over its playgrounds, had abandoned its elfin stragglers, and all of it was being impossibly, miraculously shunted back into the present through Jeffty. Revivified, updated, the traditions maintained but contemporaneous. Jeffty was the unbidding Aladdin whose very nature formed the magic lampness of his reality.

And he took me into his world.

Because he trusted me.

We had breakfast of Quaker Puffed Wheat Sparkies and warm Ovaltine we drank out of *this* year's little Orphan Annie Shake-Up Mugs. We went to the movies and while everyone else was seeing a comedy starring Goldie Hawn and Ryan O'Neal, Jeffty and I were enjoying Humphrey Bogart as the professional thief Parker in John Huston's brilliant adaptation of the Donald Westlake novel, *Slayground*. The second feature was Spencer Tracy, Carole Lombard and Laird Cregar in the Val Lewton-produced film of *Leinengen Versus the Ants*.

Twice a month we went down to the newsstand and bought the current pulp issues of *The Shadow, Doc Savage* and *Startling Stories*. Jeffty and I sat together and I read to him from the magazines. He particularly liked the new short novel by Henry Kuttner, "The Dreams of Achilles," and the new Stanley G. Weinbaum series of short stories set in the subatomic particle universe of Redurna. In September we enjoyed the first installment of the new Robert E. Howard Conan novel, ISLE OF THE BLACK ONES, in *Weird Tales*; and in August were only mildly disappointed by Edgar Rice Burroughs' fourth novella in the Jupiter series featuring John Carter of Barsoom—"Corsairs of Jupiter." But the editor of *Argosy All-Story Weekly* promised there would be two more stories in the series, and it was such an unexpected revelation for Jeffty and me, that it dimmed our disappointment at the lessened quality of the current story.

We read comics together, and Jeffty and I both decided—

separately, before we came together to discuss it—that our favorite characters were Doll Man, Airboy and The Heap. We also adored the George Carlson strips in *Jingle Jangle Comics,* particularly the Pie-Face Prince of Old Pretzleburg stories, which we read together and laughed over, even though I had to explain some of the subtler puns to Jeffty, who was too young to have that kind of subtle wit.

How to explain it? I can't. I had enough physics in college to make some offhand guesses, but I'm more likely wrong than right. The laws of the conservation of energy occasionally break. These are laws that physicists call "weakly violated." Perhaps Jeffty was a catalyst for the weak violation of conservation laws we're only now beginning to realize exist. I tried doing some reading in the area—muon decay of the "forbidden" kind: gamma decay that doesn't include the muon neutrino among its products—but nothing I encountered, not even the latest readings from the Swiss Institute for Nuclear Research near Zurich gave me an insight. I was thrown back on a vague acceptance of the philosophy that the real name for "science" is *magic.*

No explanations, but enormous good times.

The happiest time of my life.

I had the "real" world, the world of my store and my friends and my family, the world of profit and loss, of taxes and evenings with young women who talked about going shopping or the United Nations, of the rising cost of coffee and microwave ovens. And I had Jeffty's world, in which I existed only when I was with him. The things of the past he knew as fresh and new, I could experience only when in his company. And the membrane between the two worlds grew ever thinner, more luminous and transparent. I had the best of both worlds. And knew, somehow, that I could carry nothing from one to the other.

Forgetting that, for just a moment, betraying Jeffty by forgetting, brought an end to it all.

Enjoying myself so much, I grew careless and failed to consider how fragile the relationship between Jeffty's world and my world really was. There is a reason why the present begrudges the existence of the past. I never really understood. Nowhere in the beast books, where survival is shown in battles between claw and fang, tentacle and poison sac, is there recognition of the ferocity the present always brings to bear on the past. Nowhere is there a detailed statement of how the present lies in wait for What-Was, waiting for it to become Now-This-Moment so it can shred it with its merciless jaws.

Who could know such a thing...at any age...and certainly not at my age...who could understand such a thing?

I'm trying to exculpate myself. I can't. It was my fault.

It was another Saturday afternoon.

"What's playing today?" I asked him, in the car, on the way downtown.

He looked up at me from the other side of the front seat and smiled one of his best smiles. "Ken Maynard in *Bullwhip Justice* an' *The Demolished Man.*" He kept smiling, as if he'd really put one over on me. I looked at him with disbelief.

"You're *kid*ding!" I said, delighted. Bester's THE DEMOLISHED MAN?" He nodded his head, delighted at my being delighted. He knew it was one of my favorite books. "Oh, that's super!"

"Super *duper*," he said.

"Who's in it?"

"Franchot Tone, Evelyn Keyes, Lionel Barrymore and Elisha Cook, Jr." He was much more knowledgeable about movie actors than I'd ever been. He could name the character actors in any movie he'd ever seen. Even the crowd scenes.

"And cartoons?" I asked.

"Three of 'em, a *Little Lulu*, a *Donald Duck* and a *Bugs Bunny*. An' a *Pete Smith Specialty* an' a *Lew Lehr Monkeys is da C-r-r-raziest Peoples.*"

"Oh boy!" I said. I was grinning from ear to ear. And then I looked down and saw the pad of purchase order forms on the seat. I'd forgotten to drop it off at the store.

"Gotta stop by the Center," I said. "Gotta drop off something. It'll only take a minute."

"Okay," Jeffty said. "But we won't be late, will we?"

"Not on your tintype, kiddo," I said.

When I pulled into the parking lot behind the Center, he decided to come in with me and we'd walk over to the theater. It's not a large town. There are only two movie houses, the Utopia and the Lyric. We were going to the Utopia, only three blocks from the Center.

I walked into the store with the pad of forms, and it was bedlam. David and Jan were handling two customers each, and there were people standing around waiting to be helped. Jan turned a look on me and her face was a horror-mask of pleading. David was running from the stockroom to the showroom and all he could murmur as he whipped past was, "Help!" and then he was gone.

"Jeffty," I said, crouching down, "listen, give me a few minutes. Jan and David are in trouble with all these people. We won't be late, I promise. Just let me get rid of a couple of these customers." He looked nervous, but nodded okay.

I motioned to a chair and said, "Just sit down for a while and I'll be right with you."

He went to the chair, good as you please, though he knew what was happening, and he sat down.

I started taking care of people who wanted color television sets. This was the first really substantial batch of units we'd gotten in—color television was only now becoming reasonably priced and this was Sony's first promotion—and it was bonanza time for me. I could see paying off the loan and being out in front for the first time with the Center. It was business.

In my world, good business comes first.

Jeffty sat there and stared at the wall. Let me tell you about the wall.

Stanchion and bracket designs had been rigged from floor to within two feet of the ceiling. Television sets had been stacked artfully on the wall. Thirty-three television sets. All playing at the same time. Black and white, color, little ones, big ones, all going at the same time.

Jeffty sat and watched thirty-three television sets, on a Saturday afternoon. We can pick up a total of thirteen channels including the UHF educational stations. Golf was on one channel; baseball was on a second; celebrity bowling was on a third; the fourth channel was a religious seminar; a teen-age dance show was on the fifth; the sixth was a rerun of a situation comedy; the seventh was a rerun of a police show; eighth was a nature program showing a man flycasting endlessly; ninth was news and conversation; tenth was a stock car race; eleventh was a man doing logarithms on a blackboard; twelfth was a woman in a leotard doing sitting-up exercises; and on the thirteenth channel was a badly-animated cartoon show in Spanish. All but six of the shows were repeated on three sets. Jeffty sat and watched that wall of television on a Saturday afternoon while I sold as fast and as hard as I could, to pay back my Aunt Patricia and stay in touch with my world. It was business.

I should have known better. I should have understood about the present and the way it kills the past. But I was selling with both hands. And when I finally glanced over at Jeffty, half an hour later, he looked like another child.

He was sweating. That terrible fever sweat when you have stomach flu. He was pale, as pasty and pale as a worm, and his little hands were gripping the arms of the chair so tightly I could see his knuckles in bold relief. I dashed over to him, excusing myself from the middle-aged couple looking at the new 21″ Mediterranean model.

'Jeffty!"

He looked at me, but his eyes didn't track. He was in absolute terror. I pulled him out of the chair and started toward the front door with him, but the customers I'd deserted yelled at me, "Hey!" The middle-aged man said, "You wanna sell me this thing or don't you?"

I looked from him to Jeffty and back again. Jeffty was like a zombie. He had come where I'd pulled him. His legs were rubbery and his feet dragged. The past, being eaten by the present, the sound of something in pain.

I clawed some money out of my pants pocket and jammed it into Jeffty's hand. "Kiddo...listen to me...get out of here right now!" He still couldn't focus properly. "*Jeffty,*" I said as tightly as I could, "*listen* to me!" The middle-aged customer and his wife were walking toward us. "Listen, kiddo, get out of here right this minute. Walk over to the Utopia and buy the tickets. I'll be right behind you." The middle-aged man and his wife were almost on us. I shoved Jeffty through the door and watched him stumble away in the wrong direction, then stop as if gathering his wits, turn and go back past the front of the Center and in the direction of the Utopia. "Yes sir," I said, straightening up and facing them, "yes, ma'am, that is one terrific set with some sen*sa*tional features! If you'll just step back here with me..."

There was a terrible sound of something hurting, but I couldn't tell from which channel, or from which set, it was coming.

• • •

Most of it I learned later, from the girl in the ticket booth, and from some people I knew who came to me to tell me what had happened. By the time I got to the Utopia, nearly twenty minutes later, Jeffty was already beaten to a pulp and had been taken to the Manager's office.

"Did you see a very little boy, about five years old, with big brown eyes and straight brown hair ... he was waiting for me?"

"Oh, I think that's the little boy those kids beat up?"

"What!?! *Where is he?*"

"They took him to the Manager's office. No one knew who he was or where to find his parents—"

A young girl wearing an usher's uniform was placing a wet paper towel on his face.

I took the towel away from her and ordered her out of the office. She looked insulted and snorted something rude, but she left. I sat on the edge of the couch and tried to swab away the blood from the lacerations without opening the wounds where the blood had caked. Both his eyes were swollen shut. His mouth was ripped badly. His hair was matted with dried blood.

He had been standing in line behind two kids in their teens. They started selling tickets at 12:30 and the show started at 1:00. The doors weren't opened till 12:45. He had been waiting, and the kids in front of him had had a portable radio. They were listening to the ballgame. Jeffty had wanted to hear some program, God knows what it might have been, *Grand Central Station, Land of the Lost,* God only knows which one it might have been.

He had asked if he could borrow their radio to hear the program for a minute, and it had been a commercial break or something, and the kids had given him the radio, probably out of some malicious kind of courtesy that would permit them to take offense and rag the little boy. He had changed the station ... and they'd been unable to get it to go back to the ballgame. It was locked into the past, on a station that was broadcasting a program that didn't exist for anyone but Jeffty.

They had beaten him badly ... as everyone watched.

And then they had run away.

I had left him alone, left him to fight off the present without sufficient weaponry. I had betrayed him for the sale of a 21″ Mediterranean console television, and now his face was pulped meat. He moaned something inaudible and sobbed softly.

"Shhh, it's okay, kiddo, it's Donny. I'm here. I'll get you home, it'll be okay."

I should have taken him straight to the hospital. I don't know why I didn't. I should have. I should have done that.

When I carried him through the door, John and Leona Kinzer just stared at me. They didn't move to take him from my arms. One of his hands was hanging down. He was conscious, but just barely. They stared, there in the semi-darkness of a Saturday afternoon in the present. I looked at them. "A couple of kids beat him up at the theater." I raised him a few inches in my arms and extended him. They stared at me, at both of us, with nothing in their eyes, without movement. "Jesus Christ," I shouted, "he's been beaten! He's your son! Don't you even want to touch him? What the hell kind of people are you?!"

Then Leona moved toward me very slowly. She stood in front of us for a few seconds, and there was a leaden stoicism in her face that was terrible to see. It said, *I have been in this place before, many times, and I cannot bear to be in it again; but I am here now.*

So I gave him to her. God help me, I gave him over to her.

And she took him upstairs to bathe away his blood and his pain.

John Kinzer and I stood in our separate places in the dim living room of their home, and we stared at each other. He had nothing to say to me.

I shoved past him and fell into a chair. I was shaking.

I heard the bath water running upstairs.

After what seemed a very long time Leona came downstairs, wiping her hands on her apron. She sat down on the sofa and after a moment John sat down beside her. I heard the sound of rock music from upstairs.

"Would you like a piece of nice pound cake?" Leona said.

I didn't answer. I was listening to the sound of the music. Rock music. On the radio. There was a table lamp on the end table beside the sofa. It cast a dim and futile light in the shadowed living room.

Rock music from the present, on a radio upstairs? I started to say something, and then knew...

I jumped up just as the sound of hideous crackling blotted out the music, and the table lamp dimmed and dimmed and flickered. I screamed something, I don't know what it was, and ran for the stairs.

Jeffty's parents did not move. They sat there with their hands folded, in that place they had been for so many years.

I fell twice rushing up the stairs.

There isn't much on television that can hold my interest. I bought an old cathedral-shaped Philco radio in a second-hand store, and I replaced all the burnt-out parts with the original tubes from old radios I could cannibalize that still worked. I don't use transistors or printed circuits. They wouldn't work. I've sat in front of that set for hours sometimes, running the dial back and forth as slowly as you can imagine, so slowly it doesn't look as if it's moving at all sometimes.

But I can't find *Captain Midnight* or *The Land of the Lost* or *The Shadow* or *Quiet Please*.

So she did love him, still, a little bit, even after all those years. I can't hate them: they only wanted to live in the present world again. That isn't such a terrible thing.

It's a good world, all things considered. It's much better than it used to be, in a lot of ways. People don't die from the old diseases any more. They die from new ones, but that's progress, isn't it?

Isn't it?

Tell me.

Somebody please tell me.

# The Bagful of Dreams
## by Jack Vance

*Jack Vance has been building the mythos of The Dying Earth throughout his writing career; when he was in the Navy during World War II, Vance began writing evocative stories of the distant future of our people, when science has been so long forgotten that it's returned to the status of magic, and even the sun is guttering and dying. Those early stories, rewritten to form a mosaic of the far future, were published together as The Dying Earth in 1950; though the book appeared as an obscure paperback from a short-lived publishing company, The Dying Earth was quickly recognized as a classic by aficionadoes and led to a sequel in 1966, The Eyes of the Overworld, which followed the adventures of the rogue-adventurer Cugel the Clever in this strange world.*

*Vance has recently returned to writing of Cugel and his twilight world, and The Bagful of Dreams is one of the new cycle of stories that will eventually make up a third book. The magic is still here ... along with wit, colorful imagination, and a certain realistic cynicism about the follies of humanity that will remain as long as people are people.*

From Troon the road wandered apparently at random among those curious hills known as the Chaim Purpure, sometimes in wan maroon sunlight, as often in the cold black shadow cast by the northern slopes. Cugel, noting the crumbled tombs, the straggling copses of black yew, the inexplicable clefts and wafts of unfamiliar odors, marched at best speed, and presently, without incident, descended upon the Tsombol Marsh. Cugel heaved a sigh of relief, then in the same breath muttered an imprecation against the Tsombol Marsh and the vicissitudes to be expected from a region so bleak and dank.

As before the road went by an indirect route, swinging around bogs and stagnant ponds, detouring to follow the bed of an ancient highway, sometimes swerving and veering for no obvious purpose whatever. To the further annoyance of Cugel, a cold wind now blew down from the north, bending the reeds, rippling water, flapping the cloak past Cugel's legs. Pulling the long-billed hat over his ears, he hunched his shoulders and walked at a bent-kneed lope, the better to evade the chill.

The wind blew the sky clear of all obscurity; the landscape was presented to the eye as if under a fine lens, with remarkable detail, contrast and clarity; but Cugel took no satisfaction in the silence and scope of this ancient peneplain, and when he scanned the dark blue sky, he noted only a far *pelgrane,* cruising down the wind. Cugel halted and stood frozen until the creature had disappeared, then continued even more briskly than before.

As the afternoon advanced the wind became capricious, blowing first in gusts, then stopping short for periods of unnatural quiet. During these intervals, Cugel thought to hear water-wefkins, hiding behind tussocks and calling to him in the sweet voices of unhappy maidens: "Cugel, oh Cugel! why do you travel in haste? Come to my bower and comb my beautiful green hair!" And "Cugel, oh Cugel! where do you go? Take me with you, to share the pleasure of your journey!" And "Cugel, beloved Cugel! The day is dying, the year is at an end! Come visit me behind the tussock, and we will console each other's grief!"

Cugel walked only the faster, ever more anxious to discover shelter for the night; and as the sun trembled at the edge of Tsombol Marsh he found a small inn, secluded under five dire oaks. He gratefully took accommodation for the night, and the innkeeper, a tall man with a pompous abdomen and a round red face folded into creases of chronic joviality, set out an adequate supper of stewed herbs, glisters, reed-cake, and thick warm acorn beer. As Cugel ate, the innkeeper put a question: "I see by your garments that you are a man of style and dignity; still you cross Tsombol Marsh on foot: is this not an incongruity?"

"No doubt," said Cugel, "but sometimes I consider myself the single honorable man in a world of rogues and tricksters. Under such circumstances it is hard to accumulate wealth."

The innkeeper pulled thoughtfully at his chin. "Your difficulties have aroused my sympathy. Tonight I will consider on the matter."

The innkeeper was as good as his word and on the morning, after Cugel had finished his breakfast, he brought forward a large dun-colored beast with powerful hind legs, a tufted tail, and a broad snout, already bridled and saddled for riding. "The least I can do to ease your plight," said the innkeeper, "is to sell you this beast at a nominal figure. Agreed, it lacks elegance, and in fact is a hybrid of dounge and felukhary. Still it moves with an easy stride; it feeds upon inexpensive wastes, and is notorious for its stubborn loyalty."

"All very well," said Cugel. "I appreciate your altruism, but for so ungainly a creature any price whatever is bound to be excessive. Notice the sores at the base of the tail, the eczema along the back, and unless I am mistaken the creature lacks an eye."

"Trifles!" declared the innkeeper. "Do you want a dependable steed to carry you across the Plain of Standing Stones, or an adjunct to your vanity? The beast becomes your property for a mere thirty terces."

Cugel jumped back in shock. "When a fine Cambalese wheriot sells for twenty? My dear fellow, your generosity outreaches my capacity to pay!"

The innkeeper's face expressed only patience and affability. "Here, in the middle of Tsombol Marsh, you will buy not even the smell of a dead wheriot."

"The discussion has become abstract and farfetched," said Cugel. "On a practical level, I insist that your price is outrageous."

For an instant the innkeeper's face lost its genial cast and he spoke in a grumbling voice: "Every person to whom I sell this steed takes the same advantage of my kindliness."

Cugel found the remark somewhat cryptic but nevertheless, detecting irresolution, he pressed his advantage. "In spite of a dozen misgivings I offer a generous twelve terces."

"Done!" cried the innkeeper almost before Cugel had finished speaking. "I repeat, you will discover this beast to be totally loyal, even beyond your expectations."

Cugel paid over twelve terces and gingerly mounted the creature. The landlord gave him a benign farewell. "May you enjoy a safe and comfortable journey!"

Cugel replied in like fashion: "May your enterprises prosper!" In order to make a brave departure, he tried to rein the beast around and about in a caracole, but it merely hunched low to the ground, and padded out upon the road.

A mile Cugel rode in comfort, and another, and taking all with all, was favorably impressed with his acquisition. "No question but what the beast walks on soft feet; now let us discover if it will canter at speed."

He shook out the reins; the beast set off down the road, its gait a unique prancing strut, with tail arched and head held high, which Cugel thought must surely make him the object of ridicule. He kicked his heels into the creature's heaving flanks. "Faster then, at all speed; let us test your mettle!"

The beast sprang forward with great energy, and the breeze blew Cugel's cloak flapping behind his shoulders. A massive dire oak stood beside a bend in the road, an object which the beast seemed to identify as a landmark. It increased its pace, only to stop suddenly short and elevate its hindquarters, projecting Cugel into the ditch. When he managed to stagger back up on the road, he discovered the beast cavorting across the marsh, in the general direction of the inn.

"A loyal creature indeed!" growled Cugel. "It is unswervingly faithful to the comfort of its barn." He found his black and green hat, clapped it back upon his head and trudged south along the road.

During the late afternoon he came to a village of a dozen mud huts populated by a squat long-armed folk, distinguished by great shocks of whitewashed hair, arranged in original and fanciful styles. Cugel gauged the height of the sun, then examined the terrain ahead, which extended in a dreary succession of tussocks and ponds to the edge of vision. Putting aside all fastidiousness, he approached the largest and most pretentious of the huts.

He found the master of the house sitting on a bench to the side, whitewashing the hair of one of his children into a style of long radiating tufts, like the petals of a white chrysanthemum, while a number of other urchins played nearby in the mud. "Good afternoon," said Cugel. "I am anxious to learn if you can provide me food and lodging for the night, naturally for adequate recompense."

"I will feel privileged to do so," replied the householder. "This is the most commodious hut of Sampsetiska, and I am notorious across the village for my fund of anecdotes. Do you care to inspect the premises?"

"I would be pleased to rest an hour in my chamber before indulging myself in a hot bath."

His host blew out his cheeks, and wiping the whitewash from his hands beckoned Cugel into the hut, where he pointed to a heap of reeds at the side of the room. "There is your bed; recline at your convenience for as long as you wish. As for a bath, the ponds of the swamp are infested with threlkoids and wire-worms, and cannot be recommended."

"In that case," said Cugel, "I will do without. However, I have not eaten since breakfast, and I am willing to take my evening meal as soon as possible."

"My spouse has gone trapping in the swamp," said his host. "It is premature to discuss supper until we learn what she has gleaned from her toil."

In due course the woman returned carrying a wet sack and a wicker basket. She built up a fire and prepared the evening meal, while Erwig the householder brought forth a two-string guitar and all through the twilight entertained Cugel with ballads of the region.

At last the woman called Cugel and Erwig into the hut, where she served bowls of gruel, dishes of fried moss and ganions, lumps of black bread.

After the meal Erwig thrust his spouse and children out into the night. "What we have to say is unsuitable for unsophisticated ears," he explained. "This gentleman is an important traveler and does not wish to measure his every word." Bringing out an earthenware jug, Erwig poured two tots of arrak, one of which he placed before Cugel, then disposed himself for conversation. "Whence came you and where are you bound?"

Cugel tasted the arrak, which scorched the entire interior of his glottal cavity. "I am native to that noble land known as Almery, and I return to this same locality."

"Almery?" mused Erwig. "This is a name beyond my knowing."

"It lies a far distance to the south, with many regions intervening."

Erwig scratched his head in perplexity. "I am accounted a sagacious man; still I cannot divine why you travel so far and so perilously only to return again to the same place."

"In this regard I must blame the malice of my enemies. They have dealt me incalculable harm, and upon my return to Almery I intend to exact a remarkable revenge."

"Nothing is more soothing to the spirit," Erwig agreed. "An immediate obstacle to your plans, however, is the Plain of Standing Stones, by reason of the grues and asms which haunt this particular tract. I might add that pelgrane rove the skies. When you pass beyond the plain and enter the land of Ombalique, you may count yourself a lucky man."

Cugel gave the heavy-bladed knife he had taken from the slaughterhouse at Troon a meaningful twitch. "I am known as Cugel the Clever, and I am not without experience of such creatures. Still I prefer to avoid them. What is the distance to the Plain of Standing Stones, and how long is required to cross?"

"Two miles south the ground rises and the plain begins. The road proceeds in an erratic fashion from sarsen to sarsen for a distance of fifteen miles. A stout-hearted wayfarer will cross the plain in four to five hours, assuming that he is not delayed or halted totally by interference from the creatures I have mentioned. The town Cuirnif is then another hour beyond."

"It is said that an inch of foreknowledge is worth ten miles of afterthought—"

"Well spoken!" cried Erwig, swallowing a gulp of arrak.

"—and in this regard, may I inquire your opinion of Cuirnif? What reception may I expect? Are the folk notably eccentric?"

"To some extent," replied Erwig. "They use no whitewash in their hair; and they are slack in their religious observances, making obeisance to Divine Wiulio with the right hand on the abdomen, instead of upon the left buttock, which we here consider a slipshod practice. What is your opinion?"

"The rite should be conducted as you describe," said Cugel. "No other method carries weight."

Erwig refilled Cugel's glass. "I consider this an important endorsement of our views, coming as it does from you, an expert traveler!"

The door opened and Erwig's spouse looked into the hut. "The night is dark, a bitter wind blows from the north, and a black beast prowls at the edge of the marsh."

"Stand among the shadows; Divine Wiulio protects his own. It is unthinkable that you and your brats should annoy our guest."

The woman grudgingly closed the door and returned into the night. Erwig pulled himself forward on his stool and swallowed a quantity of arrak. "The folk of Cuirnif, as I say, are strange enough, but their ruler, Duke Orbal, surpasses them in every category. He devotes himself to the study of marvels and prodigies, and every wandering phantasmagorian, each jack-leg magician with two spells in his head is feted and celebrated and treated to the best of the city."

"A bizarre predilection indeed!" declared Cugel.

Again the door opened and the woman looked into the hut. Erwig put down his glass and frowned over his shoulder. "Well, woman, what is it this time?"

"The beast is now moving among the huts. For all we know it also worships Wiulio."

Erwig attempted argument, but the woman's face became obdurate. "Your guest might as well forego his niceties now as later, since we all, in any event, must sleep on the same heap of reeds." She threw wide the door and commanded her urchins into the hut. Erwig, assured that no further conversation was possible, threw himself upon the reeds, and Cugel followed soon after.

In the morning Cugel breakfasted on ash-cake and herb tea, and prepared to take his departure. Erwig accompanied him to the road. "You have made a favorable impression upon me, and I will assist you across the Plain of Standing Stones. At the first opportunity take up a large pebble the size of your fist and make the trigrammatic sign upon it. If you are attacked, hold high the pebble and cry out: 'Stand aside! I carry a sacred object!' At the first sarsen, deposit the stone and select another from the pile, again make the sign and carry it to the second sarsen, and so across the plain. You still must avoid the notice of pelgrane, as they lack all religious feeling. So then: farewell, and the next time you pass be certain to halt at my hut."

"I suspect that you will never see me again," declared Cugel. "However, if all goes well, a certain Iucounu, known as the Laughing Magician, may in due course come past and I will recommend him to your hospitality."

"It shall be as you wish."

Cugel set forth down the road, which presently angled up to a flat gray plain studded at intervals with twelve-foot pillars of gray stone. Cugel found a large pebble, and placing his right hand on his left buttock made a profound salute to the object. He intoned: "I commend this pebble to the attention of Wiulio! I request that it protect me across this dismal plain!"

He scrutinized the landscape, but aside from the sarsens and the long black shadows laid by the cool red morning sun, he discovered nothing worthy of attention, and thankfully set off along the road.

He had traveled no more than a hundred yards when he felt a presence and whirling about discovered an asm of eight fangs almost on his heels. Cugel held high the pebble and cried out: "Away with you! I carry a sacred object and I do not care to be molested!"

The asm spoke in a soft blurred voice: "Wrong! You carry an ordinary pebble. I watched and you scamped the rite. Flee if you wish; I need the exercise."

"Does the wrath of Wiulio mean nothing to you?" demanded Cugel.

"The question is irrelevant." The asm advanced. Cugel threw the stone with all his force; it stuck the broad black forehead between the bristling antennae, and the asm fell flat; before it could rise Cugel had severed its head.

He started to proceed, then turned back and took up the stone. "Who knows who guided the throw so accurately? Wiulio deserves the benefit of the doubt."

At the first sarsen, he exchanged stones as the peasant had recommended and continued across the plain and so the day went. The sun lurched up to the zenith in a series of asthenic spasms, rested quietly a period, then descended westward with exaggerated caution, like a rheumatic old man groping his way down an untrustworthy ladder.

Whether or not by virtue of his sacred stones, Cugel marched unmolested from sarsen to sarsen, though on several occasions he noted pelgrane sliding across the sky and flung himself flat to avoid attention. Ahead a line of low hills appeared and Cugel discerned the shadow of a steep-sided valley. He increased his pace, gratified to have crossed the plain in safety, and so perhaps relaxed his vigilance, for high in the sky behind him sounded a scream of wild triumph.

Cugel fled in a panic and plunged over the edge of the ravine, where he dodged among rocks and pressed himself into the shadows. Down swooped the pelgrane, past and beyond, warbling with joyful excitement: a sound now joined by a human voice raised in outcries and curses.

Cugel stole forward and discovered that, not fifty yards distant, the pelgrane had alighted and now pursued a portly black-haired man in a loose suit of black-and-white diaper. The man took refuge behind an olophar tree, and the pelgrane chased him this way and that, clashing its fangs, snatching with its great clawed hands.

Cugel cautiously crept out upon a little bluff and hid himself in the shrubbery. For all his rotundity, the man showed remarkable deftness in evading the lunges of the pelgrane, although sweat trickled down his plump cheeks and into the short beard which hung below his chin.

The pelgrane, becoming frustrated, began to scream incoherent invective; it halted to glare through the crotch in the tree and snap with its great maw. On a whimsical impulse Cugel stole down the bank until he reached a point directly above the pelgrane; selecting an appropriate moment, he jumped, to land with both feet on the creature's head, forcing the neck down into the crotch.

"Now," said Cugel to the startled man, "if you will be good enough to fetch a stout cord we will bind this abominable beast securely in place."

"Why show it such mercy?" cried the man. "Did you see how it pursued me? It must be killed and instantly! Move your foot, so that I may hack away its head."

"Not so fast," said Cugel. "For all its faults, it is a valuable specimen to which I have laid claim, and I intend to protect my interests."

"Your claim is not altogether valid," stated the man after a moment of reflection. "I lured it down within reach and I was just about to stun it when you interfered."

Cugel shrugged. "As you like. I will take my weight off the creature's neck and go my way."

The man in the black-and-white suit made an irritable gesture. "Why go to ridiculous extremes merely to score a rhetorical point? I have a suitable cord over yonder."

The two men dropped a branch over the pelgrane's head and

bound it securely in place. The man, who had introduced himself as Iolo the Dream-taker, asked: "Exactly what value do you place upon this creature, and why?"

"It has come to my attention," said Cugel, "That Orbal, Duke of Ombalique is an amateur of oddities. Surely he would pay well for such a monster, perhaps as much as a hundred terces."

"Your remarks are to the point," Iolo admitted. "Are you sure that the bonds are secure?"

Cugel tested the ropes and in so doing noticed an ornament consisting of a gold chain and blue glass egg attached to the creature's crest. Cugel reached to remove the object but Iolo's hand was there almost as soon. Cugel shouldered Iolo aside and disengaged the amulet, but Iolo instantly caught hold of the chain and the two glared eye to eye.

"I beg you to release your avid grip upon my property," said Cugel in an icy voice.

"Have you no respect for justice?" demanded Iolo. "The object is mine since I saw it first."

"You are talking mischievous nonsense," said Cugel. "If you recall, I removed the trinket from the pelgrane's crest, and you tried to snatch it from my hand."

Iolo stamped his foot in a fury. "I refuse to be domineered!" And Iolo sought to wrest the object from Cugel's grasp. The two men stumbled and fell against the bank; the blue glass egg fell to the ground and shattered in an explosion of blue smoke, to create a hole into the hillside from which a golden-gray tentacle instantly thrust forth to seize Cugel's leg.

Iolo sprang back and watched Cugel's attempts to avoid being drawn into the hole. Cugel called out: "Quick! Fetch a cord and tie the tentacle to yonder stump; otherwise it will drag me into the hill!"

Iolo spoke in a measured voice: "Avarice has brought this fate upon you; I am reluctant to interfere. Additionally, I have but one cord: that binding the pelgrane."

"Kill the pelgrane," panted Cugel. "Put the cord to its more immediate need!"

"All is not so simple," said Iolo. "You have valued this pelgrane at a hundred terces, of which my share is fifty. The rope I assess at ten terces—"

"What!" roared Cugel. "Ten terces for a length of cord worth at most a few coppers?"

"Value is not an immutable quality," Iolo pointed out. "I believe this to be one of the basic doctrines of commerce."

"Very well," said Cugel, gritting his teeth against the tension of the tentacle. "Ten terces for the rope, but I cannot pay fifty for the pelgrane; I carry only forty-five terces."

"So be it," said Iolo. "I will accept as surety the jeweled clip in your hat. Please pay over the forty-five terces."

Cugel, seeing no value in argument, managed to toss his wallet to the ground. Iolo demanded the clip, but Cugel refused to relinquish the jewel until the tentacle had been tied off. With poor grace Iolo hacked the head off the pelgrane, brought over the rope and secured the tentacle to the stump, thus easing the strain upon Cugel's leg. "Now then," said Iolo, "the clip if you please." And he poised his knife significantly near the rope.

Cugel tossed over the clip. "Now, since you have gained all my wealth, be so good as to extricate me from this tentacle."

Iolo ignored the remark and set about making camp for the night.

Cugel called out plaintively: "Are you bereft of compassion? Do you not recall how I rescued you from the pelgrane?"

"Indeed I do, and I note the consequences of this act. An anomalous object grips your leg and you have lost your wealth. There is a lesson to be learned here, to this effect: never disturb the stasis unless well reimbursed in advance."

"True," agreed Cugel. "Still, a serious disequilibrium now exists which thoughtful men would wish to adjust: you by prying loose the tentacle, I by extricating my leg."

"There is something in what you say," remarked Iolo. "In the morning, when I am rested, I will cast a wisp and locate the truth."

Cugel expostulated but Iolo turned him a deaf ear and built up a campfire over which he cooked a stew of herbs and grasses, which he ate with half a cold fowl and draughts of wine from a leather bottle, after which he stoppered the bottle and leaning back against a tree gave his attention to Cugel. "No doubt you are on your way to Duke Orbal's great Exposition of Marvels?"

Cugel made a sign in the negative. "I am a traveler, no more. What is this exposition?"

"Each year Duke Orbal presides over a competition of wonder-workers, the grand prize of which is a thousand terces. This year I intend to win the prize with my Bagful of Dreams."

"Interesting! Your 'Bagful of Dreams' is of course no more than a romantic metaphor?"

"Absolutely not!" declared Iolo in a voice of outraged dignity.

"A kaleidoscopic projection? A set of amusing impersonations? A hallucinatory gas?"

"None of these. I carry a quantity of pure unadulterated dreams, coalesced and crystallized." From his satchel Iolo brought forth a sack of soft gray leather, from which he extracted an object like a snowflake two inches in diameter. He held it up into the firelight where Cugel could admire its fleeting lusters. "With these dreams I will ply Duke Orbal and how can I fail to win over all contestants?"

"Your chances are not inconsequential. How, may I ask, do you obtain these dreams?"

"The process is complicated and secret. Still, I see no reason why I should not describe the general procedures. I live beside Lake Lucanor in the land of Daipassant. On calm nights the surface of the water becomes coated with a dusty skein which reflects the stars as small globules of shine. By using a suitable incantation I am able to lift up impalpable threads composed of pure starlight and waterweft. I weave this thread into nets and then I go forth in search of dreams. I hide in valances, I crouch on roofs, I wander through sleeping houses, I am always ready to net the dreams as they drift by. Each morning I carry these wonderful wisps to my laboratory and there I sort them out and contrive my various minglements. In due course I achieve a crystal of a hundred dreams, and with these confections I hope to enthrall Duke Orbal and win a thousand terces."

"I would offer congratulations were it not for this tentacle gripping my leg," said Cugel.

"Yes, that is a matter we must carefully explore." Iolo fed several logs into the fire, chanted a spell of protection against creatures of the night, and composed himself for sleep.

An hour passed. Cugel tried in vain to ease the grip of the tentacle. He listened to the sounds from the valley and heard the fluting of a night jar. Four black moths fluttered about the fire, then—disturbed perhaps by Iolo's snores—spiraled up one after the other into the gloom and were gone. Cugel reached to the ground for a twig, with which he was able to drag close a long branch, which allowed him to reach another of equal length. Tying the two together with a length of string from his pouch he contrived a pole exactly long enough to reach Iolo's recumbent form. Working with exquisite precision he drew the satchel across the ground, to within reach of his fingers. First he drew forth Iolo's wallet containing two hundred terces which he transferred to his own pouch, then the jeweled clip to his hat, then the soft gray leather bagful of dreams. The satchel contained nothing more of value, save that half of cold fowl which Iolo had reserved for his breakfast and the leather bottle of wine, both of which Cugel put aside for his own use. He returned the satchel to where he had found it, then he separated the branches and tossed them aside. Lacking a better hiding place for the bagful of dreams, Cugel tied the string to the bag and lowered it into the mysterious hole. He ate the fowl and drank the wine, then made himself as comfortable as possible.

In due course the night passed, and the sun swam up into a plum-colored sky. Iolo roused himself, yawned, belched, blew up the fire and added fuel, after which he gave Cugel a civil good morning. "And how passed the night?"

"As well as could be expected. It is useless, after all, to complain against that which may not be altered."

"Precisely correct!" Iolo went to the satchel for his breakfast and discovered the loss of his property. He leapt erect and stared at Cugel. "My money, my dreams—gone! How do you account for this?"

"Easily. At approximately midnight a robber came out of the woods and pillaged your satchel."

Iolo tore at his black beard. "My precious dreams! Why did you not raise an outcry?"

Cugel scratched his head. "This was not the scope of our understanding; at no time did you give me such instructions, and in all candor I did not care once again to disturb the stasis. Additionally, the robber seemed a kindly man; after taking possession of your belongings, he presented me with half a cold fowl and a bottle of wine, the provenance of which I saw no need to inquire. We held a brief conversation and I learned that like ourselves he is bound for Cuirnif and the Exposition of Marvels."

"Aha! Would you recognize this robber were you to see him again?"

"Without a doubt."

"Well then, let us see as to this tentacle. Perhaps we can pry it loose." Iolo seized the tip of the golden-gray member and bracing himself managed to lift it from Cugel's leg. For twenty minutes he struggled, kicking and thrusting, heaving and prying, and paying no heed to Cugel's roars of pain. Finally the tentacle fell away and Cugel crawled to safety.

With great caution Iolo approached the hole and peered down into the dark depths. "I see only a glimmer of far lights. The hole is mysterious... What is this bit of string fastened to the root which leads into the hole?"

"I tied a rock to the end and attempted to find a bottom to the cavity," Cugel explained. "It amounts to nothing."

Iolo tugged at the string, which first yielded, then resisted, then broke, and Iolo was left looking at the frayed end. "Odd! The string appears to have corroded, as if through contact with some acrid substance. But let us hasten into Cuirnif and there identify the villain who sequestered my valuables."

The two proceeded along a road, past garden plots, fields and vineyards. The peasants working their soil looked up in interest as the two wayfarers passed along the road: the portly round-faced Iolo in his suit of black-and-white diamonds, jowls quivering, beard jerking; and beside him the lean long-legged Cugel, his saturnine visage turned first to this side, then that. Along the way Iolo put ever more searching questions in regard to the robber. Cugel had lost interest in the subject and returned vague, ambiguous, or even contradictory answers, and Iolo's voice became ever sharper.

They entered the town, Cuirnif, crossed the square, and Cugel noted an inn which seemed to offer comfortable accommodations. "Here our paths diverge," he told Iolo. "I plan to take a chamber in the inn yonder."

"The Five Owls? It is the dearest inn of Cuirnif; how will you pay the score?"

Cugel made a confident gesture. "Is not a thousand terces the grand prize at the exposition of Marvels?"

"Indeed, but what marvel do you propose to display? I warn you, the Duke has no patience with charlatans."

"Events will order themselves," said Cugel. "Meanwhile, I wish you comfortable roofs and the finest of dreams for your net." He performed a courteous salute and took his leave of Iolo.

At the Five Owls Cugel was assigned a pleasant chamber suitably furnished, where he refreshed himself and ordered his attire. Then, descending to the common room, he commanded the best meal the house could afford, together with a decanter of amber sack. Upon completion of his meal he summoned the innkeeper and commended the quality of his table. "In fact, all taken with all, Cuirnif must be considered a place favored by the elements. The prospect is pleasant, the air is bracing, and Duke Orbal appears to be an indulgent ruler."

"Aha then! You have met Duke Orbal?"

"I noticed him across the square, no more. He seems mild and equable."

The innkeeper nodded somewhat noncommittally. "As you say, Duke Orbal is not easily exasperated, until he encounters refractory conduct, whereupon his mildness deserts him. Glance at the crest of the hill; what do you see?"

"Four tubes, or stand-pipes, approximately thirty yards tall and something less than one yard in diameter."

"Your eye is accurate. Into these tubes are dropped insubordinate members of society, without regard for who stands below or who may be coming after. Hence, while you may converse with Duke Orbal or even venture a modest pleasantry or two, never ignore his commands."

Cugel made an airy gesture. "Such strictures will hardly apply to me, a stranger in town."

The innkeeper gave a skeptical grunt. "I assume that you come to witness the Exposition of Marvels?"

"Even better! I intend to claim the grand prize. In this regard, can you recommend a dependable hostler?"

"Certainly." The innkeeper provided explicit directions.

"I also wish to hire a gang of strong and willing workers," said Cugel. "Where may these be recruited?"

The innkeeper pointed across the street to a rather dingy tavern. "In the yard of The Blue Cuckoo all the riffraff in town take counsel together. Here you will find workers sufficient to your purposes."

"While I visit the hostler, please be good enough to send a pot-boy across to hire twelve of these sturdy fellows."

"As you wish."

At the hostler's Cugel rented a large six-wheeled wagon and a team of draught animals. Returning with the wagon to the Five Owls, he found waiting a work force of twelve miscellaneous types, including a man not only senile and racked with ague, but also lacking a leg. Another, in the throes of intoxication, fought away imaginary insects. Cugel discharged these two on the spot. Another in the group was Iolo the Dream-taker, who scrutinized Cugel with the liveliest suspicion.

Cugel asked: "My good friend Iolo, what do you do in such sordid company?"

"I take employment in order to buy sustenance," said Iolo with dignity. "May I ask how you obtained funds to embark on such an ambitious program? Also, I notice that you wear in your hat that jeweled clip which only yesterday was my property!"

"It is the second of a pair," said Cugel. "The robber took the first along with your other valuables."

Iolo curled his lips in scorn. "Do you take me for a fool? Also, why do you require this wagon and this gang of workers?"

"If you care to earn the very substantial wage I propose to pay, you will soon find out for yourself," said Cugel, with which Iolo was forced to be content.

Cugel drove the wagon and the gang of workers out of Cuirnif along the road to the mysterious hole, where he found all as before. He ordered trenches dug into the hillside; crating was installed, after which that block of soil surrounding and including the hole was dragged up on the bed of the wagon, with the protruding tentacle still tied to the stump. During the middle stages of the project Iolo's manner changed. He began calling orders to the workmen and addressed Cugel with great cordiality. "A noble idea, Cugel! We shall profit greatly!"

Cugel raised his eyebrows. "I hope indeed to win the grand prize. Your wage however will be relatively modest, or even scant, unless you work more briskly."

"What!" stormed Iolo. "Surely you agree that this hole is half my property!"

"I agree to nothing of the sort. Please say no more of the matter, or I will be forced to discharge you."

Grumbling and fuming Iolo returned to work, and in due course Cugel conveyed the block of soil, with the hole and tentacle, back to

Cuirnif. Along the way he purchased an old tarpaulin with which he concealed the hole, the better to magnify the impact of his display.

At the site of the exposition Cugel slid his exhibit off the wagon and into the shelter of a pavilion, after which he paid off his men, to the dissatisfaction of those who had cultivated extravagant hopes. Cugel gave short shrift to the complaints. "The pay is adequate, and were it ten times as much, the money would still find its way into the till at the Blue Cuckoo."

"One moment!" cried Iolo in a passion. "You and I must arrive at an understanding!"

Cugel merely jumped up on the wagon and drove it back to the hostelry. Some of the men pursued him a few steps; others threw stones, without effect.

On the following day trumpets and gongs announced the formal opening of the exposition. Duke Orbal arrived at the plaza splendid in a robe of old rose trimmed with white feathers, and a hat of pale blue velvet two feet in diameter, with silver tassels around the brim and a cockade of silver puff. Mounting to a rostrum, Duke Orbal addressed the crowd. "As all know, I am considered a visionary eccentric, what with my enthusiasm for marvels and prodigies, but, after all, when the preoccupation is analyzed, is it all so absurd? Think back across the aeons to the times of the Vapurials, the Green and Purple College, the mighty magicians among whose number we include Amberlin, the second Chidule of Porphyrhyncos, Morreion, Calanctus the Calm, and of course the Great Phandaal. These were the days of power, and they are not likely to return except in nostalgic recollection. Hence this, my Exposition of Marvels.

"I see by my schedule that we have a remarkable and stimulating program, and no doubt I will find difficulty in awarding the grand prize." Duke Orbal glanced at a paper. "We will inspect Zaraflam's 'Nimble Squadrons', Gazzard's 'Unlikely Musicians', Xallops and his 'Compendium of Universal Knowledge'. Iolo will offer his 'Bagful of Dreams', and, finally, Cugel will present for our amazement that to which he gives the tantalizing title: 'Nowhere'. A most provocative program! And now without further ado we will proceed to evaluate Zaraflam's 'Nimble Squadrons'."

The crowd surged around the first pavilion and Zaraflam brought forth his 'Nimble Squadrons': a parade of cockroaches smartly turned out in red, white, and black uniforms. The sergeants brandished swords, the foot soldiers carried muskets; the squadrons marched and countermarched in intricate evolutions. "Halt!" bawled Zaraflam. The cockroaches stopped short.

"Present arms!" The cockroaches obeyed.

"Fire a salute in honor of Duke Orbal!"

The sergeants raised their swords, the footmen elevated their muskets. Down came the swords; the muskets exploded emitting little puffs of white smoke.

"Excellent!" declared Duke Orbal. "Zaraflam, I commend your painstaking accuracy!"

"A thousand thanks, your Grace! Have I won the grand prize?"

"It is still too early to predict eventualities. Now, to Gazzard and his 'Unlikely Musicians'!"

The spectators moved on to the second pavilion from which Gazzard presently appeared, his face woebegone. "Your Grace and noble citizens of Cuirnif! My 'Unlikely Musicians' were fish of the Gelid Sea, and I was assured of the grand prize when I brought them to Cuirnif. However, during the night a leak drained the tank dry and the fish are dead . . . I still wish to remain in contention for the prize; hence I will simulate the songs of my former troupe. Please adjudicate the music on this basis."

Duke Orbal made an austere sign. "Impossible. Gazzard's exhibit is hereby declared invalid. We now move on to Xallops and his remarkable 'Compendium'."

Xallops stepped forward from his pavilion. "Your Grace, ladies and gentlemen of Cuirnif! My entry at this exposition is truly remarkable; however, unlike Zaraflam and Gazzard, I can take no personal credit for its existence. By trade I am a ransacker of ancient tombs, where the risks are great and rewards few. By great good luck I chanced upon that crypt where ten aeons ago the Sorcerer Zinqzin was laid to rest. From this dungeon I rescued the volume which I now display to your astounded eyes." Xallops whisked away a cloth to reveal a great book bound in black leather. "On command this volume must reveal information of any and every sort; it knows each trivial detail, from the moment the Cosmic dung-beetle propelled the planets into orbit around the Sun to the present date. Ask; you shall be answered!"

"Remarkable!" declared Duke Orbal. "Present before us the Lost

Ode of Psyrme!"

"Certainly." The book threw back its covers to reveal a page covered with crabbed and undecipherable characters.

Duke Orbal spoke in a perplexed voice: "This is beyond my comprehension; be so good as to furnish a translation."

"The request is denied," said the book. "Such poetry is too sweet for ordinary ilk."

Duke Orbal glanced haughtily at Xallops, who spoke quickly to the book: "Show us scenes from aeons past."

"With pleasure. Reverting to the Nineteenth Aeon of the Fifty-second Cycle, I display a view across Linxfade Valley, toward Singhapura's Tower of Frozen Blood."

"Magnificent!" declared Duke Orbal. "I am curious to gaze upon the semblance of Singhapura himself."

"As you wish. Here is a scene on Thrungstone Terrace at the Temple at Yan. Singhapura stands beside the flowering wail-bush. In the chair sits the Empress Noxon, now in her hundred and fortieth year. She has tasted no water in her entire lifetime, and eats only bitter glossom, with occasionally a morsel or two of boiled eel."

"Bah!" said Duke Orbal. "A most hideous old creature! Show us rather a beautiful court lady of the Yellow Age."

The book uttered a petulant syllable in an unknown language. The page turned to reveal a marble promenade running beside a placid river. "Notice the vegetation," said the book, indicating with a luminous arrow a row of golden-pewter trees clipped into globular shapes. "Those are irix, the sap of which may be used as an effective vermifuge. The species is now extinct. Along the concourse you will observe a multitude of persons. Those with black stockings are Alulian slaves, whose ancestors arrived from far Canopus. In the middle distance stands a beautiful woman, indicated by a red dot over her head, although her face is turned toward the river."

"This is hardly satisfactory," grumbled Duke Orbal. "Xallops, can you not control the perversity of your exhibit?"

"I fear not, your Grace."

Duke Orbal gave a sniff of displeasure. "A final question! Who among the folk now residing in Cuirnif presents the greatest threat to the welfare of my realm?"

"I am a repository of information, not an oracle," stated the book.

"However, I will remark that among those present stands a certain long-legged vagabond with a crafty expression—"

Cugel leapt forward and pointed across the square. "The robber! I believe that I saw him skulking yonder! There he goes now! Summon the constables! Sound the gong!"

While all turned to look, Cugel, slamming shut the book, dug his knuckles meaningfully into the cover. The book grunted in annoyance.

Duke Orbal turned around with a frown of perplexity. "I saw no one."

"Ah well, perhaps I was mistaken. But yonder waits Iolo with his famous Bagful of Dreams!"

The Duke moved on to Iolo's pavilion, followed by the enthralled onlookers. Duke Orbal said: "Iolo the Dream-taker, your fame has preceded you all the far distance from Daipassant. I hereby tender you an official welcome and assure you that your remarkable demonstrations will receive our most sympathetic attention."

Iolo answered in a sullen voice: "Your Grace, I have sorry news to report. For the whole of one year I prepared for this day, hoping of course to win the grand prize. The blast of midnight winds, the outrage of householders, the terrifying attentions of ghosts, shrees, roof-runners and fermins: all of these have caused me discomfort. I have roamed the dark hours in pursuit of my dreams. I have lurked beside dormers, crawled through attics, hovered over couches; I have suffered frights, vicissitudes; never have I counted the cost if through my enterprise I were able to capture some particularly choice specimen. Each dream trapped in my star-shine net I carefully examined and gauged its worth; for every dream cherished and saved, I have released a dozen, and finally from my store of superlatives I fashioned my wonderful crystals, and these I brought down the long road from Daipassant. Then, only last night, under the most mysterious circumstances, my property was sequestered. My precious goods were rifled by a robber whom only Cugel claims to have seen. I therefore make this urgent representation; and I point out that the dreams, whether near or far, represent marvels of superlative quality, and I feel that a careful description of the items—"

Duke Orbal held up his hand. "I must reiterate the judgment rendered upon the good Gazzard. One of our most stringent rules stipulates that neither imaginary nor purported marvels may qualify for the competition. You are hereby extended official condolences for the misfortune you have suffered; perhaps we will have the opportunity to adjudicate your remarkable dreams on another occasion. We will now pass on to Cugel's pavilion and investigate his provocative 'Nowhere'."

Cugel stepped up on the dais before his exhibit. "Your Grace, I present for your inspection a legitimate marvel: not a straggle of untidy insects, not an insolent and pedantic almanac, but an authentic wonderment." Cugel whisked away the cloth. "Behold!"

The Duke made a puzzled sound. "A pile of dirt? A stump? What is that odd-looking member emerging from the hole?"

Cugel spoke in tones of compelling fervor. "Your Grace, I will describe the provenance of this marvel. As I departed the Plain of Standing Stones, a pelgrane swooped from the sky which I attacked and killed. On its helm it wore a qandar-egg, a notable source of diasmatic concentrate. In order to deny another baleful creature this power, which conceivably might be used against the best interests of your Grace and all Ombalique, I hurled the qandar-egg to the ground; it exploded and burst a hole into an unknown and mysterious space."

Iolo ran forward sputtering in indignation. "Come, Cugel, I beg you, be accurate in your tale!" He turned to Duke Orbal. "I grappled the pelgrane; Cugel reached from behind a tree and purloined the qandar-egg, but as he turned to flee, it fell from his hands."

Cugel spoke in a lofty voice: "Pay no heed to Iolo's distortions; I fear that he has ingested too many of his own dreams. Be so good as to inspect this tentacle which pulses with the life of another cosmos! Notice the golden luster of the dorsal surface, the green and lavender of these scales, which are formed of proscedel, or some other wonderful substance. And on the underside you will discover three colors of a sort never before seen!"

With a nonplussed expression Duke Orbal pulled at his chin. "This is all very well, but where is the rest of the creature? You present not a marvel, but the fraction of a marvel! I can make no judgment on the basis of a tail, or hinderquarters, or proboscis, whatever the member may be. Additionally, you claim that the hole enters a far cosmos; still I see only a hole, resembling nothing so much as the den of a wysen-imp."

Iolo thrust himself forward. "May I venture an opinion? As I reflect upon events, I have become convinced that Cugel himself stole my Bagful of Dreams, and also my purse containing well over two hundred terces. He ascribed this deed to a robber whom he characterized—to use his words—as a 'vulgar vicious person, with a red nose and large nostrils'. Now mark this well: as we entered the precincts of Cuirnif, Cugel positively identified your Grace as the robber!"

"One moment!" cried Cugel in outrage. "As usual Iolo deals inaccurately with the facts! True, we entered Cuirnif in each other's company. Agreed, the appearance of the robber was the subject of our conversation. Then, as soon as your Grace appeared, Iolo turned me a bland face and pointed with insulting familiarity in your direction. "That fellow yonder,' said Iolo, 'examine him well. He has a questionable reputation. Could he be the robber?' I said, "The gentleman to whom you refer appears noble and dignified, hence—'"

Iolo uttered a jeering laugh. "To the contrary, you spoke only of 'turpitude' and masks of hypocrisy'."

"Your remarks are not at all helpful," said Cugel. "Kindly hold your tongue while I continue my demonstration."

Iolo was not to be subdued so easily. He turned to Duke Orbal and cried in a poignant voice: "Hear me out, if you will! I am convinced that the 'robber' is no more than a figment of this rogue's imagination! He took my dreams and hid them, and where else but in the hole? For evidence I cite that length of string which leads into the hole. For what purpose? Obviously to suspend my Bag of Dreams!"

Duke Orbal inspected Cugel with a frown. "Are these accusations valid? Answer exactly, since all can be verified."

Cugel chose his words with care. "I can only affirm what I myself know. Quite conceivably the robber hid Iolo's dreams in the hole while I was otherwise occupied. For what purpose? Who can say? Again, assume as a hypothesis that Iolo, troubled by the paltriness of his exhibit, tossed aside his dreams in disgust. Is this so incredible? Not at all."

Iolo held up clenched fists to the sky, but before he could respond, Duke Orbal asked in a gentle voice: "Has anyone thought to search the hole for this elusive 'Bag of Dreams'?"

Cugel gave an indifferent shrug. "I have never forbidden Iolo access into the hole. He may enter now and search to his heart's content."

"You claim this hole!" returned Iolo. "It therefore becomes your duty to protect the public. Please return to me my property!"

For several minutes an animated argument took place, until Duke Orbal intervened. "Both parties have raised persuasive points; however, on the whole, I must find against Cugel. I therefore decree that he make an effort to recover the missing dreams."

Cugel disputed the decision with such vigor that Duke Orbal turned to glance along the skyline of the ridge, whereupon Cugel moderated his position. "The judgment of your Grace of course must prevail, and if I must, I will cast about for Iolo's lost dreams, although his theories are clearly absurd."

Cugel obtained a long pole, to which he attached a grapple. Gingerly thrusting his contrivance through the hole, he raked back and forth, but succeeded only in stimulating the tentacle, which thrashed from side to side.

Iolo suddenly cried out in excitement. "I notice a remarkable fact! The block of earth is at most six feet in breadth, yet Cugel plunges into the hole a pole twelve feet in length! What trickery does he practise now?"

Cugel replied in even tones: "I promised Duke Orbal a marvel and a wonderment, and I believe that I have done so. I can no more explain the matter than Zaraflam can elucidate the mental processes of his cockroaches."

Duke Orbal nodded gravely. "Well said, Cugel! Your exhibit indeed entitles you to serious consideration for the grand prize. Still—and this is an important qualification—you offer us only a tantalizing glimpse: a bottomless hole, a length of tentacle, to the effect that your exhibit seems somewhat makeshift and improvised. Contrast, if you will, the precision of Zaraflam's cockroaches!" He held up his hand as Cugel started to expostulate. "You display a hole: good enough. But how is this hole different from any other? Can I in justice offer a thousand terces on such a vague basis!"

"The matter may be resolved in a manner to satisfy us all," said Cugel. "Let Iolo enter the hole, to assure himself that his dreams are indeed elsewhere. Then, on his return, he will bear witness to the truly marvelous nature of my exhibit."

Iolo made an instant protest. "Cugel claims the exhibit; let him make the exploration!"

Cugel offered a heated rejoinder, to which Iolo responded in kind, until Duke Orbal raised his hand for silence. "I pronounce an official decree to the effect that Cugel must immediately enter his extraordinary aperture in search of Iolo's properties, and likewise make a careful study of the environment, for the benefit of us all."

"Your Grace!" protested Cugel. "This is no simple matter! The tentacle almost fills the hole!"

"I see sufficient room for an agile man to slide past."

"Your Grace, to be candid, I do not care to enter the hole, by reason of extreme fear."

Duke Orbal again glanced up at the tubes which stood in a sinister line along the ridge of the hill. He spoke over his shoulder to a burly man in a maroon and black uniform. "Which of the tubes is most suitable for use at this time?"

"The second tube from the right, your Grace, is only one-quarter occupied."

Cugel declared in a trembling voice: "I fear, but I have conquered my fear! I will seek Iolo's lost dreams!"

"Excellent," said Duke Orbal with a tight-lipped grin. "Please do not delay; my patience wears thin."

Cugel tentatively thrust a leg into the hole, but the motion of the tentacle caused him to snatch it out again. Duke Orbal muttered a few words to his sheriff, who brought up a winch. The tentacle was hauled forth from the hole a good five yards. "Now," Duke Orbal instructed Cugel, "straddle the tentacle, seize it with hands and legs and it will draw you back through the hole."

In desperation Cugel clambered upon the tentacle. The tension of the winch was relaxed and Cugel was pulled into the hole.

The light of Earth veered away from the opening and made no entrance; Cugel was plunged into a condition of near-total darkness, where, however, by some paradoxical condition he was able to sense the scope of his new environment in detail.

He stood on a surface at once flat, yet rough with rises and dips and hummocks like the face of a windy sea. The substance underfoot seemed a black spongy stuff, pitted by small cavities and tunnels in which Cugel sensed the motion of innumerable near-invisible points of light. Where the sponge rose high, the crest curled over like breaking surf, or stood ragged and crusty; in either case, the fringes glowed with a phosphorescence of red, pale blue, and several colors

Cugel had never before observed. No horizon could be detected and the laws of perspective were notably distorted; the local concepts of distance, proportion, and size were organized by conventions foreign to Cugel's understanding.

Overhead hung dead numb Nothingness. The single feature of note, a large disk the color of rain floated at the zenith, an object so dim as to be almost invisible. At some indeterminate distance—a mile? ten miles? a hundred yards?—a hummock of some bulk overlooked the entire panorama. On closer inspection Cugel saw this hummock to be a prodigious mound of gelatinous flesh, inside which floated a globular organ apparently analogous to an eye. From the base of this creature a hundred tentacles extended far and wide across the black sponge. One of these tentacles passed near Cugel's feet, through the intracosmic gap, and out upon the soil of Earth.

At this moment Cugel noted Iolo's Bag of Dreams, not three feet distant. The black sponge, bruised by the impact, had welled an acrid liquid which had dissolved a hole in the leather, allowing the star-shaped dreams to spill out upon the sponge. In groping with the pole, Cugel had damaged a growth of brown palps. The resulting exudation had dripped upon the dreams and when Cugel picked up one of the fragile flakes, he saw that its edges glowed with eery fringes of color. The combination of oozes which had permeated the object caused his fingers to itch and tingle.

A score of small luminous nodes swarmed around his head, and a soft voice addressed him by name. "Cugel, dear Cugel—what a pleasure that you have come to visit us! What is your opinion of our pleasant land?"

Cugel sprang about in wonder; how could a denizen of this inaccessible place know his name? Not far distant, upon a crust of black sponge, rested a small creature not unlike the monstrous bulk with the floating eye. The luminous nodes circled his head and the voice sounded in his ears: "You are perplexed, but needlessly. We transfer our thoughts in small quanta; if you look closely you will see them speeding through the fluxion: dainty little animalcules eager to unload their weight of enlightenment. There! Notice! Directly before your eyes hovers an excellent example. It is a thought of your own regarding which you are dubious; hence it hesitates, and awaits your decision."

"What if I speak?" asked Cugel. "Will this not facilitate affairs?"

"To the contrary! Sound is considered offensive and everyone deplores the slightest murmur."

"This is all very well," grumbled Cugel, "but—"

"Silence, please! Send forth animalcules only!"

Cugel dispatched a whole host of luminous purports: "I will do my best. Perhaps you can inform me how far this land extends?"

"Not with certainty. At times I send forth animalcules to explore the far places; they report an infinite landscape similar to that which you see."

"Duke Orbal of Ombalique has commanded me to gather information and he will be interested in your remarks. Are valuable substances to be found here?"

"To a certain extent. There is proscedel and diphany and an occasional coruscation of zamanders."

"My first concern, of course, is to collect information for Duke Orbal, and I must also rescue Iolo's Bag of Dreams; still I would be pleased to acquire a valuable trinket or two, if only to remind myself of our pleasant association."

"Understandable! I sympathize with your objectives."

"In that case, how may I obtain a quantity of these valuable substances?"

"Nothing could be more straightforward. Simply send off animalcules to gather up your requirements." The creature emitted a whole host of pale plasms which darted away in all directions and presently returned with several dozen small spheres sparkling with a frosty blue light. "Here are zamanders of the first water," said the creature. "Accept them with my compliments."

Cugel placed the gems in his pouch. "This is a most convenient system for accumulating wealth. I also wish to obtain a certain amount of diphany."

"Send forth animalcules! Why exert yourself needlessly?"

"We think along similar lines." Cugel dispatched several hundred animalcules which presently returned with twenty small ingots of the precious metal.

Cugel examined his pouch. "I find that I still have room for a quantity of proscedel. If you will take an indulgent attitude toward my acquisitiveness, I will send out the requisite animalcules."

"I would not dream of interfering in your affairs," asserted the creature.

The animalcules sped forth, and before long returned with sufficient proscedel to fill Cugel's pouch. The creature said thoughtfully, "This is at least half of Uthaw's treasure; however, he appears not to have noticed its absence."

"Uthaw?" inquired Cugel. "Do you refer to yonder monstrous hulk?"

"Yes, that is Uthaw, who is as peremptory as he is irascible."

Uthaw's eye rolled toward Cugel and bulged through the outer membrane. A tide of animalcules arrived pulsing with significance. "I notice that Cugel has stolen my treasure, which I denounce as an abuse of hospitality! In retribution, he must dig twenty-two zamanders from below the Shivering Hills. He must then sift eight pounds of prime proscedel from the Dust of Time. Finally he must scrape eight pounds of diphany bloom from the face of the High Disk."

Cugel sent forth animalcules. "Lord Uthaw, the penalty is harsh but just. A moment while I go to fetch the necessary tools!" He gathered up the Bagful of Dreams and sprang to the aperture. Seizing the tentacle he cried through the hole: "Pull the tentacle, work the winch! I have rescued the Bagful of Dreams!"

The tentacle convulsed and thrashed, effectively blocking the opening. Cugel turned and putting his fingers to his mouth emitted a piercing whistle. Uthaw's eye rolled upward and the tentacle fell limp.

The winch heaved at the tentacle and Cugel was drawn back through the hole. Uthaw, recovering his senses, jerked his tentacle so violently that the rope snapped; the winch was sent flying; and several persons were swept from their feet. Uthaw jerked back his tentacle and the hole immediately closed.

Cugel cast the Bagful of Dreams contemptuously at the feet of Iolo. "There you are, ingrate! Take your vapid hallucinations and let us hear no more of you!"

Cugel turned to Duke Orbal. "I am now able to render a report upon the other cosmos. The ground is composed of a black spongelike substance and flickers with phosphorescence. My research revealed no limits to the extent of the land. A pale disk, barely visible, covers a quarter of the sky. The denizens are, first and foremost, an ill-natured hulk named Uthaw, and others more or less similar. No sound is allowed, and meaning is conveyed by animalcules, which also procure the necessities of life. In essence, these are my discoveries, and now, with utmost respect, I claim the grand prize of one thousand terces."

From behind his back Cugel heard Iolo's mocking laughter. Duke Orbal shook his head. "My dear Cugel, what you suggest is impossible. To what exhibit do you refer? The boxful of dirt yonder? It lacks all pretensions to uniqueness."

Cugel cried out in a passionate voice: "But you saw the hole! With your winch you pulled the tentacle! In accordance with your orders I entered the hole and explored the region!"

"True enough, but hole and tentacle are both vanished. I do not for a moment suggest mendacity, but your report is not easily verified. I can hardly grant a prize to an entity so fugitive as the memory of a hole. I fear that on this occasion I must pass you by. The prize will be awarded to Zaraflam and his remarkable cockroaches."

"A moment, your Grace!" called Iolo anxiously. "I am entered in the competition and at last I am able to display my products! Observe these prime specimens, and here is a particularly choice item, distilled from a hundred dreams captured early in the morning from a bevy of beautiful maidens asleep in a bower of fragrant vines."        .

"Very well," said Duke Orbal. "I will delay the award until I test the quality of your visions. What is the procedure? Must I compose myself for slumber?"

"Not at all! The ingestion of the dream during waking hours produces not a hallucination, but a mood: a sensibility fresh, new and sweet; an allurement of the faculties, an indescribable exhilaration. Still, why should you not be comfortable as you test my dreams? You there! Fetch a couch! And you, a cushion for his Grace's noble head. You! Be good enough to take his Grace's hat."

Cugel saw no profit in remaining and moved to the outskirts of the throng. Iolo brought forth his dream and for a moment seemed puzzled by the ooze still adhering to the object, but then decided to ignore the matter. Cugel, with eyes possibly sensitized by his visit to the subcosmos, thought to glimpse fringes of acid blue luminosity about the object, but Iolo paid no heed, except to rub his fingers as if after contact with some viscid substance.

Making a series of grand gestures, Iolo approached the great chair where Duke Orbal sat at his ease. "I will arrange the dream for its most convenient ingestion," said Iolo. "I place a quantity into each ear; I insert a trifle up each nostril; I arrange the balance under your Grace's illustrious tongue. Now, if your Grace will relax, in half a minute you will experience the quintessence of a hundred exquisite dreams."

Duke Orbal became rigid. His fingers clenched the arms of the chair; his back arched and his eyes bulged from their sockets. He turned over backward, then rolled, jerked, pranced and bounded about the plaza before the amazed eyes of his subjects.

Iolo called out in a brassy voice: "Where is Cugel? Fetch hither that scoundrel Cugel!"

But already Cugel had departed Cuirnif and was nowhere to be found.

# The Cat From Hell
## by Stephen King

*In the past few years Stephen King has emerged as an accomplished, best-selling writer of such novels as* Carrie, 'Salem's Lot, *and* The Shining, *genuine scarers set in contemporary times. He's equally effective in short stories, as this story of a professional murderer and a demonic animal will show.*

Halston thought the old man in the wheelchair looked sick, terrified, and ready to die. He had experience in seeing such things. Death was Halston's business; he had brought it to eighteen men and six women in his career as an independent hitter. He knew the death look.

The house—mansion, actually—was cold and quiet. The only sounds were the low snap of the fire on the big stone hearth and the low whine of the November wind outside.

"I want you to make a kill," the old man said. His voice was quavery and high, peevish. "I understand that is what you do."

"Who did you talk to?" Halston asked.

"With a man named Saul Loggia. He says you know him."

Halston nodded. If Loggia was the go-between, it was all right. And if there was a bug in the room, anything the old man—Drogan—said was entrapment.

"Who do you want hit?"

Drogan pressed a button on the console built into the arm of his wheelchair and it buzzed forward. Close-up, Halston could smell the yellow odors of fear, age, and urine all mixed. They disgusted him, but he made no sign. His face was still and smooth.

"Your victim is right behind you," Drogan said softly.

Halston moved quickly. His reflexes were his life and they were always set on a filed pin. He was off the couch, falling to one knee, turning, hand inside his specially tailored sport coat, gripping the handle of the short-barrelled .45 hybrid that hung below his armpit in a spring-loaded holster that laid it in his palm at a touch. A moment later it was out and pointed at...a cat.

For a moment Halston and the cat stared at each other. It was a strange moment for Halston, who was an unimaginative man with no superstitions. For that one moment as he knelt on the floor with the gun pointed, he felt that he knew this cat, although if he had ever seen one with such unusual markings he surely would have remembered.

Its face was an even split: half black, half white. The dividing line ran from the top of its flat skull and down its nose to its mouth, straight-arrow. Its eyes were huge in the gloom, and caught in each nearly circular black pupil was a prism of firelight, like a sullen coal of hate.

And the thought echoed back to Halston: *We know each other, you and I.*

Then it passed. He put the gun away and stood up. "I ought to kill you for that, old man. I don't take a joke."

"And I don't make them," Drogan said. "Sit down. Look in here." He had taken a fat envelope out from beneath the blanket that covered his legs.

Halston sat. The cat, which had been crouched on the back of the sofa, jumped lightly down into his lap. It looked up at Halston for a moment with those huge dark eyes, the pupils surrounded by thin green-gold rings, and then it settled down and began to purr.

Halston looked at Drogan questioningly.

"He's very friendly," Drogan said. "At first. Nice friendly pussy has killed three people in this household. That leaves only me. I am old, I am sick...but I prefer to die in my own time."

"I can't believe this," Halston said. "You hired me to hit a cat?"

"Look in the envelope, please."

Halston did. It was filled with hundreds and fifties, all of them old. "How much is it?"

"Six thousand dollars. There will be another six when you bring me proof that the cat is dead. Mr. Loggia said twelve thousand was your usual fee?"

Halston nodded, his hand automatically stroking the cat in his lap. It was asleep, still purring. Halston liked cats. They were the only animals he did like, as a matter of fact. They got along on their own. God—if there was one—had made them into perfect, aloof killing machines. Cats were the hitters of the animal world, and Halston gave them his respect.

"I need not explain anything, but I will," Drogan said. "Forewarned is forearmed, they say, and I would not want you to go into this lightly. And I seem to need to justify myself. So you'll not think I'm insane."

Halston nodded again. He had already decided to make this peculiar hit, and no further talk was needed. But if Drogan wanted to talk, he would listen.

"First of all, you know who I am? Where the money comes from?"

"Drogan Pharmaceuticals."

"Yes. One of the biggest drug companies in the world. And the cornerstone of our financial success has been this." From the pocket of his robe he handed Halston a small, unmarked vial of pills. "Tri-Dormal-phenobarbin, compound G. Prescribed almost exclusively for the terminally ill. It's extremely habit-forming, you see. It's a combination pain-killer, tranquilizer, and mild hallucinogen. It is remarkably helpful in helping the terminally ill face their conditions and adjust to them."

"Do you take it?" Halston asked.

Drogan ignored the question. "It is widely prescribed throughout the world. It's a synthetic, was developed in the fifties at our New Jersey labs. Our testing was confined almost solely to cats, because of the unique quality of the feline nervous system."

"How many did you wipe out?"

Drogan stiffened. "That is an unfair and prejudicial way to put it."

Halston shrugged.

"In the four-year testing period which led to FDA approval of Tri-Dormal-G, about fifteen thousand cats... uh, expired."

Halston whistled. About four thousand cats a year. "And now you think this one's back to get you, huh?"

"I don't feel guilty in the slightest," Drogan said, but that quavering, petulant note was back in his voice. "Fifteen thousand test animals died so that hundreds of thousands of human beings—"

"Never mind that," Halston said. Justifications bored him.

"That cat came here seven months ago. I've never liked cats. Nasty, disease-bearing animals...always out in the fields...crawling around in barns...picking up God knows what germs in their fur...always trying to bring something with its insides falling out into the house for you to look at...it was my sister who wanted to take it in. She found out. She paid." He looked at the cat sleeping on Halston's lap with dead hate.

"You said the cat killed three people."

Drogan began to speak. The cat dozed and purred on Halston's lap under the soft, scratching strokes of Halston's strong and expert killer's fingers. Occasionally a pine knot would explode on the hearth, making it tense like a series of steel springs covered with hide and muscle. Outside the wind whined around the big stone house far out in the Connecticut countryside. There was winter in that wind's throat. The old man's voice droned on and on.

Seven months ago there had been four of them here—Drogan, his sister Amanda, who at seventy-four was two years Drogan's elder, her lifelong friend Carolyn Broadmoor ("of the Westchester Broadmoors," Drogan said), who was badly afflicted with emphysema, and Dick Gage, a hired man who had been with the Drogan family for twenty years. Gage, who was past sixty himself, drove the big Lincoln Mark IV, cooked, served the evening sherry. A day-maid came in. The four of them had lived this way for nearly two years, a dull collection of old people and their family retainer. Their only pleasures were *The Hollywood Squares* and waiting to see who would outlive whom.

Then the cat had come.

"It was Gage who saw it first, whining and skulking around the house. He tried to drive it away. He threw sticks and small rocks at it, and hit it several times. But it wouldn't go. It smelled the food, of course. It was little more than a bag of bones. People put them out beside the road to die at the end of the summer season, you know. A terrible, inhumane thing."

"Better to fry their nerves?" Halston asked.

Drogan ignored that and went on. He hated cats. He always had. When the cat refused to be driven away, he had instructed Gage to put out poisoned food. Large, tempting dishes of Calo cat food spiked with Tri-Dormal-G, as a matter of fact. The cat ignored the food. At that point Amanda Drogan had noticed the cat and had insisted they take it in. Drogan had protested vehemently, but Amanda had gotten her way. She always did, apparently.

"But she found out," Drogan said. "She brought it inside herself, in her arms. It was purring, just as it is now. But it wouldn't come near me. It never has ... yet. She poured it a saucer of milk. 'Oh, look at the poor thing, it's starving,' she cooed. She and Carolyn both cooed over it. Disgusting. It was their way of getting back at me, of course. They knew the way I've felt about felines ever since the Tri-Dormal-G testing program twenty years ago. They enjoyed teasing me, baiting me with it." He looked at Halston grimly. "But they paid."

In mid-May, Gage had gotten up to set breakfast and had found Amanda Drogan lying at the foot of the main stairs in a litter of broken crockery and Little Friskies. Her eyes bulged sightlessly up at the ceiling. She had bled a great deal from the mouth and nose. Her back was broken, both legs were broken, and her neck had been literally shattered like glass.

"It slept in her room," Drogan said. "She treated it like a baby...'Is oo hungwy, darwing? Does oo need to go out and do poopoos?' Obscene, coming from an old battle-axe like my sister. I think it woke her up, meowing. She got his dish. She used to say that Sam didn't really like his Friskies unless they were wetted down with a little milk. So she was planning to go downstairs. The cat was rubbing against her legs. She was old, not too steady on her feet. Half-asleep. They got to the head of the stairs and the cat got in front of her ... tripped her ..."

Yes, it could have happened that way, Halston thought. In his mind's eye he saw the old woman falling forward and outward, too shocked to scream. The Friskies spraying out as she tumbled head over heels to the bottom, the bowl smashing. At last she comes to rest at the bottom, the old bones shattered, the eyes glaring, the nose and ears trickling blood. And the purring cat begins to work its way down the stairs, contentedly munching Little Friskies...

"What did the coroner say?" He asked Drogan.

"Death by accident, of course. But I knew."

"Why didn't you get rid of the cat then? With Amanda gone?"

Because Carolyn Broadmoor had threatened to leave if he did, apparently. She was hysterical, obsessed with the subject. She was a sick woman, and she was nutty on the subject of spiritualism. A Hartford medium had told her (for a mere twenty dollars) that Amanda's soul had entered Sam's feline body. Sam had been Amanda's, she told Drogan, and if Sam went, *she* went.

Halston, who had become something of an expert at reading between the lines of human lives, suspected that Drogan and the old Broadmoor bird had been lovers long ago, and the old dude was reluctant to let her go over a cat.

"It would have been the same as suicide," Drogan said. "In her mind she was still a wealthy woman, perfectly capable of packing up that cat and going to New York or London or even Monte Carlo with it. In fact she was the last of a great family, living on a pittance as a result of a number of bad investments in the sixties. She lived on the second floor here in a specially-controlled, super-humidified room. The woman was seventy, Mr. Halston. She was a heavy smoker until the last two years of her life, and the emphysema was very bad. I wanted her here, and if the cat had to stay..."

Halston nodded and then glanced meaningfully at his watch.

"Near the end of June, she died in the night. The doctor seemed to take it as a matter of course... just came and wrote out the death certificate and that was the end of it. But the cat was in the room. Gage told me."

"We all have to go sometime, man," Halston said.

"Of course. That's what the doctor said. But I knew. I remembered. Cats like to get babies and old people when they're asleep. And steal their breath."

"An old wives' tale."

"Based on fact, like most so-called old wives' tales," Drogan replied. "Cats like to knead soft things with their paws, you see. A pillow, a thick shag rug... or a blanket. A crib blanket or an old person's blanket. The extra weight on a person who's weak to start with..."

Drogan trailed off, and Halston thought about it. Carolyn Broadmoor asleep in her bedroom, the breath rasping in and out of her damaged lungs, the sound nearly lost in the whisper of special humidifiers and air-conditioners. The cat with the queer black-and-white markings leaps silently onto her spinster's bed and stares at her old and wrinkle-grooved face with those lambent, black-and-green eyes. It creeps onto her thin chest and settles its weight there, purring...and the breathing slows...slows... and the cat purrs as the old woman slowly smothers beneath its weight on her chest.

He was not an imaginative man, but Halston shivered a little.

"Drogan," he said, continuing to stroke the purring cat. "Why don't you just have it put away? A vet would give it the gas for twenty dollars."

Drogan said, "The funeral was on the first of July. I had Carolyn buried in our cemetery plot next to my sister. The way she would have wanted it. Only July third I called Gage to this room and handed him a wicker basket...a picnic hamper sort of thing. Do you know what I mean?"

Halston nodded.

"I told him to put the cat in it and take it to a vet in Milford and have it put to sleep. He said, 'Yes, sir,' took the basket, and went out. Very like him. I never saw him alive again. There was an accident on the turnpike. The Lincoln was driven into a bridge abutment at better than sixty miles an hour. Dick Gage was killed instantly. When they found him there were scratches on his face."

Halston was silent as the picture of how it might have been formed in his brain again. No sound in the room but the peaceful crackle of the fire and the peaceful purr of the cat in his lap. He and the cat together before the fire would make a good illustration for that Edgar Guest poem, the one that goes: "The cat on my lap, the hearth's good fire/ ... A happy man, should you enquire."

Dick Gage moving the Lincoln down the turnpike toward Milford, beating the speed limit by maybe five miles an hour. The wicker basket beside him—a picnic hamper sort of thing. The chauffeur is watching traffic, maybe he's passing a big cab-over Jimmy and he doesn't notice the peculiar black-on-one-side, white-on-the-other face that pokes out of one side of the basket. Out of the driver's side. He doesn't notice because he's passing the big trailer truck and that's when the cat jumps onto his face, spitting and clawing, its talons raking into one eye, puncturing it, deflating it, blinding it. Sixty and the hum of the Lincoln's big motor and the other paw is hooked over the bridge of the nose, digging in with exquisite, damning pain—maybe the Lincoln starts to veer right, into the path of the Jimmy, and its airhorn blares ear-shatteringly, but Gage can't hear it because the cat is yowling, the cat is spread-eagled over his face like some huge furry black spider, ears laid back, green eyes glaring like spotlights from hell, back legs jittering and digging into the soft flesh of the old man's neck. The car veers wildly back the other way. The bridge abutment looms. The cat jumps down and the Lincoln, a shiny black torpedo, hits the cement and goes up like a bomb.

Halston swallowed hard and heard a dry click in his throat.

"And the cat came back?"

Drogan nodded. "A week later. On the day Dick Gage was buried, as a matter of fact. Just like the old song says. The cat came back."

"It survived a car crash at sixty? Hard to believe."

"They say each one has nine lives. When it comes back...that's when I started to wonder if it might not be a...a ..."

"Hellcat?" Halston suggested softly.

"For want of a better word, yes. A sort of demon sent..."

"To punish you."

"I don't know. But I'm afraid of it. I feed it, or rather, the woman who comes in to do for me feeds it. She doesn't like it either. She says that face is a curse of God. Of course, she's local." The old man tried to smile and failed. "I want you to kill it. I've lived with it for the last four months. It skulks around in the shadows. It looks at me. It seems to be...waiting. I lock myself in my room every night and still I wonder if I'm going to wake up one early morning and find it...curled up on my chest...and purring."

The wind whined lonesomely outside and made a strange hooting noise in the stone chimney.

"At last I got in touch with Saul Loggia. He recommended you. He called you a stick, I believe."

"A one-stick. That means I work on my own."

"Yes. He said you'd never been busted, or even suspected. He said you always seem to land on your feet...like a cat."

Halston looked at the old man in the wheelchair. And suddenly his long-fingered, muscular hands were lingering just above the cat's neck.

"I'll do it now, if you want me to," he said softly. "I'll snap its neck. It won't even know—"

"No! Drogan cried. He drew in a long, shuddering breath. Color had come up in his sallow cheeks. "Not... not here. Take it away." Halston smiled humorlessly. He began to stroke the sleeping cat's head and shoulders and back very gently again. "All right," he said. "I accept the contract. Do you want the body?" "No. Kill it. Bury it." He paused. He hunched forward in the wheelchair like some ancient buzzard. "Bring me the tail," he said. "So I can throw it in the fire and watch it burn."

Halston drove a 1973 Plymouth with a custom Cyclone Spoiler engine. The car was jacked and blocked, and rode with the hood pointing down at the road at a twenty-degree angle. He had rebuilt the differential and the rear end himself. The shift was a Pensy, the linkage was Hearst. It sat on huge Bobby Unser Wide Ovals and had a top end of a little past one-sixty.

He left the Drogan house at a little past 9:30. A cold rind of crescent moon rode overhead through the tattering November clouds. He rode with all the windows open, because that yellow stench of age and terror seemed to have settled into his clothes and he didn't like it. The cold was hard and sharp, eventually numbing, but it was good. It was blowing that yellow stench away.

He got off the turnpike at Placer's Glen and drove through the silent town, which was guarded by a single yellow blinker at the intersection, at a thoroughly respectable thirty-five. Out of town, moving up S.R. 35, he opened the Plymouth up a little, letting her walk. The tuned Spoiler engine purred like the cat had purred on his lap earlier this evening. Halston grinned at the simile. They moved between frost-white November fields full of skeleton cornstalks at a little over seventy.

The cat was in a double-thickness shopping bag, tied at the top with heavy twine. The bag was in the passenger bucket seat. The cat had been sleepy and purring when Halston put it in, and it had purred through the entire ride. It sensed, perhaps, that Halston liked it and felt at home with it. Like himself, the cat was a one-stick.

Strange hit, Halston thought, and was surprised to find that he was taking it seriously *as* a hit. Maybe the strangest thing about it was that he actually liked the cat, felt a kinship with it. If it had managed to get rid of those three old crocks, more power to it... especially

Gage, who had been taking it to Milford for a terminal date with a crewcut veterinarian who would have been more than happy to bundle it into a ceramic-lined gas chamber the size of a microwave oven. He felt a kinship, but no urge to renege on the hit. He would do it the courtesy of killing it quickly and well. He would park off the road beside one of these November-barren fields and take it out of the bag and stroke it and then snap its neck and sever its tail with his pocket knife. And, he thought, the body I'll bury honorably, saving it from the scavengers. I can't save it from the worms, but I can save it from the maggots.

He was thinking these things as the car moved through the night like a dark blue ghost and that was when the cat walked in front of his eyes, up on the dashboard, tail raised arrogantly, its black-and-white face turned toward him, its mouth seeming to grin at him.

"Sssshhhh—" Halston hissed. He glanced to his right and caught a glimpse of the double-thickness shopping bag, a hole chewed—or clawed—in its side. Looked ahead again . . . and the cat lifted a paw and batted playfully at him. The paw skidded across Halston's forehead. He jerked away from it and the Plymouth's big tires wailed on the road as it swung erratically from one side of the narrow blacktop to the other.

Halston batted at the cat on the dashboard with his fist. It was blocking his field of vision. It spat at him, arching its back, but it didn't move. Halston swung again, and instead of shrinking away, it leaped at him.

*Gage,* he thought. *Just like Gage—*

He stamped the brake. The cat was on his head, blocking his vision with its furry belly, clawing at him, gouging at him. Halston held the wheel grimly. He struck the cat once, twice, a third time. And suddenly the road was gone, the Plymouth was running down into the ditch, thudding up and down on its shocks. Then, impact, throwing him forward against his seatbelt, and the last sound he heard was the cat yowling inhumanly, the voice of a woman in pain or in the throes of sexual climax.

He struck it with his closed fist and felt only the springy, yielding flex of its muscles.

Then, second impact. And darkness.

•  •  •

The moon was down. It was an hour before dawn.

The Plymouth lay in a ravine curdled with groundmist. Tangled in its grille was a snarled length of barbed wire. The hood had come unlatched, and tendrils of steam from the breached radiator drifted out of the opening to mingle with the mist.

No feeling in his legs.

He looked down and saw that the Plymouth's firewall had caved in with the impact. The back of that big Cyclone Spoiler engine block had smashed into his legs, pinning them.

Outside, in the distance, the predatory squawk of an owl dropping onto some small, scurrying animal.

Inside, close, the steady purr of the cat.

It seemed to be grinning, like Alice's Cheshire had in Wonderland.

As Halston watched it stood up, arched its back, and stretched. In a sudden limber movement like rippled silk, it leaped to his shoulder. Halston tried to lift his hands to push it off.

His arms wouldn't move.

*Spinal shock,* he thought. *Paralyzed. Maybe temporary. More likely permanent.*

The cat purred in his ear like thunder.

"Get off me," Halston said. His voice was hoarse and dry. The cat tensed for a moment and then settled back. Suddenly its paw batted Halston's cheek, and the claws were out this time. Hot lines of pain down to his throat. And the warm trickle of blood.

Pain.

*Feeling.*

He ordered his head to move to the right, and it complied. For a moment his face was buried in smooth, dry fur. Halston snapped at the cat. It made a startled, disgruntled sound in its throat—*yowk!*—and leaped onto the seat. It stared up at him angrily, ears laid back.

"Wasn't supposed to do that, was I?" Halston croaked.

The cat opened its mouth and hissed at him. Looking at that strange, schizophrenic face, Halston could understand how Drogan might have thought it was a hellcat. It—

His thoughts broke off as he became aware of a dull, tingling feeling in both hands and forearms.

*Feeling. Coming back. Pins and needles.*

The cat leaped at his face, claws out, spitting.

Halston shut his eyes and opened his mouth. He bit at the cat's belly and got nothing but fur. The cat's front claws were clasped on his ears, digging in. The pain was enormous, brightly excruciating. Halston tried to raise his hands. They twitched but would not quite come out of his lap.

He bent his head forward and began to shake it back and forth, like a man shaking soap out of his eyes. Hissing and squalling, the cat held on. Halston could feel blood trickling down his cheeks. It was hard to get his breath. The cat's chest was pressed over his nose. It was possible to get some air in by mouth, but not much. What he did get came through fur. His ears felt as if they had been doused with lighter fluid and then set on fire.

He snapped his head back, and cried out in agony—he must have sustained a whiplash when the Plymouth hit. But the cat hadn't been expecting the reverse and it flew off. Halston heard it thud down in the back seat.

A trickle of blood ran in his eye. He tried again to move his hands, to raise one of them and wipe the blood away.

They trembled in his lap, but he was still unable to actually move them. He thought of the .45 special in its holster under his left arm.

*If I can get to my piece, kitty, the rest of your nine lives are going in a lump sum.*

More tingles now. Dull throbs of pain from his feet, buried and surely shattered under the engine block, zips and tingles from his legs—it felt exactly the way a limb that you've slept on does when it's starting to wake up. At that moment Halston didn't care about his feet. It was enough to know that his spine wasn't severed, that he wasn't going to finish out his life as a dead lump of body attached to a talking head.

*Maybe I had a few lives left myself.*

Take care of the cat. That was the first thing. *Then get out of the wreck*—maybe someone would come along, that would solve both problems at once. Not likely at 4:30 in the morning on a back road like this one, but barely possible. And—

And what was the cat doing back there?

He didn't like having it on his face, but he didn't like having it behind him and out of sight, either. He tried the rear-view mirror, but that was useless. The crash had knocked it awry and all it reflected was the grassy ravine he had finished up in.

A sound from behind him, like low, ripping cloth.

Purring.

*Hellcat my ass. It's gone to sleep back there.*

And even if it hadn't, even if it was somehow planning murder, what could it do? It was a skinny little thing, probably weighed all of four pounds soaking wet. And soon... soon he would be able to move his hands enough to get his gun. He was sure of it.

Halston sat and waited. Feeling continued to flood back into his body in a series of pins-and-needles incursions. Absurdly (or maybe in instinctive reaction to his close brush with death) he got an erection for a minute or so. *Be kind of hard to beat off under present circumstances,* he thought.

A dawn-line was appearing in the eastern sky. Somewhere a bird sang.

Halston tried his hands again and got them to move an eighth of an inch before they fell back.

*Not yet. But soon.*

A soft thud on the seatback beside him. Halston turned his head and looked into the black-white face, the glowing eyes with their huge dark pupils.

Halston spoke to it.

"I have never blown a hit once I took it on, kitty. This could be a first. I'm getting my hands back. Five minutes, ten at most. You want my advice? Go out the window. They're all open. Go out and take your tail with you."

The cat stared at him.

Halston tried his hands again. They came up, trembling wildly. Half an inch. An inch. He let them fall back limply. They slipped off his lap and thudded to the Plymouth's seat. They glimmered there palely, like large tropical spiders.

The cat was grinning at him.

*Did I make a mistake?* he wondered confusedly. He was a creature of hunch, and the feeling that he had made one was suddenly overwhelming. Then the cat's body tensed, and even as it leaped, Halston knew what it was going to do and he opened his mouth to scream.

The cat landed on Halston's crotch, claws out, digging.

At that moment, Halston wished he *had* been paralyzed. The pain was gigantic, terrible. He had never suspected that there could be such pain in the world. The cat was a spitting coiled spring of fury, clawing at his balls.

Halston *did* scream, his mouth yawning open, and that was when the cat changed direction and leaped at his face, leaped at his mouth. And at that moment Halston knew that it was something more than a cat. It was something possessed of a malign, murderous intent.

He caught one last glimpse of that black-and-white face below the flattened ears, its eyes enormous and filled with lunatic hate. It had gotten rid of the three old people and now it was going to get rid of John Halston.

It rammed into his mouth, a furry projectile. He gagged on it. Its front claws pinwheeled, tattering his tongue like a piece of liver. His stomach recoiled and he vomited. The vomit ran down into his windpipe, clogging it, and he began to choke.

In this extremity, his will to survive overcame the last of the impact paralysis. He brought his hands up slowly to grasp the cat. *Oh my God,,* he thought.

The cat was forcing its way into his mouth, flattening its body, squirming, working itself further and further in. He could feel his jaws creaking wider and wider to admit it.

He reached to grab it, yank it out, destroy it...and his hands clasped only the cat's tail.

Somehow it had gotten its entire body into his mouth. Its strange, black-and-white face must be crammed into his very throat.

A terrible thick gagging sound came from Halston's throat, which was swelling like a flexible length of garden hose.

His body twitched. His hands fell back into his lap and the fingers drummed senselessly on his thighs. His eyes sheened over, then glazed. They stared out through the Plymouth's windshield blankly at the coming dawn.

Protruding from his open mouth was two inches of bushy tail... half-black, half-white. It switched lazily back and forth.

It disappeared.

A bird cried somewhere again. Dawn came in breathless silence then, over the frost-rimmed fields of rural Connecticut.

● ● ●

The farmer's name was Will Reuss.

He was on his way to Placer's Glen to get the inspection sticker renewed on his farm truck when he saw the late morning sun twinkle on something in the ravine beside the road. He pulled over and saw the Plymouth lying at a drunken, canted angle in the ditch, barbed wire tangled in its grille like a snarl of steel knitting.

He worked his way down, and then sucked in his breath sharply. "Holy moley," he muttered to the bright November day. There was a guy sitting bolt upright behind the wheel, eyes open and glaring emptily into eternity. The Roper organization was never going to include him in its presidential poll again. His face was smeared with blood. He was still wearing his seatbelt.

The driver's door had been crimped shut, but Reuss managed to get it open by yanking with both hands. He leaned in and unstrapped the seatbelt, planning to check for ID. He was reaching for the coat when he noticed that the dead guy's shirt was rippling, just above the belt-buckle. Rippling ... and bulging. Splotches of blood began to bloom there like sinister roses.

"What the Christ?" He reached out, grasped the dead man's shirt, and pulled it up.

Will Reuss looked—and screamed.

Above Halston's navel, a ragged hole had been clawed in his flesh. Looking out was the gore-streaked black-and-white face of a cat, its eyes huge and glaring.

Reuss staggered back, shrieking, hands clapped to his face. A score of crows took cawing wing from a nearby field.

The cat forced its body out and stretched in obscene languor.

Then it leaped out the open window. Reuss caught sight of it moving through the high dead grass and then it was gone.

It seemed to be in a hurry, he later told a reporter from the local paper.

As if it had unfinished business.

# Black As the Pit,
# From Pole to Pole
## by Steven Utley and Howard Waldrop

*Frankenstein's monster has fascinated readers—and writers—ever since Mary Shelley's classic novel was first published in 1818. But no one has ever satisfactorily explained what happened to the creature after its disappearance at the end of that novel—till this delightful novella by two young Texas writers. The adventures they imagine for the monster evoke memories not only of Shelley but also of H. P. Lovecraft, Robert E. Howard, and Herman Melville, to name only three. This is one of those rare stories, a genuine* tour de force—*a tour that leads directly through the center of the Earth and into stranger lands than might have been imagined by any one author, or even two.*

## I

In an early American spring, the following circular was sent to learned men, scholars, explorers, and members of the Congress. It was later reprinted by various newspapers and magazines, both in the United States and abroad.

St. Louis, Missouri Territory, North America
April 10, 1818
   I declare that the earth is hollow; habitable within; containing a number of solid concentric spheres; one within the other, and that it is open at the pole twelve or sixteen degrees. I pledge my life in support of this truth, and am ready to explore the hollow if the world will support and aid me in the

undertaking. John Cleves Symmes of Ohio, Late Captain of Infantry.

N.B. I have ready for the press a treatise on the Principles of Matter, wherein I show proofs on the above proposition, account for various phenomena, and disclose Dr. Darwin's "Golden Secret."

My terms are the patronage of this and the new world; I dedicate to my wife and her ten children.

I select Dr. S.L. Mitchel, Sir H. Davy, and Barron Alexander Von Humboldt as my protectors. I ask 100 brave companions, well-equipped to start from Siberia, in the fall season, with reindeer and sledges, on the ice of the frozen sea; I engage we find a warm and rich land, stocked with thrifty vegetables and animals, if not men, on reaching one degree northward of latitude 82; we will return in the succeeding spring. J.C.S.

From the Introduction to *Frankenstein; or, The Modern Prometheus*, revised edition, 1831, by Mary Wollstonecraft Shelley:

Many and long were the conversations between Lord Byron and Shelley, to which I was a devout but nearly silent listener. During one of these, various philosophical doctrines were discussed, and among others the nature of the principle of life, and whether there was any possibility of its ever being discovered and communicated. They talked of the experiments of Dr. Darwin (I speak not of what the Doctor really did, or said that he did, but, as more to my purpose, of what was then spoken of as having been done by him) who preserved a piece of vermicelli in a glass case, 'til by some extraordinary means it began to move with a voluntary motion. Not thus, after all, would life be given. Perhaps a corpse would be reanimated; galvanism had given token of such things; perhaps the component parts of a creature might be manufactured, brought together and imbued with vital warmth...

*It ends here.*

The creature's legs buckled. His knees crunched through the crust as he went down. The death's-head face turned toward the sky. The wind swept across the ice cap, gathering up and flinging cold dust into his eyes.

The giant, the monster, the golem, closed his fine-veined eyelids and fell sideways. He could go no farther. He was numb and exhausted. He pressed his face down into the snow, and his thin, black lips began to shape the words of an unvoiced prayer:

It ends here, Victor Frankenstein. I am too weary to go on. Too weary even to cremate myself. Wherever you are now, whether passed into Heaven, Hell, or that nothingness from which you summoned me, look upon me with pity and compassion now. I had no choice. It ends here. At the top of the world, where no one shall ever come to remark on the passing of this nameless, forsaken wretch. It ends here, and the world is rid of me. Once again, Victor, I beseech you. Forgive me for my wicked machinations. Even as I forgave you yours.

He waited for death, his ears throbbing with the ever-slowing beat of his handseled heart. Spots of blackness began to erupt in his head and spread, overtaking and overwhelming the astonishingly vivid assortment of memories which flickered through his mind. Such a pretty little boy. I will not eat you, do not scream. Be quiet, please. I mean you no harm. Please. I want to be your friend. Hush now. Hush. Hush. I didn't know that he would break so easily. There is open sea not far from where I sprawl in the snow, awaiting death. The sea is the mother of all life. Save mine. The young man's name was Felix, and he drove me away. I could have crushed his skull with a single casual swat with the back of my hand. And I let him drive me away. Such a pretty little boy. Such a pretty little boy. Why was I not made pretty? Tell me now, Frankenstein. It is important that I know. Do I have a soul? Felix. Felix. I will be with you on your wedding night. I will be with you. Do I have a *soul,* Victor Frankenstein?

He suddenly pushed himself up on his elbows and shook ice from his eyelids. He could see the sea before him, but it was too bright to gaze upon. It seemed to burn like molten gold, and it was as though the very maw of Hell were opening to receive him.

He collapsed, burying his face in the snow, and lay there whimpering, no strength left now, no sensation in his legs and hands. *Do I have a soul?* he demanded a final time, just as he felt himself sliding, sliding, about to take the plunge into oblivion. There was time enough for a second question. *If so, where will it go?* And then there was no time at all.

· · ·

He had not felt so disoriented since the night of his first awakening. He sat up painfully and glared around in confusion. Then tears streamed from his eyes and froze upon his cheeks, and he shrieked with rage and frustration.

"Fiend! Monster! *Damn you!*"

He struggled to his feet and tottered wildly, flailing the air with his mismatched fists. And he kept screaming.

"*This* is the full horror of your great achievement! Death won't have me, Frankenstein! Hell spews me forth! *You made me better than you thought!*"

His thickly wrapped legs, aching with the slow return of circulation, began to pump stiffly, driving him across the ice. He kicked up clouds of cold snow dust. Then glass-sliver pain filled his lungs, and his mad run slowed to a walk. Fury spun and eddied in his guts, hotter by far than the fire in his chest, but it was fury commingled with sorrow. He sat down abruptly, put his face into his hands, and sobbed.

Death had rejected him again.

At the instant of his birth on a long-ago, almost forgotten midnight, he had drawn his first puzzled breath, and Death had bowed to Life for the first time, had permitted a mere man to pry its fingers from the abandoned bones and flesh of the kirkyard and the charnel house. Death had never reclaimed that which had been taken from it. Time and again, Death had chosen not to terminate his comfortless existence.

I was never ill, Frankenstein. I survived fire and exposure. I sustained injuries which would have killed or at least incapacitated even the hardiest of human beings. Even you could not kill me, you who gave me life. That should make you proud. You shot me at point-blank range after I killed your beautiful Elizabeth. You couldn't kill me, though. Perhaps nothing can kill me.

His sobbing subsided. He sat in the snow and dully rolled the bitter thought over and over in his mind. Perhaps nothing can kill me. Perhaps *nothing* can kill me. When Victor Frankenstein had shot him, the ball struck him low in the left side of the back and emerged a couple of inches above and to the right of the incongruous navel. The impact had knocked him from the sill of the château window through which he had been making an escape. Doubled up on the ground beneath the window, he had heard Frankenstein's howl of anguish over the murdered Elizabeth. Then, clutching his abdomen, he had lurched away into the night.

The bleeding had ceased within minutes. The wounds were closed by the following morning and, at the end of a week's time, were no more than moon-shaped, moon-colored scars. He had wondered about his regenerative powers but briefly, however, for his enraged creator was breathing down his neck in hot, vengeful pursuit. There had been no time for idle speculation during the trek across Europe, across Siberia, into the wind-swept Arctic.

He pushed his tongue out and licked his frostbitten lips. Words started to rumble up from the deep chest, then lost all life of their own, and emerged dull-sounding and flat. "You cheated me, Victor Frankenstein. In every way, you cheated me."

He paused, listening. The wind moaned like the breath of some immense frost-god wrapped in unpleasant dreams. Muffled thunder rolled across the ice from the direction of the now-leaden sea.

"I owe you nothing, Victor. *Nothing.*"

He got to his feet again and began moving toward the edge of the ice. Plucking bits of ice from his face and hair, his mind bubbling and frothing, he was suddenly stopped in his tracks by a particularly vicious gust of wind. His eyes filled with salt water. The cold cut through his parka, flesh and bone, and he cried out in pure animal misery. He sucked on his frozen fingers and tried to stamp warmth back into his limbs. In the sky, its bottom half under the horizon, the heatless, useless sun mocked him. He snarled at it, shook his fist at it, turned his back on it.

And could not believe what he saw before him.

Hanging between the northern edge of the world and the zenith was a second, smaller sun.

## II

In the year 1818, *Frankenstein; or, The Modern Prometheus* was published. Mary Shelley was twenty-one years old.

John Cleves Symmes, late of the Ohio Infantry, published his treatise about the hollow earth. He was a war hero and a Missouri storekeeper. He was thirty-eight years old.

Herman Melville would not be born for another year.

Jeremiah N. Reynolds was attending Ohio University but would soon become a doctor and a scientist. He would also fall under the spell of Symmes.

Edgar Allan Poe, nine years old, was living with his foster parents.

Percy Shelley, Lord Byron, and Dr. Polidori sailed as often as possible in the sloop *Ariel* on Lake Como.

In New Bedford, Massachusetts, young Arthur Gordon Pym sailed around the harbor in his sloop, also christened *Ariel*. His one burning desire was to go to sea.

In the South Seas, Mocha Dick, the great white whale, was an age no man could know or guess. Mocha Dick was not aware of aging, nor of the passing of time. It knew only of the sounding deeps and, infrequently, of the men who stuck harpoons into it until it turned on them and broke apart their vessels.

Victor Frankenstein's patchwork man was similarly unaware of the passing of time. The creature did not know how long he had slept in the ice at the top of the world, nor was he able to mark time within earth.

It became subtly warmer as the mysterious second sun rose in time with the ice cap's apparent northerly drift. The creature kept telling himself that what he saw was impossible, that there could be no second sun, that it was merely an illusion, a reflected image of the sun he had always known, a clever optical trick of some sort. But he was too miserable to ponder the phenomenon for very long at a time.

He subsisted on the dried meat which he had carried with him from Siberia in the pouch of his parka. He had little strength for exercise, and the circulation of his vital fluids often slowed to the point where he was only semiconscious. His eyes began playing other tricks on him. The horizon started to rise before him, to warp around him outrageously, curving upward and away in every direction, as though he had been carried over the lip of an enormous bowl and was slowly, lazily sliding toward its bottom. He could account for none of it.

He was dozing, frozen, in the shelter of an ice block when a shudder passed through the mass beneath him. He blinked, vaguely aware of something being wrong, and then he was snapped fully awake by the sight and *sound* of a gigantic blossom of spray at the edge of the sea. The thunder of crumbling ice brought him up on hands and knees. He stared, fascinated, as the eruption of water hung in the air for a long moment before falling, very slowly, very massively, back into the sea.

Then panic replaced fascination. He realized what was happening.

The ice was breaking up. He spun, the motion consuming years, took two steps and sank, howling, into snow suddenly turned to quicksand. He fell and scrambled up in time to see an ice ridge explode into powder. The shelf on which he stood pitched crazily as it started to slide down the parent mass's new face. The scraping walls of the fissure shook the air with the sound of a million tormented, screaming things. Dwarfed to insignificance by the forces at play around him, the giant was hurled flat. The breath left his lungs painfully.

He pushed himself up on elbows and sucked the cold, cutting air back into his tormented chest. The world beyond his clenched fists seemed to sag, then dropped out of sight. A moment later, clouds of freezing seawater geysered from the abyss as the shelf settled and rolled, stabilizing itself.

The creature turned and crawled away from the chasm. He kept moving until he was at the approximate center of the new iceberg. He squatted there, alternately shaking and going numb with terror.

He had seen the abyss open inches from him.

He had looked down the throat of the death he had wanted.

He had felt no temptation.

He cursed life for its tenacity. He cursed, again, the man whose explorations into the secrets of life had made it impossible for him to simply lie down, sleep and let the Arctic cold take him.

He could not help but brood over his immunity to death. What would have happened, he wondered, had he been precipitated into the fissure when the shelf broke off? Surely he would have been smeared to thin porridge between the sliding, scraping masses. But—

There was another rumble behind him. He turned his head and saw a large section of the berg drop out of sight, into the sea.

It doesn't matter, he reflected as he dug into his parka for a piece of meat. The ice is going to melt, and I will be hurled into the sea. I wonder if I can drown.

He did not relish the prospect of finding out.

His virtually somnambulistic existence resumed. He ate his dried meat, melted snow in his mouth to slake his thirst, and fully regained consciousness only when the berg shook him awake with the crash and roar of its disintegration. The sun he had known all of his life, the one which he could not think of as other than the *real* sun, at last disappeared behind him, while the strange second sun now seemed fixed unwaveringly at zenith. The horizon was still rising, rolling up the sky until it appeared behind occasional cloud masses and, sometimes, above them. It was as though the world were trying to double over on itself and enfold him.

He amused himself with that image between naps. Nothing was strange to him anymore, not the stationary sun, not the horizonless vista. He was alive, trapped on a melting iceberg. He was in Hell.

It was only when he began to make out the outlines of a coast in the sky that he experienced a renewed sense of wonder. In the time which followed, a time of unending noon, of less sleep and more terror as the berg's mass diminished, the sight of that concave, stood-on-edge land filled him with awe and a flickering sort of hope which even hunger, physical misery, and fear could not dispel.

He was alive, but merely being alive was not enough. It had never been enough.

He was alive, and here, sweeping down out of the sky, rolling itself out toward him in open invitation was . . . what?

He stood at the center of his iceberg and looked at his hands. He thought of the scars on his body, the proofs of his synthesis, and he thought:

What *was* my purpose, Victor Frankenstein? Did you have some kind of destiny planned for me when you gave me life? Had you not rejected me at the moment of my birth, had you accepted responsibility for my being in the world, would there have been some sort of fulfillment, some use, for me in the world of men?

The berg shivered underfoot for a second, and he cried out, went to his knees, hugged a block of ice desperately. The dark land mass swam in the air. When the tremor had subsided, he laughed shakily and got to his feet. His head spun, grew light, filled with stars and explosions. He reached for the ice block in an effort to steady himself but fell anyway and lay in the snow, thinking.

Thinking, This is no natural land before me, Frankenstein, and perhaps there are no men here.

Thinking, I could be free of men here, free of everything.

Thinking, This is going to be *my* land, Frankenstein.

Thinking, This is no natural land, and I am no natural man.

Thinking.

The berg had begun crunching its way through drifting sheets of pack ice when the creature spotted something else which stood out against the brilliant whiteness of the frozen sea. He watched the thing for a long time, noting that it did not move, before he was able to discern the sticklike fingers of broken masts and the tracery of rigging. It looked like some forgotten, bedraggled toy, tossed aside by a bored child.

The ship was very old. Its sides had been crushed in at the waterline, and the ice-sheathed debris of its rigging and lesser masts sat upon the hulk like a stand of dead, gray trees. A tattered flag hung from the stern, frozen solid, looking to be fashioned from thick glass.

When his iceberg had finally slowed to an imperceptible crawl in the midst of the pack, the creature cautiously made his way down to the sheet and walked to the ship. When he had come close enough, he called out in his ragged voice. There was no answer. He had not expected one.

Below decks, he found unused stores and armaments, along with three iron-hard corpses. There were flint, frozen biscuits, and salt pork, kegs of frozen water and liquor. There was a wealth of cold-climate clothing and lockers packed with brittle charts and strange instruments.

He took what he could carry. From the several armaments lockers, he selected a long, double-edged dagger, a heavy cutlass and scabbard, a blunderbuss and a brace of pistols to supplement the one he had carried throughout his Siberian trek. There had been two pistols originally—he had stolen the set before leaving Europe and had used them on a number of occasions to get what he needed in the way of supplies from terrified Siberian peasants. One of the pistols had been missing after his departure from the whaling vessel. He supposed that it had fallen from his belt when he leaped from the ship to the ice.

There was enough powder in several discarded barrels to fill a small keg. He found shot in a metal box and filled the pouch of his parka.

He did not bother himself with thoughts about the dead men or their vanished comrades. Whoever they had been, they had left in a hurry, and they had left him their goods. He was still cold, tired and hungry, but the warm clothing was now his, and he could rest in the shelter of the derelict. He had hardtack and meat and the means to make fire. And he had weapons.

He returned to the deck for a moment and contemplated the upward-curving landscape ahead.

*In this world, perhaps, there are no men.*

He waved the cutlass, wearily jubilant, and, for the first time in his life, he began to feel truly free.


## III


John Cleves Symmes published a novel in 1820, under the name Adam Seaborn. Its title was *Symzonia: A Voyage of Discovery*, and it made extensive use of Symmes's theories about the hollow world and the polar openings. In the novel, Captain Seaborn and his crew journeyed to the inner world, where they discovered many strange plants and animals and encountered a Utopian race. The explorers eventually emerged from the interior and returned to known waters. They became rich as traders, exchanging Symzonian goods for cacao and copra.

In 1826, James McBride wrote a book entitled *Symmes' Theory of Concentric Spheres*. Meanwhile, Congress was trying to raise money to finance an expedition to the North Pole, largely to find out whether or not there were indeed openings at the northern verge.

Symmes traveled about the United States, lecturing on his theory and raising funds from private donors in order to finance his proposed expedition to the north. The Russian government offered to outfit an expedition to the Pole if Symmes would meet the party at St. Petersburg, but the American did not have the fare for the oceanic crossing. He continued to range throughout the Midwest and New England, lecturing and raising money. His disciple, Jeremiah N. Reynolds, accompanied him during the last years of his life. During his winter lecture tour of 1828, Symmes fell ill and returned to Hamilton, Ohio, where he died on May 29, 1829.

The ice pack eventually yielded to snow-covered tundra, spotted here and there with patches of moss and lichens. In a matter of a long while, he entered a land marked by ragged growths of tough grass and stunted, wind-twisted trees. There was small game here, mainly rodents of a kind he did not recognize. They appeared to have no fear of him. Killing them was easy.

Larger game animals began to show themselves as he put still more distance between the ice-bound sea and himself. He supplemented his diet of biscuits, salt pork, and rodents with venison. He walked unafraid until he saw a distant pack of wolves chase down something which looked like an elk. But wolves and elk alike looked far too large, even from where he observed them, to be the ones he had known in Europe.

After that, he kept his firearms cleaned, loaded, and primed at all times, and he carried his cutlass like a cane. When he slept, he slept ringed by fires. For all of his apprehensions, he had only one near-fatal encounter.

He had crested a hillock, on the trail of giant elk, when he saw several dozen enormous beasts grazing some distance away. The animals looked somewhat like pictures of elephants he had seen, but he recalled that elephants were not covered with shaggy reddish-brown hair, that their tusks were straighter and shorter than the impressively curved tusks of these woolly beasts.

The creature pondered the unlikelihood of his blunderbuss bringing down one of the beasts and decided to skirt the herd in the direction of a thicket.

He was almost in the shadow of the ugly trees when he heard a bellow and a crash. A massive, shaggy thing as large as a coach charged him, mowing down several small trees as it burst from the thicket. Frankenstein's man dropped his blunderbuss and cutlass and hurled himself to one side as his attacker thundered past, long head down, long horn out. The beast did not turn. It galloped straight past and disappeared over the hillock. In the thicket, something coughed. Retrieving his weapons, the creature decided to skirt the thicket.

Below the ice and snow, beyond the pine forests that were the domain of strange and yet familiar mammals, beyond glaciers and a ring of mountains were the swampy lowlands. The bottom of the bowl-shaped continent turned out to be a realm of mist and semigloom, of frequent warm rains and lush growth. Cinder cones and hot springs dotted the landscape.

It was a realm of giants, too, of beasts grander and of more appalling aspect than any which the creature had previously thought possible.

He saw swamp-dwelling monsters six times larger than the largest of the odd woolly elephants. Their broad black backs broke the surface of fetid pools like smooth islets, and their serpentine necks rose and fell rhythmically as they nosed through the bottom muck, scooping up masses of soft plants, then came up to let gravity drag the mouthfuls down those incredibly long throats.

He saw a hump-backed quadruped festooned with alternating rows of triangular plates of bone along its spine. Wicked-looking spikes were clustered near the tip of the thing's muscular tail. It munched ferns and placidly regarded him as he circled it, awed, curious, and properly respectful.

He saw small flying animals which, despite their wedge-shaped heads, reminded him irresistibly of bats. There were awkward birds with tooth-filled beaks here, insects as big as rats, horse-sized lizards with ribbed sails sprouting along their spines, dog-sized salamanders with glistening polychromatic skins and three eyes. He could not set his boot down without crushing some form of life underfoot. Parasites infested him, and it was only by bathing frequently in the hot springs that he could relieve himself of his unwanted guests. Clouds of large dragonflies and other, less readily named winged things exploded from the undergrowth constantly as he slogged across the marshy continental basin, driven by the compulsion to explore and establish the boundaries of *his* world. There was life everywhere in the lowlands.

And there was the striding horror that attacked him, a hissing, snapping reptile with a cavernous maw and sharklike teeth as long as his fingers. It was the lord of the realm. When it espied the wandering patchwork man, it roared out its authority and charged, uprooting saplings and small tree ferns with its huge hind feet.

The creature stood his ground and pointed the blunderbuss. Flint struck steel, the pan flared, and, with a boom and an echo which stilled the jungle for miles, the charge caught the predator full in its lowered face.

The reptile reared and shrieked as the viscid wreckage of its eyes dribbled from its jowls and dewlap. Lowering its head again, it charged blindly and blundered past its intended victim, into the forest, where it was soon lost from sight, if not from hearing.

The creature quickly but carefully reloaded the blunderbuss and resumed his trek. A short while later, one of the blinded monster's lesser cousins, a man-sized biped with needlelike teeth and skeletal fingers, attacked. The blunderbuss blew it to pieces.

He got away from the twitching fragments as quickly as he could and watched from a distance as at least half a dozen medium-large bipeds and sail-backed lizards converged unerringly upon the spot. He turned his back on the ensuing free-for-all and, cradling the blunderbuss in his arms, looked longingly at the ice-topped mountains encircling the basin.

He had found the cold highlands infinitely more to his liking. He could not comprehend mountain-big reptiles who did nothing but eat. He was tired of being bitten and stung by insects, sick to death of mud and mist and the stench of decaying vegetation. He was, he frankly admitted to himself, not at all willing to cope with the basin's large predators on a moment-to-moment basis. The beasts of the highlands had been odd but recognizable, like parodies of the forms of that other world, the world of men.

He chuckled mirthlessly, and when he spoke, his voice sounded alien, out of place, amid the unceasing cacophony of the basin denizens' grunting, bellowing, shrilling, croaking, screeching, chittering.

What he said was, "We are all parodies here!"

It was extremely easy to become lost in the lowlands. The mists rose and fell in accordance with a logic all their own. He walked, keeping the peaks before him whenever he could see them, trusting in his sense of direction when he could not. Encounters with predatory reptiles came to seem commonplace. His blunderbuss was capable of eviscerating the lesser flesh-eating bipeds, and the cutlass was good for lopping off heads and limbs. He could outrun the darting but quickly winded sail-backed lizards. He made very wide detours around the prowling titans.

And he got lost.

He began to notice many holes in the ground as he blundered through the land of mist. He supposed that these might lead back to the world of men, but he did not care to find out. He knew where he wanted to be. He would be more than glad to let the basin's carnivorous lords have their murky realm, just as he was happy to leave men to their own world.

He finally came to a cave-pocked escarpment. Two great rivers emptied noisily into hollows at the base of the towering formation. The basalt mass rose into the mists, higher than he could see. It was isolated from his yearned-for mountains. There was no point in attempting to scale it.

He ranged back and forth across the base of the escarpment for some time, from one river to the other. He ate the eggs of the flying reptiles who made their nests on the cliff face. He slept in the caves. He sulked.

At last, he began to explore the caves which honeycombed the escarpment.

## IV

Jeremiah N. Reynolds stood at the aft rail of the *Annawan* as she slid from the harbor into the vast Atlantic, windy already in October, and cold. But the *Annawan* was bound for much colder waters: those of the Antarctic.

To starboard was the *Annawan's* sister, the *Seraph*. Together, they would cross the Atlantic along its length and sail into the summer waters of the breaking ice pack. Reynolds hoped to find Symmes's southern polar opening. He was not to have much luck.

The *Annawan* and *Seraph* expedition got as far as 62⁰ South—far south indeed, but Antarctica had already been penetrated as deeply as 63⁰45' by Palmer in 1820. A landing party was sent out toward the Pole, or, as Reynolds hoped, toward the southern verge. Symmes had thought that the concavities toward the interior world would be located at or just above latitude 82°. Reynolds and his party had come so close, but bad weather forced them to wait, and then supplies ran low. The party was rescued just in time. The expedition headed northward before the Antarctic winter could close on them.

It was while Reynolds was with his ill-fated landing party that John Cleves Symmes died in Ohio, but Reynolds was not to learn this for nearly a year. Off the coast of Chile, the *Seraph's* crew mutinied, put Reynolds and the officers ashore, and took off for a life of piracy.

Jeremiah N. Reynolds devoted the next three or four years to various South Seas expeditions, to whaling, to botanical and zoological studies in the Pacific. He continued to defend Symmes's theories and traveled about the United States to gain support, as Symmes had done before him, for a gigantic assault upon the interior world.

The creature went down.

He lost his way a second time and could only wander aimlessly through the caves, and he went down.

Into another world.

Into the world containing the great open sea, fed by the two great rivers that drained into hollows beneath the great escarpment. This second interior world was illuminated by electrical discharges and filled with constant thunder. There was a fringe of land populated by a few small animals and sparse, blighted plants.

The creature could not find his way back up to the basin. He had no choice but to pass through the world of the great open sea, into a third interior world.

There was a fourth world, a fifth, a sixth, and probably more which were not in line with his burrowing course. He moved constantly, eating what he could find, amazed and appalled by the extremes represented by the various worlds. He caught himself dreaming of the sun and moon, of days and nights. But, if he ever felt the old stirrings of loneliness now, he did not admit as much to himself. Good or bad, he told himself, these worlds were his to claim if he chose to do so. He did not need companionship.

Even so, even so, he left his mark for others to see.

There was an ape in one of the interior worlds. It was the largest ape that had ever lived in or on the earth, and, though it was an outsider to all of the ape tribes in its cavernous habitat, it ruled over them like some human monarch. It came and went freely from band to band. What it wanted, it took. This ranged from simple backrubs to sexual favors. While it was at one of the females in a given band, the erstwhile dominant males would go off to bite mushroom stalks or shake trees or do some other displacement activity. Had they interfered, the great ape would have killed them.

Frankenstein's creature tripped over the ape as the latter slept in a tangle of dead plant stalks.

The patchwork man lost the third finger on his left hand.

The great ape lost its life, its hide, and some of its meat. A pack of lesser pongids came across the carcass after the victor had departed. They gave the place a wide berth thereafter, for they reasoned among themselves—dimly, of course—that no animal had done this. No animal could have skinned the great ape that way. Something new and more terrible stalked the world now, something too dangerous, too wild, for them to understand.

They heard from other tribes that the thing which had taken the skin carried it over its shoulders. The thing looked much like a hairless ape. It made the lightning-flames with its hands and placed meat in the fire before eating it.

They would nervously look behind themselves for generations to come, fearing the new thing infinitely more than they had ever feared the great ape whose skin it had taken.

## V

The Franklin expedition set out for the North Pole in the summer of 1844. Sir John Franklin took with him two ships, the *Erebus* and the *Terror*. These were powerful, three-masted vessels with steam screws. They were made to conquer the Arctic.

The Franklin expedition was lost with all 129 members. The Arctic was the scene of a search for survivors for more than forty years afterward. During the course of these rescue missions, more of the north was mapped than had previously been dreamed possible.

In the 1860s, an American lived for several years among the Esquimaux to the north and west of Hudson Bay. He continually troubled them with questions, perhaps in the hope of learning something of the last days of the Franklin expedition.

He finally came to a village in which the storyteller, an old woman, told him of a number of white men who had pulled a boat across the ice. The American plied the storyteller with questions and soon realized that she was not talking about survivors of the Franklin expedition of fifteen years before. She was recounting the story of some survivors of one of Frobisher's voyages, 300 years before, in search of the Northwest Passage.

The creature fought his way through other lands, and somewhere he passed by the middle of the earth and never knew it.

The next world he conquered, for human beings lived there.


## VI

Some Navaho, all of the Hopi, and the Pueblo Indians of the American Southwest each have a legend about the Under-Earth People, their gods.

The legends all begin:

It was dark under the earth, and the people who lived there wanted to come up. So they came up through the holes in the ground, and they found this new world with the sun in the sky. They went back down and returned with their uncles and their cousins. Then, when they all got here, they made us.

In the center of the villages are *kivas*, underground structures in which religious ceremonies are held. In the center of the floor of each kiva is a well, going far down out of sight. It is from the wells that the first men are said to have come to the outside world.

The memory of the Hopi may be better than that of the Esquimaux. The Hopi remember further back than Frobisher. If you ask them, they will tell of Esteban, the black slave of Cabeza de Vaca. They will tell of the corn circle they made when Coronado came, and of the fight in the clouds of the highest pueblo, and how many had to jump to their deaths when the village was set afire by the Spaniards.

But, mostly, the Hopi remember Esteban, the second outsider whom they ever saw. Esteban was tall and black. He had thick lips, and he loved to eat chili peppers, they will tell you.

That was 1538.

And in the center of each pueblo is a kiva, where the first men came from inside the earth.

He saw them first as they paddled animal-hide boats through the quietness of a calm lake where he drank. They were indistinct blobs of men, difficult to see in the perpetual twilight of this new interior world. But they were men.

The creature withdrew into the shadows beneath the grayish, soft-barked trees and watched thoughtfully as the men paddled past and vanished into the gloom.

Men. Men *here*. In *his* world. *How?* He weighed the blunderbuss in his hands. Could mere men have fought their way this far into the earth? Even with ships in which to cross the Arctic sea, even with firearms and warm clothing and the strength of numbers, could poor, weak human beings do what he had done? How could there be men here? How? Were they native to this subterranean world? He shrugged in his ape-hide cloak, and a frown creased his broad forehead.

I know what to expect of men. I will leave this place and go . . .

Where? Back to the cavern of the apes? Back to the land of heat and molten rock? Back to the great open sea?

No, he thought, then said the word aloud. "No." The inner world belongs to me. All of it. I won't share it with men. He made a careful check of his firearms, shouldered the blunderbuss and set out to find these human beings.

He tried to remain alert and wary as he walked, for there were dangers other than men in this world. Once, from a safe distance, he had seen a vaguely bearlike beast tearing at a carcass. Another time, he had watched as an obviously large flying reptile, larger by far than the delicate horrors he had observed in the basin, glided past, a black silhouette against the swirling gray murk overhead. Yet another time, he had happened upon the spoor of a four-footed animal whose clawtipped paws left impressions six inches wide. Only a fool would not have been cautious here. But, still, his mind wandered.

I could attack these men, he told himself. I have weapons, and I have my great strength. And I cannot die by ordinary means. I would have the element of surprise in my favor, too. I could charge into their camp and wipe them out easily. And then, once again, I would be free to come and go as I please. If I do not kill them now, when the odds favor me, they'll find out about me eventually, and then I'll have to fight them anyway. They will not tolerate my existence once they know.

*But* . . . He stopped, perplexed by a sudden thought. But what if these men are different from those I knew before? Idiotic notion! Don't delude yourself. You know what men are like. They hate you on sight. You don't belong with men. You aren't a man, and you have no place among men. But what if? . . .

He had eaten several times and slept twice when he finally located a squalid village built on the shore of a deep inlet. From a vantage point among the trees, the creature could see that the village consisted of perhaps two dozen lodges, crudely fashioned of poles and hides. He saw women smoking fish on racks and chewing animal skins to soften them while the men repaired their ungainly boats at the water's edge. Naked children ran among the lodges, chasing dogs and small piglike animals.

The men, he noted, were armed mainly with spears, though a very few also had what appeared to be iron swords of primitive design at their sides. He smiled grimly, envisioning the psychological impact his blunderbuss's discharge might have upon such poorly armed opponents.

He was thinking about tactics when a long, low craft hove into view at the mouth of the inlet and sped toward the beach. The men on the shore shouted and waved. The women put aside their skins, and the children raced a yelping horde of dogs to the water's edge. As soon as the canoe had been beached, its passengers—about ten men—were mobbed. The sounds were jubilant. The sounds were of welcome. In his place of hiding, Frankenstein's man unexpectedly found himself sick at heart.

Now, whispered a part of himself. Creep down now, and begin killing them while their attention is diverted.

He regarded the blunderbuss in his hands. At close range, it could probably kill two or three people at once, and possibly maim others. He felt the pistols digging into his skin where his belt held them against his abdomen. He closed his eyes and saw heads and bellies splitting open as he strode through the village, swinging the cutlass in devastating arcs. He saw all of the villagers dead and mutilated on the ground before him. The palms of his hands started to itch. Kill them off.

A celebration was getting underway in the village. Eyes still closed, the creature listened to the thin, shrill laughter, to the bursts of song. Something twisted a knife in his heart, and he knew that he was helpless to do anything to these people.

He wanted to go down into the village. He wanted to be with these people. He wanted to be of them. He had not known that he was so painfully lonely. I still want people, he bleakly admitted to himself. Frankenstein made me a fool. I am a monster who wants friends. I want to have a place among men. It isn't right that I should be so alone.

Cold reason attempted to assert itself. *These people will kill you if they have the chance. They don't need you. They don't want you. Your own creator turned his back on you. Frankenstein put his curse on you. Frankenstein made you what you are, and that is all you can be. A monster. An abomination in the eyes of men. A—*

Frankenstein is dead.

*His work lives on.*

Frankenstein has no power over me now. I control my own life.

He was on his feet, walking into the village, and, within himself, there were still screams. *Will you throw your life away so easily? Will you—*

I want people. I want friends. I want what other men have.

Bearlike in his shaggy cloak of ape skin, he entered the village.

If Victor Frankenstein had made him a monster, the blunderbuss made him a god.

The men who had arrived in the long boat were obviously home from a fairly successful raiding trip. A quantity of goods had been heaped at the approximate center of the village. Nearby was a smaller pile of grislier trophies: severed heads, hands, feet, and genitals. The villagers had started drinking from earthen vessels, and many of them were already inebriated.

But one of the children spotted the creature as he stepped out of the shadows. A cry of alarm went up. The women and youngsters scattered. The men lurched forward with spears and swords at the ready.

The creature had stopped dead in his tracks as soon as the commotion began. Now he swung the blunderbuss up and around. He blew a patch of sod as big around as his head from the ground in front of the warriors, then watched, immensely gratified, as the spears and swords slipped, one and two at a time, from trembling hands.

"We are going to be friends," he said. And laughed with wicked delight. "Oh, Victor, were you but here!"

The creature had just had an inspired thought.

Before eighteen months had passed in the outer world, the creature was the leader of the largest war party ever seen in the interior. His firearms, coupled with his demonic appearance, guaranteed him godhood, for the barbarians who lived on the shores of the great lake were a deeply superstitious lot. They dared not incur his wrath. Their petty animosities were forgotten, or at least ignored, as he conquered village after village, impressing the inhabitants into his service.

With 300 warriors at his back, he finally left the lake and followed a lazily winding river until he came to the first of the city-states. It was called Karac in the harsh tongue of the inner world, and it was almost magnificent after the rude villages of the lake dwellers. Karac sent an army of 500 men to deal with the savages howling around the walls. The creature routed Karac's army, slept and marched into the city.

Ipks fell next, then Kaerten, Sandten, Makar, until only Brasandokar, largest of the city-states, held against him by the might of its naval forces.

Against that city the creature took with him not only his mob of warriors but also the armies of his conquered city-states, ripe for revenge. They had been under the domination of Brasandokar for a long time, and they wanted its blood. Under the creature, they got it. Two thousand men attacked in the dim twilight, from the land, from the great river. They swarmed over the gates and walls, they swept the docks and quays. Flames lit the air as the raiders ran through the stone-paved streets. They plundered, and Frankenstein's man ravaged with them.

He stopped them only when he saw the woman.

Her name was Megan, and she was the second daughter of the War Leader of Brasandokar. The creature looked up from his pillaging and saw her in the window of a low tower toward which invaders were sweeping. He stopped the rapine and went to the tower and escorted her down. He could not say why he did this. He knew that not even the woman whom his accursed creator had begun to fashion for him had moved him so much. Megan had stood in the tower window, her head turned to the side, listening to the battle raging below. Brave? Foolish?

It took him a moment after he found her in the tower to realize that she was blind. He placed her small, pale hand upon his arm and silently led her down the stairs. Together, they entered the courtyard, and his panting, blood-spattered men parted to let him pass, and all that he could think was, I have found my destiny.

Glow-lamps fashioned from luminous weed hung everywhere. The city-state of Brasandokar seemed laid out for a masked ball, but there were still embers to be found in the fire-gutted buildings, and the streets were still full of the stench of drying blood. Widows sat in doorways and sang songs of mourning. The sounds of their grief were punctuated by shouts and hammerings.

In the tower where he had first seen her, the creature sat across from Megan. She toyed restlessly with his gift, a black jewel taken from the coffers of Sandten.

I have never before seen such a beautiful woman, he thought. And then that dark and seething part of himself which had once urged the extermination of the villagers whispered, *Fool, fool* . . . He shook his head angrily. No. Not this time. Not a fool. Not a monster. A man. An emperor. A god.

A god in love for the first time in his life.

"Sir," said the Lady Megan, setting the jewel aside.

"Yes?"

"I ask you not to go on with this suit."

There was a mocking laugh inside his head. He shuddered and ground his teeth together. "Do I offend you?" he asked, and his voice sounded thick and strange.

"You are a conqueror, sir, and Brasandokar is yours to do with as you please. Your power is unlimited. A word from you, and your armies—"

"I am finished with this city, Lady Megan. I am finished with my armies. Brasandokar will show no sign of having been invaded within a matter of..." He trailed off helplessly. There were no weeks in a timeless world.

She nodded slightly. "I hear people working outside. But I hear wives crying for their husbands, too. My father is still abed with his wounds, and my brother-in-law is still dead. You are still a conqueror. I cannot consider your suit. Take me as is your right, but—"

"*No.*"

Lady Megan turned her blind eyes in the direction of his voice. "You may be thought a weak king otherwise, sir."

He rose to his full height and began pacing back and forth across the room. Not much of an emperor after all, he thought bitterly. Certainly not much of a god.

"Why do you not take me?" Lady Megan asked quietly.

Because. Because. "Because I am in love with you. I don't want to take you against your will. Because I am very ugly."

Because I am a monster. Life without soul. A golem. A travesty. Thing. It. Creature. He stopped pacing and stood by the window from which she had listened to the sack of Brasandokar. At his orders, his followers labored alongside the citizens to repair the damage inflicted upon the city. His empire would bear few scars.

Ashes in my mouth. Shall I leave now? Take away their god, and these people will soon go back to their squabbles and raids. And where can a god go now? Yes. Downriver. To the great flat river beyond Brasandokar. Into new worlds. Into old hells.

He started when he felt her hands upon his back. He turned and looked down at her, and she reached up as far as she could to run her fingers across his face and neck.

"Yes," Lady Megan said. "You are very ugly. All scars and seams." She touched his hands. "You are mismatched. Mismatched also is your heart. You have the heart of a child in the body of a beast."

"Shall I leave you, Lady Megan?"

She backed away and went unerringly to her seat. "I do not love you."

"I know."

"But, perhaps, I could come to love you."


## VII

Edgar Allen Poe's first published story, "MS Found in a Bottle," was about Symmes' Hole, although Poe did not know it at the time. It wasn't until 1836, while editing Arthur Gordon Pym's manuscript, that Poe came across one of Jeremiah N. Reynolds's speeches to the U.S. House of Representatives, urging them to outfit an expedition to the South Seas. In the same issue which carried the opening installment of Pym's memoirs, Poe had an article defending both Reynolds and the theories of the late Captain Symmes.

A year after the publication of *The Narrative of Arthur Gordon Pym*, Reynolds published his book on whaling in the South Pacific, memoirs of his days as expedition scientist aboard the *Annawan*. In this book, he gave the first complete accounts of the savage white whale, Mocha Dick, who terrorized whaling fleets for half a century.

Poe and Reynolds never met.

They were married in Brasandokar. The creature had to wear his wedding signet on his little finger, since his ring finger had been bitten off by the great ape. After the ceremony, he took his Lady Megan to the tallest tower in the city and gently turned her face up so that her dead eyes peered into the murk.

"There should be stars there," he told her, "and the moon. Lights in the air. A gift to you, were I able to make it so."

"It sounds as if it would be wonderful to see."

If only I could make it so.

Sex was difficult for them, owing to the way he had been made. They managed nonetheless, and Lady Megan bore him a stillborn son. She was heartbroken, but he did not blame her. He cursed himself, his creator, the whole uncaring universe, and his own words to Victor Frankenstein came back to haunt him: "I shall be with you on your wedding night."

Frankenstein would always be with him, though he was long since dead.

In what would have been, in the outer world, the third year of their love, Kaerten revolted. Within Brasandokar, there was dissent: his generals wanted him to launch an all-out attack and raze Kaerten to the ground.

He stood in his tower and spoke to them.

"You would be as I once was. You would kill and go on killing. Otherwise, all this land would have been empty with my rage. Do you understand? I would not have stopped until everyone was dead. Then my men and I would have turned on each other. I have come to know a stillness in my soul. It came when I stopped killing. We can do the same as a people."

Still they pressed for war. The armies were restless. An example needed to be made of Kaerten, lest the other cities regard his inaction as a mark of weakness. Already, conspiracies were being hatched in Karac, in Ipks, in Makar. Brasandokar itself was not without troublemakers.

"If you want so badly to kill," he finally snarled, "come to me. I'll give you all the killing you can stomach!"

Then he stomped away to his chambers.

Lady Megan took his giant hand in both of hers and kissed it. "They will learn," she said soothingly. "You'll show them. But, for now, they can't stand that you've taught yourself not to kill."

He remained pessimistic.

"War! War! War!"

He felt Megan shiver alongside him. He drew her closer and hugged her gently, protectively. Her head rested upon his shoulder, and her hand lay upon his pale, scarred chest.

In the courtyard below, the army continued to chant. "War! War! War! War!"

He had left his bed at one point to look down upon them. Many of his original followers were in the crowd. He had shaken his fist at them.

"I'm afraid now," Megan confessed. "I remember listening at my window in my father's house when you took the city. I was frightened then, but I was curious, too. I didn't quite know what to expect, even when you came in and escorted me down. Now I'm afraid, really afraid. These men were your friends."

"Hush. Try to sleep. I've sent word to my officers. I'll make them disperse the soldiers. Or, if worse comes to worst, I'll call on the units that are still loyal to me."

He kissed her forehead and lay back, trying to shut out the chant. Let the army level Kaerten. Let the empire shudder at my wrath. But leave me in peace.

The chant abruptly broke off into a bedlam of yells punctuated by the clang of swords. The creature rolled away from the Lady Megan and sprang to the window in time to see his personal guards go down before the mob. Shrieks and curses began to filter up from the floors below.

Lady Megan sat up in bed and said, quietly, "It's happened, hasn't it?"

He made no reply as he pulled on his breeches and cloak, then went to an ornately carved wooden cabinet.

"What are you going to do?" she asked when she heard the rattle of his cutlass in its scabbard. There was a rising note of terror in her voice now.

"They still fear the firearms," he growled as he began loading the pistols. There was just enough powder and shot to arm each of the weapons, including the blunderbuss. He tossed the keg and the tin box aside, thrust the pistols and a dagger into his belt, and cradled the blunderbuss in the crook of his arm. The sounds of battle were closer. Too close.

"Stay here until I return. Bolt—"

The door bulged inward as something heavy was slammed against it on the other side. Lady Megan screamed. The creature held the muzzle of the blunderbuss a foot away from the door and fired. Within the confines of his bedchamber, the roar of the discharge hurt his eardrums, but it failed to completely drown out cries of agony.

A spear poked through one of the several holes he had blown in the door. He grabbed it away and thrust the barrel of a pistol through the hole. A second spear snaked through another hole and jabbed him in the wrist. A third stabbed him shallowly in the left side. He roared with fury and emptied his pistols into the attackers. When he had run out of firearms, he stepped back, stooped, and picked up the spear he had previously snatched.

Then the door came off its hinges and fell into the room, followed by the heavy iron bench which had battered it down. The creature impaled the first man through the door. A sword nicked him across the forearm as he whipped the cutlass out of its scabbard, catching the swordsman in the sternum. Assassins spilled into the room, stumbling over the bench and the corpses, losing hands and arms and the tops of skulls, falling and creating greater obstacles for those behind. A blade drove through his side, snapping ribs. A spear slid under his sword arm, into his belly. Another sword went into his thigh. He howled. And swung the cutlass, grunting as something crunched beneath the blade. There was no end to them. They kept coming, more than he could count, faster than he could kill them. He swung the cutlass and missed, and someone stabbed him in the groin. He swung and missed again, and someone caught him on the cheek with the flat of a blade. He swung and missed and dropped the cutlass, and something hot and sharp pierced him high in the chest, and he went down. They had killed him for the time being.

Flanked by his bodyguards, he lumbered through the streets of one of his cities. The Lady Megan, second daughter of the War Leader of Brasandokar, rode at his side in a litter borne by four strong men who panted and grumbled as they tried to match his long stride. From time to time, he would glance at the woman and smile fleetingly. She did not love him, but she had told him that she might come to love him. That was enough for now, he kept telling himself.

His people, on the other hand, would probably never learn to love him. He had their respect and their obedience. But they could not love what they feared. Their children ran away at the sight of him, and the hubbub of the marketplace diminished noticeably as he passed through. Nevertheless, he enjoyed touring the city afoot, and he was happy that Lady Megan had agreed to accompany him. He paused occasionally to describe things to her. The luster of jewels from

Sandten. The patterns in cloth woven in Ipks. The iridescent scales of strange fish hauled up from the river's bottom. He took her by the quays and told her of an incredible motley of vessels, skin-hulled canoes, sail-less galleys, freight barges, flatboats, and rafts.

And one rose on the docks to confront him, and that one was Victor Frankenstein, a pale corpse with opaque eyes, frostbitten cheeks, and ice beaded on the fur of his parka.

I am waiting for you to join me, Frankenstein said. His voice was the same one which had lurked in the creature's head, calling him fool, urging him to commit monstrous deeds.

I see you at last, the creature replied.

Frankenstein looked past him to Lady Megan. You will lose everything, he told the creature, not taking his eyes from the beautiful blind woman. Even as I lost everything. We two are joined at the soul, monster, and our destinies run parallel to each other.

You're dead, Frankenstein, and I am free. Go back to the grave.

Not alone, demon. Not alone. Frankenstein laughed shrilly and, without taking a step, reached forward, his arm elongating nightmarishly, his hand darting past the creature's head toward Lady Megan's face.

Yes! Alone! He tore Victor Frankenstein to pieces on the spot, then led Lady Megan back to her tower.

The top of Megan's head came to his breastbone. She had long, fine hair of a light, almost silvery hue. Her flesh was pale, the color of subtly tinted porcelain. She had small, pointed breasts, a firm, delicately rounded belly, and slim hips. She was not much more than a girl when he married her, but she knew about sexual technique—there was no premium set on virginity in Brasandokar—and she did not mock him for his virtually total ignorance of such matters. She was the first woman he had ever seen naked.

And after their first clumsy copulation, Victor Frankenstein materialized at the foot of the bed to regard him scornfully. Megan seemed oblivious to the apparition.

Even in this respect you are a travesty, said Frankenstein, pointing at the creature's flaccid penis. You remove the beauty from all human functions.

The sin is with my maker.

The sin is that you have broken the promise you made at my deathbed. You live on, monster.

I have little choice in the matter. The creature rolled from the bed to drive the ghost away, but his knee buckled as soon as he put his weight on it, and he went sprawling on the floor. Pain exploded in his head, his torso, his limbs. He lay upon his face and gasped for breath. The earth closed in and smothered him.

It took him forever to claw his way up to the surface. The closer he got, the worse the pain became. The taste of blood was in his mouth. He moaned, raised his head, and dully looked around at the carnage. Nothing made any sense. A splintered door, knocked from its hinges. An iron bench. A litter of weapons. Blood everywhere. He dropped his head back into his hands and puzzled together the things he had seen.

Megan. Lady Megan. Where was the Lady Megan?

Horror began to gnaw within him. He dragged himself forward across the floor until he reached the corner of the bed, pushed himself up on hands and knees. Looked. Looked. Looked. Looked.

Until the sight of the bloody meat on the bed doubled him up on the floor. Until he saw only a huge swimming red ocean before him. Until he heard himself scream in animal pain and loss.

They heard him in the streets below, heard a sound like all of the demons in whom they half-believed set loose at once, and some of them unsheathed swords and made as though to return to the tower in which they had slain the conqueror, his woman, his few supporters. They stopped when they saw him at his window.

"I'll show you war!" he howled, and a metal bench crashed into their midst. Cries and moans filled the courtyard. He disappeared from the window. Moments later, a heavy cabinet sailed through the window and shattered on the pavement. It was followed by chairs, a wardrobe, the bodies of warriors.

Then he came down with his cutlass in his hand, and they broke and ran in the face of his fury, casting away their weapons, trampling those who fell. He flew at their backs, his wounds forgotten. He drove them before him, killing all whom he could reach.

He raged the breadth of Brasandokar. He demolished booths and slaughtered penned animals in the marketplace. He overturned braziers and kicked over tables laden with goods. He smashed open casks of liquor and heaved a disemboweled soldier into a public well. He grabbed a torch and set fires everywhere, and the city's burning began to light the cavern sky for miles around. He dragged people from their homes and butchered them in the gutters.

At last, he staggered to the docks, dazed, exhausted, in shock. Lowering himself onto a raft, he cut it loose and entered the current. Behind him, Brasandokar blazed, and he was tiredly certain that he had destroyed it for all time. He shook his fist at the flames.

"No scars on the face of my empire!" he shouted, but there was no feeling of triumph in his heart. Megan was still dead. Megan was dead.

Screaming, crying, he fell to the bottom of the raft. It drifted toward the great flat river where men did not go.

The creature awoke just before the river entered a low, dark cavern.

How long he had drifted to this, he did not know, nor could he tell how long and how far he traveled through the cave. The river flowed smoothly. The raft sometimes nudged an invisible bank, sometimes floated aft-foremost along the water. The walls of the cavern sometimes glowed with the balefire of mushroom clusters, sometimes with a wonder of animals shining on the ceiling like moving stalactites.

More often than not, though, there was the darkness, impenetrable before and behind.

From one hell to another I go, he thought, dipping up a handful of water from the river. The water was cooler now, but were not underground streams always cool? Had he not lived in caves before, hunted by men, despised by all natural things, and had not the underground waters been cool then? He could hardly remember but decided that the matter was unimportant anyway.

What is important is that this river leads somewhere, away from the lands of men, where I can be free of their greeds, their fears. I am warm in my cloak. My wounds heal. I still have my cutlass. I am still free. He curled up on the raft and tried to ignore the first pangs of hunger. The top of Lady Megan's head comes to my breastbone. She has long, fine hair of a light, almost silvery hue. Her flesh is . . .

He eventually noticed the river's current slowing and its bed becoming wider and shallower. He peered into the gloom and, from the corner of his eye, saw the movement of light. He turned his head. The light vanished. The waters lay black around him.

The light reappeared in front of the raft. He stared into the water. There were small movements below: a series of dots undulated, darted away, returned. He put his hand into the water. The dots flashed away into the depths. He kept his hand in the water. Presently, the dots snaked into sight again. He lunged, felt contact, and squeezed. Something struggled in his hand. He hauled his long arm up and over and smashed its heavy burden against the deck. The thing tried to flop away. He slammed it against the deck a second time, and it lay still. Its glow faded swiftly.

He looked around and saw more of the dots moving in the water. There was a noisy splash behind the raft. The lights winked out.

Soon the raft entered another lighted place. The light was from bracket mushrooms halfway up the walls of the cavern. The creature poled close to the bank and, as he passed, snapped off a piece of fungus. Some of its luminescence came off on his hand.

He poled back to the middle of the river, then knelt to examine the thing he had dragged from the water. It was a salamander, perhaps three feet long. Along its dorsal side was the row of phosphorescent dots that had given it over to death. The skull was flat and arrowheadlike.

He ate it happily. With his hunger quelled, he took more notice of his surroundings. The walls of the cavern were gradually curving away to the sides. The bracket mushrooms grew more thickly as he drifted farther, and the waters frequently parted where fish broke the surface. The river grew shallower, though there were places where his pole could not touch bottom. He let the weakening current carry him past these places. He wondered what might dwell at the bottoms of those deep places.

He was poling the raft forward at one point when he heard the sloshing of a large thing ahead. The water stretched flat and unbroken before him. Nothing moved below the surface. Something had frightened away the salamanders and fish. There was another splashing noise. He raised the pole like a harpoon and waited, but nothing happened. Gradually, the dotted lines reappeared in the water.

In a little while, the sides of the river slid out of sight. There was almost no current. Overhead were faint smudgy patches of light, arcing out forever before and to either side of him. Here, he thought, was the end of the great river. A vast subterranean lake. Perhaps it drained into other worlds. Perhaps it opened up to the exterior. He shrugged, willing to accept anything, and lay down on the deck to rest.

He was awakened by soft, dry rain pelting his face. He opened his eyes and, for the first time in many years, thought he saw the stars. But underground? And rain? In a cave?

The creature sat up and shook his head to clear it. This was a rain such as men had never seen. Tiny luminous things bounced off the deck of the raft. Fish swirled and turned in the water and flopped onto the deck in attempts to get the things.

He reached into his hair and drew out a pupal case, then looked up again, blinking against the cascade. From the dimly lit ceiling was falling a faintly glowing snow, and tiny winged shapes fluttered beneath the ceiling.

The creature rolled the pupal case in his hand. The worms were hatching, and the fish were going crazy with gluttony. He scooped up and killed the larger fish that flopped onto the raft, brushed piles of insect cases into the water and left the rain of pupal cases as unexpectedly as he had entered it. As he started to eat one of his fish, he heard splashes of panic behind him as something large wallowed through the feeding schools. He could see nothing.

But, later, he was sure that he saw hazy white shapes swim past at a distance.

## VIII

The dark-haired little man was dying, in delirium.

Two ward heelers had gotten him drunk that election day in Baltimore, Maryland, and taken him from place to place and had him vote under assumed names. It was common practice to gather up drunks and derelicts to swell the election rolls.

Neither of the two men knew who it was that they dragged, moaning and stumbling, between them. The man was Edgar Allan Poe, but Poe so far gone into the abyss that even the few friends he had would not have recognized him. Opium and alcohol had done their work on a mind already broken by a life of tragic accidents. They left Poe in a doorway when the polls closed. He was found there by a policeman and taken to a small hospital. He burned with fever, he tossed in his bed, he mumbled. The hospital staff could not keep him quiet.

Early the next morning, Edgar Allan Poe stiffened and sat up in bed.

"Reynolds!" he said. "Reynolds!"

And lay back and died.

Have you no name, sir? the Lady Megan asked.

I have been called Demon, the creature replied. And worse, he added to himself. My soldiers call me the Bear, or the Ape, or the Shatterer.

But a *name*, she persisted, a real name. I cannot call you Bear or Ape.

Victor Frankenstein did not christen me.

Who was Vitter Frang—? She shook her head, unable to utter the odd syllables. Who was he? She? A friend, a god?

He told her. She looked horrified, then disappeared.

He lay on the raft and felt tears on his face. He had been crying in his sleep.

He heard their raucous cries long before he saw them. The high, worm-lit cavern ceiling sloped down before him, brightening ahead. The sounds grew louder as he drifted toward the sloping roof, and he glimpsed indistinct white shapes in the water from time to time.

He stripped the rope from one end of the pole and sharpened it with his dagger. It would make a crude but lethal spear.

White shapes awaited his coming. They screamed at him and began piling into the water on either side of his raft. They were as tall as men, with large beaks, webbed feet, and the merest vestiges of wings.

Behind them was a circle of brighter light. He bellowed his challenge at the things splashing around him and poled forward. They were too heavy to climb onto the raft, but they managed to slow his advance by massing in his path. He stabbed at them with the pole until he felt the raft crunch against the bottom. Then he leaped into the calf-deep water and sloshed toward the circle of light, swinging the pole like a club, beating a path through a cawing mass of white feathers and beaks. The light was a cool white circle ahead: the mouth of a tunnel. Eggs cracked under his feet, young birds squirmed and died as he passed.

One of the giant birds rose to block his path. A shock ran up his arm as he broke the improvised spear over its skull. Leaping over the carcass, he dashed toward the light, into the tunnel. Into a world of nightmare-polished stone of deepest ebony.

A wave of white horrors pursued him. He ran through corridors chiseled out of the rock by something far older than human beings. He glimpsed carvings on the walls and sculptures which no human hand had made, but he did not slow his feet until he had emerged into the light of a large central opening. Tunnels yawned to right and left. Above the opening was a grayish sheet of ice. It arched to form a dome. The floor of the chamber was littered with the rubble which must once have formed the roof. The creature heard the vengeful white birds screeching at his back and plunged into one of the tunnels to find himself at the foot of a spiral ramp. It was cold there, and it had the smell of dust and antiquity. It had the smell of tumble-down churches he had seen, of dark mold and dead leaves on the forest floor. He shivered in spite of himself as he began to ascend.

He came out in a hall of glass cases and strode, wondering, past incomprehensible displays and strange machinery. Here were strangely curved hand tools, levers, and wheels in riotous profusion, brassy colors, iron, gold, silver. In one case was a curve-bladed cutting tool like a halberd-pike. The creature banged on the glass with the stump of his pole, to no effect. He put his arms around the case and toppled it, and one pane broke with a peculiarly metallic crash.

It was followed by a dim, echoing sound. A gong was being struck somewhere.

The creature pulled the pike-ax from its mountings and examined it. It was made entirely of metal. It was curiously balanced. It had never been designed to be hefted by a being with hands. He was pleased with it, nonetheless, and when the first of the white birds burst into the hall and charged him, he sheared its head off with a casual swing. The gong continued to clang, and the sound was everywhere now. He ran. The decapitated bird thrashed on the floor.

Its angry, squawking brethren flowed into the room.

It was in a second ascending tunnel that he first saw the beings that the clangor had summoned. Shapes out of nightmare; sight beyond reason. They were paralleling his course through the tunnel. There were few of them at first, but each time he came to a lighted connecting tunnel, there were more, blocking the paths so that he could not turn aside. Their voices piped and echoed through the halls and tunnels, and he saw tentacles, cilia, myriad dim eyes as he ran.

He turned a corner, and three of the things stood in his way, their pikes raised, their bodies hunched as low as barrel-thick cones could be lowered.

His halberd chopped into the nearest of the things just below its bunched eyestalks and cilia. The top of the cone described a green-bleeding arc and richocheted off the wall, and the trunk toppled forward, the pike slipping from tentacles. Five sets of leathery wings, like the tin arms of a starfish, began to beat and buzz spasmodically.

The creature did not pause with that ax-stroke but stepped closer and caught the second cone with his backswing. The blade stuck in the trunk. It swung its pike at his head.

He dived to the floor as the halberd whistled past, grabbed the base, and heaved. The thing went backward into the third cone. Both fell into a struggling heap. He threw himself upon them, seized bunches of eyestalks in his hands, and ripped them free. The cones' high, distressed pipings ceased when he opened the trunks with a pike. It was like splitting melons.

Then he was on his way once more, his feet slippery with green ichor. More pipings sounded ahead, commingled with the raucous voices of the great white birds.

Twice he turned aside when the cones blocked his way. The third time, he realized that they were desperate to keep him out of the interconnecting tunnels. Were they guarding something? Their ruler? Their children?

He was on another group before they knew it. Piping screams of warning came too late to save the first two guards in his path. He was through them before they recovered. The pipings behind him rose in pitch and volume as he raced through the tunnel. He saw movement ahead: there was a room at the end, and two cones were slashing the air with their pikes, warning him away. Behind them, a third cone seized a wheel with its tentacles and turned it. A panel began to slide from the ceiling and close off the room.

He yelled and leaped. The cones dropped their pikes and fled. He watched them go, then looked around at the chamber. At the far side of the room was a huge metal door, studded with bolts, deadplates, and slides leading . . . where? Into darker recesses? Hell? A weapons room, a nursery? The machinery in the room gave him no clue.

The creature abruptly noted a thick, sickening smell which overlay the place's scent of antiquity. The odor seemed to be coming through cracks in that gigantic door. He stepped nearer and heard a sloshing, rolling sound, as if a putrefying carcass of vast size were being dragged. He raised his halberd.

Two cones appeared to one side. They saw him approaching the door and started to hoot and honk, their tentacles and cilia beating, their wings buzzing, their eyestalks writhing, as though imploring him to stay away from the portal. Whatever lay beyond the door, they obviously did not want him to see it. He sought only escape. Perhaps it lay there.

One of the cones threw a flask at him but missed. There was a pop and an explosion as the vial hit the wall, and fire spread an orange tongue across the floor.

For an instant, the creature felt panic, then saw that the fire separated him from the two cones but not a panel of levers and dials set in the wall next to the door. He seized levers and threw his weight upon them. Nothing happened. He tried other levers. Nothing. The helpless cones wailed with terror.

And the room began to shake.

The door through which he had come reopened. Past the snakes of flame, he saw masses of the cones pour in from the tunnel. One threw a small hatchet at him. It smashed dials near his hand. Far, far below, tremors rocked some gigantic machinery. The huge door groaned, the groan rising to a shriek of protesting metal, and, slowly, ponderously, opened. It swung away on huge rollers and hinges, and a smell of death and rotting things filled the room.

The creature, huddled to one side, poised to leap through the flames, through the door to safety, stared in horror as something oozed from the opening. It flowed out forever, skirting the flames behind which he stood, moving faster and faster until it reached the hindmost of the cones now trying to escape through side tunnels. There was a greasy sucking sound, and a cone disappeared into the mass. Other cones screamed. Some fluttered their wings, rose from the floor, circled, banged into the walls like blinded canaries. They fell, and sticky edges of the gelatinous horror covered them.

There was an explosion somewhere below, and the floor sagged, cracked, yawned open. The oozing thing rippled and twisted, then slid into the fissure. As it fell from sight, another mass emerged through the door, skirted both fire and fissure, and squeezed its bulk into one of the tunnels. Screams and whistles ended in mid-note. A third horror came through, then a fourth, a fifth. The earth trembled, and a seam ran from the hole in the floor to the wall and upward. Dust sifted down from the ceiling.

The creature, driven back by the fire, saw the crack open. It reached the roof of the chamber and stopped, a forty-five-degree slash up the wall. He bounded forward, squeezed himself into the rent, and started making his way up, away from the flames, away from the shapeless nightmares from behind the great portal. The pike hampered him, but he refused to abandon it.

He climbed through the ceiling and found himself in another circular chamber. The place shook and rocked, a bedlam of moving things, shrieks and groans in the air and in the earth. Smoke billowed up from below. Piping cones swept past him and paid him no attention. He ran with them, into tunnels that led upward. Always upward. He passed machinery noisily tearing itself to pieces. He passed the flightless white birds and did not bother to wonder whether they had invaded the tunnels en masse to find him or were merely some sort of livestock maintained by the cones.

Once, he saw a cone run past the mouth of a side tunnel. Pseudopodia shot out of the tunnel, snared it, and pulled it back out of sight. Once, the earth heaved and smashed him to the floor.

Upward. Always upward.

Upward, into the sunlight.

The creature followed some of the birds through a rent into a light-filled tunnel whose ceiling had fallen in. Clouds of ash fell all around. In the distance, a volcano sputtered and spat. There was a sound of continuous thunder in the air, and of masses of ice breaking up, of water turning to steam, of the earth sundering.

He screamed as the white, hot ash touched him. The birds squawked as if on fire beneath the deadly rain. The snow steamed. He hurled himself down and rolled in the snow, trying to escape, and as he rolled, he heard a roar that drowned out everything else. His ears turned his eyes in the direction of the roar. He gasped.

A crack had opened in the world. It ran straight and true across the ice cap, and down the crack came a wall of water. Roiling and seething, the waters swept past with the speed of a tornado.

He thought of the spewing volcano and of the unbridled energy which would be released when the cold water met the magma. He picked himself up, the halberd still clasped in his fist, and slogged away. The ash swirled about his head, blinding him, and covered him from head to foot.

There was a sound like the universe breaking. A giant hand struck him from behind and threw him headlong into the steaming snows. Broken white birds tumbled past. He was rolled and carried by the sound. Steam, slivers of ice, and hot ash blew past in a gale. New furies of cinders fell on him.

He picked himself up and ran. For the sea, for water, for relief from the falling hellish rain which scoured his skin. It lay ahead, a troubled line of gray against the white tongues of the land. The crack through which the cataract ran pointed like the finger of God to escape from the ash. He ran, covered with hot dust. He ran, and, overhead, birds appeared, disturbed from some ethereal rookery or nest, giving voice to harsh echoing cries as they made their way through the burning air. He ran, and the flightless birds from the caverns below fled with him. He ran, and the ghost of Victor Frankenstein uncoiled in his head, a serpent rising to sink its fangs into him.

Welcome to the Pit, Frankenstein said. And laughed. And the white ash continued to fall.

## IX

Herman Melville published *Moby Dick; or, The Whale* in 1851, to generally scathing notices. Less than 4,000 copies of the novel were sold during the next three and one-half decades; it was not until 1921 that the book began to receive plaudits, and by 1921, Melville had been dead for thirty years.

The cataract worked terror on the land through which it tore. The white banks gave way and caved in. Behind was a mountain-sized wall of steam, at the heart of which could be seen the reddish glow of the volcano's maw.

Looking like a snowman built by crazy children, the creature came at last to the coast. Two miles to his left was the mouth of the crack. Most of the waddling white birds had struck out for the torrent at once, drawn by the lure of cold water. There was no doubt in his mind that the current had swept them back toward the depths below.

It must close, he thought, watching as hillocks of ice bobbed and shattered in the cataract. It must close, or the sea will fill the interior of the earth. He imagined the dark waters rushing through the tunnels of the underground city, engorging the great river, backing up to flood Brasandokar, Sandten, to the cavern of the great apes, to the cavern of magma. Another explosion, another cataclysm. The world bursting open like a ripe fruit. Good riddance to it all.

He turned and began to run around the headland, away from the roaring river. After a time, its roar diminished noticeably. He sat down on the ice, exhausted, and stared out to sea, oblivious even to the cinders which continued to fall. He could go no farther.

Welcome to the Pit, Frankenstein said again.

Go away, he thought wearily, burning with the torment of the white ash.

This is where it ends, said Frankenstein. Feel the heat of the ash, demon. Listen to the thunder of water rushing to meet magma. Hell, demon. Hell. You are home

The creature peered into the darkness gathering over the sea. On the waters was a canoe. It was being carried toward the cataract.

He clambered to his feet, picked up the halberd, and stumbled to the edge of the sea. Two figures could be seen in the canoe, one seated in the prow, the other aft. As the canoe drew nearer, he saw that the men looked haggard, listless, and did nothing to try to alter their course. The one in the prow seemed more active, turning his face to stare at the creature on the shore.

The canoe crunched nose-first against the shore, spun in the current, rocking and heaving as it cartwheeled through the choppy waters.

The creature swung the pike-ax high over his head, out over the water, and snagged a gunwale. The ice beneath his feet threatened to crumble as he strained backward, drawing the unwieldly vessel with him, fighting the craft's weight and momentum and the pull of the current. He growled inarticulately, feeling pain in his shoulder sockets, the corded muscles of his back and legs. Wounds in his thighs opened and seeped blood.

But the canoe came out of the water, onto the shelf.

The man at the bow was too stunned to resist. He could only stare, wide-eyed. Then the creature grabbed him and hurled him onto the ice. The man landed heavily and did not move.

The man in the stern called out feebly, his voice barely more than a croak, as the creature dragged the canoe farther inland. Ice dust lifted as the shelf shuddered and cracked, letting chunks of itself swirl away toward the cataract.

When he had gained safety, the creature wrenched the halberd from the gunwale. The man in the stern waved an oar, weakly menacing. The pike clove him from pate to clavicle.

There was a dead black man in the bottom of the canoe. He pulled out both corpses, lay the halberd in the boat, and started dragging it across the ice cap, away from the cataract, away from the ash and heat. Victor Frankenstein appeared at his side, keeping pace.

You can still kill after all, Frankenstein noted with satisfaction.

Yes. I can still kill.

Where now, demon? Hell is not to your liking?

There isn't room here for both of us, Victor.

Birds passed overhead on their way out to sea. *Tekeli-li,* they screamed. *Tekeli-li.*

## X

Late in June, 1863, Professor Otto Lidenbrock, of the University of Hamburg, arrived with his nephew Axel and a guide on the rim of the Icelandic volcano Sneffel. They descended into the crater, determined to reach the interior of the earth by way of a chimney on the crater floor.

A Frenchman edited Axel Lidenbrock's subsequent account of the expedition, and it appeared in *Hetzell's Young People's Magazine for Education and Recreation* in 1864.

In New England, seventeen-year-old Abner Perry read geology and paleontology texts and tinkered together curious little inventions in the attic of his father's house.

He sculled the canoe for a long time. Even this far out, he could not rest, for the current still nibbled gently at the boat. If he rested, he might lose ground. Somehow, he had to keep paddling until he outran the pull of the waterfall to the center of the earth.

The ragged curtain of fire and ash in the air had begun to settle. The air seemed full of dust. The sun hung on the horizon like a sinking ship. It was dim and the color of blood.

He turned his gaze toward the prow and saw what he at first took to be a similarly blood-red island. A calved ice cake, perhaps, like the one which had borne him into the earth—how many years before?

Then the island sank from sight, to reemerge a hundred yards off the port gunwale. Twin corkscrews of foam rose and fell. The creature watched in awe.

The whale went under with hardly a ripple, as smoothly as a surgeon's blade slides under the skin. For a few seconds, the sea was flat, like glass, with only a few dimples as ash sifted onto it.

The whale broke the sea into a million liquid mirrors as it breached. It was huge, huge, and it stood in the air like a trout fighting to free itself of a hook. Its eyes were tiny in comparison with its bulk, and it took in the world to each side: on this, the calm sea; on that, one of the hated boats. But the boat did not pursue. A single creature stood in it.

The whale was white, white as land ice, marbled with patches like sooted snow. Its redness came from the setting sun. To the monster, the patchwork being in the boat, it was the biggest thing in the universe. It stood apart from heaven and earth. In its side were innumerable harpoons and lances, tangled lines, all covered with barnacles, unlike the whale's smooth white skin. It hung in the air like a heavy cloud, then slowly, so slowly, went back into the ocean.

The creature's heart leaped with it, and he danced in the stern of the boat.

"Free!" he yelled as the whale breached a second time, farther away. "Free! Free! Free!"

He watched, smiling, until the great whale was lost to sight. It seemed to him that God had passed through this part of the world and found it good.

A long twilight began as the sun slipped behind the horizon. The creature sculled with the sweeps, ignoring the Antarctic cold which was finally displacing the heat of the recent cataclysm. He was bound northward for the lands of men.

The stars came out slowly. Above, the twin smudges of the Magellanic Clouds shone dimly. They had lighted the way for sailors for 300 years. They would light his.

He rowed happily, willing, for the moment, to accept whatever lay ahead. And Victor Frankenstein sat in the prow, frowning. And could say nothing.

# The Kugelmass Episode
## by Woody Allen

*Woody Allen isn't known as a writer of fantastic stories, despite
writing and starring in the movie* Sleeper. *He's a humorist, as
anyone will tell you—but his humor has always been based on a
kind of* reductio ad absurdum *fantasy that finds expression, in
this balloon-pricking story, in the misadventures of a man who
wanted more "magic" in his life—and found it in an unlikely
affair with Emma Bovary.*

*Madame Bovary isn't much like Frankenstein's monster, but
there are amusing parallels here with the Utley-and-Waldrop
story: two very different revivifications of famous characters, in
settings for which they were never made.*

Kugelmass, a professor of humanities at City College, was unhappily
married for the second time. Daphne Kugelmass was an oaf. He also
had two dull sons by his first wife, Flo, and was up to his neck in
alimony and child support.

"Did I know it would turn out so badly?" Kugelmass whined to his
analyst one day. "Daphne had promise. Who suspected she'd let
herself go and swell up like a beach ball? Plus she had a few bucks,
which is not in itself a healthy reason to marry a person, but it doesn't
hurt, with the kind of operating nut I have. You see my point?"

Kugelmass was bald and as hairy as a bear, but he had soul.

"I need to meet a new woman," he went on. "I need to have an
affair. I may not look the part, but I'm a man who needs romance. I
need softness, I need flirtation. I'm not getting younger, so before it's
too late I want to make love in Venice, trade quips at '21,' and

exchange coy glances over red wine and candlelight. You see what I'm saying?"

Dr. Mandel shifted in his chair and said, "An affair will solve nothing. You're so unrealistic. Your problems run much deeper."

"And also this affair must be discreet," Kugelmass continued. "I can't afford a second divorce. Daphne would really sock it to me."

"Mr. Kugelmass—"

"But it can't be anyone at City College, because Daphne also works there. Not that anyone on the faculty at C.C.N.Y. is any great shakes, but some of those coeds..."

"Mr. Kugelmass—"

"Help me. I had a dream last night. I was skipping through a meadow holding a picnic basket and the basket was marked 'Options.' And then I saw there was a hole in the basket."

"Mr. Kugelmass, the worst thing you could do is act out. You must simply express your feelings here, and together we'll analyze them. You have been in treatment long enough to know there is no overnight cure. After all, I'm an analyst, not a magician."

"Then perhaps what I need is a magician," Kugelmass said, rising from his chair. And with that he terminated his therapy.

A couple of weeks later, while Kugelmass and Daphne were moping around in their apartment one night like two pieces of old furniture, the phone rang.

"I'll get it," Kugelmass said. "Hello."

"Kugelmass?" a voice said. "Kugelmass, this is Persky."

"Who?"

"Persky. Or should I say The Great Persky?"

"Pardon me?"

"I hear you're looking all over town for a magician to bring a little exotica into your life? Yes or no?"

"Sh-h-h," Kugelmass whispered. "Don't hang up. Where are you calling from, Persky?"

Early the following afternoon, Kugelmass climbed three flights of stairs in a broken-down apartment house in the Bushwick section of Brooklyn. Peering through the darkness of the hall, he found the door he was looking for and pressed the bell. I'm going to regret this, he thought to himself.

Seconds later, he was greeted by a short, thin, waxy-looking man.

"*You're* Persky the Great?" Kugelmass said.

"The Great Persky. You want a tea?"

"No, I want romance. I want music. I want love and beauty."

"But not tea, eh? Amazing. O.K., sit down."

Persky went to the back room, and Kugelmass heard the sounds of boxes and furniture being moved around. Persky reappeared, pushing before him a large object on squeaky roller-skate wheels. He moved some old silk handkerchiefs that were lying on its top and blew away a bit of dust. It was a cheap-looking Chinese cabinet, badly lacquered.

"Persky," Kugelmass said, "what's your scam?"

"Pay attention," Persky said. "This is some beautiful effect. I developed it for a Knights of Pythias date last year, but the booking fell through. Get into the cabinet."

"Why, so you can stick it full of swords or something?"

"You see any swords?"

Kugelmass made a face and, grunting, climbed into the cabinet. He couldn't help noticing a couple of ugly rhinestones glued onto the raw plywood just in front of his face. "If this is a joke," he said.

"Some joke. Now, here's the point. If I throw any novel into this cabinet with you, shut the doors, and tap it three times, you will find yourself projected into that book."

Kugelmass made a grimace of disbelief.

"It's the emess," Persky said. "My hand to God. Not just a novel, either. A short story, a play, a poem. You can meet any of the women created by the world's best writers. Whoever you dreamed of. You could carry on all you like with a real winner. Then when you've had enough you give a yell, and I'll see you're back here in a split second."

"Persky, are you some kind of outpatient?"

"I'm telling you it's on the level," Persky said.

Kugelmass remained skeptical. "What are you telling me—that this cheesy homemade box can take me on a ride like you're describing?"

"For a double sawbuck."

Kugelmass reached for his wallet. "I'll believe this when I see it," he said.

Persky tucked the bills in his pants pocket and turned toward his bookcase. "So who do you want to meet? Sister Carrie? Hester

Prynne? Ophelia? Maybe someone by Saul Bellow? Hey, what about Temple Drake? Although for a man your age she'd be a workout."

"French. I want to have an affair with a French lover."

"Nana?"

"I don't want to have to pay for it."

"What about Natasha in 'War and Peace'?"

"I said French. I know! What about Emma Bovary? That sounds to me perfect."

"You got it, Kugelmass. Give me a holler when you've had enough." Persky tossed in a paperback copy of Flaubert's novel.

"You sure this is safe?" Kugelmass asked as Persky began shutting the cabinet doors.

"Safe. Is anything safe in this crazy world?" Persky rapped three times on the cabinet and then flung open the doors.

Kugelmass was gone. At the same moment, he appeared in the bedroom of Charles and Emma Bovary's house at Yonville. Before him was a beautiful woman, standing alone with her back turned to him as she folded some linen. I can't believe this, thought Kugelmass, staring at the doctor's ravishing wife. This is uncanny. I'm here. It's her.

Emma turned in surprise. "Goodness, you startled me," she said. "Who are you?" She spoke in the same fine English translation as the paperback.

It's simply devastating, he thought. Then, realizing that it was he whom she had addressed, he said, "Excuse me. I'm Sidney Kugelmass. I'm from City College. A professor of humanities. C.C.N.Y.? Uptown. I—oh, boy!"

Emma Bovary smiled flirtatiously and said, "Would you like a drink? A glass of wine, perhaps?"

She is beautiful, Kugelmass thought. What a contrast with the troglodyte who shared his bed! He felt a sudden impulse to take this vision into his arms and tell her she was the kind of woman he had dreamed of all his life.

"Yes, some wine," he said hoarsely. "White. No, red. No, white. Make it white."

"Charles is out for the day," Emma said, her voice full of playful implication.

After the wine, they went for a stroll in the lovely French

countryside. "I've always dreamed that some mysterious stranger would appear and rescue me from the monotony of this crass rural existence," Emma said, clasping his hand. They passed a small church. "I love what you have on," she murmured. "I've never seen anything like it around here. It's so...so modern." "It's called a leisure suit," he said romantically. "It was marked down." Suddenly he kissed her. For the next hour they reclined under a tree and whispered together and told each other deeply meaningful things with their eyes. Then Kugelmass sat up. He had just remembered he had to meet Daphne at Bloomingdale's. "I must go," he told her. "But don't worry, I'll be back."

"I hope so," Emma said.

He embraced her passionately, and the two walked back to the house. He held Emma's face cupped in his palms, kissed her again, and yelled, "O.K., Persky! I got to be at Bloomingdale's by three-thirty.

There was an audible pop, and Kugelmass was back in Brooklyn.

"So? Did I lie?" Persky asked triumphantly.

"Look, Persky, I'm right now late to meet the ball and chain at Lexington Avenue, but when can I go again? Tomorrow?"

"My pleasure. Just bring a twenty. And don't mention this to anybody."

"Yeah. I'm going to call Rupert Murdoch."

Kugelmass hailed a cab and sped off to the city. His heart danced on point. I am in love, he thought, I am the possessor of a wonderful secret. What he didn't realize was that at this very moment students in various classrooms across the country were saying to their teachers, "Who is this character on page 100? A bald Jew is kissing Madame Bovary?" A teacher in Sioux Falls, South Dakota, sighed and thought, Jesus, these kids, with their pot and acid. What goes through their minds!

Daphne Kugelmass was in the bathroom-accessories department at Bloomingdale's when Kugelmass arrived breathlessly. "Where've you been?" she snapped. "It's four-thirty."

"I got held up in traffic," Kugelmass said.

Kugelmass visited Persky the next day, and in a few minutes was again passed magically to Yonville. Emma couldn't hide her excitement at seeing him. The two spent hours together, laughing and talking about their different backgrounds. Before Kugelmass left, they made love. "My God, I'm doing it with Madame Bovary!" Kugelmass whispered to himself. "Me, who failed freshman English."

As the months passed, Kugelmass saw Persky many times and developed a close and passionate relationship with Emma Bovary. "Make sure and always get me into the book before page 120," Kugelmass said to the magician one day. "I always have to meet her before she hooks up with this Rodolphe character."

"Why?" Persky asked. "You can't beat his time?"

"Beat his time. He's landed gentry. Those guys have nothing better to do than flirt and ride horses. To me, he's one of those faces you see in the pages of *Women's Wear Daily*. With the Helmut Berger hairdo. But to her he's hot stuff."

"And her husband suspects nothing?"

"He's out of his depth. He's a lacklustre little paramedic who's thrown in his lot with a jitterbug. He's ready to go to sleep by ten, and she's putting on her dancing shoes. Oh, well... See you later."

And once again Kugelmass entered the cabinet and passed instantly to the Bovary estate at Yonville. "How you doing, cupcake?" he said to Emma.

"Oh, Kugelmass," Emma sighed. "What I have to put up with. Last night at dinner, Mr. Personality dropped off to sleep in the middle of the dessert course. I'm pouring my heart out about Maxim's and the ballet, and out of the blue I hear snoring."

"It's O.K., darling. I'm here now," Kugelmass said, embracing her. I've earned this, he thought, smelling Emma's French perfume and burying his nose in her hair. I've suffered enough. I've paid enough analysts. I've searched till I'm weary. She's young and nubile, and I'm here a few pages after Léon and just before Rodolphe. By showing up during the correct chapters, I've got the situation knocked.

Emma, to be sure, was just as happy as Kugelmass. She had been starved for excitement, and his tales of Broadway night life, of fast cars and Hollywood and TV stars, enthralled the young French beauty.

"Tell me again about O.J. Simpson," she implored that evening, as she and Kugelmass strolled past Abbé Bournisien's church.

"What can I say? The man is great. He sets all kinds of rushing records. Such moves. They can't touch him."

"And the Academy Awards?" Emma said wistfully. "I'd give anything to win one."

"First you've got to be nominated."

"I know. You explained it. But I'm convinced I can act. Of course, I'd want to take a class or two. With Strasberg maybe. Then, if I had the right agent—"

"We'll see, we'll see. I'll speak to Persky."

That night, safely returned to Persky's flat, Kugelmass brought up the idea of having Emma visit him in the big city.

"Let me think about it," Persky said. "Maybe I could work it. Stranger things have happened." Of course, neither of them could think of one.

"Where the hell do you go all the time?" Daphne Kugelmass barked at her husband as he returned home late that evening. "You got a chippie stashed somewhere?"

"Yeah, sure, I'm just the type," Kugelmass said wearily. "I was with Leonard Popkin. We were discussing Socialist agriculture in Poland. You know Popkin. He's a freak on the subject."

"Well, you've been very odd lately," Daphne said. "Distant. Just don't forget about my father's birthday. On Saturday?"

"Oh, sure, sure," Kugelmass said, heading for the bathroom.

"My whole family will be there. We can see the twins. And Cousin Hamish. You should be more polite to Cousin Hamish—he likes you."

"Right, the twins," Kugelmass said, closing the bathroom door and shutting out the sound of his wife's voice. He leaned against it and took a deep breath. In a few hours, he told himself, he would be back in Yonville again, back with his beloved. And this time, if all went well, he would bring Emma back with him.

At three-fifteen the following afternoon, Persky worked his wizardry again. Kugelmass appeared before Emma, smiling and eager. The two spent a few hours at Yonville with Binet and then remounted the Bovary carriage. Following Persky's instructions, they held each other tightly, closed their eyes, and counted to ten. When they opened them, the carriage was just drawing up at the side door of the Plaza Hotel, where Kugelmass had optimistically reserved a suite earlier in the day.

"I love it! It's everything I dreamed it would be," Emma said as she swirled joyously around the bedroom, surveying the city from their window. "There's F.A.O. Schwarz. And there's Central Park, and the Sherry is which one? Oh, there—I see. It's too divine."

On the bed there were boxes from Halston and Saint Laurent. Emma unwrapped a package and held up a pair of black velvet pants against her perfect body.

"The slacks suit is by Ralph Lauren," Kugelmass said. "You'll look like a million bucks in it. Come on, sugar, give us a kiss."

"I've never been so happy!" Emma squealed as she stood before the mirror. "Let's go out on the town. I want to see 'Chorus Line' and the Guggenheim and this Jack Nicholson character you always talk about. Are any of his flicks showing?"

"I cannot get my mind around this," a Stanford professor said. "First a strange character named Kugelmass, and now she's gone from the book. Well, I guess the mark of a classic is that you can reread it a thousand times and always find something new."

The lovers passed a blissful weekend. Kugelmass had told Daphne he would be away at a symposium in Boston and would return Monday. Savoring each moment, he and Emma went to the movies, had dinner in Chinatown, passed two hours at a discothèque, and went to bed with a TV movie. They slept till noon on Sunday, visited SoHo, and ogled celebrities at Elaine's. They had caviar and champagne in their suite on Sunday night and talked until dawn. That morning, in the cab taking them to Persky's apartment, Kugelmass thought, It was hectic, but worth it. I can't bring her here too often, but now and then it will be a charming contrast with Yonville.

At Persky's, Emma climbed into the cabinet, arranged her new boxes of clothes neatly around her, and kissed Kugelmass fondly. "My place next time," she said with a wink. Persky rapped three times on the cabinet. Nothing happened.

"Hmm," Persky said, scratching his head. He rapped again, but still no magic. "Something must be wrong," he mumbled.

"Persky, you're joking!" Kugelmass cried. "How can it not work?"

"Relax, relax. Are you still in the box, Emma?"

"Yes."

Persky rapped again—harder this time.

"I'm still here, Persky."

"I know, darling. Sit tight."

"Persky, we *have* to get her back," Kugelmass whispered. "I'm a married man, and I have a class in three hours. I'm not prepared for anything more than a cautious affair at this point."

"I can't understand it," Persky muttered. "It's such a reliable little trick."

But he could do nothing. "It's going to take a little while," he said to Kugelmass. "I'm going to have to strip it down. I'll call you later."

Kugelmass bundled Emma into a cab and took her back to the Plaza. He barely made it to his class on time. He was on the phone all day, to Persky and to his mistress. The magician told him it might be several days before he got to the bottom of the trouble.

"How was the symposium?" Daphne asked him that night.

"Fine, fine," he said, lighting the filter end of a cigarette.

"What's wrong? You're as tense as a cat."

"Me? Ha, that's a laugh. I'm as calm as a summer night. I'm just going to take a walk." He eased out the door, hailed a cab, and flew to the Plaza.

"This is no good," Emma said. "Charles will miss me."

"Bear with me, sugar," Kugelmass said. He was pale and sweaty. He kissed her again, raced to the elevators, yelled at Persky over a pay phone in the Plaza lobby, and just made it home before midnight.

"According to Popkin, barley prices in Kraków have not been this stable since 1971," he said to Daphne, and smiled wanly as he climbed into bed.

The whole week went by like that. On Friday night, Kugelmass told Daphne there was another symposium he had to catch, this one in Syracuse. He hurried back to the Plaza, but the second weekend there was nothing like the first. "Get me back into the novel or marry me," Emma told Kugelmass. "Meanwhile, I want to get a job or go to class, because watching TV all day is the pits."

"Fine. We can use the money," Kugelmass said. "You consume twice your weight in room service."

"I met an Off Broadway producer in Central Park yesterday, and he said I might be right for a project he's doing," Emma said.

"Who is this clown?" Kugelmass asked.

"He's not a clown. He's sensitive and kind and cute. His name's Jeff Something-or-Other, and he's up for a Tony."

Later that afternoon, Kugelmass showed up at Persky's drunk.

"Relax," Persky told him. "You'll get a coronary."

"Relax. The man says relax. I've got a fictional character stashed in a hotel room, and I think my wife is having me tailed by a private shamus."

"O.K., O.K. We know there's a problem." Persky crawled under the cabinet and started banging on something with a large wrench.

"I'm like a wild animal," Kugelmass went on. "I'm sneaking around town, and Emma and I have had it up to here with each other. Not to mention a hotel tab that reads like the defense budget."

"So what should I do? This is the world of magic," Persky said. "It's all nuance."

"Nuance, my foot. I'm pouring Dom Perignon and black eggs into this little mouse, plus her wardrobe, plus she's enrolled at the Neighborhood Playhouse and suddenly needs professional photos. Also, Persky, Professor Fivish Kopkind, who teaches Comp Lit and who has always been jealous of me, has identified me as the sporadically appearing character in the Flaubert book. He's threatened to go to Daphne. I see ruin and alimony jail. For adultery with Madame Bovary, my wife will reduce me to beggary."

"What do you want me to say? I'm working on it night and day. As far as your personal anxiety goes, that I can't help you with. I'm a magician, not an analyst."

By Sunday afternoon, Emma had locked herself in the bathroom and refused to respond to Kugelmass's entreaties. Kugelmass stared out the window at the Wollman Rink and contemplated suicide. Too bad this is a low floor, he thought, or I'd do it right now. Maybe if I ran away to Europe and started life over . . . Maybe I could sell the *International Herald Tribune,* like those young girls used to.

The phone rang. Kugelmass lifted it to his ear mechanically.

"Bring her over," Persky said. "I think I got the bugs out of it."

Kugelmass's heart leaped. "You're serious?" he said. "You got it licked?"

"It was something in the transmission. Go figure."

"Persky, you're a genius. We'll be there in a minute. Less than a minute."

Again the lovers hurried to the magician's apartment, and again

Emma Bovary climbed into the cabinet with her boxes. This time there was no kiss. Persky shut the doors, took a deep breath, and tapped the box three times. There was the reassuring popping noise, and when Persky peered inside, the box was empty. Madame Bovary was back in her novel. Kugelmass heaved a great sigh of relief and pumped the magician's hand.

"It's over," he said. "I learned my lesson. I'll never cheat again, I swear it." He pumped Persky's hand again and made a mental note to send him a necktie.

Three weeks later, at the end of a beautiful spring afternoon, Persky answered his doorbell. It was Kugelmass, with a sheepish expression on his face.

"O.K., Kugelmass," the magician said. "Where to this time?"

"It's just this once," Kugelmass said. "The weather is so lovely, and I'm not getting any younger. Listen, you've read 'Portnoy's Complaint'? Remember The Monkey?"

"The price is now twenty-five dollars, because the cost of living is up, but I'll start you off with one freebie, due to all the trouble I caused you."

"You're good people," Kugelmass said, combing his few remaining hairs as he climbed into the cabinet again. "This'll work all right?"

"I hope. But I haven't tried it much since all that unpleasantness."

"Sex and romance," Kugelmass said from inside the box. "What we go through for a pretty face."

Persky tossed in a copy of "Portnoy's Complaint" and rapped three times on the box. This time, instead of a popping noise there was a dull explosion, followed by a series of crackling noises and a shower of sparks. Persky leaped back, was seized by a heart attack, and dropped dead. The cabinet burst into flames, and eventually the entire house burned down.

Kugelmass, unaware of this catastrophe, had his own problems. He had not been thrust into "Portnoy's Complaint," or into any other novel, for that matter. He had been projected into an old textbook, "Remedial Spanish," and was running for his life over a barren, rocky terrain as the word *tener* ("to have")—a large and hairy irregular verb—raced after him on its spindly legs.

# Manatee Gal Ain't You Coming Out Tonight

by Avram Davidson

*Avram Davidson has won a Hugo Award from the World Science Fiction Convention and an Edgar Award from the Mystery Writers of America, but he remains surprisingly little-known to the majority of readers in any field. If you've never encountered his writing before, you have a treat coming, for Davidson (currently writer-in-residence at William and Mary College) is one of the finest writers in any genre today, or ever.*

*That's extravagant praise but fully deserved, as this atmospheric and scary tale of half-forgotten mysteries in the richly-imagined Central American country called British Hidalgo will show. (Read this one slowly: it's to be savored.)*

The Cupid Club was the only waterhole on the Port Cockatoo waterfront. To be sure, there were two or three liquor booths back in the part where the tiny town ebbed away into the bush. But they were closed for siesta, certainly. And they sold nothing but watered rum and warm soft-drinks and loose cigarettes. Also, they were away from the breezes off the Bay which kept away the flies. In British Hidalgo gnats were flies, mosquitoes were flies, sand-flies—worst of all—were flies—*flies* were also flies: and if anyone were inclined to question this nomenclature, there was the unquestionable fact that mosquito itself was merely Spanish for little fly.

It was not really cool in the Cupid Club (Alfonso Key, prop., LICENSED TO SELL WINE, SPIRITS, BEER, ALE, CYDER AND PERRY). But it was certainly less hot than outside. Outside the sun burned the Bay, turning it into molten sparkles. Limekiller's boat stood at mooring, by very slightly raising his head he could see her, and every so often he did raise it. There wasn't much aboard to tempt thieves, and there weren't many thieves in Port Cockatoo, anyway. On the other hand, what was aboard the *Sacarissa* he could not very well spare; and it only took one thief, after all. So every now and then he did raise his head and make sure that no small boat was out by his own. No skiff or dory.

Probably the only thief in town was taking his own siesta.

"Nutmeg P'int," said Alfonso Key. "You been to Nutmeg P'int?"

"Been there."

Every place needs another place to make light fun of. In King Town, the old colonial capital, it was Port Cockatoo. Limekiller wondered what it was they made fun of, down at Nutmeg Point.

"What brings it into your mind, Alfonso?" he asked, taking his eyes from the boat. All clear. Briefly he met his own face in the mirror. Wasn't much of a face, in his own opinion. Someone had once called him "Young Count Tolstoy." Wasn't much point in shaving, anyway.

Key shrugged. "Sometimes somebody goes down there, goes up the river, along the old bush trails, buys carn. About now, you know, mon, carn bring good price, up in King Town."

Limekiller knew that. He often did think about that. He could quote the prices Brad Welcome paid for corn: white corn, yellow corn, cracked and ground. "I know," he said. "In King Town they have a lot of money and only a little corn. Along Nutmeg River they have a lot of corn and only a little money. Someone who brings down money from the Town can buy corn along the Nutmeg. Too bad I didn't think of that before I left."

Key allowed himself a small sigh. He knew that it wasn't any lack of thought, and that Limekiller had had no money before he left, or, likely, he wouldn't have left. "May-be they trust you down along the Nutmeg. They trust old Bob Blaine. Year after year he go up the Nutmeg, he go up and down the bush trail, he buy carn on credit, bring it bock up to King *Town*."

Off in the shadow at the other end of the barroom someone began to sing, softly.

> *W'ol' Bob Blaine, he done gone.*
> *W'ol' Bob Blaine, he done gone.*
> *Ahl, ahl me money gone—*
> *Gone to Spahnish Hidalgo...*

In King Town, Old Bob Blaine had sold corn, season after season. Old Bob Blaine had bought salt, he had bought shotgun shells, canned milk, white flour, cotton cloth from the Turkish merchants. Fish hooks, sweet candy, rubber boots, kerosene, lamp *chim*ney. Old Bob Blaine had returned and paid for corn in kind—not, to be sure, immediately after selling the corn. Things did not move that swiftly even today, in British Hidalgo, and certainly had not Back When. Old Bob Blaine returned with the merchandise on his next buying trip. It was more convenient, he did not have to make so many trips up and down the mangrove coast. By and by it must almost have seemed that he was paying in advance, when he came, buying corn down along the Nutmeg River, the boundary between the Colony of British Hidalgo and the country which the Colony still called Spanish Hidalgo, though it had not been Spain's for a century and a half.

"Yes mon," Alfonso Key agreed. "Only, that one last time, he *not* come bock. They say he buy one marine engine yard, down in Republican waters."

"I heard," Limekiller said, "that he bought a garage down there."

The soft voice from the back of the bar said, "No, mon. Twas a coconut walk he bought. Yes, mon."

Jack wondered why people, foreign people, usually, sometimes complained that it was difficult to get information in British Hidalgo. In his experience, information was the easiest thing in the world, there—all the information you wanted. In fact, sometimes you could get more than you wanted. Sometimes, of course, it was contradictory. Sometimes it was outright wrong. But that, of course, was another matter.

"Anybody else ever take up the trade down there?" Even if the information, the answer, if there was an answer, even if it were negative, what difference would it make?

"No," said Key. "No-body. May-be you try, eh, Jock? May-be they trust you."

There was no reason why the small cultivators, slashing their small cornfields by main force out of the almighty bush and then burning the slash and then planting corn in the ashes, so to speak—maybe they would trust him, even though there was no reason *why* they should trust him. Still... Who knows... They might. They just might. Well... some of them just might. For a moment a brief hope rose in his mind.

"Naaa ... I haven't even got any crocus sacks." There wasn't much point in any of it after all. Not if he'd have to tote the corn wrapped up in his shirt. The jute sacks were fifty cents apiece in local currency; they were as good as money, sometimes even better than money.

Key, who had been watching rather unsleepingly as these thoughts were passing through Jack's mind, slowly sank back in his chair. "Ah," he said, very softly. "You haven't got any crocus sack."

"Een de w'ol' days," the voice from the back said, "every good 'oman, she di know which bush yerb good fah wyes, fah kid-ney, which bush yerb good fah heart, which bush yerb good fah fever. But ahl of dem good w'ol' 'omen, new, dey dead, you see. Yes mon. Ahl poss ahway. No-body know bush medicine nowadays. Only *bush-doc-tor*. And dey very few, sah, very few."

"What you say, Captain Cudgel, you not bush *doc*-tor you w'own self? Nah true, Captain?"

Slowly, almost reluctantly, the old man answered. "Well sah. Me know few teeng. Fah true. Me know few teeng. Not like in w'ol' days. In w'ol' days, me dive fah conch. Yes mon. Fetch up plan-ty conch. De sahlt wah-tah hort me eyes, take bush-yerb fah cure dem. But nomah. No, mon. Me no dive no mah. Ahl de time, me wyes hort, stay out of strahng sun now ... Yes mon. ..."

Limekiller yawned, politely, behind his hand. To make conversation, he repeated something he had heard. "They say some of the old-time people used to get herbs down at Cape Manatee."

Alfonso Key flashed him a look. The old man said, a different note suddenly in his voice, different from the melancholy one of a moment before, "Mon-ah-*tee*. Mon-ah-*tee* is hahf-*mon*, you know, sah. Fah true. Yes sah, mon-ah-*tee* is hahf-*mon*. Which reason de lah w'only allow you to tehk one mon-ah-*tee* a year."

Covertly, Jack felt his beer. Sure enough, it was warm. Key said, "Yes, but who even bother nowadays? The leather is so tough you can't even sole a boot with it. And you dasn't bring the meat up to the Central Market in King *Town*, you *know*."

The last thing on Limekiller's mind was to apply for a license to shoot manatee, even if the limit were one a week. "How come?" he asked. "How come you're not?" King Town. King Town was the reason that he was down in Port Cockatoo. There was no money to be made here, now. But there was none to be lost here, either. His creditors were all in King Town, though if they wanted to, they could reach him even down here. But it would hardly be worth anyone's while to fee a lawyer to come down and feed him during the court session. Mainly, though, it was a matter of, Out of sight, somewhat out of mind. And, anyway—who knows? The Micawber Principle was weaker down here than up in the capital. But still and all: something might turn up.

"Because, they say it is because Manatee have teats like a woman."

"One time, you know, one time dere is a mahn who mehk mellow wit ah mon-ah-tee, yes, sah. And hahv pickney by mon-ah-tee." It did seem that the old man had begun to say something more, but someone else said, *"Ha-ha-ha!"* And the same someone else next said, in a sharp, all-but-demanding voice, "Shoe *shine?* Shoe *shine?*"

"I don't have those kind of shoes," Limekiller told the boy.

"Suede *brush?* Suede *brush?*"

Still no business being forthcoming, the bootblack withdrew, muttering.

Softly, the owner of the Cupid Club murmured, "That is one bod bobboon."

Limekiller waited, then he said, "I'd like to hear more about that, Captain Cudgel..."

But the story of the man who "made mellow" with a manatee and fathered a child upon her would have to wait, it seemed, upon another occasion. Old Captain Cudgel had departed, via the back door. Jack decided to do the same, via the front.

The sun, having vexed the Atlantic coast most of the morning and afternoon, was now on its equal way towards the Pacific. The Bay of Hidalgo stretched away on all sides, out to the faint white line which marked the barrier reef, the great coral wall which had for so long safeguarded this small, almost forgotten nation for the British Crown and the Protestant Religion. To the south, faint and high and blue against the lighter blue of the sky, however faint, darker: Pico Guapo, in the Republic of Hidalgo. Faint, also, though recurrent, was Limekiller's thought that he might, just might, try his luck down there. His papers were in order. Port Cockatoo was a Port of Entry and of Exit. The wind was free.

But from day to day, from one hot day to another hot day, he kept putting the decision off.

He nodded politely to the District Commissioner and the District Medical Officer and was nodded to, politely, in return. A way down the front street strolled white-haired Mr. Stuart, who had come out here in The Year Thirty-Nine, to help the war effort, and had been here ever since: too far for nodding. Coming from the market shed where she had been buying the latest eggs and ground-victuals was good Miss Gwen; if she saw him she would insist on giving him his supper at her boarding-house on credit: her suppers (her breakfasts and lunches as well) were just fine. But he had debts enough already. So, with a sigh, and a fond recollection of her fried fish, her country-style chicken, and her candied breadfruit, he sidled down the little lane, and he avoided Miss Gwen.

One side of the lane was the one-story white-painted wooden building with the sign DENDRY WASHBURN, LICENCED TO SELL DRUGS AND POISONS, the other side of the lane was the one-story white-painted wooden building where Captain Cumberbatch kept shop. The lane itself was paved with the crushed decomposed coral called pipeshank—and, indeed, the stuff did look like so much busted-up clay pipe stems. At the end of the lane was a small wharf and a flight of steps, at the bottom of the steps was his skiff.

He poled out to his boat, where he was greeted by his first mate, Skippy, an off-white cat with no tail. Skippy was very neat, and always used the ashes of the caboose: and if Jack didn't remember to sweep them *out* of the caboose as soon as they had cooled, and off to one side, why, that was his own carelessness, and no fault of Skippy's.

"All clear?" he asked the small tiger, as it rubbed against his leg. The small tiger growled something which might have been "Portuguese man o'war off the starboard bow at three bells," or "Musket-men to the futtock-shrouds," or perhaps only, "Where in the Hell have *you* been, all day, you creep?"

"Tell you what, Skip," as he tied the skiff, untied the *Sacarissa,* and, taking up the boat's pole, leaned against her in a yo-heave-ho manner; "let's us bugger off from this teeming tropical metropolis and go timely down the coast . . . say, to off Crocodile Creek, lovely name, proof there really is no Chamber of Commerce in these parts . . . then take the dawn tide and drop a line or two for some

grunts or jacks or who knows what ... sawfish, maybe ... maybe ...
*some*thing to go with the rice-and-beans tomorrow ... Corn what we
catch but can't eat," he grunted, leaned, hastily released his weight
and grabbed the pole up from the sucking bottom, dropped it on
deck, and made swift shift to raise sail; *slap/slap/* ... and then he
took the tiller.

"And *thennn* ... Oh, shite and onions, *I* don't know. Out to the
Welshman's Cayes, maybe."

"Harebrained idea if ever I heard one," the first mate growled,
trying to take Jack by the left greattoe. "Why don't you cut your hair
and shave that beard and get a job and get drunk, like any decent,
civilized son of a bitch would do?"

The white buildings and red roofs and tall palms wavering along
the front street, the small boats riding and reflecting, the green mass
of the bush behind: all contributed to give Port Cockatoo and envi-
rons the look and feel of a South Sea Island. Or, looked at from the
viewpoint of another culture, the District Medical Officer (who was
due for a retirement which he would not spend in his natal country),
said that Port Cockatoo was "*gemütlich.*" It was certainly a quiet and a
gentle and undemanding sort of place.

But, somehow, it did not seem the totally ideal place for a man not
yet thirty, with debts, with energy, with uncertainties, and with a
thirty-foot boat.

A bright star slowly detached itself from the darkening land and
swam up and up and then stopped and swayed a bit. This was the
immense kerosene lamp which was nightly swung to the top of the
great flagpole in the Police yard: it could be seen, the local Baymen
assured J. Limekiller, as far out as Serpent Caye ... Serpent Caye, the
impression was, lay hard upon the very verge of the known and
habitable earth, beyond which the River Ocean probably poured its
stream into The Abyss.

Taking the hint, Limekiller took his own kerosene lamp, by no
means immense, lit it, and set it firmly between two chocks of wood.
Technically, there should have been two lamps and of different
colors. But the local vessels seldom showed any lights at all. "He see
me forst, he blow he conch-*shell;* me see *he* forst, me blow *my*
conch-shell." And if neither saw the other. "Well, we suppose to meet
each othah ... " And if they didn't? Well, there was Divine

Profidence—hardly any lives were lost from such misadventures: unless, of course, someone was drunk.

The dimlight lingered and lingered to the west, and then the stars started to come out. It was time, Limekiller thought, to stop for the night.

He was eating his rice and beans and looking at the chart when he heard a voice nearby saying,"Sheep a-high!"

Startled, but by no means alarmed, he called out, "Come aboard!"

What came aboard first was a basket, then a man. A man of no great singularity of appearance, save that he was lacking one eye. "Me name," said the man, "is John Samuel, barn in dis very Colony, me friend, and hence ah subject of de Queen, God bless hah." Mr. Samuel was evidently a White Creole, a member of a class never very large, and steadily dwindling away: sometimes by way of absorption into the non-White majority, sometimes by way of emigration, and sometimes just by way of Death the Leveler. "I tehks de libahty of bringing you some of de forst fruits of de sile," said John S.

"Say, mighty thoughtful of you, Mr. Samuel, care for some rice and beans?—My name's Jack Limekiller."

"—to weet, sour*sop*, bread*fruit*, oh-*ronge*, coco*nut*—what I care for, Mr. Limekiller, is some *rum. Rum* is what I has come to beg of you. De hond of mon, sah, has yet to perfect any medicine de superior of *rum*."

Jack groped in the cubbyhold. "What about all those bush medicines down at Cape Manatee? he asked, grunting. There was supposed to be a small bottle, a *chaparita,* as they called it. Where— Oh. It must be...No. Then it must be...

Mr. Samuel rubbed the grey bristles on his strong jaw. "I does gront you, sah, de vertue of de country yerba. But you must steep de *yerba* een de *rum,* sah. Yes mon."

Jack's fingers finally found the bottle and his one glass and his one cup and poured. Mr. Samuel said nothing until he had downed his, and then gave a sigh of satisfaction. Jack, who had found a mawmee-apple in the basket of fruit, nodded as he peeled it. The flesh was tawny, and reminded him of wintergreen.

After a moment, he decided that he didn't want to finish his rum, and, with a questioning look, passed it over to his guest. It was pleasant there on the open deck, the breeze faint but sufficient, and comparatively few flies of any sort had cared to make the voyage from shore. The boat swayed gently, there was no surf to speak of, the waves of the Atlantic having spent themselves, miles out, upon the reef; and only a few loose items of gear knocked softly as the vessel rose and fell upon the soft bosom of the inner bay.

"Well sah," said Mr. Samuel, with a slight smack of his lips, "I weesh to acknowledge your generosity. I ahsked you to wahk weet me wan mile, and you wahk weet me twain." Something splashed in the water, and he looked out, sharply.

"Shark?"

"No, mon. Too far een-shore." His eyes gazed out where there was nothing to be seen.

"Porpoise, maybe. Turtle. Or a sting-ray..."

After a moment, Samuel said, "Suppose to be ah tortle." He turned back and gave Limekiller a long, steady look.

Moved by some sudden devil, Limekiller said, "I hope, Mr. Samuel, that you are not about to tell me about some Indian caves or ruins, full of gold, back in the bush, which you are willing to go shares on with me and all I have to do is put up the money—because, you see, Mr. Samuel, I haven't got any money." And added, "Besides, they tell me it's illegal and that all those things belong to the Queen."

Solemnly, Samuel said, "God save de Queen." Then his eyes somehow seemed to become wider, and his mouth as well, and a sound like hissing steam escaped him, and he sat on the coaming and shook with almost-silent laughter. Then he said, "I sees dot you hahs been ahproached ahlready. No sah. No such teeng. My proposition eenclude only two quality: Expedition. Discretion." And he proceded to explain that what he meant was that Jack should, at regular intervals, bring him supplies in small quantities and that he would advance the money for this and pay a small amount for the service. Delivery was to be made at night. And nothing was to be said about it, back at Port Cockatoo, or anywhere else.

Evidently Jack Limekiller wasn't the only one who had creditors.

"Anything else, Mr. Samuel?"

Samuel gave a deep sigh. "Ah, mon, I would like to sogjest dat you breeng me out ah woman...but best no. Best not...not yet... Oh, Mon, I om so lustful, ahlone out here, eef you tie ah rottlesnake down fah me I weel freeg eet!"

"Well, Mr. Samuel, the fact is, I will not tie a rattlesnake down for you, or up for you, for any purpose at all. However, I will keep my eyes open for a board with a knot-hole in it."

Samuel guffawed. Then he got up, his machete slap-flapping against his side, and with a few more words, clambered down into his dory—no plank-boat, in these waters, but a dug-out—and began to paddle. Bayman, bushman, the machete was almost an article of clothing, though there was nothing to chop out here on the gentle waters of the bay. There was a splash, out there in the darkness, and a cry—Samuel's voice—

"Are you all right out there?" Limekiller called.

"Yes mon..." faintly. "Fine... bloddy Oxville tortle..."

Limekiller fell easily asleep. Presently he dreamed of seeing a large Hawksbill turtle languidly pursuing John Samuel, who languidly evaded the pursuit. Later, he awoke, knowing that he knew what had awakened him, but for the moment unable to name it. The awakeners soon enough identified themselves. Manatees. Sea-cows. The most harmless creatures God ever made. He drowsed off again, but again and again he lightly awoke and always he could hear them sighing and sounding.

Early up, he dropped his line, made a small fire in the sheet-iron caboose set in its box of sand, and put on the pot of rice and beans to cook in coconut oil. The head and tail of the first fish went into a second pot, the top of the double boiler, to make fish-tea, as the chowder was called; when they were done, he gave them to Skippy. He fried the fillets with sliced breadfruit, which had as near no taste of its own as made no matter, but was a great extender of tastes. The second fish he cut and corned—that is, he spread coarse salt on it: there was nothing else to do to preserve it in this hot climate, without ice, and where the art of smoking fish was not known. And more than those two he did not bother to take, he had no license for commercial fishing, could not sell a catch in the market, and the "sport" of taking fish he could neither eat nor sell, and would have to throw back, was a pleasure which eluded his understanding.

It promised to be a hot day and it kept its promise, and he told himself, as he often did on hot, hot days, that it beat shoveling snow in Toronto.

He observed a vacant mooring towards the south of town, recollected that it always had been vacant, and so, for no better reason than that, he tied up to it. Half of the remainder of his catch came ashore with him. This was too far south for any plank houses or tin roofs. Port Cockatoo at both ends straggled out into 'trash houses,' as they were called—sides of wild cane allowing the cooling breezes to pass, and largely keeping out the brute sun; roofs of thatch, usually of the bay or cohune palm. The people were poorer here than elsewhere in this town where no one at all by North American standards was rich, but 'trash' had no reference to that: *Loppings, twigs, and leaves of trees, bruised sugar cane, corn husks, etc.*, his dictionary explained.

An old, old woman in the ankle-length skirts and the kerchief of her generation stood in the doorway of her little house and looked, first at him, then at his catch. And kept on looking at it. All the coastal people of Hidalgo were fascinated by fish: rice and beans was the staple dish, but fish was the roast beef, the steak, the chicken, of this small, small country which had never been rich and was now—with the growing depletion of its mahogany and rosewood—even poorer than ever. Moved, not so much by conscious consideration of this as by a sudden impulse, he held up his hand and what it was holding. "Care for some corned fish, Grandy?"

Automatically, she reached out her tiny, dark hand, all twisted and withered, and took it. Her lips moved. She looked from the fish to him and from him to the fish; asked, doubtfully, "How much I have for you?"—meaning, how much did she owe him.

"Your prayers," he said, equally on impulse.

Her head flew up and she looked at him full in the face, then. "T'ank you, Buckra," she said. "And I weel do so. I weel pray for you." And she went back into her trash house.

Up the dusty, palm-lined path a ways, just before it branched into the cemetery road and the front street, he encountered Mr. Stuart— white-haired, learned, benevolent, deaf, and vague—and wearing what was surely the very last sola topee in everyday use in the Western Hemisphere (and perhaps, what with one thing and another, in the Eastern, as well).

"Did you hear the baboons last night?" asked Mr. Stuart.

Jack knew that "baboons," hereabouts, were howler-monkeys.

Even their daytime noises, a hollow and repetitive *Rrrr-Rrrr-Rrrr,* sounded uncanny enough; as for their night-time wailings—

"I was anchored offshore, down the coast, last night," he explained. "All I heard were the manatees."

Mr. Stuart looked at him with faint, grey eyes, smoothed his long moustache. "Ah, *those* poor chaps," he said. "They've slipped back down the scale... much *too* far down, I expect, for any quick return. Tried to help them, you know. Tried the Herodotus method. Carthaginians. Mute trade, you know. Set out some bright red cloth, put trade-goods on, went away. Returned. Things were knocked about, as though animals had been at them. *Some* of the items were gone, though. But nothing left in return. Too bad, oh yes, too bad..."

His voice died away into a low moan, and he shook his ancient head. In another moment, before Jack could say anything, or even think of anything to say, Mr. Stuart had flashed him a smile of pure friendliness, and was gone. A bunch of flowers was in one hand, and the path he took was the cemetery road. He had gone to visit one of "the great company of the dead, which increase around us as we grow older."

From this mute offering, laid also upon the earth, nothing would be expected in return. There are those whom we do not see and whom we do not desire that they should ever show themselves at all.

The shop of Captain Cumberbatch was open. The rules as to what stores or offices were open and closed at which times were exactly the opposite of the laws of the Medes and the Persians. The time to go shopping was when one saw the shop open. Any shop. They opened, closed, opened, closed... And as to why stores with a staff of only one closed so often, why, they closed not only to allow the proprietor to siesta, they also closed to allow him to eat. It was no part of the national culture for Ma to send Pa's "tea" for Pa to eat behind the counter: Pa came home. Period. And as for establishments with a staff of more than one, why could the staff not have taken turns? Answer: De baas, of whatsoever race, creed, or color, might trust an employee with his life, but he would never trust his employee with his cash or stock, never, never, never.

Captain Cumberbatch had for many years puffed up and down the coast in his tiny packet-and-passenger boat, bringing cargo merchandise for the shopkeepers of Port Caroline, Port Cockatoo, and—very, very semioccasionally—anywhere else as chartered. But some years ago he had swallowed the anchor and set up business as shopkeeper in Port Cockatoo. And one day an epiphany of sorts had occurred: Captain Cumberbatch had asked himself why he should bring cargo for others to sell and/or why he should pay others to bring cargo for he himself to sell. Why should he not bring his own cargo and sell it himself?

The scheme was brilliant as it was unprecedented. And indeed it had but one discernable flaw: Whilst Captain Cumberbatch was at sea, he could not tend shop to sell what he had shipped. And while he was tending his shop he could not put to sea to replenish stock. And, tossing ceaselessly from the one horn of this dilemma to the other, he often thought resentfully of the difficulties of competing with such peoples as the Chinas, Turks, and 'Paniards, who—most unfairly—were able to trust the members of their own families to mind the store.

Be all this as it may, the shop of Captain Cumberbatch was at this very moment open, and the captain himself was leaning upon his counter and smoking a pipe.

"Marneen, Jock. Hoew de day?"

"Bless God."

"Forever and ever, ehhh-men."

A certain amount of tinned corned-beef and corned-beef hash, of white sugar (it was nearer grey), of bread (it was dead white, as unsuitable an item of diet as could be designed for the country and the country would have rioted at the thought of being asked to eat dark), salt, lamp-oil, tea, tinned milk, cheese, were packed and passed across the worn counter; a certain amount of national currency made the same trip in reverse.

As for the prime purchaser of the items, Limekiller said nothing. That was part of the Discretion.

Outside again, he scanned the somnolent street for any signs that anyone might have—somehow—arrived in town who might want to charter a boat for... well, for anything. Short of smuggling, there was scarcely a purpose for which he would have not chartered the *Sacarissa*. It was not that he had an invincible repugnance to the midnight trade, there might well be places and times where he would have considered it. But Government, in British Hidalgo (here, as elsewhere in what was left of the Empire, the definite article was conspicuously absent: "Government will do this," they said—or, often as not, "Government will not do this") had not vexed him in any way and he saw no reason to vex it. And, furthermore, he had heard many reports of the accommodations at the Queen's Hotel, as the King Town "gaol" was called: and they were uniformly unfavorable.

But the front street was looking the same as ever, and, exemplifying, as ever, the observation of The Preacher, that there was no new thing under the sun. So, with only the smallest of sighs, he had started for the Cupid Club, when the clop ... clop of hooves made him look up. Coming along the street was the horse-drawn equivalent of a pickup truck. The back was open, and contained a few well-filled crocus sacks and some sawn timber; the front was roofed, but open at the sides; and for passengers it had a white-haired woman and a middle-aged man. It drew to a stop.

"Well, young man. And who are *you?*" the woman asked. Some elements of the soft local accent overlaid her speech, but underneath was something else, something equally soft, but different. Her "Man" was not *mon*, it was *mayun*, and her "you" was more like *yieww*.

He took off his hat. "Jack Limekiller is my name, ma'am."

"Put it right back on, Mr. Limekiller. I do appreciate the gesture, but it has already been gestured, now. Draft-dodger, are you?"

That was a common guess. Any North American who didn't fit into an old and familiar category—tourist, sport fisherman, sport huntsman, missionary, businessman—was assumed to be either a draft-dodger or a trafficker in "weed" ... or maybe both. "No, ma'am. I've served my time, and, anyway, I'm a Canadian, and we don't have a draft."

"Well," she said, "doesn't matter even if you are, I don't *cay*-uh. Now, sir, I am Amelia Lebedee. And this is my nephew, Tom McFee." Tom smiled a faint and abstract smile, shook hands. He was sun-dark and had a slim moustache and he wore a felt hat which had perhaps been crisper than it was now. Jack had not seen many men like Tom McFee in Canada, but he had seen many men like Tom McFee in the United States. Tom McFee sold crab in Baltimore. Tom McFee managed the smaller cotton gin in a two-gin town in Alabama. Tom McFee was foreman at the shrimp-packing plant in one of the Florida Parishes in Louisiana. And Tom McFee was railroad freight agent in whatever dusty town in Texas it was that advertised itself as "Blue Vetch Seed Capital of the World."

"We are carrying you off to Shiloh for lunch," said Amelia, and a handsome old woman she was, and sat up straight at the reins. "So you just climb up in. Tom will carry you back later, when he goes for some more of this wood. Land! You'd think it was *teak*, they cut it so slow. Instead of pine."

Limekiller had no notion who or what or where Shiloh was, although it clearly could not be very far, and he could think of no reason why he should not go there. So in he climbed.

"Yes," said Amelia Lebedee, "the war wiped us out completely. So we came down here and we planted sugar, yes, we planted sugar and we made sugar for, oh, most eighty years. But we didn't move with the times, and so that's all over with now. We plant most anything *but* sugar nowadays. And when we see a new and a civilized face, we plant them down at the table." By this time the wagon was out of town. The bush to either side of the road looked like just bushtype bush to Jack. But to Mrs. Lebedee each acre had an identity of its own. "That was the Cullen's place," she'd say. And, "The Robinson's lived there. Beautiful horses, they had. Nobody has horses anymore, just us. Yonder used to be the Simmonses. Part of the house is still standing, but, land!—you cain't see it from the road anymore. They've gone back. Most everybody has gone back, who hasn't died off..." For a while she said nothing. The road gradually grew narrower, and all three of them began thoughtfully to slap at "flies."

A bridge now appeared and they rattled across it, a dark-green stream rushing below. There was a glimpse of an old grey house in the archaic, universal-tropical style, and then the bush closed in again. "And *they*-uh," Miss Amelia gestured, backwards, "is Texas. Oh, what a fine place that was, in its day! Nobody lives there, now. Old Captain Rutherford, the original settler, he was with Hood. *Gen*eral Hood, I mean."

It all flashed on Jack at once, and it all came clear, and he wondered that it had not been clear from the beginning. They were now passing through the site of the old Confederate colony. There had been such in Venezuela, in Colombia, even in Brazil; for all he knew, there might still be. But this one here in Hidalgo, it had not been wiped out in a year or two, like the Mormon colonies in Mexico—there had been no Revolution here, no gringo-hating

Villistas—it had just ebbed away. Tiny little old B.H., "a country," as someone (who?) had said, "which you can put your arms around," had put its arms around the Rebel refugees... its thin, green arms... and it had let them clear the bush and build their houses... and it had waited... and waited... and, as, one by one, the Southern American families had "died out" or "gone back," why, as easy as easy, the bush had slipped back. And, for the present, it seemed like it was going to stay back. It had, after all, closed in after the Old Empire Mayans had so mysteriously left, and that was a thousand years ago. What was a hundred years, to the bush?

The house at Shiloh was small and neat and trim and freshly painted, and one end of the veranda was undergoing repairs. There had been no nonsense, down here, of reproducing any of the ten thousand imitations of Mount Vernon. A neatly-mowed lawn surrounded the house; in a moment, as the wagon made its last circuit, Jack saw that the lawnmowers were a small herd of cattle. A line of cedars accompanied the road, and Miss Amelia pointed to a gap in the line. "That tree that was there," she said, calmly, "was the one that fell on my husband and on John Samuel. It had been obviously weakened in the hurricane, you know, and they went over to see how badly—that was a mistake. John Samuel lost his left eye and my husband lost his life."

*Discretion...* Would it be indiscreet to ask—? He asked.

"How long ago was this, Miss Amelia?" All respectable women down here were "Miss," followed by the first name, regardless of marital state.

"It was ten years ago, come September," she said. "Let's go in out of the sun, now, and Tom will take care of the horse."

In out of the sun was cool and neat and, though shady, the living room-dining room was as bright as fresh paint and flowered wall-paper—the only wall-paper he had seen in the colony—could make it. There were flowers in vases, too, fresh flowers, not the widely-popular plastic ones. Somehow the Bayfolk did not make much of flowers.

For lunch there was heart-of-palm, something not often had, for a palm had to die to provide it, and palms were not idly cut down: there was the vegetable pear, or chayote, here called cho-cho; venison chops, tomato with okra; there was cashew wine, made from the fruit of which the Northern Lands know only the seed, which they ignorantly call "nut." And, even, there was coffee, not powdered ick, not grown-in-Brazil-shipped-to-the-United-States-roasted-ground-canned-shipped-to-Hidalgo-coffee, but actual local coffee. Here, where coffee grew with no more care than weeds, hardly anyone except the Indians bothered to grow it, and what *they* grew, *they* used.

"Yes," Miss Amelia said, "it can be a very good life here. It is necessary to work, of course, but the work is well-rewarded, oh, not in terms of large sums of money, but in so many other ways. But it's coming to an end. There is just no way that working this good land can bring you all the riches you see in the moving pictures. And that is what they all want, and dream of, all the young people. And there is just no way they are going to get it."

Tom McFee made one of his rare comments. "*I* don't dream of any white Christmas," he said. "I am staying here, where it is always green. I told Malcolm Stuart that."

Limekiller said, "I was just talking to him this morning, myself. But I couldn't understand what he was talking about . . . something about trying to trade with the manatees. . . "

The Shiloh people, clearly, had no trouble understanding what Stuart had been talking about; they did not even think it was particularly bizarre. "Ah, those poor folks down at Mantee," said Amelia Lebedee; "—now, mind you, I mean *Mantee,* Cape Mantee, I am *not* referring to the people up on Manatee River and the Lagoons, who are just as civilized as you and I: I mean *Cape* Mantee, which is its correct name, you know—"

"Where the medicine herbs grew?"

"Why, yes, Mr. Limekiller. Where they grew. As I suppose they still do. No one really knows, of course, *what* still grows down at Cape Mantee, though Nature, I suppose, would not change her ways. It was the hurricanes, you see. The War Year hurricanes. Until then, you know, Government had kept a road open, and once a month a police constable would ride down and, well, at least, take a look around. Not that any of the people there would ever bring any of their troubles to the police. They were . . . well, how should I put it? Tom, how would *you* put it?"

Tom thought a long moment. "Simple. They were always simple."

What he meant by "simple," it developed, was simple-minded. His aunt did not entirely agree with that. They gave that impression, the Mantee people, she said, but that was only because their ways were so different. "There is a story," she said, slowly, and, it seemed to Jack Limekiller, rather reluctantly, "that a British man-of-war took a Spanish slave-ship. I don't know when this would have been, it was well before we came down and settled here. Well before The War. Our own War, I mean. It was a small Spanish slaver and there weren't many captives in her. As I understand it, between the time that Britain abolished slavery and the dreadful Atlantic slave-trade finally disappeared, if slavers were taken anywhere near Africa, the British would bring the captives either to Saint Helena or Sierra Leone, and liberate them there. But this one was taken fairly near the American coast. I suppose she was heading for Cuba. So the British ship brought them *here*. To British Hidalgo. And the people were released down at Cape Mantee, and told they could settle there and no one would 'vex' them, as they say here."

*Where* the slaves had come from, originally, she did not know, but she thought the tradition was that they had come from somewhere well back in the African interior. Over the course of the many subsequent years, some had trickled into the more settled parts of the old colony. "But some of them just stayed down there," she said. "Keeping up their own ways."

"Too much intermarrying," Tom offered.

"So the Bayfolk say. The Bayfolk were always, *I* think, rather afraid of them. None of them would ever go there alone. And, after the hurricanes, when the road went out, and the police just couldn't get there, none of the Bayfolk would go there at *all*. By sea, I mean. You must remember, Mr. Limekiller, that in the 1940s this little colony was very much as it was in the 1840s. There were no airplanes. There wasn't one single highway. When I say there used to be a road to Mantee, you mustn't think it was a road such as we've got between Port Cockatoo and Shiloh."

Limekiller, thinking of the dirt road between Port Cockatoo and Shiloh, tried to think what the one between Port Cockatoo and the region behind Cape Mantee must have been like. Evidently a trail, nothing more, down which an occasional man on a mule might make his way, boiling the potato-like fruit of the breadnut tree for his food and feeding his mule the leaves: a trail that had to be "chopped," had to be "cleaned" by machete-work, at least twice a year, to keep the all-consuming bush from closing over it the way the flesh closes over a cut. An occasional trader, an occasional buyer or gatherer of chicle or herbs or hides, an occasional missioner or medical officer, at infrequent intervals would pass along this corridor in the eternal jungle.

And then came a hurricane, smashing flat everything in its path. And the trail vanished. And the trail was never re-cut. British Hidalgo had probably never been high on any list of colonial priorities at the best of times. During the War of 1939-1945, they may have forgotten all about it in London. Many of Hidalgo's able-bodied men were off on distant fronts. An equal number had gone off to cut the remaining forests of the Isle of Britain, to supply anyway a fraction of the wood which was then impossible to import. Nothing could be spared for Mantee and its people; in King Town, Mantee was deemed as distant as King Town was in London. The p.c. never went there again. No missioner ever returned. Neither had a medical officer or nurse. Nor any trader. No one. Except for Malcolm Stuart...

"He did try. Of course, he had his own concerns. During the War he had his war work. Afterwards, he took up a block of land a few miles back from here, and he had his hands full with that. And then, after, oh, I don't remember how many years of stories, stories—there is no television here, you know, and few people have time for books— stories about the Mantee people, well, he decided he had to go have a look, see for himself, you know."

Were the Mantee people really eating raw meat and raw fish? He would bring them matches. Had they actually reverted to the use of stone for tools? He would bring them machetes, axes, knives. And...as for the rest of it...the rest of the rather awful and certainly very odd stories...he would see for himself.

But he had seen nothing. There had been nothing to see. That is, nothing which he could be sure he had seen. Perhaps he had thought that he had seen some few things which he had not cared to mention to Jack, but had spoken of to the Shiloh people.

They, however, were not about to speak of it to Jack.

"Adventure," said Amelia Lebedee, dismissing the matter of Mantee with a sigh. "Nobody wants the adventure of cutting bush to plant yams. They want the adventure of night clubs and large automobiles. They see it in the moving pictures. And you, Mr. Limekiller, what is it that *you* want?—coming, having come, from the land of night clubs and large automobiles..."

The truth was simple. "I wanted the adventure of sailing a boat with white sails through tropic seas," he said. "I saw it in the moving pictures. I never had a night club but I had a large automobile, and I sold it and came down here and bought the boat. And, well, here I am."

They had talked right through the siesta time. Tom McFee was ready, now, to return for the few more planks which the sawmill might—or might not—have managed to produce since the morning. It was time to stand up now and to make thanks and say good-bye. "Yes," said Amelia Lebedee, pensively "Here we are. Here we all are. We are all here. And some of us are more content being here than others."

Half-past three at the Cupid Club. On Limekiller's table, the usual single bottle of beer. Also, the three chaparitas of rum which he had bought—but they were in a paper bag, lest the sight of them, plus the fact that he could invite no one to drink of them, give rise to talk that he was "mean." Behind the bar, Alfonso Key. In the dark, dark back, slowly sipping a lemonade (all soft drinks were "lemonade"—coke was lemonade, strawberry pop was lemonade, ginger stout was lemonade... sometimes, though not often, for reasons inexplicable, there was also lemon-flavored lemonade)—in the dark rear part of the room, resting his perpetually sore eyes, was old Captain Cudgel.

"Well, how you spend the night, Jock?" Alfonso ready for a tale of amour, ready with a quip, a joke.

"Oh, just quietly. Except for the manatees." Limekiller, saying this, had a sudden feeling that he had said all this before, been all this before, was caught on the moebius strip which life in picturesque Port Cockatoo had already become, caught, caught, never would be released. *Adventure!* Hah!

At this point, however, a slightly different note, a slightly different comment from the old, old man.

"Een Eedalgo," he said, dolefully, "de monatee hahv no leg, mon. Becahs Eedalgo ees a smahl coun-*tree,* ahn every-teeng smahl. Every-teeng *weak.* Now, een Ahfrica, mon, de monatee *does* hahv leg."

Key said, incredulous, but still respectful, "What you tell we, Coptain Cudgel? *What?*" His last word, pronounced in the local manner of using it as a particular indication of skepticism, of criticism, of denial, seemed to have at least three *T*s at the end of it; he repeated: "*Whattt?*"

"Yes, mon. Yes sah. Een Ahfrica, de monatee hahv *leg,* mon. Eet be ah poerful beast, een Ahfrica, come up on de *lond,* mon."

"I tell you. *Me* di hear eet befoah. Een Ahfrica," he repeated, doggedly, "de monatee hahv leg, de monatee be ah poerful beast, come up on de *lond,* mon, no lahf, mon—"

"Me no di lahf, sah—"

"—de w'ol' people, dey tell me so, fah true."

Alfonso Key gave his head a single shake, gave a single click of his tongue, gave Jack a single look.

Far down the street, the bell of the Church of Saint Benedict the Moor sounded. Whatever time it was marking had nothing to do with Greenwich Meridian Time or any variation thereof.

The weak, feeble old voice resumed the thread of conversation. "Me grahndy di tell me dot she grahndy di tell *she.* Motta hav foct, eet me grahndy di give me me name, b'y. Cudgel. Ahfrica name. Fah true. Fah True."

A slight sound of surprise broke Limekiller's silence. He said, "Excuse me, Captain. Could it have been 'Cudjoe'...maybe?"

For a while he thought that the question had either not been heard or had, perhaps, been resented. Then the old man said, "Eet could be so. Sah, eet might be so. Lahng, lahng time ah-go... Me Christian name, Pe-tah. Me w'ol' grahndy she say. 'Pickney: you hahv ah Christian name, Pe-tah. But me give you Ahfrica name, too. Cahdjo. No fah-get, pickney? Time poss, time poss, de people dey ahl cahl me 'Cudgel,' you see, sah. So me fah-get...Sah, hoew you know dees teeng, sah?'"

Limekiller said that he thought he had read it in a book. The old captain repeated the word, lengthening it in his local speech. "Ah boook, sah. To t'eenk ahv dot. Een ah boook. Me w'own name een ah boook." By and by he departed as silently as always.

In the dusk a white cloth waved behind the thin line of white beach. He took off his shirt and waved back. Then he transferred the groceries into the skiff and, as soon as it was dark and he had lit and securely fixed his lamp, set about rowing ashore. By and by a voice called out, "Mon, where de Hell you gweyn? You keep on to de right, you gweyn wine up een *Sponeesh* Hidalgo: Mah to de lef, mon: mah to de *lef!*" And with such assistances, soon enough the skiff softly scraped the beach.

Mr. John Samuel's greeting was, "You bring de rum?" The rum put in his hand, he took up one of the sacks, gestured Limekiller towards the other. "Les go timely, noew," he said. For a moment, in what was left of the dimmest dimlight, Jack thought the man was going to walk straight into an enormous tree: instead, he walked across the enormous roots and behind the tree. Limekiller followed the faint white patch of shirt bobbing in front of him. Sometimes the ground was firm, sometimes it went squilchy, sometimes it was simply running water—shallow, fortunately—sometimes it felt like gravel. The bush noises were still fairly soft. A rustle. He hoped it was only a wish-willy lizard, or a bamboo-chicken—an iguana — and not a yellow-jaw, that snake of which it was said ... but this was no time to remember scare stories about snakes.

Without warning—although what sort of warning there could have been was a stupid question, anyway—there they were. Gertrude Stein, returning to her old home town after an absence of almost forty years, and finding the old home itself demolished, had observed (with a lot more objectivity than she was usually credited with) that there was no *there,* there. The *there,* here, was simply a clearing, with a very small fire, and a *ramada:* four poles holding up a low thatched roof. John Samuel let his sack drop. "Ahnd noew," he said, portentously, "let us broach de rum."

After the chaparita had been not only broached but drained, for the second time that day Limekiller dined ashore. The cooking was done on a raised fire-hearth of clay-and-sticks, and what was cooked was a breadfruit, simply strewn, when done, with sugar; and a gibnut. To say that the gibnut, or paca, is a rodent, is perhaps—though accurate—unfair: it is larger than a rabbit, and it eats well. After that Samuel made black tea and laced it with more rum. After that he gave a vast belch and a vast sigh. "Can you play de bon*joe?*" he next asked.

"Well.. I have been known to try... "

The    lamp    flared    and    smoked.    Samuel    adjusted it...somewhat....He got up and took a bulky object down from a peg on one of the roof-poles. It was a sheet of thick plastic, laced with raw-hide thongs, which he laboriously unknotted. Inside that was a deerskin. And inside *that,* an ordinary banjo-case, which contained an ordinary, if rather old and worn, banjo.

"Mehk I hear ah sahng...ah sahng ahv *you* country."

What song should he make him hear? No particularly Canadian song brought itself to mind. Ah well, he would dip down below the border just a bit...His fingers strummed idly on the strings. The words grew, the tune grew, he lifted up what some (if not very many) had considered a not-bad-baritone, and began to sing and play.

*Manatee gal, ain't you coming out tonight,*
*Coming out tonight, coming out tonight?*
*Oh, Manatee gal, ain't you coming out tonight,*
*To dance by the light of the—*

An enormous hand suddenly covered his own and pressed it down. The tune subsided into a jumble of chords, and an echo, and a silence.

"Mon, mon, you not do me right. I no di say, "Mehk I hear a sahng ahv *you* country?" Samuel, on his knees, breathed heavily. His breath was heavy with rum and his voice was heavy with reproof...and with a something else for which Limekiller had no immediate name. But, friendly it was not.

Puzzled more than apologetic, Jack said, "Well, it *is* a North American song, anyway. It was an old Erie Canal song. It—Oh. I'll be damned. Only it's supposed to go, *'Buffalo gal, ain't you coming out tonight,'* And I dunno what made me change it, what difference does it make?"

"What different? What different it mehk? Ah, Christ me King! You lee' buckra b'y, you not know w'ehnnah-teeng?"

It was all too much for Limekiller. The last thing he wanted was anything resembling an argument, here in the deep, dark bush, with an all-but-stranger. Samuel having lifted his heavy hand from the instrument, Limekiller, moved by a sudden spirit, began,

*Amazing grace, how sweet the sound,*
*To save a wretch like me.*

With a rough catch of his breath, Samuel muttered, "Yes. Yes. Dot ees good. Go on, b'y. No stop."

*I once was halt, but now can walk:*

*Was blind, but now I see...*

He sang the beautiful old hymn to the end: and, by that time, if not overpowered by Grace, John Samuel—having evidently broached the second and the third chaparita—was certainly overpowered: and it did not look as though the dinner-guest was going to get any kind of guided tour back to the shore and the skiff. He sighed and he looked around him. A bed rack had roughly been fixed up, and its lashings were covered with a few deer hides and an old Indian blanket. Samuel not responding to any shakings or urgings, Limekiller, with a shrug and a "Well what the hell," covered him with the blanket as he lay upon the ground. Then, having rolled up the sacks the supplies had come in and propped them under his head, Limekiller disposed himself for slumber on the hides. Some lines were running through his head and he paused a moment to consider what they were. What they were, they were, *From ghoulies and ghosties, long leggedy feasties, and bugges that go* boomp *in the night, Good Lord, deliver us*. With an almost absolute certainty that this was not the Authorized Version or Text, he heard himself give a grottle and a snore and knew he was fallen asleep.

He awoke to slap heartily at some flies, and the sound perhaps awoke the host, who was heard to mutter and mumble. Limekiller leaned over. "What did you say?"

The lines said, Limekiller learned that he had heard them before.

"Eef you tie ah rottlesnake doewn fah me, Iweel freeg eet."

"I yield," said Limekiller, "to any man so much hornier than myself. Produce the snake, sir, and I will consider the rest of the matter."

The red eye of the expiring fire winked at him. It was still winking at him when he awoke from a horrid nightmare of screams and thrashings-about, in the course of which he had evidently fallen or had thrown himself from the bedrack to the far side. Furthermore, he must have knocked against one of the roof-poles in doing so, because a good deal of the thatch had landed on top of him. He threw it off, and, getting up, began to apologize.

"Sorry if I woke you, Mr. Samuel. I don't know what —" There was no answer, and looking around in the faint light of the fire, he saw no one.

"Mr. Samuel? Mr. *Samuel?* John? oh, hey, *Johhn!?...*"

No answer. If the man had merely gone out to "ease himself," as the Bayfolk delicately put it, he would have surely been near enough to answer. No one in the colony engaged in strolling in the bush at night for fun. "Son of a bitch," he muttered. He felt for and found his matches, struck one, found the lamp, lit it, looked around.

There was still no sign of John Samuel, but what there were signs of was some sort of horrid violence. Hastily he ran his hands over himself, but, despite his fall, despite part of the roof having fallen on him, he found no trace of blood.

All the blood which lay around, then, must have been—could only have been—John Samuel's blood.

All the screaming and the sounds of something—or some things—heavily thrashing around, they had not been in any dream. They had been the sounds of truth.

And as for what else he saw, as he walked, delicate as Agag, around the perimeter of the clearing, he preferred not to speculate.

There was a shotgun and there were shells. He put the shells into the chambers and he stood up, weapon in his hand, all the rest of the night.

"Now, if it took you perhaps less than an hour to reach the shore, and if you left immediately, how is it that you were so long in arriving at Port?" The District Commissioner asked. He asked politely, but he did ask. He asked a great many questions, for, in addition to his other duties, he was the Examining Magistrate.

"Didn't you observe the wind, D. C.? Ask anyone who was out on the water yesterday. I spent most of the day tacking—"

Corporal Huggin said, softly, from the wheel, "That would be correct, Mr. Blossom."

They were in the police boat, the *George* . . . once, Jack had said to P.C. Ed Huggin, "For George VI, I suppose?" and Ed, toiling over the balky and antique engine, his clear tan skin smudged with grease, had scowled, and said, "More for bloody George III, you ask *me*. . ." At earliest daylight, yesterday, Limekiller, red-eyed and twitching, had briefly cast around in the bush near the camp, decided that, ignorant of bush-lore as he was, having not even a compass, let alone a pair of boots or a snake-bite kit, it would have been insane to attempt any explorations. He found his way along the path, found his skiff tied up, and had rowed to his boat. Unfavorable winds had destroyed his hope of being of getting back to Port Cockatoo in minimum time: it had been night when he arrived.

The police had listened to his story, had summoned Mr. Florian Blossom, the District Commissioner; all had agreed that "No purpose would be served by attempting anything until next morning." They had taken his story down, word by word, and by hand—if there was an official stenographer anywhere in the country, Limekiller·had yet to hear of it—and by longhand, too; and in their own accustomed style and method, too, so that he was officially recorded as having said things such as: *Awakened by loud sounds of distress, I arose and hailed the man known to me as John Samuel. Upon receiving no response,* etcetera.

After Jack had signed the statement, and stood up, thinking to return to his boat, the District Commissioner said, "I believe that they can accommodate you with a bed in the Unmarried Police Constables' Quarters, Mr. Limekiller. Just for the night."

He looked at the official. A slight shiver ran up and down him. "Do you mean that I am a prisoner?"

"Certainly not, Mr. Limekiller. No such thing."

"You know, if I had wanted to, I could have been in Republican waters by now."

Mr. Blossom's politeness never flagged. "We realize it and we take it into consideration, Mr. Limekiller. But if we are all of us here together it will make an early start in the morning more efficacious."

Anyway, Jack was able to shower, and Ed Huggins loaned him clean clothes. Of course they had not gotten an early start in the morning. Only fishermen and sandboatmen got early starts. Her Majesty's Government moved at its accustomed pace. In the police launch, besides Limekiller, was P.C. Huggin, D.C. Blossom, a very small and very black and very wiry man called Harlow the Hunter, Police-Sergeant Ruiz, and whitehaired Dr. Rafael, the District Medical Officer.

"I wouldn't have been able to come at all, you know," he said to Limekiller, "except my assistant has returned from his holidays a day earlier. Oh, there is so much to see in this colony! Fascinating, fascinating!"

D.C. Blossom smiled. "Doctor Rafael is a famous antiquarian, you know, Mr. Limekiller. It was he who discovered the grave-*stone* of my three or four times great-grand-sir and-grandy."

Sounds of surprise and interest—polite on Limekiller's part, gravestones perhaps not being what he would have most wished to think of—genuine on the part of everyone else, ancestral stones not being numerous in British Hidalgo.

"Yes, Yes," Dr. Rafael agreed. "Two years ago I was on *my* holidays, and I went out to St. Saviour's Caye . . . well, to what is left of St. Saviour's Caye after the last few hurricanes. You can imagine what is left of the old settlement. Oh, the Caye is dead, it is like a skeleton, bleached and bare!" Limekiller felt he could slightly gladly have tipped the medico over the side and watched the bubbles; but, unaware, on the man went. "—so, difficult though it was making my old map agree with the present outlines, still, I did find the site of the old burial-ground, and I cast about and I prodded with my iron rod, and I felt stone underneath the sand, and I dug!"

More sounds of excited interest. Digging in the sand on the bit of ravished sand and coral where the ancient settlement had been—but was no more—was certainly of more interest than digging for yams on the fertile soil of the mainland. And, even though they already knew that it was not a chest of gold, still, they listened and they murmured *oh* and *ah*. "The letters were still very clear, I had no difficulty reading them. *Sacred to the memory of Ferdinando Rousseau, a native of Guernsey, and of Marianna his Wife, a native of Mandingo, in Africa.* Plus a poem in three stanzas, of which I have deposited a copy in the National Archives, and of course I have a copy myself and a third copy I offered to old Mr. Ferdinand Rousseau in King Town—"

Smiling, Mr. Blossom asked, "And what he tell you, then, Doctor?"

Dr. Rafael's smile was a trifle rueful. "He said, 'Let the dead bury their dead'—" The others all laughed. Mr. Ferdinand Rousseau was evidently known to all of them. "—and he declined to take it. Well, I was aware that Mr. Blossom's mother was a cousin of Mr. Rousseau's mother—" ("Double-cousin," said Mr. Blossom.)

Said Mr. Blossom, "And the doctor has even been there, too, to that country. I don't mean Guernsey; in Africa, I mean; not true, Doctor?"

Up ahead, where the coast thrust itself out into the blue, blue Bay, Jack thought he saw the three isolated palms which were his landmark. But there was no hurry. He found himself unwilling to hurry anything at all.

Doctor Rafael, in whose voice only the slightest trace of alien accent still lingered, said that after leaving Vienna, he had gone to London, in London he had been offered and had accepted work in a British West African colonial medical service. "I was just a bit surprised that the old grave-stone referred to Mandingo as a country, there is no such country on the maps today, but there are such a people."

"What they like, Doc-tah? What they like, thees people who dey mehk some ahv Mr. Blossom ahn-*ces*-tah?"

There was another chuckle. This one had slight overtones.

The DMO's round, pink face furrowed in concentration among memories a quarter of a century old. "Why," he said, "they are like elephants. They never forget."

There was a burst of laughter. Mr. Blossom laughed loudest of them all. Twenty-five years earlier he would have asked about Guernsey; today...

Harlow the Hunter, his question answered, gestured towards the shore. A slight swell had come up, the blue was flecked, with bits of white. "W'over dere, suppose to be wan ahv w'ol' Bob Blaine cahmp, in de w'ol' days."

"Filthy fellow," Dr. Rafael said, suddenly, concisely.

"Yes sah." Harlow agreed. "He was ah lewd fellow, fah true, fah true. What he use to say, he use to say, 'Eef you tie ah rottle-snehk doewn fah me, I weel freeg eet...'"

Mr. Blossom leaned forward. "Something the matter, Mr. Limekiller?"

Mr. Limekiller did not at that moment feel like talking. Instead, he lifted his hand and pointed towards the headland with the three isolated palms.

"Cape Man'tee, Mr. Limekiller? What about it?"

Jack cleared his throat. "I thought that was farther down the coast... according to my chart..."

Ed Huggin snorted. "Chart! Washington chart copies London

chart and London chart I think must copy the original *chart* made by old Captain Cook. *Chart!*" He snorted again.

Mr. Florian Blossom asked, softly, "Do you recognize your landfall, Mr. Limekiller? I suppose it would not be at the cape itself, which is pure mangrove bog and does not fit the description which you gave us..."

Mr. Limekiller's eyes hugged the coast. Suppose he couldn't *find* the goddammed place? Police and Government wouldn't like that at all. Every ounce of fuel had to be accounted for. Chasing the wild goose was not approved. He might find an extension of his stay refused when next he went applying for it. He might even find himself officially listed as a Proscribed Person, trans.: haul-ass, Jack, and don't try coming back. And he realized that he did not want that at all, at all. The whole coast looked the same to him, all of a sudden. And then, all of a sudden, it didn't... somehow. There was something about that solid-seeming mass of bush—

"I think there may be a creek. Right there."

Harlow nodded. "Yes mon. Is a creek. Right dere."

And right there, at the mouth of the creek—in this instance, meaning, not a stream, but an inlet—Limekiller recognized the huge tree. And Harlow the Hunter recognized something else. "Dot mark suppose to be where Mr. Limekiller drah up the skiff."

"Best we ahl put boots *on*," said Sergeant Ruiz, who had said not a word until now. They all put boots on. Harlow shouldered an axe. Ruiz and Huggin took up machetes. Dr. Rafael had, besides his medical bag, a bundle of what appeared to be plastic sheets and crocus sacks. "You doesn't mind to cahry ah shovel, Mr. Jock?" Jack decided that he could think of a number of things he had rather carry: but he took the thing. And Mr. Blossom carefully picked up an enormous camera, with tripod. The Governments of His and/or Her Majesties had never been known for throwing money around in these parts; the camera could hardly have dated back to George III but was certainly earlier than the latter part of the reign of George V.

"You must lead us, Mr. Limekiller." The District Commissioner was not grim. He was not smiling. He was grave.

Limekiller nodded. Climbed over the sprawling trunk of the tree. Suddenly remembered that it had been night when he had first come this way, that it had been from the other direction that he had made his way the next morning, hesitated. And then Harlow the Hunter spoke up.

"Eef you pleases, Mistah Blossom. I believes I knows dees pahth bet-tah."

And, at any rate, he knew it well enough to lead them there in less time, surely, than Jack Limekiller could have.

Blood was no longer fresh and red, but a hundred swarms of flies suddenly rose to show where the blood had been. Doctor Rafael snipped leaves, scooped up soil, deposited his take in containers.

And in regard to other evidence, whatever it was evidence of, for one thing, Mr. Blossom handed the camera over to Police-Corporal Huggin, who set up his measuring tape, first along one deep depression and photographed it; then along another...another...another...

"Mountain-cow," said the District Commissioner. He did not sound utterly persuaded.

Harlow shook his head. "No, Mistah Florian. No sah. No, no."

"Well, if not a tapir: what?"

Harlow shrugged.

Something heavy had been dragged through the bush. And it had been dragged by something heavier...something much, much heavier...It was horridly hot in the bush, and every kind of "fly" seemed to be ready and waiting for them: sand-fly, bottle fly, doctor-fly. They made unavoidable noise, but whenever they stopped, the silence closed in on them. No wild parrot shrieked. No "baboons" rottled or growled. No warree grunted or squealed. Just the waiting silence of the bush. Not friendly. Not hostile. Just indifferent.

And when they came to the little river (afterwards, Jack could not even find it on the maps) and scanned the opposite bank and saw nothing, the District Commissioner said, "Well, Harlow. What you think?"

The wiry little man looked up and around. After a moment he nodded, plunged into the bush. A faint sound, as of someone—or of something?—Then Ed Huggin pointed. Limekiller would never even have noticed that particular tree was there; indeed, he was able to pick it out now only because a small figure was slowly but surely climbing it. The tree was tall, and it leaned at an angle—old enough to have experienced the brute force of a hurricane, strong enough to have survived, though bent.

Harlow called something Jack did not understand, but he followed the others, splashing down the shallows of the river. The river slowly became a swamp. Harlow was suddenly next to them. "Eet not fah," he muttered.

Nor was it.

What there was of it.

An eye in a monstrously swollen head winked at them. Then an insect leisurely crawled out, flapped its horridly-damp wings in the hot and humid air, and sluggishly flew off. There was no wink. There was no eye.

"Mr. Limekiller," said District Commissioner Blossom, "I will now ask you if you identify this body as that of the man known to you as John Samuel."

"It's him. Yes sir."

But was as though the commissioner had been holding his breath and had now released it. "Well, well," he said. "And he was supposed to have gone to Jamaica and died there. I never heard he'd come back. Well, he is dead now, for true."

But little Doctor Rafael shook his snowy head. "He is certainly dead. And he is certainly not John Samuel."

"Why—" Limekiller swallowed bile, pointed. "Look. The eye is missing, John Samuel lost that eye when the tree fell—"

"Ah, yes, young man. John Samuel did. *But not that eye.*"

The bush was not so silent now. Every time the masses and masses of flies were waved away, they rose, buzzing, into the heavy, squalid air. Buzzing, hovered. Buzzing, returned.

"Then who in the Hell—?"

Harlow wiped his face on his sleeve. "Well, sah. I cahn tell you. Lord hahv mercy on heem. Eet ees Bob Blaine."

There was a long outdrawn *ahhh* from the others. Then Ed Huggin said, "But Bob Blaine had both his eyes."

Harlow stopped, picked a stone from the river bed, with dripping hand threw it into the bush . . . one would have said, at random. With an ugly croak, a buzzard burst up and away. Then Harlow said something, as true—and as dreadful—as it was unarguable. "He not hahv either of them, noew."

• • •

By what misadventure and in what place Bob Blaine had lost one eye whilst alive and after decamping from his native land, no one knew: and perhaps it did not matter. He had trusted on "discretion" not to reveal his hideout, there at the site of his old bush-camp. But he had not trusted to it one hundred percent. Suppose that Limekiller were deceitfully or accidently, to let drop the fact that a man was camping out there. A man with only one eye. What was the man's name? John Samuel. What? John *Samuel*... Ah. Then John Samuel had not, after all, died in Jamaica, according to report. Report had been known to be wrong before. John Samuel alive, then. No big thing. Nobody then would have been moved to go down there to check up.—Nobody, now, knew why Bob Blaine had returned. Perhaps he had made things too hot for himself, down in "republican waters"—where hot water could be so very much hotter than back here. Perhaps some day a report would drift back up, and it might be a true report or it might be false or it might be a mixture of both.

As for the report, the official, Government one, on the circumstances surrounding the death of Roberto Blaine, a.k.a. Bob Blaine... as for Limekiller's statement and the statements of the District Commissioner and the District Medical Officer and the autopsy and the photographs: why, that had all been neatly transcribed and neatly (and literally) laced with red tape, and forwarded up the coast to King Town. And as to what happened to it there—

"What do you think they will do about it, Doctor?"

Rafael's rooms were larger, perhaps, than a bachelor needed. But they were the official quarters for the DMO, and so the DMO lived in them. The wide floors gleamed with polish. The spotless walls showed, here a shield, there a paddle, a harpoon with barbed head, the carapace of a huge turtle, a few paintings. The symmetry and conventionality of it all was slightly marred by the bookcases which were everywhere, against every wall, adjacent to desk and chairs. And all were full, crammed, overflowing.

Doctor Rafael shrugged. "Perhaps the woodlice will eat the papers," he said. "Or the roaches, or the *wee-wee* ants. The mildew. The damp. Hurricane... This is not a climate which helps preserve the history of men. I work hard to keep my own books and papers from going that way. But I am not Government, and Government lacks time and money and personnel, and...perhaps, also...Government has so many, many things pressing upon it...Perhaps, too, Government lacks interest."

"What were those tracks, Doctor Rafael?"

Doctor Rafael shrugged.

"You do know, don't you?"

Doctor Rafael grimaced.

"Have you seen them, or anything like them, before?"

Doctor Rafael, very slowly, very slowly nodded.

"Well...for God's sake...can you even give me a, well a *hint?* I mean: that was a rather rotten experience for me, you know. And—"

The sunlight, kept at bay outside, broke in through a crack in the jalousies, sun making the scant white hair for an instant ablaze: like the brow of Moses. Doctor Rafael got up and busied himself with a fresh lime and the sweetened lime juice and the gin and ice. He was rapt in this task, like an ancient apothecary mingling strange unguents and syrups. Then he gave one of the gimlets to his guest and from one he took a long, long pull.

"You see. I have two years to go before my retirement. The pension, well, it is not spectacular, but I have no complaint. I will be able to rest. Not for an hour, or an evening...an evening! only on my holidays, once a year, do I even have an evening all my own!—Well. You may imagine how I look forward. And I am not going to risk premature and enforced retirement by presenting Government with an impossible situation. One which wouldn't be its fault, anyway. By insisting on impossible things. By demonstrating—"

He finished his drink. He gave Jack a long, shrewd look.

"So I have nothing more to say...about *that.* If they want to believe, up in King Town, that the abominable Bob Blaine was mauled by a crocodile, let them. If they prefer to make it a jaguar or even a tapir, why, that is fine with Robert Rafael, M.D., DMO. It might be, probably, the first time in history that anybody anywhere was killed by a tapir, but that is not my affair. The matter is, so far as I am concerned, so far—in fact—as *you* and I are concerned—over. *"Do you understand?"*

Limekiller nodded. At once the older man's manner changed. "I have many, many books, as you can see. Maybe some of them would be of interest to you. Pick any one you like. Pick one at random." So saying, he took a book from his desk and put it in Jack's hands. It was just a book-looking book. It was, in fact, volume II of the Everyman edition of Plutarch's Lives. There was a wide card, of the kind on which medical notes or records are sometimes made, and so Jack Limekiller opened the book at that place.

*seasons, as the gods sent them, seemed natural to him. The Greeks that inhabited Asia were very much pleased to see the great lords and governors of Persia, with all the pride, cruelty, and*

"Well, now, what the Hell," he muttered. The card slipped, he clutched. He glanced at it. He put down vol. II of the Lives and he sat back and read the notes on the card.

It is in the nature of things [they began] for men, in a new country and faced with new things, to name them after old, familiar things. Even when resemblance unlikely. Example: *Mountain-cow* for tapir. ('Tapir' from Tupi Indian *tapira,* big beast.) Example: Mawmee-*apple* not apple at all. Ex.: *Sea-cow* for manatee. Early British settlers not entomologists. Quest.: Whence word *manatee?* From Carib? Perhaps. After the British, what other people came to this corner of the world? Ans.: Black people. Calabars, Ashantee, Mantee, Mandingo. Re last two names. Related peoples. Named after totemic animal. *Also,* not likely? *likely* — named unfamiliar animals after familiar (i.e., familiar in Africa) animals. Mantee, Mandee-hippo. Refer legend

Limekiller's mouth fell open. "Oh, my God!" he groaned. In his ear now, he heard the old, old, quavering voice of Captain Cudgel (once Cudjoe): "*Mon, een Ahfrica, de mon-ah-tee hahv leg, I tell you. Een Ahfrica eet be ah poerful beast, come up on de lond, I tell you . . . de w'ol' people, dey tell me so, fah true . . .*"
He heard the old voice, repeating the old words, no longer even half-understood: but, in some measure, at least half-true.

Refer legend of were-animals, universal. Were-wolf, were-tiger, were-shark, were-dolphin. Quest.: Were-manatee?

*"Mon-ah-tee    ees    hahlf    ah    mon...hahv    teats    like    a*
*womahn...Dere ees wahn mon, mehk mellow weet mon-ah-tee,*
*hahv pickney by mon-ah-tee..."*

And he heard another voice saying, not only once, saying,*"Mon,*
*eef you tie ah rottlesnake doewn fah me. I weel freeg eet.."*

He thought of the wretched captives in the Spanish slaveship, set
free to fend for themselves in a bush by far wilder than the one left
behind. Few, to begin with, fewer as time went on; marrying and
intermarrying, no new blood, no new thoughts. And, finally, the one
road in to them, destroyed. Left alone. Left quite alone.
Or...almost...

He shuddered.

How desperate for refuge must Blaine have been, to have sought to
hide himself anywhere near Cape Mantee—

And what miserable happenstance had brought he himself, Jack
Limekiller, to improvise on that old song that dreadful night? —And
what had he called up out of the darkness... out of the bush... out
of the mindless present which was the past and future and the timeless
tropical forever?...

There was something pressing gently against his finger, something
on the other side of the card. He turned it over. A clipping from a
magazine had been roughly pasted there.

Valentry has pointed out that, despite a seeming resemblance to
such aquatic mammals as seals and walrus, the manatee is
actually more closely related anatomically to the elephant.

...out of the bush...out of the darkness...out of the mindless
present which was also the past and the timeless tropical forever...

*"They are like elephants. They never forget."*

"Ukh," he said, though clenched teeth. "My God. Uff. Jesus...

The card was suddenly, swiftly, snatched from his hands. He
looked up still in a state of shock, to see Doctor Rafael tearing it into
pieces.

"Doña 'Sana!"

A moment. Then the house-keeper, old, all in white. "Doctór?"

"Burn this."

A moment passed. Just the two of them again. Then Rafael, in a tone which was nothing but kindly, said, "Jack, you are still young and you are still healthy. My advice to you: Go away. Go to a cooler climate. One with cooler ways and cooler memories." The old woman called something from the back of the house. The old man sighed. "It is the summons to supper," he said. "Not only must I eat in haste because I have my clinic in less than half-an-hour, but suddenly-invited guests make Dona 'Saña very nervous. Good night, then, Jack."

Jack had had two gin drinks. He felt that he needed two more. At least two more. Or, if not gin, rum. Beer would not do. He wanted to pull the blanket of booze over him, awfully, awfully quickly. He had this in his mind as though it were a vow as he walked up the front street towards the Cupid Club.

Someone hailed him, someone out of the gathering dusk.

"Jock! Hey, mon, Jock! Hey, b'y! Where you gweyn so fahst? Bide, b'y, bide a bit!"

The voice was familiar. It was that of Harry Hazeed, his principal creditor in King Town. Ah, well. He had had his chance, Limekiller had. He could have gone on down the coast, down into the republican waters, where the Queen's writ runneth not. Now it was too late.

"Oh, hello, Harry," he said, dully.

Hazeed took him by the hand. Took him by both hands. "Mon, show me where is your boat? She serviceable? She is? Good: Mon, you don't hear de news: Welcome's warehouse take fire and born up! Yes, mon. Ahl de carn in King *Town* born up! No carn ah-tahl: No tortilla, no empinada, no tamale, no carn-*cake!* Oh, mon, how de people going to punish! Soon as I hear de news, I drah me money from de bonk, I buy ahl de crocus sock I can find, I jump on de pocket-*boat*—and here I am, oh, mon, I pray fah you...I pray I fine you!"

Limekiller shook his head. It had been one daze, one shock after another. The only thing clear was that Harry Hazeed didn't seem angry. "You no understond?" Hazeed cried. "Mon! We going take your boat, we going doewn to Nutmeg P'int, we going to buy carn, mon! We going to buy ahl de carn dere is to buy! Nevah mine dat lee' bit money you di owe me, b'y! We going make plenty money, mon! And we going make de cultivators plenty money, too! What you theenk of eet, Jock, me b'y? Eh? Hey? What you theenk?"

Jack put his forefinger in his mouth, held it up. The wind was in the right quarter. The wind would, if it held up, and, somehow, it felt like a wind which would hold up, the wind would carry them straight and clear to Nutmeg Point: the clear, clean wind in the clear and starry night.

Softly, he said—and, old Hazeed leaning closer to make the words out, Limekiller said them again, louder, "I think it's great. Just great. I think it's great."

# Getting Back to Before It Began
## by Raylyn Moore

*Here's a very short story that has things both charming and trenchant to say about our dreams of The Simple Life.*

For a long time the boy was alone, riding mile after mile at the back of the bus, watching the names of things pass by outside. Calumet, Feckless Joe's, Gillette, Gilbey's, Goshen, Gretna Estates, Kent, Lake Manahawkin, Lumberville, Miracle Whip, Northend Supply, Poor Old Frank's, Prudential.

At Sacktown the girl got on. Finding the seats up front all taken, she wandered back to where he was and sat beside him. Because he was a dreamy youth and not forward at all, he let the bus go through Saugus, Stickney, String City and Suquamish before he even spoke to her, and then he only said hello and how are you?

Since she was shy too, they traveled through Tioga, Transfer, Tribble and Troy before she answered. She said I'm fine and how far are you going?

He smiled and said I'm glad you asked. I've been riding this old bus a long time just hoping someone would inquire. You see, I'm an idealist and I have a theory, and people in my position need someone around to explain things to. (As is the case with many dreamy youths who are not forward, with this boy a little encouragement went a long way.)

He said I plan to ride to the absolute end of the line, past the place where the names stop. Out there everything will be unspoiled because it's unnamed. Haven't you ever noticed that once naming begins, ruin

163

follows? Sometimes the destruction is fast, sometimes slow, but it comes. Inevitably.

She thought about it while they rode through Ulm, Uncompahgre, Underhill and Upper Black Eddy. When the bus stopped at Uz to let out some people, she said how much farther will you need to travel before you come to the place where the names run out?

I do like you very much, he said, because you ask all the right questions. And for other reasons too, he added, looking frankly for the first time at her plump round arms and cute knees and her light-bright long hair falling over the neat velveteen collar of the coat around her shoulders. In answer I would say that all the evidence seems to indicate that it can't be much farther. For one thing, notice how lots of passengers are getting off now but no one is getting on.

She watched a while with him and it was true. Riders debarked from the front of the bus in the towns of Value, Veach, Viroqua and Vultee, but in none of these places did anyone get on.

He said you will notice also that the billboards with the names of all the useless things in the world on them are getting fewer and farther between. Which is probably because these are all things one will not need to remember in the nameless country.

This was also true, the girl saw at once. The colored-up and lit-up names for tires, digestive aids, steakhouses, toothpaste, suntan oil, batteries, deodorants, household appliances and floor waxes appeared only sparingly in and near the villages of Walhonding and Wanilla, and not at all as the bus sped through Warshoal and Waverly Creek, where another clutch of passengers debarked but no one boarded.

Of course, the boy explained (eagerly now), the trick will be for us to get well past the borderline, out where there's not even the dimmest concept of propernaming things and towns, because once one place has heard of another place, so to speak, and begins distinguishing it by a name, even a name like Other, the disease has already struck, you see. The rot has set in.

*Us?* she said, harking back to the beginning of his speech. *I'm* getting off this bus in Zerba where I plan to stay with an aunt and get a job in the Zigzag Pizza Palace.

The boy said quickly oh you can't do that. You must come with me.

Which just goes to show that by now he'd discarded his backwardness completely. But already the bus was rushing through Xelto heading for Yelvington, and he knew he didn't have time for a relaxed and orderly wooing.

It was touch and go for a while, but by Zelienopolis she had made up her mind, and as they whizzed right through Zerba without stopping, bus tires singing on the pavement because the hamlet was too small even for SLOW signs, she closed her delicate, trembling eyelids and bit hard into her berry-red lower lip, but she did not pull the cord to halt the coach.

Everyone else did though, many times over. By the time the bus reached Zincville there was only one other passenger left besides themselves, an elderly gentleman in a Borsolino hat, and he got off in Zooks Spur.

After that they rode on and on, finding out it was really true and becoming more and more excited. For out of the windows everything began looking unspoiled. There were a few sparse settlements, but evidently not having heard of one another, they had no names.

The names had truly run out. Been all used up. No more billboards loomed against the horizon. No more names on mailboxes and then finally no more mailboxes, nor utility poles, nor even fences, which would imply ownership, which would require naming of places.

They were trying to choose the ideal nameless spot for themselves when the driver's patience also ran out. He said what the hell's the matter with you two? You kids better shape up and snap to and make up your mind pretty damn quick. This bus doesn't go on forever, you know.

The boy, who would never be backward again, wasn't about to be intimidated by a mere busdriver, but it so happened that at this precise moment they saw an unnamed place they both liked, a meadow with shade trees and fruit trees and a stream washing sunnily along between mossy banks.

There would not be any troublesome traffic either because several hundred yards ago the highway also had run out. In fact the bus had been having a rough go over the unspoiled earth. No wonder the driver was getting surly.

So they disembarked, not forgetting to take along the girl's handbag which contained a few items she thought she would need even here, and the boy's bedroll and rucksack of camping gear, which he swung enthusiastically down from the overhead rack.

The bus turned around lumberingly and roared away in an acrid huff of inefficiently burning fuel. But after the cool fresh breezes of the nameless place had chased away the last of the bus smell, the couple settled down to be themselves and enjoy each other and celebrate their escape.

Everyone will think that it didn't last.

It will be suspected at once that in the girl's handbag was a supply of an indispensable facecream called Sof-Karess, and when this ran out, she begged to be taken back to the place where things have proper names so she could go into a store she remembered the name of and ask the clerk for more Sof-Karess.

Or it will be imagined that after the first joyful years and several babies, the couple tired of each other and quarreled and set up separate camps. So that the children, running to and fro between the camps, could tell one another and their parents where they were going, the settlements had to be named His and Hers.

It will be thought, in other words, that the girl and boy, being human, could not after all avoid either returning to what they were accustomed to, or bringing place names to their nameless place because the seeds of corruption were in themselves. For that's the way it always works in stories.

Unless it happens to be a story that proves the original rationale itself was a shuck. In which case it would turn out that one day the couple went for a walk and discovered, just on the other side of their unspoiled meadow, a highway with a string of towns called Aaronsburg, Absaraka, Acme Junction, and so on.

But none of this kind of thing happened. Not at all.

Instead, this devoted pair lived a richly satisfactory life, an ideal life. They had some lovely children. They stayed on their land and made whatever they needed with their own hands, though they found indeed that they required very little but each other and their own place.

Their only moments of anxiety came at rare intervals when they fancied they could hear distant rumblings and were afraid the gas tax money had piled up so relentlessly back where they'd come from that to get rid of it the highway department would be forced to extend the road into their nameless place, after which of course someone would have to name the place where the road led. Or when they imagined that some other person might have stumbled onto the same hypothesis the boy had worked out and would stay on the bus beyond the end of the line, making it necessary eventually to have two settlements named Ours and Theirs.

They needn't have given these possibilities a thought, however, for the bus never went that far out again.

# Descent of Man
## by T. Coraghessan Boyle

*People who see apes and monkeys in zoos, or who have them for pets (usually only monkeys become pets, though), are always amused at how similar to us the lower orders of primates can be. But of course that's just another way of saying that we're similar to them....*
      *T. Coraghessan Boyle, who is connected with the Iowa Creative Writers Workshop and is an editor of* The Iowa Review, *has written short stories for* Esquire, North American Review, The Paris Review, Quest/77, *and* Transatlantic Review. *Several but not all of his stories are fantasies.*

I was living with a woman who suddenly began to stink. It was very difficult. The first time I confronted her she merely smiled. "Occupational hazard," she said. The next time she curled her lip. There were other problems too. Hairs, for instance. Hairs that began to appear on her clothing, sharp and black and brutal. Invariably I would awake to find these hairs in my mouth, or I would glance into the mirror to see them slashing like razor edges across the collars of my white shirts. Then too there was the fruit. I began to discover moldering bits of it about the house—apple and banana most characteristically—but plum and tangelo or even passionfruit and yim-yim were not at all anomalous. These fruit fragments occurred principally in the bedroom, on the pillow, surrounded by darkening spots. It was not long before I located their source: they lay hidden like gems in the long wild lanks of her hair. Another occupational hazard.

Jane was in the habit of sitting before the air-conditioner when she came home from work, fingering out her hair, drying the sweat from her face and neck in the cool hum of the machine, fruit bits sifting silently to the carpet, black hairs drifting like feathers. On these occasions the room would fill with the stink of her, bestial and fetid. And I would find my eyes watering, my mind imaging the dark rotting trunks of the rain forest, stained sienna and mandalay and hooker's green with the excrements dropped from above. My ears would keen with the whistling and crawing of the jungle birds, the screechings of the snot-nosed apes in the branches. And then, slack-faced and tight-boweled, I would step into the bathroom and retch, the sweetness of my own intestinal secrets a balm against the potent hairy stench of her.

One evening, just after her bath (the faintest odor lingered, yet still it was so trenchant I had to fight the impulse to get up and urinate on a tree or a post or something), I lay my hand casually across her belly and was suddenly startled to see an insect flit from its cover, skate up the swell of her abdomen, and bury itself in her navel. "Good Christ," I said.

"Hm?" she returned, peering over the cover of her Yerkish reader.

"That," I said. "That bug, that insect, that vermin."

She sat up, plucked the thing from its cachette, raised it to her lips and popped it between her front teeth. "Louse," she said, sucking. "Went down to the old age home on 13th Street to pick them up."

I anticipated her: "Not for—?"

"Why certainly, potpie—so Konrad can experience a tangible gratification of his social impulses during the grooming ritual. You know: you scratch my back, I scratch yours."

I lay in bed that night sweating, thinking about Jane and those slippery-fingered monkeys poking away at her, and listening for the lice crawling across her scalp or nestling their bloody little siphons in the tufts under her arms. Finally, about four, I got up and took three doriden. I woke at two in the afternoon, an insect in my ear. It was only an earwig. I had missed my train, failed to call in at the office. There was a note from Jane: Pick me up at 4. Konrad sends love.

The Primate Center stood in the midst of a macadamized acre or two, looking very much like a school building: faded brick, fluted columns, high mesh fences. Finger paintings and mobiles hung in the windows, misshapen ceramics crouched along the sills. A flag raggled at the top of a white-washed flagpole. I found myself bending to examine the cornerstone: Asa Priff Grammar School, 1939. Inside it was dark and cool; the halls were lined with lockers and curling watercolors; the linoleum gleamed like a shy smile. I stepped into the BOYS' ROOM. The urinals were a foot and a half from the floor. Designed for little people, I mused. Youngsters. Hardly big enough to hold their little peters without the teacher's help. I smiled, and situated myself over one of the toy urinals, the strong honest scent of Pine-Sol in my nostrils. At that moment the door wheezed open and a chimpanzee shuffled in. He was dressed in shorts, shirt and bowtie. He nodded to me, it seemed, and made a few odd gestures with his hands as he moved up to the urinal beside mine. Then he opened his fly and pulled out an enormous slick red organ like a peeled banana. I looked away, embarrassed, but could hear him urinating mightily. It hissed against the porcelain like a thunderstorm, rattled the drain as it went down. My own water wouldn't come. I began to feel foolish. The chimp shook himself daintily, zippered up, pulled the plunger, crossed to the sink, washed and dried his hands, and left. I found I no longer had to go.

Out in the hallway the janitor was leaning on his flathead broom. The chimp stood before him gesticulating with a manic dexterity: brushing his forehead and tugging his chin, slapping his hands under his armpits, tapping his wrist, his tongue, his ear, his lip. The janitor watched intently. Suddenly—after a particularly virulent flurry—the man burst into laughter, rich braying globes of it. The chimp folded his lip and joined in, adding his weird nasal snickering to the janitor's barrel-laugh. I stood by the door to the BOYS' ROOM in a quandary. I began to feel that it might be wiser to wait in the car—but then I didn't want to call attention to myself, darting in and out like that. The janitor might think I was stealing paper towels or something. So I stood there, thinking to have a word with him when the chimp moved on—with the expectation that he could give me some grass-roots insight into the nature of Jane's job. But the chimp didn't move on. The two continued laughing, now harder than ever. The janitor's face was tear-streaked. Each time he looked up the chimp produced a gesticular flurry that would stagger him again. Finally the janitor wound down a bit, and still chuckling, held out his hands, palms up. The chimp flung his arms up over his head and then heaved them down again, rhythmically slapping the big palms with his own. "Right on! Mastuh Konrad," the janitor said, "Right on!" The chimp grinned, then hitched up his shorts and sauntered off down the hall. The janitor turned back to his broom still chuckling.

I cleared my throat. The broom began a geometrically precise course up the hall toward me. It stopped at my toes, the ridge of detritus flush with the pinions of my wingtips. The janitor looked up. The pupil of his right eye was fixed in the corner, beneath the lid, and the white was red. There was an ironic gap between his front teeth. "Kin ah do sumfin fo yo, mah good man?" he said.

"I'm waiting for Miss Good."

"Ohhh, Miz *Good*," he said, nodding his head. "Fust ah taught yo was thievin paypuh tow-els out'n de Boys' Room but den when ah sees yo standin dere rigid as de Venus de Milo ah thinks to mahsef: he is some kinda new sculpture de students done made is what he is." He was squinting up at me and grinning like we'd just come back from sailing around the world together.

"That's a nice broom," I said.

He looked at me steadily, grinning still. "Yo's wonderin what me and Mastuh Konrad was jivin bout up dere, isn't yo? Well ah tells yo: he was relatin a hoomerous anecdote, de punch line o which has deep cosmic implications in dat it establishes a common ground between monks and ho-mo sapiens despite dere divergent ancestries." He shook his head, chortled. "Yes in-deed, dat Mastah Konrad is quite the wit."

"You mean to tell me you actually understand all that lip-pulling and finger-waving?" I was beginning to feel a nameless sense of outrage.

"Oh sartinly, mah good man. Dat ASL."

"What?"

"ASL is what we was talkin. A-merican Sign Language. De-veloped for de deef n dumb. Yo sees, Mastuh Konrad is sumfin of a genius round here. He can comoonicate de mos esoteric ideas in bof ASL and Yerkish, re-spond to and translate English, French, German and Chinese. Fack, it was Miz Good was tellin me dat

Konrad is workin right now on a Yerkish translation o Darwin's *De-scent o Man*. He is mainly into Anthro-pology, yo knows, but he has cultivated a in-ter-ess in udder fields too. Dis lass fall he done undertook a Yerkish translation o Chomsky's *Language and Mind* and Nietzsche's *Janseits von Gut und Böse*. And dat's some pretty heavy shit, Jackson."

I was hot with outrage. "Stuff," I said. "Stuff and nonsense."

"No sense in feelin personally treatened by Mastuh Konrad's chievements, mah good fellow—yo's got to rea-lize dat he is a genius."

A word came to me: "Bullhonk," I said. And turned to leave. The janitor caught me by the shirtsleeve. "He is now scorin his turd opera," he whispered. I tore away from him and stamped out of the building.

Jane was waiting in the car. I climbed in, cranked down the sunroof and opened the airvents.

At home I poured a water-glass of gin, held it to my nostrils and inhaled. Jane sat before the air-conditioner, her hair like a urinal mop, stinking. Black hairs cut the atmosphere, fruit bits whispered to the carpet. Occasionally the tip of my tongue entered the gin. I sniffed and tasted, thinking of plastic factories and turpentine distilleries and rich sulphurous smoke. On my way to the bedroom I poured a second glass.

In the bedroom I sniffed gin and dressed for dinner. "Jane?" I called. "Shouldn't you be getting ready?" She appeared in the doorway. She was dressed in her work clothes: jeans and sweatshirt. The sweatshirt was gray and hooded. There were yellow stains on the sleeves. I thought of the lower depths of animal cages, beneath the floor-meshing. "I figured I'd go like this," she said. I was knotting my tie. "And I wish you'd stop insisting on baths every night—I'm getting tired of smelling like a coupon in a detergent box. It's unnatural. Unhealthy."

In the car on the way to the restaurant I lit a cigar, a cheap twisted black thing like half a pepperoni. Jane sat hunched against her door, unwashed. I had never before smoked a cigar. I tried to start a conversation but Jane said she didn't feel like talking: talk seemed so useless, such an anachronism. We drove on in silence. And I reflected that this was not the Jane I knew and loved. Where, I wondered, was the girl who changed wigs three or four times a day and sported nails like a Chinese emperor?—and where was the girl who dressed like an Arabian Bazaar and smelled like the trade winds?

She was committed. The project, the study, grants. I could read the signs: she was growing away from me.

The restaurant was dark, a maze of rocky gardens, pancake-leafed vegetation, black fountains. We stood squinting just inside the door. Birds whistled, carp hissed through the pools. Somewhere a monkey screeched. Jane put her hand on my shoulder and whispered in my ear. "Siamang," she said. At that moment the leaves parted beside us: a rubbery little fellow emerged and motioned us to sit on a bench beneath a wicker birdcage. He was wearing a soiled loincloth and eight or ten necklaces of yellowed teeth. His hair flamed out like a brushfire. In the dim light from the braziers I noticed his nostrils—both shrunken and pinched, as if once pierced straight-through. His face was of course inscrutable. As soon as we were seated he removed my socks and shoes, Jane's sneakers, and wrapped our feet in what I later learned were plantain leaves. I started to object—I bitterly resent anyone looking at my feet—but Jane shushed me. We had waited three months for reservations.

The maitre d' signed for us to follow, and led us through a dripping stonewalled tunnel to an outdoor garden where the flagstones gave way to dirt and we found ourselves on a narrow plant-choked path. He licked along like an iguana and we hurried to keep up. Wet fronds slapped back in my face, creepers snatched at my ankles, mud sucked at the plantain leaves on my feet. The scents of mold and damp and long-lying urine hung in the air, and I thought of the men's room at the subway station. It was dark as a womb. I offered Jane my hand, but she refused it. Her breathing was fast. The monkey chatter was loud as a zoo afire. "Far out," she said. I slapped a mosquito on my neck.

A moment later we found ourselves seated at a bamboo table overhung with branch and vine. Across from us sat Dr. and Mrs. U-Hwak-Lo, director of the Primate Center and wife. A candle guttered between them. I cleared my throat, and then began idly tracing my finger around the circular hole cut in the table's center.

The Doctor's ears were the size of peanuts. "Glad you two could make it," he said. "I've long been urging Jane to sample some of our humble fare." I smiled, crushed a spider against the back of my chair. The Doctor's English was perfect, pure Martha's Vineyard—he sounded like Ted Kennedy's insurance salesman. His wife's was weak: "Yes," she said, "nussing cook here, all roar." "How exciting!" said Jane. And then the conversation turned to primates, and the Center.

Mrs. U-Hwak-Lo and I smiled at one another. Jane and the Doctor were already deeply absorbed in a dialogue concerning the incidence of anal retention in chimps deprived of frisbee coordination during the sensorimotor period. I gestured toward them with my head and arched my eyebrows wittily. Mrs. U-Hwak-Lo giggled. It was then that Jane's proximity began to affect me. The close wet air seemed to concentrate her essence, distill its potency. The U-Hwak-Los seemed unaffected. I began to feel queasy. I reached for the fingerbowl and drank down its contents. Mrs. U-Hwak-Lo smiled. It was coconut oil. Just then the waiter appeared carrying a wooden bowl the size of a truck tire. A single string of teeth slapped against his breastbone as he set the bowl down and slipped off into the shadows. The Doctor and Jane were oblivious—they were talking excitedly, occasionally lapsing into what I took to be ASL, ear and nose and lip-picking like a manager and his third base coach. I peered into the bowl: it was filled to the rim with clean-picked chicken bones. Mrs U-Hwak-Lo nodded, grinning: "No on-tray," she said. "Appeticer." At that moment a simian screamed somewhere close, screamed like death itself. Jane looked up. "Rhesus," she said.

On my return from the men's room I had some difficulty locating the table in the dark. I had already waded through two murky fountains and was preparing to plunge through my third when I heard Mrs. U-Hwak-Lo's voice behind me. "Here," she said. "Make quick, repass now serve." She took my hand and led me back to the table. "Oh, they're enormously resourceful," the Doctor was saying as I stumbled into my chair, pants wet to the knees. "They first employ a general anaesthetic—a distillation of the chu-bok root— and then the chef (who logically doubles as village surgeon) makes a circular incision about the macaque's cranium, carefully peeling back the already-shaven scalp, and stanching the blood-flow quite effectively with maura-ro, a highly absorbent powder derived from the tamana leaf. He then removes both the frontal and parietal plates to expose the brain..." I looked at Jane: she was rapt. I wasn't really listening. My attention was directed toward what I took to be the main course, which had appeared in my absence. An unsteady pinkish mound now occupied the center of the table, completely obscuring the circular hole—it looked like cherry vanilla yogurt, a carton and a half, perhaps two. On closer inspection I noticed several black hairs peeping out from around its flaccid edges. And thought immediately of the bush-headed maitre d'. I pointed to one of the hairs, remarking to Mrs. U-Hwak-Lo that the rudiments of culinary hygiene could be a little more rigorously observed among the staff. She smiled. Encouraged, I asked her what exactly the dish was. "Much delicacy," she said. "Very rare find in land of Lincoln." At that moment the waiter appeared and handed each of us a bamboo stick beaten flat and sharpened at one end.

"...then the tribal elders or visiting dignitaries are seated around the table," the Doctor was saying. "The chef has previously of course located the macaque beneath the table, the exposed part of the creature's brain protruding from the hole in its center. After the feast, the lower ranks of the village population divide up the remnants. It's really quite efficient."

"How fascinating!" said Jane. "Shall we try some?"

"By all means... but tell me, how has Konrad been coming with that Yerkish epic he's been working up?"

Jane turned to answer, bamboo stick poised: "Oh I'm so glad you asked—I'd almost forgotten. He's finished his tenth book and tells me he'll be doing two more—out of deference to the Miltonic tradition. Isn't that a groove?"

"Yes," said the Doctor, gesturing toward the rosy lump in the center of the table. "Yes it is. He's certainly—and I hope you won't mind the pun—a brainy fellow. Ho-ho."

"Oh Doctor," Jane laughed, and plunged her stick into the pink. Beneath the table, in the dark, a tiny fist clutched at my pantleg.

I missed work again the following day. This time it took five doriden to put me under. I had lain in bed sweating and tossing, listening to Jane's quiet breathing, inhaling her fumes. At dawn I dozed off, dreamed briefly of elementary school cafeterias swarming with knickered chimps and weltered with trays of cherry vanilla yogurt, and woke stale-mouthed. Then I took the pills. It was three-thirty when I woke again. There was a note from Jane: Bringing Konrad home for dinner. Vacuum rug and clean toilet.

Konrad was impeccably dressed—long pants, platform wedgies, cufflinks. He smelled of eau de cologne, Jane of used litter. They arrived during the seven o'clock news. I opened the door for them. "Hello Jane," I said. We stood at the door, awkward, silent. "Well?" she said. "Aren't you going to greet our guest?" "Hello Konrad," I said. And then: "I believe we met in the boys' room at the Center the other day?" He bowed deeply, straight-faced, his upper lip like a halved canteloupe. Then he broke into a snicker, turned to Jane and juggled out an esoteric series of gestures. Jane laughed. Something caught in my throat. "Is he trying to say something?" I asked. "Oh potpie," she said, "it was nothing—just a little quote from Yeats."
"Yeats?"
"Yes, you know: 'An aged man is but a paltry thing.'"

Jane served watercress sandwiches and animal crackers as hors d'oeuvres. She brought them into the living room on a cut-glass serving tray and set them down before Konrad and me, where we sat on the sofa, watching the news. Then she returned to the kitchen. Konrad plucked up a tiny sandwich and swallowed it like a communion wafer, sucking the tips of his fingers. Then he lifted the tray and offered it to me. I declined. "No thank you," I said. Konrad shrugged, set the plate down in his lap and carefully stacked all the sandwiches in its center. I pretended to be absorbed with the news: actually I studied him, half-face. He was filling the gaps in his sandwich-construction with animal crackers. His lower lip protruded, his ears were rubbery, he was balding. With both hands he crushed the heap of crackers and sandwiches together and began kneading it until it took on the consistency of raw dough. Then he lifted the whole thing to his mouth and swallowed it without chewing. There were no whites to his eyes.

Konrad's only reaction to the newscast was a burst of excitement over a war story—the reporter stood against a wasteland of treadless tanks and recoilless guns in Thailand or Syria or Chile: huts were burning, old women weeping. "Wow-wow! eeeeeeee! er-er-er-er," Konrad said. Jane appeared in the kitchen doorway, hands dripping. "What is it, Konrad?" she said. He made a series of violent gestures. "Well?" I asked. She translated: "Konrad says that 'the pig oppressors' genocidal tactics will lead to their mutual extermination and usher in a new golden age. . .'"—here she hesitated, looked up at him to continue (he was springing up and down on the couch, flailing his fists as though they held whips and scourges)—"'. . . of freedom and equality for all, regardless of race, creed, color—or genus.' I wouldn't worry," she added, " it's just his daily slice of revolutionary rhetoric. He'll calm down in a minute—he likes to play Che, but he's basically non-violent."

Ten minutes later Jane served dinner. Konrad, with remarkable speed and coordination, consumed four cans of fruit cocktail, thirty-two spareribs, half a dozen each of oranges, apples and pomegranates, two cheeseburgers and three quarts of chocolate malted. In the kitchen, clearing up, I commented to Jane about our guest's prodigious appetite. He was sitting in the other room, listening to *Don Juan,* sipping brandy. Jane said that he was a big, active male and that she could attest to his need for so many calories. "How much does he weigh?" I asked. "Stripped," she said, "one-eighty-one. When he stands up straight he's four-eight-and-three-quarters." I mulled over this information while I scraped away at the dishes, piled them in the dishwasher, neat ranks of blue china. A few moments later I stepped into the living room to observe Jane stroking Konrad's ears, his head in her lap. I stand five-seven, one-forty-three.

When I returned from work the following day, Jane was gone. Her dresser drawers were bare, the closet empty. There were white rectangles on the wall where her Rousseau reproductions had hung. The top plank of the bookcase was ribbed with the dust-prints of her Edgar Rice Burroughs collection. Her girls' softball trophy, her natural foods cookbook, her oaken cudgel, her moog, her wok: all gone. There were no notes. A pain jabbed at my sternum, tears started in my eyes. I was alone, deserted, friendless. I began to long even for the stink of her. On the pillow in the bedroom I found a fermenting chunk of pineapple. And sobbed.

• • •

By the time I thought of the Primate Center the sun was already on the wane. It was dark when I got there. Loose gravel grated beneath my shoes in the parking lot; the flag snapped at the top of its pole; the lights grinned lickerishly from the Center's windows. Inside the lighting was subdued, the building hushed. I began searching through the rooms, opening and slamming doors. The linoleum glowed all the way up the long corridor. At the far end I heard someone whistling "My Old Kentucky Home." It was the janitor. "Howdedo," he said. "Wut kin ah do fo yo at such a inauspicious hour o de night?"

I was candid with him. "I'm looking for Miss Good."

"Ohhh, she leave bout fo-turdy evy day—sartinly yo should be well apprised o dat fack."

"I thought she might be working late tonight."

"Noooo, no chance o dat." He was staring at the floor.

"Mind if I look for myself?"

"Mah good man, ah trusts yo is not intimatin dat ah would dis-kise de troof... far be it fum me to pre-varicate jus to proteck a young lady wut run off fum a man dat doan unnerstan her needs nor 'low her to spress natchrul inclinations o her soul."

At that moment a girlish giggle sounded from down the hall. Jane's girlish giggle. The janitor's right hand spread itself across my chest. "Ah wooden insinuate mahsef in de middle o a highly sinificant speriment if ah was yo, Jackson," he said, hissing through the gap in his teeth. I pushed by him and started down the corridor. Jane's laugh leaped out again. From the last door on my left. I hurried. Suddenly the Doctor and his wife stepped from the shadows to block the doorway. "Mr. Horne," said the Doctor, arms folded against his chest, "take hold of yourself. We are conducting a series of experiments here that I simply cannot allow you to—"

"A fig for your experiments," I shouted. "I want to speak to my, my—roommate." I could hear the janitor's footsteps behind me. "Get out of my way, Doctor," I said. Mrs. U-Hwak-Lo smiled. I felt panicky. Thought of the Tong Wars. "Is dey a problem here, Doc?" the janitor said, his breath hot on the back of my neck. I broke. Grabbed the Doctor by his elbows, wheeled around and shoved him into the janitor. They went down on the linoleum like spastic skaters.

I applied my shoulder to the door and battered my way in, Mrs. U-Hwak-Lo's shrill in my ear: "You make big missake, Misser!" Inside I found Jane, legs and arms bare, pinching a lab smock across her chest. She looked puzzled at first, then annoyed. She stepped up to me, made some rude gestures in my face. I could hear scrambling in the hallway behind me. Then I saw Konrad—in a pair of baggy BVD's. I grabbed Jane. But Konrad was there in an instant—he hit me like the grill of a Cadillac and I spun across the room, tumbling desks and chairs as I went. I slumped against the chalkboard. The door slammed: Jane was gone. Konrad swelled his chest, swayed toward me, the fluorescent lights hissing overhead, the chalkboard cold against the back of my neck. And I looked up into the black eyes, teeth, fur, rock-ribbed arms.

# Probability Storm
## by Julian Reid

*Fantasy writers have a great fondness for telling stories of the surprising things that can happen in bars: de Camp and Pratt's Gavagan's Bar stories are famous among these, as are Arthur C. Clarke's tales of the White Hart. To these odd gathering-places we now add Rafferty's* Why Not? *Tavern, an establishment plagued by gremlins and peopled by characters who aren't necessarily there. Inevitably, matters sometimes get out of hand...*

*Julian Reid is a tall and slender young man who attended the first Clarion Science Fiction Writers' Workshop in Seattle; he lives in Victoria, British Columbia, where he works as a journalist.* Probability Storm *was his first published story, and he reports that several others are in the works.*

If you've never been to Rafferty's, you won't believe a word of this—I'm warning you right off, because disbelieving can be dangerous. Look what happened to Howard Hopper and General Wilbur Prescott and Lady Beatrice Annabelle Scraggs; you've heard of *them*, I'm sure. Or remember how dynasties used to topple when Edward Everett Peaslake let his mind wander, and how the Dow-Jones Average dropped thirteen whole points the day Isadora Edison discovered a minor compositor's error at the bottom of the third column on page forty-three of the Sunday *New York Times*. And then there was the infamous Barnabas Tobin with his terrible Exopsychic Deontologizer, which was on the verge of reducing the entire world to a state of primordial chaos by the time the Duly Constituted Authorities belatedly intervened. There are things I could tell you about Barnabas Tobin... but I'd better not. After all, a word to the wise is sufficient.

181

So maybe, before you read the rest of this, you ought to drop in at Rafferty's. Tonight, if you can make it; or if you can't, tomorrow at the very latest. You'll have no difficulty finding the place: just drive north on Twenty-ninth until you come to the big wrought-iron gates of the North American Institute of Parapsychic Technology. Then slow down and shift to the outside lane, if you aren't in it already. It's only another three blocks, and then you swing right onto Washington Avenue—which is named after *the* Washington, George Henry I mean, the man who invented the Transcendental Impulsifier. Keep going for two more blocks and you're there.

The sign over the entrance is small and tastefully discreet, but you can't possibly miss it if you have your eyes open and your wits about you. It reads *"Rafferty's* WHY NOT? *Tavern,"* and the "WHY NOT?" is in Old Gothic Black-letter while the rest is in flowing Spencerian script. The words are carved into a varnished slab of Oregon cedar, which is said to come from the very tree that Rafferty's grandfather chopped down a century ago in order to release the dryad who later became his wife. It's illuminated from below by two small spotlights which have been burning steadily for twenty-seven years now, ever since the day Rafferty and his bride Moira first took over the establishment. Rafferty screwed in one bulb and Moira the other, and they both together pulled the switch that made the power flow. Some say there's magic in those lights, but there isn't—you have my word for that. What makes them glow is electricity, and there's nothing magical about electricity.

Anyway, as I said before, you can't possibly miss the place—unless, of course, there are gremlins around. But you know how gremlins are, and you're in a pretty sad state if you haven't learned yet how to get on with them. Just be patient and keep your wits about you, and above all don't lose your temper—if you don't let them ruffle you, they'll tire of the game soon enough. Still, maybe I should warn you that if you're one of those smug, stuffy types who can't stand gremlins, you'd best stay away from Rafferty's. There's usually a whole crowd of them in the neighborhood, you see; they seem to like the place. Myself, I'm glad they do; I'd be pretty lonely without them. But that's an opinion you're not obligated to share.

So anyway, now you're at Rafferty's; and there's not much point in having gone that far unless you stop and go inside. Fortunately, parking is no problem; the City has seen to that. There are meters all down the street, both sides, and you shouldn't have much trouble finding one that isn't full yet and paying to have your car dematerialized for as long as you plan to stay. Of course, sometimes the gremlins take it into their minds to interfere with the meters, so there's an off-chance that your spanking new Cadillac Eldorado might rematerialize as a cranky old Volkswagen Beetle. But it's only a very off-chance, and it won't happen unless one of them takes a personal dislike to you. And anyway, the loss will be covered by your insurance, if you've been sensible enough to take out one of those new policies that cover Acts of Gremlins as well as Acts of God.

And that's the last of my warnings, even though there are one or two other points I might perhaps have mentioned. But don't worry about them—they don't concern you, not unless you happen to be a white-headed man with a red beard or an illegitimate descendant of Oliver Cromwell or the thirteenth daughter of the seventh daughter of a thirteenth son. Which isn't likely, these days; and besides, if you *are* one of these things, you've already learned that you've got to tread carefully. If you hadn't, you'd never have managed to survive this long, as Charles Darwin made himself famous by pointing out.

So from this point on, you're on your own. Once you're inside Rafferty's, literally anything might happen—provided, of course, it's permitted by both the Laws of Nature and the Constitution of these United Sates of America, together with the rules Rafferty himself has laid down for the conduct of a decent, well-run establishment. Even the gremlins respect those; they know they'll be thrown out if they don't. There aren't many people who can say *No* to an obstreperous gremlin and make it stick, but Rafferty is one of them. It's his dryad ancestry, I suspect—that and his marriage to Moira. No one would want to offend Moira, not even a gremlin. And besides, Moira is the seventh daughter of a seventh daughter, and you know what *that* means.

Now, on this particular night I'm telling you about, it just so happened that there weren't any gremlins around—not at first, anyway. Rafferty was there, of course, and Moira was upstairs washing the dinner dishes, and Soleful Susie, the barmaid, was sitting in the rear booth with her feet up, resting, and amusing herself by tickling the tummy of James Clerk Maxwell, the cat. It was early in the evening, sevenish, and there were still only half a dozen customers in the place. Old John Edgar Harding, the retired professor of 'Pataphysics who used to head the department at Miskatonic, was sitting at one end of the bar, discoursing ponderously to Rafferty on his theory of the Unrequited Middle. At the other end Louella van Doren, a red-headed three-times-divorcee who writes a monthly column on Creative Marriage Management for *Fortune* magazine, was conversing animatedly with Isherwood Foster, a handsome stockbroker some twenty years younger than herself. In the center booth on the left was Byron Wilcox, the Neo-Dadaist poet, who always insists that he doesn't come to Rafferty's in search of inspiration, as other poets might, but only to get stinking drunk. And finally, in the last-but-one booth on the right, were two of the young whiz kids from the North American Institute, engrossed in a game of three-dimensional chess. Their names were Spassky and Fischer— but they weren't the Spassky and Fischer you're thinking of, nor even their *doppelgängers,* but two different people entirely. It's just a coincidence that they were both chess players, so don't worry about it: these things happen sometimes, especially in Rafferty's.

And that's the lot—more or less, because *I* was there too, of course. But *I* don't count, not really, because I wasn't corporeally present. I seldom am; I come and go, you see. But don't let that bother you—*I* don't, not any more. I'm used to it by now.

So anyway, that's how things were when The Fat Man came in. I call him The Fat Man because you wouldn't be interested in his family name, not if you know what's good for you, and he wasn't the type you'd care to be on first-name terms with. All you need to know about him is that he was ugly-fat, with jowls that oozed down the sides of his face like candle drippings. And he was mean, too—you could tell that just by looking at him. It's said that inside of every fat man there's a thin man crying to get out; well, the thin man inside of this one had been swallowed up entirely and he wasn't even screaming any more. You can't get any meaner than that; it's positively cannibalistic.

It goes without saying that The Fat Man wasn't a regular at Rafferty's—for one thing, the gremlins would never have stood for him; and for another, he wasn't the sort who'd survive for long with a whole passel of gremlins around. But it just so happened, as I've already told you, that there weren't any gremlins there, not just then. So The Fat Man waddled up to the bar, all sticky-pink and for now unmolested, and heaved himself up onto one of the stools and sat squinting around. When he spotted Rafferty he crooked his finger and called out: "Hey! How about some service, eh?" His voice was gruff and grunty, like all the rest of him.

So Rafferty came over and said, as politely as he could manage: "Well, sir, what can I do for you?"

"You can get me a drink," said The Fat Man. "And make it strong, hear?" He wiggled his finger as he spoke, like it was a stick he carried round with him to beat on helpless animals and children when they had the effrontery to cross his path.

"Yes, sir," said Rafferty. He didn't ask what kind of drink it was that The Fat Man wanted—like all good bartenders, Rafferty is prescient in these matters. And The Fat Man knew this; I'm not sure how, but he knew.

So Rafferty mixed up a double whiskey sour for him; and meantime The Fat Man sat squinting around piggily. "Nice place you got here," he said. "Funny I never noticed it before. Been here quite a while, from the looks of it."

"Twenty-seven years," said Rafferty.

"Now that's pee-cool-ier," said The Fat Man. "Twenty-seven years you been in this neighborhood, and I never noticed—not even once. Now that's what I call pee-cool-ier—*most* pee-cool-ier."

"It's been known to happen," said Rafferty, feeling obliged to comment. "Some people just ain't observant—you know how it is." He knew that it must be gremlins' work, of course; but he wasn't going to say that to The Fat Man's face—Rafferty is a great believer in Etiquette. "That'll be a buck twenty-five," he added, setting down the whiskey sour.

"You don't say," said The Fat Man, hauling out his wallet. "But take *me*, now," he went on, "I've always considered myself a pretty observant guy." He handed Rafferty a ten. "No sir, I don't make a habit of missing things, not me. I'd never of gotten where I am today if I hadn't of kept my eyes peeled all the way, Now this is a real nice place you got here—yes sir, it surely is. Does pretty good business, too, if I don't miss my bet."

"Not bad," said Rafferty, ringing up on the cash-register and counting out The Fat Man's change.

"Of course," said The Fat Man, "it *could* be better—now ain't that so?"

"Could be," said Rafferty. "Here's your change."

"That's what I thought," said The Fat Man, taking it. "Wouldn't take much, neither, to jack your earnings up quite a bit. A little sprucing up here and there, maybe a little music to keep things lively—now take me, for instance, I'm a sentimental sort, I like a little music when I drink. Which reminds me," he added, picking up his glass. "Cheers."

"Don't mention it," said Rafferty.

The Fat Man set down his glass. "Good stuff," he said, smacking his lips, which set his jowls to quivering like custard. "The very best, if I'm not mistaken. Yes sir, a guy like me appreciates the best—and you know, there's a lot more out there like me. Good liquor, good music, and good-looking women—we got a taste for those things. Now take her, for instance"—he jerked a thumb toward Soleful Susie, who had just emerged from the booth at the back—"not bad, not bad at all. But not too good, neither, not the way she's looking at present. Now if you hoisted her skirts up another foot or so, and gave the customers a little something to gawk at. . . " He laughed, and the laugh made him quiver all over. "Well, you get my meaning, don't you?"

"I do indeed," said Rafferty, flashing a glance at Soleful Susie to see how she was taking this. Which to all intents and purposes she wasn't—taking it, I mean. Not that anybody but me could be sure, just by looking; because with Soleful Susie it's sometimes hard to tell.

"Yes, sir," said The Fat Man, "it pays to move with the times. Now this setup here, you got to admit it's kind of old-fashioned." He squinted around. "Not that I'm knocking it, mind you; it's got atmosphere, and that's an asset. But it ain't enough, not by a long shot—not in this day and age. We're living in an age of progress, see; things are changing and they're gonna keep on changing, and we've all of us got to change along with them just in order to keep up. Change is the nature of things, and there's no point holding back from it—it just don't pay, no sir, not in the long run." He leaned forward and waggled his finger at Rafferty. "You know what it is, mister, this Change thing I'm talking about? It's opportunity, that's what it is—and it's the smart guys like me that know how to cash in on it. Yes sir, I got a real nose for opportunity—I can smell it out from a mile off. I never missed a bet, friends tell me; and I daresay they're right about that."

"I daresay," said Rafferty, not batting an eyelid; but I could feel the hackles rising on the back of his neck. Mine would have been rising, too, if I'd happened to have any—which I didn't, not being corporeal just at that moment. That's dangerous talk, you see, the same kind that Barnabas Tobin used in selling his Exopsychic Deontologizer to his backers. *I* should know, seeing as how it was that same talk got me where I am now—not that I'm complaining, mind you, since I only got my just deserts; but all things considered, I can't honestly recommend it, not to those of you who don't have any just deserts coming to you.

The fact was, I sensed a storm brewing. Everything added up to that, now that I stopped to think about it: The Fat Man, the two whiz kids named Fischer and Spassky, and above all the absence of gremlins. It all added up because it *didn't* add up, if you get what I mean. There was no pattern to it that I could see, and that worried me: in a well-run universe like this one there's always a pattern, unless something has gone wrong somewhere.

Maybe I was just imagining things, but I didn't think so. In any case, I figured I'd better check into it, just in case Causality was beginning to get a little out of hand. So I gathered my energies together, concentrating myself, so to speak; and then gave myself a Moebius twist, reversing parity; and all at once I'd slipped over, and was on The Other Side.

I was right about the storm; it was still only in the early stages, building up, but I could tell right away that it was going to be a real humdinger. Even now, when things had hardly got started, it was pretty impressive: great waves of statistical anomaly roaring in to smash and spatter against the frame of Objective Reality like breakers along a rocky coast; and the gremlins were whooping and hollering and skeering in on the wave crests like California surfers gone berserk with the sheer power of it all. It was a great game for them, no doubt about it; but for me it was different—I didn't dare let myself get carried away. I clung like a limpet to Objective Reality, gluing as much of my attention as I could spare on Rafferty's and its inhabitants and the whole firm, solid, not-quite-unshakable continuum of which they were a part, at the same time keeping a weather eye peeled to take in the storm which was battering at their foundations.

Well, I'm exaggerating a little—actually it wasn't as bad as all that. I mean, the foundations were safe enough, at least in this neighborhood; the chaos threatening us fell somewhere short of being primordial, if that was any consolation. Not like the storm Barnabas Tobin kicked up, when all but one or two of the Eternal Verities were temporarily knocked for a loop and the entire Orderly Frame of Things was teetering on the edge of collapse—this time, I could tell, we were nowhere near the center of the disturbance. Elsewhere, maybe, a galaxy or two would blink out of existence, or a few dozen stars go supernova, or a planet shatter and dissolve; maybe they had already, maybe that was what this tempest was all about. But here on the outskirts nothing much would happen, relatively speaking— things would be shaken up, of course, but no worse than a plague of mischievous gremlins could manage if they set their minds to it; and after a while the forces of Natural Law and Order would slowly but surely reassert themselves. That didn't bother me particularly; the world's survived worse. Maybe it'd even be a good thing, shaking The Fat Man and all the others like him out of their customary self-satisfied complacency—though in most cases, I'm afraid, it'd take more than a mere Probability Storm to manage *that*. Look at what it took to enlighten *me* for instance, and how much it cost me...

But I'm digressing. It's a bad habit of mine—sort of hard to avoid, though, when you're smeared out like I am into a subcorporeal slur of low-order probabilities. But a bad one all the same.

So anyway, there I was, hanging on tight to Reality as if my continued existence depended on it, while all around me waves of Uncertainty beat and shattered. Everything was blurred and kind of hazy, as it always is on The Other Side, and with each wave that came it blurred some more and shimmered out of focus as if it were getting ready to melt and run; and then, as the wave passed, it would kind of waver back again into almost-but-not-quite sharpness, only to shimmer and smear once again as the next wave came. Every now and then a gremlin would come skeering past me, or maybe even through me, and I'd feel it is as a sort of electric tingle of joyously untrammeled irresponsibility that didn't have a care in this or any other world. I wouldn't have been human (or ex-human, or whatever you want to call me) if a part of me hadn't leapt at the touch of it and yearned wildly to respond. They were like children at play, all glory and mischief and irrepressible energy rolled up into a tight little frenzy of marvelously uninhibited innocence; and if I was unable to join them in their game I was the poorer for it. But I hung back because I had to—I *couldn't* join in; my sense of responsibility to the Scheme of Things said otherwise.

And besides, I was thinking of Rafferty's and what would soon be happening over there—if it hadn't started already. I wasn't too worried about the rest of the world; all they'd have to contend with was a sudden upsurge of statistical anomalies. Maybe half a million normally level-headed New Yorkers would all at once take it into their minds to go for a drive through the Lincoln Tunnel, and maybe a couple of hundred thousand bridge players all around the world would pick up their hands and discover they'd been dealt thirteen spades, and maybe all the babies who happened to be conceived on this particular night would be born identical triplets with genius-grade IQ's, and maybe all the cars stacked in all the world's parking meters would be shuffled together so that when their owners paid to retrieve them they'd get back some rather interesting hybrids. Little things like that are none too serious; people take them in their stride, after the initial shock.

But Rafferty's, you see, is a kind of focal point—that's what gives the place its special charm, or a part of it anyway. There are statistical fields just as there are magnetic ones, and they too have poles, and Rafferty's happens to be located smack-dab on top of one of those poles. "The still point of the turning world," old John Edgar Harding calls it sometimes—but only when it's late in the evening and he's getting maudlin. Maybe it's second sight on his part, or maybe it's only the liquor; but anyway, he's right, after a manner of speaking.

So that's why, just then, the Probability Waves were rolling in on me from all directions at once. Don't try to figure out the geometry of it—you can't, because geometry on The Other Side is different from anything you could ever conceive of. You'd have to be crazy to try, like Ludwig Kleinsdorfer was—you know what his formulas did to *him,* and he was nowhere near the truth of it.

But I'm wandering again, which is exactly what I was hanging on trying *not* to do at this time I'm telling you about. Confusion was compounding itself all around me; the last thing in the world I wanted to do was let any of it spill over into myself. Even if old Kleinsdorfer had been there in person, which he wasn't at that particular moment, I'd have done my best to ignore him; I'd have known I was being impolite, him being an old friend of mine, but the last thing I needed just then was a Disturbing Influence, and if there's one thing that can be said of old Kleinsdorfer in spades, it's that he's very much a Disturbing Influence. So instead of him I concentrated on The Fat Man, because I sensed that in some way he was the key to all this, at least in its local manifestations. Either he was a Disturbing Influence himself, a kind of statistical Typhoid Mary, which didn't seem too likely; or else the Scheme of Things was seeking to regain its equilibrium by throwing him in as a counterbalance. If so, God only knew what would happen to him in the end, because the Scheme of Things isn't much concerned about the ultimate fate of its uncomprehending counterbalances, as I know all too well. But anyway, I focused on The Fat Man, and did another Moebius twist, and flipped back over into Our Side.

It was a pretty nauseating experience. I found myself coextensive with The Fat Man, interpenetrating his body so to speak, and I didn't like it. He *felt* as mean as he looked, mean clear through, in every joint and flabby muscle of his body. Sinking into him was like drowning in a pool of warm Jello. But it had to be done, so I gritted my incorporeal teeth and did it.

Something in him felt my presence and resisted. He gave a little twitch, spilling some of the drink he was holding in his hand, and I felt his eyes cross, mean and narrowly calculating. He had stopped talking to Rafferty, somewhere in midsentence, as I slipped into him. Rafferty didn't say anything, but bent to wipe the spilled drink from the counter.

"*Jee*-zus!" said The Fat Man suddenly. I had an inside view of the fact that he wasn't feeling too good.

At the other end of the bar, old John Edgar Harding turned and looked toward us. "It is you, my good man, is it not?" he said.

"Uh-huh," I said, struggling to control The Fat Man's vocal cords. "It's me, all right—Quintus MacDonald. At your service."

Old John Edgar rose and came strolling over to us. The Fat Man sat rigid, mainly because I was holding him that way—and quite an effort it took, I assure you. John Edgar stopped in front of us. "I gather that there is a Storm brewing," he said deliberately.

"That's right," I said around The Fat Man's greasy tongue. "A big one, coming this way."

"Thank you," John Edgar said. "It is good to be warned." He inclined his head to one side. "You heard, Rafferty?"

"I heard," said Rafferty.

"Perhaps you had best fetch Moira down," said John Edgar. "I have noticed that she frequently exerts a calming influence on such occasions."

"You're right," said Rafferty. He turned and went out through the door behind the bar to call Moira.

"A Storm, you say?" said Louella van Doren from the other end of the bar. She turned to Isherwood Foster. "You've never been here during a Probability Storm, have you, darling? It's really quite thrilling—a once-in-a-lifetime experience."

Isherwood Foster looked as if he hoped to hell it would be.

"You may rely on us," John Edgar assured me. "Even in the moment of crisis we shall not lose our heads."

"Better not," I warned him—with some difficulty, because already I could feel my control over The Fat Man's body slipping; he was stronger than I'd expected. "Gotta be going—'bye."

"Good-bye," said John Edgar. "And good luck."

I couldn't respond, because I was already engaged in decorporealizing. I exploded out of The Fat Man, and fragments of me spread like ripples to every corner of Rafferty's. For a moment parts of me were simultaneously caught up in the consciousnesses of Soleful Susie, John Edgar Harding, Fischer and Spassky, Byron Wilcox, Isherwood Foster, Louella van Doren, and James Clerk Maxwell, the cat. It was like being jerked in eight different directions at once. Then I caught hold of myself and pulled myself back together. It felt good—you have to have been split eight ways simultaneously to appreciate just how good being a decorporealized microstatistical smear can feel.

Rafferty had just returned, with Moira following him. The Fat Man sat quivering piggishly in front of them. "Something just happened to me, didn't it?" he said in an accusing tone. "Don't deny it—I *felt* it happening to me!"

"Maybe," Rafferty said. "I didn't notice."

"You're lying," said The Fat Man. "I could *feel* it all through me!"

"Don't be foolish," said John Edgar Harding superciliously. "It is nonsense to speak of 'feelings' in reference to a swinish creature like you." He turned and marched back to his stool.

Byron Wilcox stuck his head out from his booth. "Hey, Susie," he wailed, "don't dry up on me! I need another shot."

"Coming," called Soleful Susie. She went behind the bar.

Louella van Doren was explaining loudly to Isherwood Foster just what the last Probability Storm at Rafferty's had been *like*. James Clerk Maxwell was curled up asleep in the rear booth. Undisturbed, the whiz kids Spassky and Fischer continued their game of three-dimensional chess. That's the way things are in Rafferty's: the habitués have learned to take just about anything in their stride.

The Fat Man shuddered. "You could at least call a doctor," he said. "For all you know, I might be dying."

"There's a phone in back," said Rafferty. "You can use it if you want."

The Fat Man closed his eyes. "*Jee*-zus! he said again.

At this point something in me tingled, and I became aware that there was a gremlin in the room. Maybe he'd followed me across from The Other Side, or maybe he was one of the regulars who were here most nights—I couldn't say, because I often have difficulty telling one gremlin from another. In any case, I felt a whoop of joy that kind of shimmered in the atmosphere as he spotted The Fat Man. That's torn it, I thought to myself; the trouble's about to start.

The Fat Man shifted on his barstool. Now maybe I'd better tell you that Rafferty's isn't one of those places that have modern-type barstools which are screwed down to the floor; Rafferty insists that his customers prefer the old-fashioned wooden kind that you can tilt backward or forward if you want to. So The Fat Man's stool wasn't fixed down, and there was this little depression in the floor right behind it where it had been worn down over the years; the chances were maybe one in a million that The Fat Man's shifting would slide one leg of the stool into this depression in just such a way that the stool would topple right over—but what's a one-in-a-million chance to a gremlin? I felt the little bugger seize it and give it a sort of a twist; and then it had materialized and The Fat Man was sprawling on the floor, all pink and tumbled like a stranded jellyfish. He'd let out a sort of porcine squeal as he went down, and it seemed to hang in the air and mingle with the silvery tintinnabulation of the gremlin's laughter.

Soleful Susie rushed around the end of the bar and helped him to his feet. The Fat Man sort of leaned on her as he got up; it was like his gross flabby self was oozing around her to swallow her up, just like it had already swallowed up the thin man who was no longer screaming inside. Then he let go of her and leaned panting against the bar. "Jee-*zus!*" he said. "You oughta do something about those goddamn stools—I might of been killed!"

"It ain't the stools," said Rafferty. "It's the gremlins."

"I oughta sue," said The Fat Man. "I'd be within my rights."

"Don't be silly," said Moira. "You can't sue a gremlin."

"An interesting point," said John Edgar Harding from the end of the bar. "Is the proprietor of a respectable establishment such as this one legally responsible for the acts of such gremlins as might be said to haunt it?"

"He isn't," Louella van Doren volunteered. "There was an article about it in *Fortune* just last month. Isn't that right, Ishy darling?"

"That's right," said Isherwood Foster. "I read it myself."

"You see?" said Rafferty to The Fat Man. "Gremlins is classed as an Act of God, so I ain't legally responsible for how they behave "

"That's right, Raffy," said Louella van Doren cheerfully. "I told you this 'ud be fun," she added in a loud aside to Isherwood Foster.

The Fat Man quivered all over with piggy indignation. "What kind of a place *is* this?" he demanded.

"A nice, clean, decent one," said Moira.

"As you can see," added Rafferty.

"Jee-zus *Christ!*" said The Fat Man.

"Here," said Soleful Susie, "if you'll just move aside I'll get your stool set up for you again."

The Fat Man turned and glared at her, like he was contemplating using her for a toilet-plunger, then stumped over to the booth behind Byron Wilcox and eased himself into it. "I could use another drink," he said, obviously doing his best to keep himself under control. "How about it, sister?"

"Be right with you, sir," said Soleful Susie. She upended the stool and set it back in place.

The Fat Man sat glowering. He hadn't left yet, though, in spite of the utmost provocation—which meant that he hadn't just dropped by casually, like he'd tried to make it appear. So he had something on his mind—business, probably; I've had enough experience with businessmen that I can tell. It wasn't good, clean, open-and-aboveboard business, either; otherwise he'd have come right out with it in the first place. I smelled a rat, in other words—a big, pink, slimy one.

I also smelled a couple more gremlins, who'd presumably been whistled up by their friend to come and join in the fun at The Fat Man's expense; they sort of flashed and glittered in the air, like Christmas-tree tinsel. And there was a kind of electric tension building up, as the Probability Storm began to spill over from The Other Side. I felt all taut and tingly and keyed-up; I knew inside that something was about to break.

Two of the gremlins darted over to The Fat Man's booth; I couldn't see what they were doing, but from the way The Fat Man was acting I guessed that they were amusing themselves by triggering off all sorts of itches and twitches and aches in his internal organs. The third gremlin drifted across to the booth where the two whiz kids were sitting; and I drifted over, too, being kind of interested in what might happen to their game. Spassky was bent over the board, about to move a pawn, when the gremlin got to him. He hesitated, then suddenly darted his hand across and shifted his queen one space to the left. Fischer frowned; the move didn't make sense to him. It wouldn't have made sense to me, either, if the gremlin hadn't brushed against me as it left, so I picked up the fact that this particular move would lead inevitably to a mate twenty-three turns later, unless Fischer happened to make exactly the right countermove eleven turns from now. Which he probably would, knowing the way gremlins work; in any case, I was sure this game would be one that would go down in the history books, at least the kind of history books that are read by three-dimensional chess freaks.

Then one of the bottles behind the bar seemed to pick itself up and begin to shake itself. It was the molecules of the air doing it—I knew that—and the odds against its happening spontaneously were an uncountable number of trillions to one. There were no gremlins behind the bar—Moira is very strict on keeping them out from there—so I knew it was the antistatistical chaos from The Other Side beginning to spill over. Isherwood Foster was watching the bottle bug-eyed, while Louella van Doren was prattling along beside him giving a highly inaccurate running commentary on just *exactly* what was happening. The Fat Man in his booth didn't pay any attention; he was lost in his own miseries.

Rafferty picked the bottle from the air and set it down carefully on the shelf. It stayed put. Rafferty has The Power, so he's quite capable of handling that sort of thing.

Soleful Susie was carrying a couple of drinks across to The Fat Man and Byron Wilcox; suddenly she slipped, and the two glasses flew off her tray as neatly as if they'd been aimed and cascaded their contents down the front of The Fat Man's suit. That was gremlins' work—I could tell. Moira could, too, and she waggled an admonitory finger in their general direction; she doesn't like to have gremlins taking advantage of poor Susie. The Fat Man was too immersed in his internal indignities to pay much attention to what was happening to him.

More bottles started dancing on the shelves, clinking together; the sound gradually formed into the opening bars of Mozart's *Eine kleine Nachtmusik*. The chance of that happening naturally was infinitesimal. I knew then that the Storm was upon us.

And with it came a flurry of gremlins, tens and hundreds of them. There were so many that from now on I wasn't able to distinguish between what was gremlins' doings and what was caused by the Probability Storm itself. Maybe it didn't make any difference, anyway; after all, old Ludwig Kleinsdorfer has always claimed that gremlins are merely improbabilities personified, much as I am now; and while Kleinsdorfer may be crazy, he isn't so crazy that he isn't absolutely right every now and then. But be that as it may, Rafferty's was chaos from this point on.

For *me* it was pretty chaotic, too, since I couldn't avoid being sucked into it. I corporealized and decorporealized, bunched up and spread out into a spiral wave form, bobbing in and out of various people's consciousnesses, all in a sort of cosmic waltz that whirled me up and dissolved me into dancing almost like a cloud of midges. But my being never quite disintegrated, and I retain all my memories intact—so you can take my word for everything I'm going to tell you.

As a matter of fact, I was never the least bit confused—which is quite an accomplishment, and one that I have the right to be proud of. In the beginning, I've got to admit, I *almost* slipped into confusion. Everything seemed sort of hazy and distorted, as if I were seeing it through waves of flowing water. Everybody except Rafferty and Moira was all out of focus, as if they were on the edge of dissolving into the other people they might have been if their lives had gone otherwise than they actually had. Even the thin man that The Fat Man had swallowed up inside him was back, screaming his head off to be let out—I don't mean screaming out loud, because he had no vocal cords of his own; it was an etheric scream, which only I and the gremlins could hear. Rafferty's flowed too—not the walls themselves, which were solid and secure enough, but the bar and the booths and the stools and all the fixtures, which *might* have been set up subtly otherwise even by a masterhand such as Rafferty's. But all this was only at first; then I began to catch the rhythm and flow with it, and everything became clearer.

But only for a moment. Then suddenly I was bunched up and concentrated inside the consciousness of James Clerk Maxwell. I'd never been corporealized in a cat before; and believe me, it's quite an experience. I was curled up in the rear booth, peacefully dreaming of my happy kittenhood, when all of a sudden it struck me that there were dozens of she-cats I'd known that I might have had but for one reason or another hadn't. The specters of all those might-have-been shes rose *en masse* in my mind as if they were all physically present, a great roiling phalanx of them; the air was redolent with their rich musky scent. That scent was calling me, and I was horny as hell, and I rose and arched my back and yawned and spread out all my front claws, and then I settled back onto my haunches and let out a deep musical yowl that was compounded half of excitement and half of sheer unalloyed frustration at all those golden opportunities that seemed almost palpably present but I knew somehow I'd had the misfortune to miss forever. Then my eyes happened to light on Louella van Doren, who was also emitting a rich musky odor of civet that I could pick up even from here (I suppose it was her perfume; not being gifted with a sense of smell when I'm in my decorporeal state, I hadn't noticed it before); and then all at once, willy-nilly, I was *her* instead of James Clerk Maxwell.

It took me a moment to realize I'd made the shift, because as far as the quality of their minds went, there wasn't too much difference—I'd never realized before how much of a cat Louella is. I spread my claws and clutched them tight on Isherwood Foster's forearm; the poor dear was as rigid as a tight girdle, but that didn't seem to bother me. "Isn't this exciting, darling?" I purred into his ear. And all the while I was tautly aware of the deep masculine musk of him, and of the delectable way his stiff rough whiskers prickled me as I rubbed my cheek against his. I flexed my muscles, and part of me didn't like what was on my mind—the *me* part of me, I mean; after all, I was male once, and I never went in for perversions. But the Louella part of me was positively aglow with excitement, and brimming with a caldron of plans for poor Ishy that fell a long way short of what *I* would consider Creative Marriage Management. "I'm frightened, darling," I whispered, lying through my false teeth. "Hold me close; I'm *scared* what might happen next." And Isherwood Foster held me close, in a kind of death grip. I raked my claws down his forearm. "Oh, *darling,*" I said, "you're so *strong!*"

And then, thank God, I was free of Louella and exploding outward. For a moment I was coextensive with the whole of Rafferty's, my consciousness multifaceted as if I had myriad eyes, like an insect. Rafferty, I could see, was breasting the Storm, with Moira at his side; and the two whiz kids, Fischer and Spassky, were completely oblivious to it, immersed in their game. Byron Wilcox had been seized with what he saw fit to term inspiration, and was scribbling down a poem on the napkin that had come with his last drink. The others were more overtly affected. Soleful Susie had collapsed into the arms of Old John Edgar Harding, who was stroking her hair and whispering to her something about the Fallacy of the Interminable Asymptote. Louella van Doren and Isherwood Foster... well, I already told you something of what was happening there, and I won't go into any further details in case they might embarrass you. The Fat Man in his booth was quivering and twitching like a stuck pig, totally unable to cope with the force of the primal scream that was rising from the thin man trapped inside him. The outlines of the bar and the booths were all blurred, and dancing like a swarm of mayflies above a pond. And through the midst of it all stalked James Clerk Maxwell, his fur bristling, wailing like a banshee for all the loves he had lost and was currently engaged in seeking out again.

There was more, of course, but there's a limit to how much the human mind can assimilate in a single instant—even a deontologized human mind like mine. And I was fast approaching that limit. So with a determined spasm that spread spiraling outward to all the semidissociated parts of me, I pulled myself together. For a moment I found myself concentrated behind the bar, down near Moira's feet. I kind of huddled there, drinking solace and security from the sweet female presence of her. It really *does* mean something to be the seventh daughter of a seventh daughter; it gives one a kind of radiant selfhood that communicates itself like comfort to all those around one. I suppose I'm more or less in love with Moira because of that radiance of hers; I think everybody who's ever met her is, a little, except maybe for The Fat Man. If I was still human I might try to make something of it—I used to have sufficient gall. But then, of course, there's Rafferty, who's not the sort to stand for any nonsense. And anyway, I'm no longer human, at least not in the conventional sense of the word, so there's no point mooning over *that* particular impossibility.

So anyway, there I was, bunched up and feeling all bittersweet sad and almost sorry for myself—about not being Rafferty, I mean, so I could have Moira for my very own—and then another wave of anomalies hit me, and all at once I was scattered every which way once again. I scrabbled to collect myself, and all of a sudden found myself half-materialized amongst the bottles behind the bar; but I caught myself in time to keep from knocking them down from the shelf, and managed to waver into somewhat indistinct materiality on top of the bar, directly in front of John Edgar Harding and Soleful Susie.

Susie let out a kind of half-shriek and shrank back, but John Edgar just looked unperturbedly up at me and said: "Well, my good man, you're here in the flesh, I see."

"More or less," I said, panting. "I'll have to be going soon."

"When we must go, we must go," said John Edgar sagely. "That is the way of the world; but we might as well make the best use of the little time available to us. Let me see, now—the last time we met face to face we were conversing about Barnabas Tobin, were we not?"

"That's right," I said.

"Perhaps we could continue with that conversation," said John Edgar, "for the duration of this brief span that has been vouchsafed to us. The subject is one of professional interest to me, as you doubtless are cognizant."

"I am," I said. But perhaps at this point I should stop a moment and explain that, back in my corporeal existence, I, Quintus MacDonald, was Barnabas Tobin's leading financial backer. That's what got me into the spot I'm in now; and it's also why I'm such an authority on the Exopsychic Deontologizer and its untoward effects.

"Well," I said to John Edgar, "after the Duly Constituted Authorities cracked down, old Barnabas went kind of off his head, as I'm sure you remember."

"I remember it well," said John Edgar, nodding.

"He was convinced people were plotting against him," I said. "Behind his back, as he put it. Which wasn't true; they were being quite open about it, actually. But it didn't make any difference; it just made him feel all the more certain that universal deontologization was the only solution to all the world's problems. So he came to me and begged my support to help him continue his experiments in secret." I shook my head wryly. "And I was fool enough to agree."

"Foolish indeed," said John Edgar. "I would have expected that a person of your acumen would have learned his lesson by that point."

"Well, I hadn't," I said, put on the defensive. "I was merely the twelfth richest man in the world, remember; I'd never developed a head for anything more recondite than making money. And I've got to confess that the idea of deontologization still appealed to me. So it went against the cosmic grain—so what? I was always a contrary-minded sort; it was contrariness that got me where I was then, Lord help me."

"And He did, did He not?" said John Edgar. "He finally demonstrated to you the error of your ways, which was all you ever had any right to ask of Him. But continue, please."

"I'm trying to," I said—a trifle impatiently, because I could already feel the prickling sensation that indicated I was on the edge of dematerializing again. "So anyway, to cut it short, we built another Exopsychic Deontologizer—in secret, of course. It was a small model, distinctly underpowered—it ran on two Eveready dry cells, as

I remember—but Barnabas got old Ludwig Kleinsdorfer to check over his calculations, and they both agreed that it would be just barely strong enough to turn the cosmic tide."

"Fascinating," said John Edgar. "Absolutely fascinating. I had never realized that Kleinsdorfer himself was involved..." He broke off, perhaps because I was frowning impatiently at him. "But continue."

"So I was there in person," I said, "when Barnabas turned it on. As his backer I'd insisted—the more fool I. It might've worked, too, if we hadn't both of us been overenthusiastic. I insisted that he try it at the top setting—Kleinsdorfer had warned us against that, but we both of us forgot it in the heat of the moment. That was what saved the world, I guess—our overenthusiasm—because the photon tube blew as soon as he threw the switch. So Barnabas and I were the only persons caught in the field during the one brief moment it existed; and of course we were deontologized immediately, and shot straight off to opposite statistical poles, Barnabas off in the Andromeda Galaxy somewhere, and me..." I shrugged. "Well, here I am." I was going to say more, but with my shrug a shudder passed through me, and I felt myself starting to disintegrate. I had just time to shout: "Gotta go—'bye for now"—and then I was dematerialized once again, spreading in a wave front that pulsed briefly outward to take in the whole of Rafferty's, the whole continent, the whole world, the whole cosmos.

Infinitely attenuated, I was aware of John Edgar saying: "Farewell, my friend; we must resume our conversation on some more propitious occasion." Simultaneously, I was aware of myriad statistical anomalies taking place throughout the cosmos: a mass outbreak of the screaming meemies in a department store in Newark, New Jersey; a convocation of several hundred laughing hyenas around a half-dry waterhole in Central Africa; a whole rookery of penguins dancing the barcarole in the Falkland Islands; a sudden subsidence of the outermost fringes of Jupiter's Great Red Spot; an indescribably vivid auroral display above the northern hemisphere of the variform planet, Organon; thirty million Casseflavian jub-jubs all sporulating at the identical instant on a world somewhere in the Lesser Magellanic Cloud; further out yet, in an uncharted galaxy well beyond the range of Earth's most powerful telescopes, ten thousand synchronized supernovae spelling out the Velantian ideogram for Mystic Happiness—and countless more, enough so that I could fill a dozen books simply listing them all. Then, with a swirl, I contracted again, and found myself back in Rafferty's.

This time I had locked into the consciousness of Byron Wilcox. He had just completed his poem, and was sitting gazing bemusedly down at it. Along with him I read it over once again:

> It happened one frosty look of trees
> waving gracefully against the wall:
> the cat, the king and I there found surcease
> in conscience bound to weary seneschal.
> I forget whether he went on and on,
> yet go he did; and in the morning spoke
> briefly of love and pity—there were none
> who mourned for him, and few cared where he woke.
> He said her head shook vertically aligned
> in sequences he could not comprehend,
> but joy it was to kneel here unconfined
> and flex his wings and call his God his friend.
> Eve loved intensely all men who must die,
> and bowed her hands and closed one weeping eye.

Well, I thought, it rhymes and scans, so it isn't exactly Neo-Dadaist. But I liked it anyway, in spite of the fact that it almost made sense. Briefly I contemplated submitting it to *The New Yorker,* who had been begging for a new Byron Wilcox poem recently; but then I decided against it. This was the kind of verse that could ruin my carefully maintained reputation as the nation's foremost Neo-Dadaist. The critics would unanimously accuse me of deserting The Cause—and they might well be right, at that. Rhyme, meter, and sense—those were the three things that I, Byron Wilcox, had sworn to stand foursquare against. Reluctantly I scrumpled up the napkin on which the poem was written and dropped it onto the floor, where I ground it determinedly beneath my feet.

The other part of me—the *me* part—was trying to calculate the stupendous improbability of Byron Wilcox's ever coming up with a poem that even verged on comprehensibility. But there was no way of figuring the odds against it, so presently I gave up.

And then I was free of Byron Wilcox, and temporarily pretty much in control of myself. The eye of the storm must have just reached us, I figured, so that there was a brief lull going on. I decided to drop over to the whiz kids' booth and see how their game was developing.

It was as I'd expected: Fischer had made the right countermove to Spassky's shift of the queen a dozen or so turns back, and now the game was developing into a very interesting contest that represented a situation which could rise only once in a trillion games between even the most masterly players. Every conceivable move had an indefinite number of potentially interesting game situations branching out from it, and there was no way of telling which player had the advantage. Gremlins apart, I suspected it would lead ultimately to a stalemate; but there was no way to know for sure.

I expanded my consciousness outward, to take in the general situation. For the time being, it seemed, everything had settled down: Rafferty and Moira were ensconced firmly behind the bar, Byron Wilcox was at work on another poem, Soleful Susie had detached herself from John Edgar Harding and got out her compact and was engaged in fixing up her tear-streaked face, Louella van Doren was gently stroking the arm of the still-rigid Isherwood Foster and whispering sweet nothings into his flushing ear, James Clerk Maxwell had given up on his love quest and returned to his booth and was curled up there licking himself, and The Fat Man was collapsed across his table and muttering obscurely to himself something about "Gimpy" and how he should have listened to him while he still had the chance. Even the gremlins were resting, for the moment; but I knew that wouldn't keep up for long.

It didn't. Pretty soon one of them swooped over in the direction of The Fat Man, and the others followed—there must have been a dozen of them or more. They amused themselves by resuming their torment of him. Suddenly he sat back with a yelp and all his buttons popped off, to clatter down on the table in front of him in the shape of a neat exclamation mark. His jacket and shirt bulged open, to reveal a hairless pink expanse of flabby chest underneath. He grabbed at it and started scratching himself furiously, as if he'd just contracted the hives.

Then all the bottles behind the bar started dancing again—this time to the tune of "Waltzing Matilda." The second installment of the Storm was upon us.

I felt everything waver and go hazy, as it had before. Then, before it even had a chance to clarify, a wave picked me up from behind and hurled me straight into the consciousness of Soleful Susie. All at once I found myself decidedly down in the dumps about some bastard named Sam, who'd cut out three years ago and left me in the lurch. I hated Sam; and at the same time, in that particular moment, I couldn't help loving him, because marching across my mind, arm-in-arm with myriad smiling avatars of me, were all the Sams-that-might-have-been, kind, generous, and above all lovingly warm. I realized that I wanted from the bottom of my heart to have Sam back, and to forgive him for everything he had ever done to me. But at the same time I didn't *want* to feel this way, because I knew damn well that the real-life Sam was an unmitigated bastard—and if I needed proof of that, all I had to do was remember all the filthy things he'd done to me before he finally turned tail and ran out. Thinking of Sam brought tears to my eyes, and I reached up and tried to blot them away before they ran and spoiled my makeup. And then old John Edgar Harding was alongside me, and he put his arm around my shoulders and said: "There, there, my dear girl, there's no need to cry; just remember what Plotinus said. . . " And I couldn't care less about Plotinus, whoever in the hell *he* was; but at the same time I was grateful to the old man for at least trying to comfort me—and above all for calling me a "girl," because I knew damn well that I was getting close to the wrong side of forty.

And meanwhile I—the Quintus MacDonald I—was feeling very embarrassed about all this, because I liked Susie and felt somewhat guilty about this forceful sharing of those innermost secrets she never shared with anybody. I struggled to extricate myself before my embarrassment got worse, and finally I succeeded. I flew out of Susie's mind like a cork from a champagne bottle—and fetched up, of course, exactly where I'd least wanted to go, back in the consciousness of The Fat Man.

It was just as slimy as ever, if not more so—like halfcoagulated grease in a frying pan. Sinking into it, I could feel the thin man inside screaming at me to let go of him, and I knew a kind of vicious joy in holding him squeezed off. I hated him: he was a pretty decent sort, really, and I hated anything right and decent on principle, because that kind of thing was always standing in my way.

All this was just the general tone of me—by which I mean The Fat Man, from whom I wish to dissociate myself just as far as I possibly can. Unfortunately, that wasn't possible, not at that moment. Like it or not, I *was* The Fat Man, and that meant I was one of the medium-big wheels in something I'm going to call The Syndicate—you know what I mean, and you also know that if you dig too deeply into the subject it's not likely to be good for you. Just look at what happened to Francis Ford O'Donnell and Efrem Z. Weaver...but I'm digressing again, aren't I? That's because this particular part of the story is one I don't feel too happy telling; I'd rather not remember it at all. Being inside The Fat Man isn't the kind of thing you want to write home about: I felt like I was going to be swallowed up in slime at any moment.

But anyway, there I was; and right now I was lost in a kind of gibbering terror, shot through with flashes of memory of a talk I'd had this afternoon with a little squirt called Gimpy. Gimpy, I gathered, had warned me against coming to this place, and like a fool I hadn't paid him any heed. It's haunted, he'd told me; and I'd sat there quivering with laughter at him because he was superstitious enough to believe in ghosts. I didn't believe in them myself, you see; I was an incorrigible skeptic about anything I couldn't buy or latch onto by my own nefarious means. And this *Rafferty's* joint was in a good location—I was mad as hell at Gimpy and my stooges for never even mentioning it before—because if we set up a connection there we could use it to move in on the lucrative trade in grimoires and such with the students at the North American Institute of Parapsychic Technology, who must be ripe for the picking if they were fool enough to fall for the crap peddled in a nuthouse like that. I saw money in it, big money, if it could be handled right. Just get an in with the owner, and pretty soon I'd have him eating out of the palm of my hand—I knew all the tricks; I could do it in my sleep if need be. And here was this meek little milksop of a Gimpy, and he had the nerve to argue with me and say it wasn't worth it, not if it meant going inside that *Rafferty's* joint again; and I sat there laughing and told him that if he was *that* yellow he didn't have to come with me, I was smart enough to look after myself and I'd like to see the ghost that was smart enough to hold *me* back from what promised to be a pretty hot deal.

And now I was scared yellow myself, and wishing to hell that I'd taken Gimpy just a trifle more seriously. As a matter of fact, I was scared out of my own filthy mind, and right now I was coward enough to admit it. I wanted to get out of here with my skin intact, and once I was out I'd figure some way of getting my own back—I had some boys under me who were pretty slick at arranging that sort of thing. I'd call them in and make arrangements, because nobody and nothing was going to get away with doing things like *this* to me—after all, I had my reputation to uphold. I was mean not just because I enjoyed it, but also because it paid; and I wasn't going to compromise with good business practice just because I was scared as hell right at this moment. No sir, I wasn't the type that compromised—not me.

I'm making all this sound a good deal more orderly and coherent than it actually was, because The Fat Man's mind was pretty confused at this particular moment, and what I picked up from it I picked up in bits and snatches. I fitted it all together later, just about the way I've told it to you (except that I've left out a few of the nastier details; there are some things it's better for your peace of mind not to know); but the way it actually came out, like I said, was sort of in little spurts of lucidity between the terrified gibberings, like this: *Jee*-zus, they're gonna *kill* me if they keep up with this . . . doctor says I gotta watch out for my heart . . . *Jeez,* it felt like it stopped just then . . . should of listened to that goddamn Gimpy . . . if I can only get out of here, I'm gonna call up the Creep—*he'll* know what to do . . . burn the place up, maybe; no, burning's too good for them . . . *owww,* that hurt! . . . gotta get outa here . . . remember what happened to the Don: heart attack, the doc said . . . shows what *he* knows . . . the Creep knows some pretty clever tricks . . . don't leave no traces, neither; nothing for the goddamn cops to latch onto . . . that goddamn bartender: maybe I could get my hands on that wife of his . . . *Jee*-zus, that hurts! . . . oughta be a law against them ghosts or goblins or whatever they're called . . . they got no right to treat *me* like this! ... *oooow,* the pain, the pain, the pain ... Kee-*rist,* I feel like I'm gonna *die* or something ... gotta get outa here ... gotta get out ... get out ...

Well, you get the general idea. Only I can't find words to make you feel the rancid sliminess of it all, or the cold hard meanness that writhed beneath it—there aren't any words for that; you have to be trapped in the midst of it to know what it's like. As I was just then—drowning in slime, it felt like. And meanwhile the Probability Storm was raging on all around me (every now and then I could feel little side-eddies from it pulsing through me), and anomalies were pyramiding up in incredibly implausible sequences—and there I was, missing all the fun, stuck there inside of The Fat Man and screaming to get out.

I don't know how long it took, because I lost track of time in there. I struggled and struggled, but he seemed determined to suck me down. God, he was strong in his meanness!—toward the end I was beginning to feel desperately afraid that he was even stronger than I was. And then I thought of Moira, and that thought gave me strength. It was as if she were there beside me, fighting along with me. And slowly, with her help, I fought my way up to the surface.

And then, at last, I'd made it and kicked free of him. I can't tell you what a relief that was; it was like something had been suffocating me and finally I was able to breathe again. I flexed myself all over and expanded, spiralwise, almost singing with the sheer joy of being able to move freely once more. For a moment I felt as uninhibitedly loose and carefree as the gremlins must. You have to have been trapped inside a Fat Man, even if it's only for a few suffocating minutes, in order to appreciate what a joyous thing freedom is.

For a while I was almost dizzy with happiness. And then I began to worry. It wasn't the Storm that was bothering me: that, I could see, was beginning to die down now, and Rafferty's had stood firm, as always. I'd expected it to: Rafferty's is a good, soundly built place—it can weather practically anything. It *has* to be, of course, being located slap-bang on top of a statistical pole—for which fact you should be grateful, if you aren't already, because if it weren't for the solidity of Rafferty's and its regulars a whole lot of anomalies would come spilling out to expend themselves elsewhere, and the local citizenry would find themselves in all kinds of messes that they wouldn't even have thought possible, the very least of which would be having a whole plague of footloose gremlins on their hands. Tear down Rafferty's and all the other places like it, and the world would find itself halfway to being deontologized without the need of a Barnabas Tobin to help the process along.

And *that* was what was worrying me, because I knew what was in The Fat Man's mind, and it didn't bode well for Rafferty's. People like that are dangerous: they don't appreciate what precarious foundations Reality is built on, and they don't realize how easily the whole thing might be toppled if those foundations are undermined. They've been warned often enough, but they stubbornly refuse to believe in the pundits' warnings—which is pretty damn foolish of them, as *I'm* in a position to know. Just think what would happen if the whole world were suddenly deontologized, without any warning—and *you* along with it. Sure, *I've* adjusted to it all right— but how do you think *you'd* react? And even if you could take it, what about your Grandpa Julius and Aunt Maude and all the rest of your family and friends and acquaintances? Half of them would go crazy, at the very least; and what do you think the cosmos would be like if it were half filled with crazy subcorporeal entities, all interpenetrating and intermingling with the sane ones like you and me? It'd make Edgar Allen Schwarzkopf's worst nightmares look like a Shriners' Circus. And that state of things was precisely what The Fat Man and the others of his unbelieving ilk were working to bring on, even though their selfish little souls didn't know it. I shuddered subcorporeally at the very thought.

Something had to be done, and quickly, because I knew that if The Fat Man got out of there and followed through with his schemes, then Rafferty's was in trouble. Fortunately—or maybe it wasn't just fortunate: maybe it was The Scheme of Things using me as an instrument to right its balance—I knew precisely what to do. The trouble was, it depended on enlisting the gremlins to come to my aid.

Now that was a problem, because you can't talk reason to a gremlin. As a matter of fact, there's practically no way of persuading him to go along with anything at all, because there's no way of getting him to hold still and listen. Unless, that is, you have The Power, like Rafferty and Moira; and that was something I'd never been blessed with. The only way I could think of to get the gremlins' cooperation was to start off doing what I had in mind on my own bat, and then hope they'd see it as a new kind of game and join in just for the sheer hell of it.

So I concentrated all my energies and directed them, not toward The Fat Man, but toward the thin man inside him who was screaming to be let out. That thin man was a pretty decent sort actually, as I've already said, and there had to be a finite probability that he might have come into being in The Fat Man's place; otherwise he wouldn't have been there at all. The trouble was, that probability was mighty low; it was only the advent of the Storm that had actualized it at all. And while I had some voluntary control over probabilities, just as the gremlins did, I didn't have very good coordination of it, and I knew damn well that I didn't have the ability all on my own to realize something as inherently improbable as the thin man's having grown up in The Fat Man's place. The gremlins could manage it, if I got enough of them in there all pulling together; that was why I needed their help.

So I focused all my attention on the thin man, as I said, and tried my damnedest to imagine what he might be like. It was hard, I can tell you—and not just because, as you may already have gathered, my attention has a tendency to wander at times. It was hard apart from that, hard to imagine The Fat Man being anything other than The Fat Man, all piggish and jowly and mean, let alone to imagine him as slender and dapper and brimming with good-hearted benevolence. But that was the way it had to be.

Slowly a picture of the thin man began to build up in my mind. There was something graceful about him—something catlike and just a little bit effeminate. A delicate smile played on his face, so delicate that you almost had to look twice to be sure it was really there. There was a sort of Old World courtesy about him, and it was easy to picture him helping an old lady across the street or stopping to pat a passing child on the head (somewhat fastidiously) just because he was benevolently taken with its innocent beauty. It was obvious that he would wear a carnation in his buttonhole—a *white* carnation—and probably he'd put on white gloves when he went out for a stroll, and carry a little Charlie Chaplin cane. Yes, I decided, I definitely liked him—he was a little ridiculous, but kind and amusing. Rather like W.

Worthington Enderby, in fact...but no, I mustn't let my mind wander.

From one corner of my awareness, I noticed that a couple of gremlins had stopped by to watch what I was doing. They were definitely curious. I risked a slight flicker in their direction in order to catch their attention; but they shied away. Disappointed, I went back to my task. Presently I noticed they were back, and one or two others with them. I redoubled my efforts.

At last one of the gremlins caught on. The game amused him, as I'd hoped it would, and I felt him alongside me pitching in. The image of the thin man grew clearer in my mind, but I was still all too aware that it was The Fat Man who was in reality sitting in front of me, grunting to himself and porkily sweating beneath the strain of my efforts.

But I was lucky: my game was catching on. More of the gremlins joined in, singly at first and then by twos and threes, and I felt their whoops of excitement as they warmed to the task. Presently there were enough of them at it so that I felt safe to drop out; from now on they could do a better job without my own unskilled fumblings to interfere with what they were doing. I withdrew, distancing myself in order to get a better view of the proceedings.

At first I could see nothing out of the ordinary, except for a slight golden haze that seemed to cling to The Fat Man and blur his outlines a little. And then he started to melt. I mean that literally: great rolls of fat were oozing down from him and evaporating away into immaterial ectoplasm. Slowly what remained of him dissolved into transparency, and within it the lineaments of the thin man began to waver into form. Once, briefly, the old Fat Man seemed all at once to flicker back into being and sit there, flabbily impenetrable—I told you he was strong; and after all he was fighting for his life, such as it was. His lips were shaping the same words over and over and over, as if they were an incantation by which he hoped to save himself: "I don't believe it...I don't believe it...I don't believe it...." But he'd picked the wrong last refuge to fall back on: unbelieving can never save you, as I think I've already said. It didn't save him, certainly: all at once he blinked entirely out of existence, and the thin man was sitting there in his place. His hands were folded on the table in front of him, and a delicately self-satisfied smile was playing on his lips. I think he saw me, somehow—maybe I'd been concentrating so hard that I was partially materialized there in front of him—because he rose from the booth and picked up his cane and made a courteous little bow in my general direction. Then, after turning to brush the bench off fastidiously, he seated himself again. He was wearing white gloves, just as I'd imagined him, and a white carnation in his buttonhole.

The gremlins dispersed; they'd had their fun. One by one they flickered out; the Storm had died away now, and I guess they figured they'd find more amusement over on The Other Side where the waves wouldn't quite have spent themselves yet. I let my awareness spread outward once more to take in the whole of Rafferty's.

Rafferty himself was standing imperturbably behind the bar, with his arm around Moira. In the rear booth, James Clerk Maxwell was curled up, sound asleep; I took a peek into his mind, and he was dreaming of mice. Across from him, Spassky and Fischer were still immersed in their three-dimensional chess—it was shaping up to a stalemate, just as I'd figured, but the moves they'd been making would give them conversational material for years to come. Byron Wilcox was sitting staring vaguely off into space; I couldn't tell whether he was inspired or simply in a stupor. At the bar, Louella van Doren had her arm around Isherwood Foster; the poor fellow was still as rigid as a post, but Louella didn't seem to mind. Soleful Susie stood dabbing at her eyes—her memories of Sam hadn't quite dissolved away as yet, apparently—while in front of her John Edgar Harding sat hunched forward on the bar, with his chin cradled in his hands. I took a peek at him, and saw that he was mulling over a new insight he'd just had into the nature of the Unrequited Middle.

The thin man leaned out from his booth and waved delicately to Soleful Susie. She nodded at him, shoved her handkerchief back into her sleeve, and went behind the bar to fetch him another drink. Rafferty let go of Moira and set about mixing it. There was a smile on Moira's face as she watched him work—a smile of total devotion. I felt a pang of jealousy shimmer through me, but I held it in.

The thin man got up from his booth and walked gracefully across to the bar. He seated himself on the same stool The Fat Man had occupied earlier. "Nice place you have here," he said to Rafferty. "A very pleasant atmosphere—very pleasant indeed."

"We try to keep things cheerful," said Rafferty, and Moira nodded approvingly.

The thin man looked across at Soleful Susie. He smiled at her and she smiled weakly back. Then he turned to Moira. "An attractive young woman, that," he said to her, loud enough so that Susie could hear. "The two of you add a most agreeable touch to the decor."

"I like to think so," Moira said, smiling. And Soleful Susie flushed with pleasure.

Rafferty turned and set the drink down in front of the thin man. "That will be a dollar twenty-five, will it not?" said the thin man, reaching for his billfold.

Rafferty waved him off. "Oh, no," he said. "Tonight it ain't necessary. Tonight I got something to celebrate—drinks are on the house."

"On the house?" Louella van Doren said. "Isn't that wonderful, Ishy?" But Isherwood Foster made no reply.

Byron Wilcox overheard, too. He snapped out of his trance and waved enthusiastically at Susie. But Susie's attention was fixed on the thin man, so Moira went to take the order instead.

Old John Edgar Harding raised his head and winked at me. At least, he winked in the general direction of the shelves behind the bar, which was where my major focal node was concentrated just at that moment. I summoned up the energy to half-materialize, and gave him an ectoplasmic wink in return.

Then I decided to fade—I was interested in seeing how things were going over on The Other Side. I refocused myself, gave myself a Moebius twist, and flipped over. I was feeling more cheerful than I had in a long time—maybe I was finally beginning to get over my unrequited passion for Moira—and I wanted to see what the gremlins had come up with for their latest game. Maybe they'd let me join in; I felt like it just then.

And that's the end of this story—at least, it's as good an end as any. All endings are arbitrary, anyway; there aren't any such things in Reality. Everything that *is* stretches on and on and on.

Maybe you don't believe that; but you'll learn eventually. Howard Hopper did, after all; and so did General Wilbur Prescott and Isadora Edison and Lady Beatrice Annabelle Scraggs. Even Edward Everett Peaslake had his intimations, and Ludwig Kleinsdorfer had a theory, as usual. And then there was Barnabas Tobin, of course—*he* learned his lesson in the end; the Scheme of Things saw to that. Just as it saw to The Fat Man, and just as it's seen to me.

Unbelieving can be dangerous, as I told you before. But don't worry about that—Rafferty has a tonic for it.

You'll be around *sometime,* I know. I'm looking forward to seeing you.

# Growing Boys
## by Robert Aickman

*Robert Aickman isn't yet famous in the United States, though he's published nine books in England, most of them collections of fantastic and macabre tales. He won the World Fantasy Award for Best Short Story in 1975, and you'll easily understand why as you read this more recent novella about twin boys who are, quite literally, monsters. Aickman is blessed not only with literary talent of a high order, but also with a thorough understanding of human nature... which enables him to tell a very frightening story indeed.*

The first time it occurred to poor Millie that something might really be wrong was, on the face of it, perfectly harmless and commonplace.

Uncle Stephen, the boys' great-uncle, had found the words, conventional though the words were. "You're much too big a boy to make messes like that, Rodney. And you too, of course, Angus."

"*Angus* wasn't making a mess," Rodney had retorted. "There's no need to bite his head off too."

"Keep quiet, boy, and clean yourself up," Uncle Stephen had rejoined, exactly as if he had been father to the lads, and a good and proper father also.

In reality, however, Uncle Stephen was of course a bachelor.

"I'll take you up to the bathroom, Rodney," Millie had intervened. "If you'll excuse us for a few moments, Uncle Stephen."

Uncle Stephen had made no effort to look pleasant and social. Rather, he had grated with irritation. When Millie took Rodney out of the room, Uncle Stephen was glaring at her other son, defying him to move, to speak, to breathe, to exist except upon sufferance.

It was certainly true that the boys lacked discipline. They were a major inconvenience and burden, overshadowing the mildest of Millie's joys. Even when they were away at school, they oppressed her mind. There was nowhere else where they were ever away, and even the headmaster, who had been at London University with Phineas, declined to accept them as boarders, though he had also declined to give any precise reason. When Millie had looked very pale, he had said, as gently as he could, that it was better not to enter into too much explanation: experience had taught him that. Call it an intuition, he had explained. Certainly it had settled the matter.

She had supposed that, like so many things, the headmaster's decision might have related to the fact that the boys were twins. Twins ran in her family, and the two other cases she knew of, both much older than she was, did not seem to be happy twins. None the less, until the coming of Rodney and Angus, and though she would have admitted it to few people, she had always wished she had a twin herself: a twin sister, of course. Mixed twins were something especially peculiar. She had never herself actually encountered a case, within the family, or without. She found it difficult to imagine.

Now, Millie no longer wished for a twin. She hardly knew any longer what she wished for, large, small, or totally fantastic.

All that notwithstanding (and, of course, much, much more), Millie had never supposed there to be anything very exceptional about her situation. Most mothers had troubles of some kind; and there were many frequently encountered varieties from which she had been mercifully spared, at least so far. Think of Jenny Holmforth, whose Mikey drank so much that he was virtually unemployable! Fancy having to bring up Audrey and Olivia and Proserpina when you had always to be looking for a part-time job as well, and with everyone's eyes on you, pitying, contemptuous, no longer even lascivious!

But upstairs in the bathroom, it came to Millie, clearly and consciously for the first time, that the boys were not merely too big to make messes: they were far, far too big in a more absolute sense. Rodney seemed almost to fill the little bathroom. He had spoken of Uncle Stephen biting his head off. That would have been a dreadful transaction; like... But Millie drew back from the simile.

Of course, for years no one could have failed to notice that the boys were enormous; and few had omitted to refer to it, jocularly or otherwise. The new element was the hypothesis that the irregularity went beyond merely social considerations. It existed in a limbo where she and her husband, Phineas, might well find themselves virtually alone with it, and very soon.

Millie had read English Language and Literature and knew of the theory that Lady Wilde and her unfortunate son had suffered from acromegaly. That appeared to have been something that ran in Lady Wilde's family, the Elgees; because Sir William had been quite stunted. But of course there were limits even to acromegaly. About Rodney and Angus, Millie could but speculate.

When all the clothes had been drawn off Rodney, she was appalled to think what might happen if ever in the future she had to struggle with him physically, as so often in the past.

Re-entering the drawing room, Rodney pushed in ahead of her, as he always did.

Angus seized the opportunity to charge out, almost knocking her down. He could be heard tearing upstairs: she dreaded to think for what. It mattered more when her respected Uncle Stephen was in the house.

She looked apologetically at Uncle Stephen and managed to smile. When her heart was in it, Millie still smiled beautifully.

"Rodney," roared Uncle Stephen, "sit down properly, uncross your legs, and wait until someone speaks to you first."

"He'd better finish his tea," said Millie timidly.

"He no longer deserves anything. He's had his chance and he threw it away."

"He's a very big boy, Uncle Stephen. You said so yourself."

"*Too* big," responded Uncle Stephen. "Much *too* big."

The words had been spoken again, and Millie knew they were true.

Uncle Stephen and Millie talked for some time about earlier days and of how happiness was but a dream and of the disappearance of everything that made life worth living. They passed on to Phineas's lack of prospects and to the trouble inside Millie that no doctor had yet succeeded in diagnosing, even to his own satisfaction. Millie offered to show Uncle Stephen round the garden, now that it had almost stopped raining.

"It's quite a small garden," she said objectively.

But Uncle Stephen had produced his big, ticking watch from his waistcoat pocket, which sagged with its weight. There was this sagging pocket in all his waistcoats. It helped to confirm Uncle Stephen's identity.

"Can't be done, Millie. I'm due back for a rubber at six and it's five-eleven already."

"Oh, I'm terribly sad, Uncle Stephen. Phineas and I have raised the most enormous pelargoniums. Mainly luck, really. I should so much like you to see them." Then Millie said no more.

"My loss, Millie dear. Let me embrace my sweet girl before I go."

He crushed her for a minute or two, then stepped back, and addressed Angus.

"Stand up and give me your hand."

Angus soared upwards but kept his hands to himself.

"I mean to shake your hand," bawled Uncle Stephen, in his quarter-deck manner; even though he had never mounted a quarter-deck, except perhaps on Navy Day.

Angus extended his proper hand, and Uncle Stephen wrenched it firmly.

When Millie and he were for a moment alone together in the little hall, something that could not happen often, Uncle Stephen asked her a question.

"Have you a strap? For those two, I mean."

"Of course not, Uncle Stephen. We prefer to rely on persuasion and, naturally, love."

Uncle Stephen yelled with laughter. Then he became very serious. "Well, get one. And use it frequently. I've seen what I've seen in this house. I know what I'm talking about. Get two, while you're about it. The Educational Supply Association will probably help you."

"Phineas will never use anything like that."

"Then you'd better consider leaving him, Millie dear, because there's trouble coming. You can always make a home with me and bring the boys with you. You know that, Millie. There's a welcome for you at any time. Now: one more kiss and I must vamoose."

As soon as the front door shut, Angus, who had been watching and listening to the scene through the hole the twins had made in the upstairs woodwork, almost fell on her in every sense.

Back in the drawing room she saw that Rodney, released from thrall, had resumed his tea, and had already eaten everything that had been left. Noting this, Angus began to bawl.

It might be all right later, but at that hour Millie was afraid lest the neighbors intervene: Hubert and Morwena Ellsworthy, who were ostentatiously childless.

"Don't cry, Ang," said Rodney, putting his arm tightly around Angus's shoulder. "Uncle Stephen always hogs the lot. You know that."

Angus's rage of weeping failed to abate.

Rodney gave him a tender and succulent kiss on the cheek.

"We'll go to the Lavender Bag," he said. "I'm still hungry too. I think I've got the worms. I expect you have as well. Race you. Ready Steady...Go."

As the race began on the spot, the picking up and clearing up for Millie to do were not confined to the tea things.

The Lavender Bag was a café at the other end of The Parade. It was run by the Misses Palmerston, four of them. It was a nice enough place in its way, and useful for the release through long lunchtimes and teatimes of high spirits or low spirits, as the case might be. Millie went there often, and so did her friends, though soon she would have no friends. Some of them distrusted her already because they knew she had a degree.

Now, Millie suddenly set down the cake tray she was holding. She took care not to let the large crumbs fall to the carpet.

"Oh God," gulped Millie, sinking to the edge of the settee; and almost to her knees. "God, please, God. What have I done to be punished? Please tell me, God, and I'll do something else."

Only some outside intervention could possibly avail.

She had never been very good at having things out with anyone, not even with girl friends, and Phineas had undoubtedly weakened her further. All the same, something simply had to be attempted, however recurrent, however foredoomed.

To make a special occasion of it, she put on a dress, even though it had to be a dress that Phineas would recognize: at least, she supposed he must. The boys were still rampaging about at the Lavender Bag, which in the summer remained open for light snacks until 8 p.m. They liked to run round the tables wolfing everything that others had left on plates and in saucers. The Misses Palmerston merely looked on with small, lined smiles. Simultaneously the boys were normal children and flashing young blades.

"Why *should* you feel at the end of your tether?" enquired Phineas. "After all, every day's your own. Certainly far more than my days are mine."

If only one could give him a proper drink before one attempted to talk seriously with him; that is to talk about oneself!

"It's the boys, Phineas. You don't know what it's like being at home with them all day."

"The holidays won't last for ever."

"After only a week, I'm almost insane." She tried to rivet his attention. "I mean it, Phineas."

Millie knew extremely well that she herself would be far more eloquent and convincing if Phineas's abstinence had not years ago deprived her too, though with never the hint of an express prohibition, but rather the contrary. When she was reading, she had learned of the Saxons never taking action unless the matter had been considered by the council, first when sober and then when drunk. It was the approach that was needed now.

"What's the matter with the boys this time?" asked Phineas.

Millie twitched. "They're far too tall and big. How long is it since you looked at them, Phineas?"

"Being tall's hardly their fault. I'm tall myself and I'm their father."

"You're tall in a different way. You're willowy. They're like two great red bulls in the house."

"I'm afraid we have to look to *your* family for that aspect of it. Consider your Uncle Nero, if I may venture to mention him."

"I don't like him being called that."

"But you can't deny he's bulky. There's no one of his build anywhere up my family tree, as far as I am aware. For better or for worse, of course. There are more troublesome things than sturdiness, especially in growing boys."

Millie did not have to be told. She had often reflected that Phineas, seeping tiredly over the settee at the end of the day's absence, was like an immensely long anchovy, always with the same expression at the end of it; and in the next bed it was, of course, far worse.

"Then you're not prepared to help in any way? Suppose I have a breakdown?"

"There'd be no danger of that, Millie, if only you could persuade yourself to eat more sensibly."

"Perhaps you could persuade your sons of that?"

"I shall try to do so when they are older. At present, they are simply omnivorous, like all young animals. It is a stage we go through, and then try to pass beyond."

"Then you do admit that they *are* like animals?"

"I suppose it depends partly upon which animals."

Millie knew perfectly well, however, that for her they were not like animals, or not exactly; and despite what she had said to Phineas. They were like something far more frightening.

"Uncle Stephen was very upset by them before you came home."

Phineas merely smiled at her. He had all but finished the lactose drink which he consumed every evening before their meal.

"Uncle Stephen said we ought to see what discipline could do."

"Discipline would hardly prevent the boys growing up," observed Phineas.

And it was still a matter of hours before it was even sunset.

The boys could be heard approaching in what had become their usual way. They stumbled in through the open French window.

"Got any good grub in your pockets, Dad?" shouted Rodney.

With a smile, Phineas produced a dun-coloured bag of huge, gluey toffees: something he would never have put into his own mouth.

The boys fell into chairs and began to pass the bag from hand to hand.

"Mum going to cook supper soon?"

"I expect so, Angus."

"What's it going to be, Dad?"

"Better ask her, Rodney."

It was not, she knew, that he aimed to instil manners. It was merely that he could not care less.

One thing Millie had particularly resented was that every single evening she had to produce two very different meals, and then be silently sneered at if she herself chose the more exciting one, or consumed any scrap of it.

Now Millie was past resentment. Panic had taken its place.

"We need food, Dad. You don't want us to outgrow our strength."

"Besides we're twins," said Angus.

It was hard to see where that came in, but Millie knew quite well that somewhere it very much did.

Everything was fundamentally her own fault. She was perfectly well aware of that. Everything always is one's own fault.

"Our reports come yet, Dad?"

"I don't think so, Rodney."

"You can't put them on the fire this time, because it's summer, but you *will* put them down the *topos*?"

"Unopened, Dad?" put in Angus. He was half on his feet again, and redder than ever.

"*Unopened*, Dad," insisted Rodney, though perhaps more calmly.

"Torn up, if you like," said Angus.

"We shall have to see," said Phineas. "Shan't we? When the time comes, that is."

He rose from the settee and walked quietly from the room.

"Oh Mum," said Rodney, jumping up and down. "Do get on with it."

The patience of the young is soon exhausted.

"We're hungry," Angus confirmed. "Remember we only had salad for lunch. Muck we called it."

It had been a cut-up which Phineas had not eaten the previous evening. One could not simply throw it away; and Phineas would never accept such things unless they were completely fresh. It was the trouble with food of that kind that no one ever wanted it all, and it then became useless. Nor was the household made of money. Phineas not only lacked prospects: he lacked a suitable income also. Unhappily, Phineas was an intellectual without either creativity or judgment. Millie had realized it even during those early days in the Camargue; when Rodney and Angus were being conceived.

In the kitchen, she was shaking so much she gashed the index finger of her left hand. It would, of course, have mattered more if she had been lefthanded, as were Phineas and the boys; but it was a nasty enough cut, which bled far too much, so that fair-sized gouts fell on the newly prepared vegetable matter, which thereupon had to be slowly picked over a further time. Blood oozed through Millie's handkerchief and spotted the dress she had specially put on.

At the same time, the big fry-up for the boys was beginning to run out of fat.

In the end, they came charging in. Millie was weeping, of course, and in more and more of a muddle. Once she had never muddled things, but quite the contrary: perhaps that was why she wept now.

"For God's sake, Mum! we're hungry. We told you."

"Hungry as hunters."

What had that originally meant? A kind of horse? A kind of tiger? A kind of man?

"What is it, Mum? What are we getting?"

"Chops and liver and bacon and things," replied Millie in a very low voice, possibly inaudible above the sizzle. "I've hurt my finger."

"We could eat the entire animal," said Angus.

Phineas always lay on his bed while a major meal was in prepara- tion,  and Millie had to ascend and summon him, because the boys simply did not do it, however often she asked them.

Four days later, Millie's finger was as bad as ever, and her left hand almost unusable. She knew that incurable illness often first manifested itself through minor injuries which failed to clear up.

"Oh Mum, do get better!" admonished Angus at breakfast when she let slip the teapot.

"It's entirely a matter of eating the right things," observed Phineas mildly; "though, naturally, it'll take some months before you can expect to enjoy the benefits."

Phineas himself was eating a small quantity of muesli in skim milk. He always used a tiny teaspoon for such purposes.

The flap of the front-door letter-box was heard: presage everywhere of Charon's final shoulder-tap, bone against bone.

The boys made a dash, as they did each day; but this time Millie had reached the door of the room before them. She stood there facing them.

"We're going for the post, Mum."

"I'm going for it this morning. You both sit down, please."

"It may be our reports, Mum."

"I'm going this morning, Angus."

They were only a foot or two away, but before they could lay hands on her, she had not merely whipped open the door but also snatched the key out of the lock, flashed from the room, and managed to lock the door on the other side: all this with the real use of one hand only.

For the moment she had proved as effective as she used to be, but there had been something strange about the incident; which had all begun with a vivid dream she had had the previous night, so vivid that she remembered it (or imagined it) still, and in detail: a small dream really, but prophetic.

For the moment Phineas had been left to manage the two roaring boys. The French window was in the drawing room, but soon the boys would be out through the dining-room casements and making mischief of some kind. Happily, the big drawing room window was never opened until after breakfast. The boys had never as yet intentionally smashed their way in or out, but Millie dreaded to see their huge faces gazing at her, diminishing her, from the world outside.

None the less, Millie paused for a moment, and quite consciously. Much was at stake if her dream could be taken at all seriously.

It could. Millie had advanced into the hall and the delivery had proved to consist of two accounts rendered and a packet with the school crest upon the envelope.

Millie went back into the drawing room, and, sitting down, even straightened the crease in her jeans. Then, while in the locked room the abominable hubbub raged on, she calmly opened the boys' reports.

Reports they had been in her dream, and dire ones: at once a burden, but also, in certain ways, a release, or a faint hope of release. The actual packet proved, however, simply to contain a letter, together with some appeal forms for reconditioning the school chapel. The letter, addressed to Phineas, was from the deputy headmaster. Millie read it.

Dear Mr. Morke,

I know you will forgive my writing on behalf of the Headmaster, who has unfortunately been in Hospital since the middle of the Spring Term, as you may possibly have heard from your Sons.

I very much regret to tell you that the Trustees, to whom the matter has been referred in the absence of the Headmaster, take the view that no useful purpose would be served by the return of your Sons to the School at the commencement of the Term now ahead, that is to say, the Autumn Term.

It is the view of the Trustees, in which I am bound to say I fully concur, that the Boys are too physically mature to benefit from the ordinary course of Tuition in Class, however excellent. Perhaps they may be regarded as outside and beyond the normal school disciplines.

In the circumstances, there would seem no advantage to our delivering the usual Reports upon the conduct of the Boys during the Summer Term, just past. Doubtless you will have drawn your own conclusions from the Reports relating to previous Terms, and will scarcely be surprised by the Decision which the Trustees have reached.

It is the custom of the School to extend Best Wishes to all its Old Boys when finally they move towards New Fields of Endeavour; and I am sure that the Headmaster, with whom, as I understand, you are on terms of long-standing and personal friendship, would wish me to make no exception in the present cases.

May I venture to remind you of the Outstanding Account in respect of the Boys' attendance during the Summer Term, and including a number of important Extras? The Bursar requests me to take this opportunity of remarking that he would be most grateful for a settlement during the next seven days, as he is keeping his Books open for this single item, and is being pressed by the School's Honorary Accountants. I am sure you will understand.

Yours sincerely,
PHILIP DE SODA
(Revd., M.A., B.D.)

Millie rose, unlocked the door, and re-entered the dining room, holding the letter high above her head.

"There are no reports, Phineas. They've been expelled."

When the boys had been much younger, it might have availed to hold the letter up there, but now it was pointless, because they were far taller than she was, as well as in every way more brawny. The letter was out of her hands in a flash.

It was very unlikely that they could understand it, and doubtful if they could even read all of it, but she herself had provided the clue, and at least they could take in the signature.

"It's the Sod!" cried Angus. "The Sod wrote it."

"Give it here," commanded Rodney. Within seconds the floor was littered with tiny scraps of paper, and the boys were standing shoulder to shoulder against the world, completely obscuring the framed photograph of their mother on a horse.

"What are you going to do now, Phineas?" enquired Millie.

Phineas was, as always, making a point of being undisturbed. He continued to chase the last particles of saturated muesli with his toy teaspoon.

"Well?" enquired Millie. "Our sons have been expelled from their school. You'll have to do something with them."

"Was the term 'expulsion' actually employed in the letter?"

"Of course not. Schoolmasters don't use it nowadays. They're afraid of libel actions."

"Well then, we mustn't exaggerate. It's not at all uncommon for a headmaster to reach the view that a boy would fare better in some other school. Nowadays, there's no question of a stigma at all. The change in itself is often entirely beneficial."

He drew a crispbread from the packet, broke it in half, returned one half to the packet, and began to break up the other into reasonably symmetrical pieces on his plate.

Each of the boys now had his arm around the other's shoulder, in the style of Tweedledum and Tweedledee. But they had no other resemblance to Tweedledum and Tweedledee.

"If you don't do something, Uncle Stephen will," said Millie.

The boys extended their thick red tongues at her, but Phineas' eye was glancing at the *Guardian* which lay on the table for him alone to read and take to work.

Millie went upstairs, locked the door of the bedroom, and began looking through her old address book. It had little to offer, apart from varying shades and intensities of nostalgia and regret

She lay down on her unmade bed, turning her back on Phineas's unmade bed.

She could not think while the boys were in the house; or, for different reasons, Phineas either.

She could hear birds singing, and, from the next house, screeching music for early housewives. She knew that they were supposed to choose the records for themselves.

Then, duly, there was the din of the boys leaving. At the moment their craze was to do something with dogs in the local wood—any dogs, as she understood it.

She had no idea what it was that they did, nor did she wish to know. The wood was of course deserted on a weekday morning, apart from the usual misfits straying about, and unlikely to present much of a problem to boys such as Rodney and Angus.

Millie gave it a little longer, lest she walk into Phineas; then she unlocked the door and went down.

Phineas had departed for work, with all the others. She had feared that the letter from Mr. de Soda might have held him back. She began to collect the torn pieces into a small plastic bag that was lying about, because she proposed to keep them. It was a surprisingly long job: she could not but remember that the mills of God tear exceeding small. Then she began to clear up, and, later, to wash up. She could count on a little tranquillity until the boys returned, raging for their midday meal.

But the bell rang, and then there was that same flop from the letter-box: somewhat less menacing, however, when it is presumably a matter not of a postal delivery, but more probably of a harmless circular.

Millie went out quite calmly. Duly, it was a publicity leaflet, a throwaway.

Your Fortune is in your Hands
Consult
Thelma Modelle
NOW

Modern Palmistry
Absolutely Private and Confidential
Normally no need for an appointment
Nothing spooky    Nothing embarrassing

## 4 The Parade

"There is no reason why the human hand
should not provide as good a guide to
individual destiny as any other."

The concluding quotation was unascribed. Millie fancied that it came from Aldous Huxley. She seemed to remember encountering something of the kind when trying to read one of Huxley's works at Oxford. The leaflet was inexpensively produced in simple black on simple white. It was quite small.

Millie had almost finished her immediate chores. There was little incentive to embellish the tasks. She stuffed the bag of torn-up paper into her handbag, because she could think of nothing else to do with it at the moment and set forth for 4 The Parade. Reason and careful thought had proved alarmingly unfruitful. The moment had come to give the subliminal a trial; if that was the applicable word. An omen was an omen, and there were few of them.

The Parade was her own fish shop, selling rough vegetables and packet cheese as well. She had never previously had occasion to heed the number. Upstairs had lived the rheumatism lady, who went round all the old folk in her little car. Millie was aware that lately the rheumatism lady had moved to a proper clinic, paid for by the ratepayers; because everyone was talking about it. Now at the foot of the stairs there was an arrow, with a curious curve in it pointing upwards, and the name THELMA MODELLE newly painted at the heart of it in grey. Plain THELMA would, perhaps, have been too much like an unregulated fairground; and changing times were rendering the title "Madame" obsolete even in such cases as this. There was nothing to do but ascend.

Perhaps, have been too much like an unregulated fairground; and changing times were rendering the title "Madame" obsolete even in such cases as this. There was nothing to do but ascend.

Thelma Modelle came out on to the little landing. Her jeans were pale green and she wore a sleeveless grey jumper which looked as if it were woven from used raffia. As promised, there was to be no attempt at formality or mystification.

Thelma Modelle had a smooth dark brown mop, falling over one side of her angular, sallow face; and the enormous, rather empty eyes of the seer or pythoness.

Indeed, at first she stared at Millie for a perceptibly long time without uttering a word.

"Well, come in," she said at last, as if there had been some demur.

They were in the rheumatism lady's small sitting room, though already it looked much more run down. The rheumatism lady's little water-colors had been replaced by wall cards bearing emblems of the zodiac; somewhat stained, and by no means a complete set. There was a round black table in the center of things, with two black composition chairs opposite one another.

"Sit down," said Thelma Modelle, still a little petulantly, "and call me Thelma."

Millie sat, as one does at such times; but Thelma continued to stand. She was observing Millie.

"Would you prefer to smoke?"

"I've given it up. My husband made me stop it."

"Then why are you carrying a packet of Players in your handbag?"

Millie felt that she had turned pale and puce at the same time.

"It's an unopened packet. I suppose you can see that too."

"One thing I can't see is why you're here. What are you looking for?"

"Your leaflet came through my door. Just this moment, in fact. So will you please read my palm, or whatever it is you do?" Millie extended her hand across the table.

"That's the wrong one," said Thelma. "But never mind. It would be no good with you in any case. I'll see what the cards have to say."

She picked up a working pack from the mantel behind her. Millie would have supposed there would be shuffling, perhaps cutting, certainly a careful and symmetrical laying out. But all Thelma did was chuck six or seven apparently random cards across the surface of the table.

"You're in trouble right enough," said Thelma.

"What sort of trouble?" asked Millie steadily.

"You'll know the details best."

"What's going to happen about it?"

"It's going to get worse."

"Yes, I suppose it's bound to do that."

"I should try running away, if I were you. Hide. Change your name. Change your appearance. Change everything."

"Join the raggle-taggle gypsies, in fact?" After all, one must at times seek some proportion of things.

"Please!" exclaimed Thelma, "I *am* a gypsy."

"I'm so sorry." But that was wrong too. "I wasn't meaning to be rude."

"The gypsies wouldn't *have* you."

"Why ever not?" But Millie was by now hardly surprised, hardly capable of surprise.

"You're marked."

"In what way? How am I marked? You don't mean that lacrosse accident?"

"No. Not that."

Millie reflected silently for a moment. If Thelma Modelle would sit down, as consultants normally do, it could be that much easier.

Millie spoke again. "Please tell me more."

"The cards won't go any further."

"Well, something else then." After all, there was a crystal on the mantel too, though Millie had never seen one in her life before (it was smaller than she had supposed); and some sort of large, shapeless thing leaning against the wall.

"If you want to know more, it will have to be sex."

Millie had heard at Oxford of "sex magic," and its alleged dangers. "I don't think I want that," she said.

"That's quite all right," said Thelma rather nastily. "I shouldn't advise you to find out more anyway."

"Why ever not? Is it really as terrible as all that?"

"It might make you mad."

The familiar Shakespearian phrase was really too much. Millie rose to her feet.

"How much do I owe you?"

Thelma's expression had become very odd.

"No money. Just look in again. While you still have time of your own."

"You've made a mistake there," said Millie. "The boys aren't going back. They've been expelled."

"I've never claimed to be right every time."

Millie managed to smile a little. "Please take some money. I have profited by your frankness."

"Not from you," said Thelma. "I've told you what you can do."

"I'll think about it," said Millie.

"You can come and live here if you've nowhere else to go."

"I can go to my Uncle Stephen. Actually he's pressing me."

"You can do whatever you like," said Thelma.

There was a scuffling up the stairs, and another client appeared. It was Dawn Mulcaster, mature, frustrated, and twittery as ever. She and Millie exchanged very faint smiles but no words. Millie sped downwards.

The curious thing was that, though nothing could have been more depressing and foreboding than Thelma's insights, yet Millie felt noticeably more buoyant than on her outward journey. As in the matter she had last night dreamed of, the burden was at the same time a release, or a faint hope of release. She was even able to muse smilingly upon a fortune-teller's obvious need of a receptionist; and upon the positively comical discrepancy between this particular fortune-teller's publicity and her performance. Perhaps the discrepancy was mainly in tone. All the same, surely the interview had been "spooky" in the extreme? Dawn Mulcaster would certainly be finding it so. Millie felt that she had done better than Dawn was likely to be doing. In fairness to Thelma Modelle's publicity person, Millie had to acknowledge that she did not feel in the least "embarrassed."

She stopped in the street for a moment. A more precise thought had struck her. Her cut finger was completely healed. Somehow she had even parted with the unpleasant bandage. She smiled; and continued homewards.

The boys stormed back, wolfed their food without a word to Millie, and stormed out again.

Millie washed up after the three of them; circulated round The Parade and The Avenue, shopping, meditating; put together two totally different evening meals; and then went upstairs to lie on her bed, in order to prepare for another confrontation with Phineas. She must keep up the pressure or go mad, as Thelma Modelle had predicted.

Indeed, when Millie fell asleep, she found she was dreaming of

Thelma's establishment, where she, Millie, now appeared to have a job of some kind, as she was seated at the toilet table in what had been the rheumatism lady's bathroom, and sorting through hundreds, perhaps thousands, of invoices in the desperate hope of finding her own. The invoices were on paper of different sizes and textures, and in many different handwritings, mostly illegible. Millie was amazed by the mental processes that must lie behind the ways in which many of the bills were laid out. Only those which had been drafted by Uncle Stephen were fully orderly. When Millie awoke, it occurred to her to wonder whether Thelma herself could write at all, or whether she relied mainly on bluff, as did Rodney and Angus though no one ever dared to mention it.

There was the noise of creeping about downstairs. Then Phineas's voice floated up the stairwell: "Millie!" She shrivelled. "Millie, where are you?"

It was far, far too early for his return. Could he have lost his job? That might be yet another burden which was not a burden entirely, but very faintly a forerunner.

Millie threw off the eiderdown, pulled on a jacket, and sauntered downstairs.

Phineas was positively prancing from room to room. It was impossible that he could have been promoted, because, in his position, there was no real promotion. His step seemed light and gay, as with the man in the ballad.

"I've been adopted!" cried Phineas, unable to contain himself until she had reached the ground floor, terra firma.

"Whatever for?"

"As Liberal candidate, of course. At North Zero."

"Where's that?"

"It's in Cornwall and Anew MacAndrew says I should have every chance."

She had been perfectly well aware that Phineas was frequenting the local Liberal Association and bringing their literature home. It was one of various activities of his that resulted in her being so often left alone with the boys.

"Does the Party find the money for your deposit, or do you have to do it?"

"I haven't the slightest idea. I haven't thought about it."

"Perhaps the boys can go down and canvass for you?"

"They're too young, as you can perfectly well imagine for yourself. I'm afraid I shall have to sacrifice much of my family life, and leave the boys more in the hands of their mother. I notice that you haven't congratulated me, Millie."

"If it's what you want, I'm pleased for you, Phineas. Provided, that is, that you find a new school for the boys before you set out."

"I haven't been able to think much about that, as you can imagine. I feel it is something their mother can perfectly well do for them, if the necessity should arise."

"I can and shall do nothing of the kind, Phineas. Finding a school for boys like that is the father's job. I mean it, Phineas."

She was almost glowing with resolution. She realized that to display moral qualities demands practice, just as much as intellectual and manual qualities. She had never really attended when, down the years, such truths had been hammered into her. But she also knew that much of her relied upon the boys being out of the house.

"I had hoped you might be pleased for me," said Phineas, entering the sitting room, and draping himself. "Could I have my lactose, please?"

"It's too early. It's only just past teatime." Phineas eschewed tea, because of the tannin, which affected both his colon and his autonomic structure.

"I'm going to get myself a cup of tea," said Millie. "And then I want to go on talking seriously."

In her heart, she was not in the least surprised to find, when she returned, that Phineas had taken himself off. Perhaps he had gone out to look for the boys. He liked to delude himself that he could "join in" their play, though Millie knew better, knew that he was accepted on the very thinnest of sufferance, for short periods only, and only for ulterior reasons. In the boys' eyes, there was very little to choose between Phineas's status and hers. She knew that, even if he did not.

Millie took her little tray upstairs, locked the bedroom door, took off her jacket once more, and wriggled beneath the eiderdown. She had brought up the Family Size packet of Playmate biscuits, really meant for the boys.

But, contrary to expectation, Phineas drifted back in no time. Elation at the thought of the new and more fulfilling life that lay before him had probably made him restless. Soon, he was tapping at their bedroom door.

"Let me in, please."

"I'm having a rest. I'll come out when it's time for your supper."

"Where are the boys?"

"In the wood with the dogs, as far as I know."

"It might be better if they were encouraged to stay more in their own home."

"That's their father's job."

"Millie, what are you doing in there?"

"I'm lying down, and now I'm going back to sleep." She knew that by now there was not a hope of it, though she had spoken as positively as she could.

So positively, indeed, that there was quite a pause. Then Phineas said, "I might as well have my lactose now. I've had a lot to think about today."

Grumpily, Millie emerged. Rest and peace had gone, as well as slumber.

"Let me carry the tray," said Phineas. "It's right that I should do these things when I'm here."

He was not at all used to the work, and had to descend the stairs very slowly, like a stick-insect.

"What is going to happen to your job?" asked Millie, as soon as the tray was on the sink-surround, more or less in safety.

"That must come second. In life, one has to make such decisions."

"Meanwhile, what pays the boys' school fees? They won't have them at the ordinary local school. You know that."

"I shall have my Parliamentary salary in the end, and shall of course make you an allowance for things of that kind. Could I please have my lactose?"

"So you propose quite calmly to live entirely on me. On my little income from Daddy's estate?"

"Not if you do not wish it. You and the boys can do that, if necessary; and lucky we are that it should be so. I myself can apply for a maintenance grant."

"Do you mean the dole?"

"Of course not. I refer to the Applecroft Fund for supporting Liberal candidates. I did not intend to approach them but I always can if you lack all interest in your husband's career in life."

"Phineas!" Millie tried to sound positively menacing. "I tell you again that I accept no responsibility for the future of the boys, financial or otherwise. They are out of my hands."

"Well, Millie, in the very, very last resort, that's a matter for the common law, is it not? But there is no need at all for it to come to that."

"It would be bad for your chances, if it did."

"Not nowadays. Your notion of the world often seems antediluvian, Millie dear."

"The boys neither love nor want me. Not that they love or want you either."

Quite unselfconsciously, Phineas smiled. "What boys feel for their father is something a woman cannot understand, not even their mother. It's something that really *is* antediluvian, Millie."

"If you had any understanding whatever of what goes on around you, you'd know better than to talk such rubbish."

"No one is more concerned than I am about what goes on everywhere in the world."

His eyes were filled with a need for his mission to be understood and appreciated; for the lactose that by now really was due.

Millie set about preparing it.


"Where are the boys?" asked Phineas, as the sun sank in unnoticed glory.

"I expect they're at the Lavender Bag, as they were last night." Millie looked at her watch; the boys having stopped the clock so often that it no longer seemed to her worth paying for repairs. "No. The Lavender Bag will have shut some time ago."

"Perhaps it's some kind of special evening?"

"They would have come here and gorged themselves and then gone back."

"Well, what *are* we to think, Millie? It really might be better if you took more interest in what your sons do. I shan't be able to give so much time to it in the future. You must understand that."

Millie went to the record-player and put on Honegger's *Pacific 231*. The next piece on the record was Mossolov's factory music. Before the record could reach Gravini's *Homage to Marinetti,* Millie turned the machine off.

"Would you like your supper? I should like mine."

"I shall have to take more care over what I eat now that I have so much greater responsibility."

But when, shortly afterwards, the moment came, he seemed to pick and niggle very much as usual. Her own appetite was undoubtedly the more disturbed of the two.

In the end, the police arrived, though not until it was quite dark. Most unusually, it was Phineas who unwound himself and let the man in. For this reason, Millie did not learn his rank: lacked the opportunity to glance at his official card. The man was not in his blues, but dressed overall by a multiple outfitter.

"Good evening, madam. Do either of you know anything of two men named Angus Morke and Rodney Morke? They've given this address."

"They are our two sons, officer," said Phineas.

"Indeed, sir? I should hardly have thought it. Certainly not in your case, madam. These two are fully-grown men. In fact, rather more than that."

"Don't be ridiculous, officer," said Phineas. "They are our sons, and we know exactly how big they are."

"I wonder if you altogether do, sir. If you don't mind my saying so, madam. It took a whole squad to get them under any kind of control. And, even then, there are some very nasty injuries which the Court will be hearing about tomorrow, in addition to the other charges. The Sergeant is worried about whether the cells will hold them. The station isn't Parkhurst Prison. It's only intended for quiet overnight cases. But I mustn't do all the talking. I've only come to make the usual routine enquiries. The two men—boys, if you prefer, madam—do really reside here then?"

"Of course they do," said Phineas. "This is their home."

"If you say so, sir. Now, how old would each of them be?"

"They are twins. Surely you must have realized that? As far as I recall, they are rising sixteen."

"You mean that they're fifteen, sir?"

"Yes, I think that's right. Fifteen."

"It's incredible, if you don't mind my saying so, madam."

"In the course of your work," said Phineas, "you must have realized that some boys grow faster than some other boys."

It was high time for Millie to speak. "What have the two of them done?"

"What are they *alleged* to have done?" Phineas corrected. "If anything, of course."

The officer made it clear that from now on, and whatever the rule book might say, he preferred to deal with Millie.

"I'm afraid the charges are rather serious, madam. In fact, we've never before had anything to compare with it since the station first opened, which of course was when most of the houses like this one were being built. We haven't had much violence in the suburb, *serious* violence that is; though of course it's growing fast pretty well everywhere in the world."

"What have they done, officer? Please tell me. I'm perfectly able to face it." Again, the additional burden that could at the same time be a further remote prospect of freedom!

"Remember," put in Phineas, "that it's still only mere allegation. It is well known that the police exaggerate; sometimes very greatly. I speak as an adopted Parliamentary candidate."

"Do you indeed, sir? For somewhere round here, that is?"

"No, not locally. But it makes no difference."

"Well, madam," said the officer, with professional quietness, "as for the charges, they include a long list of assaults, fifteen at least so far, and we are expecting more. Some of those we already have are very serious indeed. Not what we're used to round here, as I have remarked. More like the Glasgow docks in the old days, I should have said. Then there's a lot of damage to property. A lot of damage to a lot of property, I should have put it. Doors stove in and roofs ripped about and ornaments smashed. There are a couple of attempted rapes expected to be reported soon, from what the officers say. A couple at least."

"In these times, there's no such thing as *attempted* rape," objected Phineas. "It's a rape, or it isn't a rape, and most people are very doubtful about it even if it's supposed to be proved."

"And that's not to mention the injuries inflicted on the officers, which we don't like at all, madam, especially in a quiet district like this."

"No," said Millie soberly, "I'm sure not."

"Now if I could have a few details of the education these lads have had? Supposing them to have had any, of course. But it's no matter for joking, all the same. It's an offence too, not to educate a child."

Millie realized that the night air was coming in through the front door which Phineas had left open: the night air of a hot summer. Phineas made no move, and Millie did not care to leave him just then even for a single moment. Besides, closing the outer door might lead to new suspicions.

By the end of it, and indeed long before that, Millie knew perfectly well that Phineas should have produced the whisky, but that, thanks to Phineas, there was no whisky in the house. Most assuredly she could not be absent long enough to make tea, even supposing the officer to be interested in tea at that hour.

"If the accused really are what the law calls minors," said the officer, "then a parent will be required to attend the Court."

"Of course my husband will attend the Court," said Millie.

"Perhaps you too, madam? A mother can often influence the Justices more than a father."

Millie smiled. "I shall remember that, officer."

"Not that a case of this kind is likely to remain with Petty Sessions for long. It will be simply a matter of a quick committal, as far as I can see."

"I'm sure you are once more greatly exaggerating, officer," said Phineas, smiling in his turn.

"You'll be there to hear for yourself, sir," replied the officer, entirely reasonable.

When he had gone, Millie found it almost impossible even to speak to Phineas.

"I'm not sharing a room with you," she managed to say.

"Please yourself," said Phineas. "After today's news, I've still a great deal to think about and plan, as anyone but you would see at once."

Next morning, and really quite early next morning, the childless Hubert Ellsworthy was the first with the local news; or with a bit of it.

In his old yachting jumper, with part of the Club name still on it, and shapeless gray bags splashed with oil from his garden workshop, he stood there trying to arrange his scattered locks.

"I thought I ought to tell you first, Phineas, as, after all, we are neighbors. I've heard that there are two sex maniacs on the loose.

Apparently, the authorities feel we should warn one another to keep everything bolted and barred. What times we live in! Eh, Phineas?"

Millie, who had overheard this in her nightdress, could already see, from the bathroom window, Morwena Ellsworthy sealing every aperture with passe-partout, despite the season, and even pulling down blinds.

The next arrival was young Graham, the local weekly's cub reporter, as people described him, and the only one who left the office very often. Girls tended to tell him that they liked the name "Graham."

That time, Millie opened the door.

"May I come in for a few moments, Mrs. Morke? It's really rather important."

Millie had never before spoken to him, though, like everyone else, she knew who he was. He was a nice young lad, everyone said. In any case, he was by now sufficiently practiced in his profession never to take even the hint of negation as an answer.

"Well, what is it?" asked Millie. "Do sit down."

Phineas, having dealt with Hubert Ellsworthy, had gone back to bed. In the marital bedroom: Millie had spent the night on the lounge sofa-convertible which, at the time of hire-purchase, she had, consciously or subconsciously, made sure really was long enough and wide enough to live up to its brochure.

"You've heard the news, Mrs. Morke?"

"What news in particular?"

"The police station in The Approach has been completely wrecked. I've never seen anything like it," said young Graham very seriously.

"Well, what can I do? Would you like a cup of coffee?"

"Not just at the moment, Mrs. Morke, though thanks all the same. The thing is that the Station Inspector tipped us the wink that your two boys were being held for all that damage last night. And now, presumably, they've made a getaway. Would you care to give me a statement?"

"No," said Millie.

"Are the boys here, Mrs. Morke? After all, it's their home."

"I have nothing to say," said Millie, hoping she had the formula right.

"Then, presumably, they *are* here? Don't worry, I shan't give them away. Nor do *you* have to give them away. You can just say whatever comes into your head. It doesn't much matter what it is, really."

Millie could see that he was only trying to be kind.

"Nothing. So would you please go? I'm sorry to turn you out, but I'm sure you'll understand."

"Rum tykes, aren't they? Sorry, I suppose that's not a very nice way of talking to their mother. My kid brother told me about the month or whatever it was they spent in the under-seven. They made a mark there all right, from what Matheson had to say. Marked everyone, in fact. Do please give me a statement of some kind, Mrs. Morke. Anything you like. Just anything."

"I'm sorry," said Millie. "I really am. I know you're only doing your job."

"Well, I suppose there's not much more I can do this time, but you're famous now, Mrs. Morke, and there'll be others coming fast in my footsteps. Not that I've missed a scoop. Not personally, that is. I don't suggest that."

"I'm glad," said Millie, meeting his generosity at least half way.

"And I'm sorry you're in trouble, Mrs. Morke. I really am. You're still a very nice-looking girl. If I may put it that way."

"I don't see why you shouldn't," said Millie. "Well, that's it, wouldn't you say?"

Millie opened her handbag and carefully combed her hair. She went upstairs.

Phineas lay there, reading Minutes.

"Phineas! I'm leaving you."

"Oh, please calm down, and let's have breakfast."

"Get it yourself. I'm packing and going. I'll collect the rest of my things as soon as I can. The things that are left. Before the boys smash them too."

"Millie!" cried Phineas, while she bustled around with a quiet efficiency she had not known for years. "Millie, don't you realize that this is the moment in all their lives when our sons are likely to need their mother most? Surely you must see that for yourself? The moment in their lives when *I* need you most too?"

"I've done all I can," said Millie. "You're full of educational theories. Now's the time for you to give them a real trial. You. Not me."

"At least come with me to the Court? Let's have breakfast quietly and consider what line to take. I'm sure the whole thing is quite grossly exaggerated. The police do that, you know. I keep saying so."

"It would be difficult to exaggerate in any way about the boys."

"But you're their mother, Millie!"

"Perhaps that's how I know. You learn nothing."

Replete and bursting though it was, she shut her suitcase with new strength. It still bore her maiden name: MELANIE PIGOTT. Why should she not return to that? When in due course she had left Uncle Stephen's abode and started a life of her own? The green suitcase had been a joint present from her parents on her twenty-first birthday. At the time she had wondered how long the family name would still be hers; but now it might be hers once more, and for a very indefinite period. When empty, the suitcase was delightfully weightless; when full, delightfully substantial.

"I'm not going to bother with good-bye," said Millie.

Phineas clutched at her physically. His overlong arm was as the tentacle of an undernourished octopus.

"Millie, do at least try to be sensible. Just get breakfast, and we'll talk it all over as much as you like."

She threw his elongated hand back on the bedspread.

As she bore her packed suitcase briskly up The Drive, she reflected that two days ago she could hardly have lifted the thing from the bedroom floor.

She wondered how long it would be before the inevitable reaction and collapse.


Uncle Stephen saw to it that Millie wanted for nothing.

Every morning he brought her the loveliest, most fragrant breakfast in bed. Every evening he lingered in her room, tucking her in, adjusting the ventilation and positioning of the curtains, putting away any clothes she had left about, gossiping about the small events of the day, taking away her shoes in order to give them a rub.

He prepared most of the other meals too. As he pointed out, he would have had to feed himself in any case, and having to feed her too made the whole thing into a work of joy. He had many outside engagements: bridge, bowls, the rifle and revolver ranges, the committee of the small amateur soccer club, the British Legion, the Skeleton A.R.P., the Patriotic Alliance (which was often in a state of inner schism, and therefore particularly demanding); but Millie could never for one moment doubt that she constituted the primary demand both upon his heart and even upon his time. The undiagnosed trouble inside Millie had ceased even to demand diagnosis.

"You do spoil me, Uncle Stephen. It's lovely." She lay on the settee in lounging pyjamas and matching surtout (as the manufacturers termed it). She had never been able to bother with garments of that kind before, but now Uncle Stephen had bought them for her at Katja's in the new Vanity Market, and had helped to choose them too. She had rather looked down on such shops and on such clothes, but that had been ignorance and the wrong kind of sophistication. It was almost impossible to believe that Phineas lived only eleven-and-a-half miles away as the crow flew, if any crow should be so misdirected.

"I like being spoilt, Uncle Stephen," said Millie.

"I love to do it, girl. You're all I have, you know that, and always have been."

That must have been what Phineas would have called an exaggeration, but it was true that Uncle Stephen, so far as was known, had at all times "looked after himself." Now he had a thick mop of silky white hair, like a wise old lion; and the same green eyes as his sister, Millie's mother, and as Millie herself.

"All the same, I can't stay for ever," said Millie coyly.

"Why on earth not? First, *I'll* look after *you,* and do it with love in my heart. Then, when I'm past it, *you'll* look after *me*— well, some of the time. In the end, I'll leave you all I've got. I've no one else. Remember that. It's not much. But it will be enough."

"I'll remember, Uncle Stephen, and thank you. All the same, a woman nowadays is expected to lead a life of her own. I was all set to do it."

"You've tried that sort of thing once, girl, and you've seen what happened." Uncle Stephen's eye wandered away from her, which was unusual. "I wish I could put a hand to one of the rattans I used to have."

"What are they, Uncle Stephen?" asked Millie, though really she knew fairly well.

"Disciplinary instruments, my love. Disciplinary instruments. Never had one out of my right hand during all the years I was in the Archipelago."

"I wonder if anything's happened by now?" Millie spoke a little drowsily. The wine at dinner had been South African, and she had fallen badly out of practice.

"You let sleepings dogs lie. Never trouble trouble until trouble troubles you."

She smiled at him. It would be absurd to argue about anything. "Carry me to bed, Uncle Stephen."

She dreamt that she and Thelma Modelle were climbing Everest together. They were both garbed in the latest chic, waterproof, windproof, coldproof clothing, and carried little axes, silvery in the sun. Thelma, the gypsy, was deputizing as a Sherpa. It was all exceedingly enjoyable, and not at all too steep for Millie's new energies. The summit lay straight ahead. They might have tea when they arrived there; or Thelma might have to have ideas of her own about a suitable gypsy celebration.

How many months later was it when Millie opened the *Daily Telegraph* and saw the familiar headline: "Liberal Loses Deposit"? Apparently the sitting member for North Zero had fallen over a cliff, or at least been discovered by children dashed to pieces on the rocks below. The coroner had returned an open verdict, and a by-election had followed. Previously Millie's eyes must have glided over these events.

Uncle Stephen brought her the *Daily Telegraph* or the *Sunday Telegraph* with her early morning tea; and *The Imperialist* every time there was a new issue. That day, when a little later he came up with her breakfast, two small, heavenly-smelling kippers and the perfect toast upon which she could always rely, she was pensive.

"Uncle Stephen, tell me. Did they ever catch those boys? I suspect you know all the time."

"I know nothing that you don't know, little girl."

She eyed him. "What exactly does that mean? Do you know the answer to the question I asked?" She spoke quite roguishly.

"I do not. I know what my answer would be if I only had the chance. Now eat your scrap of porridge, or it'll go cold. I'll sugar it for you."

Millie dragged herself upwards. She really preferred to eat in a sprawling position, but Uncle Stephen liked to see more of her.

"Tell me, Uncle Stephen, have there been any more happenings? Like the one on the night before I left. I simply don't read the reports of things like that."

"That's the self-protective instinct, my little love, and you could do with more of it, not less."

"But have there, Uncle Stephen? I'd rather like to know."

"Nothing that anyone could get a grip on. Or nothing that's come my way. I don't spend all day reading the newspapers. It can get hold of you as poisonously as the television, if you once let it."

"You're hiding something, Uncle Stephen."

"That I am not. There are these violences all over the world every minute of the day. Everyone's a villain without proper discipline. I haven't noticed the names of your two lads in particular."

"And you haven't heard anything locally either?"

"Not a word. I'd be out in no time if I had, after what's been done."

The last words very nearly convinced Millie.

"Let me pour your chocolate," said Uncle Stephen.

But immediately he spoilt it all by speaking further.

"They'll have shot up a lot further by this time," he observed. His eyes were searching round the room, as they always did when the subject of the boys arose.

"Thank you, Uncle Stephen," said Millie, as he stopped pouring. "It's a beautiful breakfast. When I've finished it, I'd like to sleep a little more. Then I'll come down and give you a hand."

He took the hint quite quietly. He merely said, "I see now that you're looking pale. Don't you worry about helping me. I can easily bring up your little lunch when the time comes."

"You *are* good to me, Uncle Stephen."

But, as soon as he had left the room and closed the door, Millie began to heave; and in no time, while trying to muffle the noise, she was being copiously sick into the article provided in well-found houses for that and other purposes: as sick as she had been, without cessation as it had seemed, during the long months before the two boys were born.

Really there could be no question of Millie even attempting to lead a life of her own as, like so many women, she had originally, in a vague way, intended. She was afraid to leave the house, and even more so after what Uncle Stephen had so casually said.

That she had good reason to lie low was confirmed by the episodes that followed.

It was more than a year after Millie had left Phineas, and the gold of summer was fast dissolving into the copper of autumn, when one night Millie stirred in her sleep to see a big face pressed against the panes of her first-floor bedroom window. Whether it was Angus's face or Rodney's face, which of their faces, she would probably not by now have known in any case. It was an unseemly blot on the October moonlight, then it ducked.

What was more, her window was open, as at night it always was. The boy was far too big to climb right in, but he could easily have inserted a huge arm, perhaps reached to the bed, and then strangled or humiliated her. Millie had realized from the first that the boys must have a perfectly clear idea of where she was, even though she emerged so seldom, and Uncle Stephen never recommended otherwise What had decided the boys to re-enter her life now? She had seen only one of them, but was sure that the other was there also, because the other always was. She suspected that by now their combined strength could throw down the entire house. And very possibly they were growing still. Boys by no means always cease to grow at sixteen or seventeen.

She drew on her kimono and ran to Uncle Stephen's room. She knocked on his door, as she had done before when hungry during the night, or when merely lonely.

"Come in, girl. Come in."

"Uncle Stephen. The boys are back. One of them has just looked through my window in the moonlight. I think I'm going to be sick again."

"Come in with me, little love. I'll look after you and protect you. That's what I'm doing in your life. That's what I'm here for. You know that."

Fortunately, it was a very large bed. Uncle Stephen had brought it back from the East; from gorgeous, sanctified Goa, now for ever lost.

"When I.was young, I could never in my life have even imagined anything so frightening," said Millie. "Not until the boys were born. Or actually a little before that. When Phineas and I were on our honeymoon. In France, and then in the marshes behind Ariano. I never dared to read horror stories and ghost stories." She snuggled towards Uncle Stephen.

"No man and no woman knows anything of the troubles they are going to meet with in life. Or I take it they'd succeed in dodging them," said Uncle Stephen. "They're supposed to be sent to form and mould us, but my idea is to form and mould *them* whenever possible. Remember that."

"You're the most wonderful uncle," Millie murmured, though she was still shivering and gulping.

"I'll stay with you ten minutes while you calm down and arrange your pinafore, and then I'm going hunting."

"No, Uncle Stephen! It's too dangerous. They're watching the house. They're *immense*."

"Many times in my life I've been under siege. Each time, in the end, I burst out and destroyed everything in sight. I'm hard to hold, Millie."

"Things have changed since those days, Uncle Stephen. It's sad, but it's true. *The Imperialist* admits it. That was the bit I read you, when you ordered me to stop. There's nothing for either of us to do nowadays but escape. A fortune-teller told me that last year, and now it's come true."

"I know all about times changing, none better," said Uncle Stephen, holding her close. "The fact remains that *I* have *not* changed. I am older, unfortunately, but otherwise exactly the same. Also I have weapons, I have strategy and tactics, and I have experience. I am going to give those cubs the lesson they've needed since their first birthday. I learned, my little love, to deal with growing boys in a harder school than Eton and Harrow or any of those places."

"I'm not going to let you try. You're overconfident. Those two are like children of the future." She was appalled. "Perhaps they *are* children of the future?"

"I'll admit that they're too big for their boots," said Uncle Stephen drily.

"If you go anywhere near them they'll harm you. We're just going to wait for the daylight. I'll stay with you if you'll let me. Then we'll steal away somewhere for a bit. Somewhere nice. You've always said you could afford it, if only circumstances had been different. Well, circumstances *are* different, whether we like it or not. We could go and stay in an hotel at Southhampton, and you could look at the different ships going to places. You would like that, wouldn't you?"

"And if everyone behaved in that way?" enquired Uncle Stephen. "If everyone did, what would become of our country? Things are rough enough already. You're as bad as that so-called man of yours, Millie." But he spoke affectionately, none the less, cuddling and caressing her, not meaning his comparison very seriously.

"Uncle Stephen, don't be silly. They're not ordinary boys you can either pamper or stand in the corner. They're *enormous*. I told you what the man from the police station said. They're quite beyond handling by any single individual."

"All I know is that they're boys, and that's quite enough. I don't want to leave you alone, as you know perfectly well, my little pet, but I'm going. You just lie in my bed until I'm back. And don't worry. I'm here to keep you from all harm. And I have weapons. Remember that."

He squeezed her hand, and clambered out into the night.

Soon he was on the roof, directly above her. She could hear the slotting of iron into iron, or was it nowadays steel into steel? When she had lived beside the Heath as a small child during the Second World War, the A.T.S. girls operating the antiaircraft unit concealed among the evergreen gorse had made that noise all day as they took the long guns to pieces and put them together again. Uncle Stephen possessed artillery of his own. It was included in the weapons he had mentioned; nor did it consist in a couple of squat, serio-comic muzzle-loading Peninsular War mortars, looking like pugs On the contrary, Uncle Stephen could mount at least three quite modern-looking pieces, painted not black but dark green as gorse, and palpably requiring expert knowledge to discharge satisfactorily; the kind of knowledge that the girls on the Heath had been acquiring during the daytime. He had explained to Millie that these guns were designed by the authorities primarily for withstanding a concerted rush. She wondered when he had managed to dismantle at least one of them in the room downstairs and reassemble it on the roof of the house without her hearing or noticing a thing. She might have been impressed by his foresight, but instead resurrected her suspicions that Uncle Stephen had all along known something that he had failed to pass on.

There was a flash and a crash: quite startlingly like 6.30 or 7.30 p.m. when Millie had been but a tot.

Another and another. Millie fully realized that this could not continue for long; not in the modern world. Somehow it would be stopped, however justified it might be, even by the narrowest legalistic standard of self-defense and of protecting an unarmed mother.

Concurrently, Millie was subdued by a confused mêlée of feeling about Angus and Rodney; even though she had never been able within herself to accept that they were authentically her own offspring.

A shadow passed between the moon and the casement. Surely the boys should have been intelligent enough to take cover? How, without doing so, had either of them survived Uncle Stephen's cannonade? Uncle Stephen was the least likely of men to aim and then miss. He kept in continual practice, as in so many directions.

Another flash and crash: though this time in the latter was a curious rending sound, as if the gun barrel were about to burst asunder. Millie had heard of guns soldering up through being fired continuously day and night. Probably Uncle Stephen's gun had not of late been fired often enough to be in prime condition. Millie realized the danger that Uncle Stephen might be running from the gun exploding within itself and shattering into smithereens, as she understood that guns not infrequently did.

But by now the official legions were massing. Millie could hear outer-space blastings of fire engines, of ambulances, of police cars; and between them the insect whinings of television pantechnicons and radar. It was much as the moment when an escape from a concentration camp is first notified. She ran to the window.

Functionaries were swarming over and around machines to make sure that nothing remained unaccounted for in the designated area, except criminally. It was an ideal spot for such an operation, as Uncle Stephen's house stood in comparative isolation at a corner of the woods; a public open space owned by the Council.

Millie ran back to her own room. It would be most unwise to turn on a light, and possibly the current had already been chopped at the main. In any case, public lights were beginning to range: brutal searchlights, and the torture-chamber arc lights necessary for television.

Millie tore off her nightdress. She plunged into her jeans and a thick sweater which Uncle Stephen had bought for her at the supply stores where he bought many of his own garments. She had lost her handkerchief and took out a clean one.

For these simple actions the case was cogent enough. But Millie then hesitated. Uncle Stephen had stopped firing, and Millie could but speculate upon the exact reason. She could not possibly bring herself to desert Uncle Stephen, but the thing of which she was most certain was that the two of them could not win. She suspected that Uncle Stephen really knew that as well as she did. So what then?

Cautiously, she re-entered Uncle Stephen's bedroom. The beam of light which now filled it illuminated nothing human or real. In her short absence, the room had been killed.

Millie realized that Uncle Stephen was in difficulties. The gun was refusing to fire, as cars sometimes refuse to start. Uncle Stephen was tinkering with it, bashing it, cursing it. Soon, in the nature of things, the functionaries would close in finally; nor would it be a concerted attack of the kind which the gun was designed to ward off. It would be more a matter of irresistible infiltration, worked out long before in every detail, standard practice, precluding all possibility of topographical variation.

Millie ascended the attic ladder to the rooftree. "Uncle Stephen!" she called down to him.

Absorbed though he was in his male task, he looked up at once.

"Go back," he cried out. "Go back, little Millie."

"What's up, Uncle Stephen? What's gone wrong?" Nothing else was possible than to enter into things as he saw them.

"The boys have won this round, Millie. We must admit that. They've put the gun right out of action."

"But how, Uncle Stephen?"

"It's some kind of schoolboy muck. They dropped a whole gob of it into the breech. Clever monkeys, we must admit."

Millie had almost forgotten the boys; incredible though that seemed.

"Where are they now?"

"I'll bet they've made off. They don't have much more to do, just at this moment."

Millie glanced anxiously round amid the confused and inhuman lights. But she knew that for a second she had almost wished the boys had still been there; as some kind of reassurance against all that was developing.

"I said I was here to protect you," affirmed Uncle Stephen, "and I shall do it still. I have always won the last battle. Always and always."

"Come away with me, Uncle Stephen, while there's time."

He went through burlesque bristling motions. "You don't suppose I shall knuckle down to a couple of schoolboys with their pockets full of gum." He expressed it facetiously, but of course he meant it, could hardly have meant it more.

Now that the firing had ceased for some time, the encircling host had begun to relax. Cups of tea were being consumed; ambulance workers were chatting to firemen on familiar subjects, their respective rates of pay and conditions of employment, their pension prospects, the maladies of their dear ones.

"Oh, come on, Uncle Stephen. If the boys have gone, we can go too."

To her consternation, he was not to be budged. "No, girl," he said. "This is my home, my castle, as we used to say; and perhaps by now it's your home and castle too. Wouldn't you say that's very nearly true, Millie?" He had given up fiddling with the gun, and was addressing himself to something even more important.

"The boys will return," she said. "When all the people have gone. And you'll be in endless trouble for firing that gun in any case, even though I know you did it for my sake."

"All my guns are licensed, Millie. I'm a registered holder of firearms. And as for the boys, let them come. I want nothing better. They've won a battle. They won't win the war. They're hulking brutes, but they're still only schoolboys. Look at this." Uncle Stephen displayed the mess on his hands and combat suit.

"We shan't feel the same about the house ever again, Uncle Stephen. You must know that."

"If we were all to let ideas of that kind govern our lives, we'd all be homeless." Uncle Stephen sat back on the semidismantled gun. "You mustn't suppose, girl, that I don't know what you mean. It's simply that not one thing in life is ever gained by running away. This is our home, yours and mine, and here we stay."

"I'm afraid of the boys coming back," said Millie. "I'm terrified."

The big lights were being turned out, one after another. It is often noticeable that they are in use only for a few minutes. By now Millie was unsure whether she preferred the crude glare or the deep darkness.

Someone was hammering at the front door. It was of course inevitable, sooner or later. Probably it had been going on at a lesser intensity for some time.

Millie dropped down the attic ladder and flitted through the dark house like a noctambule. She was not going to wait for any nonsense from Uncle Stephen about taking no notice. All the same, at the foot of the stairs she stood and called out. After all, it might conceivably be the boys.

"Who's there?" In the hall, the trophies were shaggy as a tropical forest.

"I'm a police officer, madam. Kindly open the door."

She knew the voice. She slipped the chain and drew the big bolts in a trice.

"We're old friends, officer."

All the same, he showed his card, and said, "Detective-Sergeant Meadowsweet." Millie smiled. "May we have some light on the scene, madam?"

"Would that be safe?"

"Safe as could be, madam. The two men have been sighted miles away, and we're closing in steadily."

"Oh!" gasped Millie. "So you know?"

"Of course we know, madam. What else did you think we were doing here? Now, I just want you to tell me all that's taken place. After that, I must have a word with the gentleman upstairs who's been treating himself to a little pistol practice."

"I hope he's not done any damage."

"No particular damage that we know of, but that's more by luck than judgment, wouldn't you say?"

"He's got all the necessary licenses."

"We know that, madam, but he happens not to have a license to fire at intruders, because no such license exists. Jobs of that kind must be left to the police. It sometimes causes hardship, but it's the law, and a gentleman with all those different licenses knows better than most what they permit him to do, and what not."

"Perhaps I should say," put in Millie, "that the gentleman's my uncle. He kindly took me in after the trouble we had a year ago. A little *more* than a year, actually."

"I could see at the time that your husband wasn't much help," said Detective-Sergeant Meadowsweet in his inimitable way; and then duly added, "If you don't mind my saying so, madam. '

"Oh no, I don't mind," said Millie. "Phineas was utterly wet from first to last. The whole thing was the biggest mistake I ever made. Not that 'mistake' is quite a strong enough word. But do sit down, Sergeant."

"I take it," said the Detective-Sergeant as he did so, "that the two men were attempting to force an entrance? Tonight, I mean."

"They're really only boys," said Millie, "absurd though it seems."

"I don't think we need to go over that ground again, madam. If you remember, we covered it very fully when Mr. Morke was there. So the two of them were attempting to force an entrance?"

"Well, not exactly, as I have to admit. What happened was simply that I saw one of them out on the lawn and rather lost my head. You know what they look like, Sergeant? How enormous they are?"

"Yes, we know very well, madam. Don't you worry about that. The approved school couldn't hold them for a week. The Tower of London would be more the thing, I'd say. So what happened then?"

"They're so strong too. I admit that I'm frightened to think about it. But of course you know about that too."

The Sergeant nodded. He had settled himself on the big black stool from somewhere in French West Africa. Millie had been given to understand that, before the French came, the potentate whose official seat it had been (perhaps even throne) had at times waded through blood almost to the knees. She had difficulty in remembering which of the different regions the different things came from; especially as Uncle Stephen had shifted in midcareer from the fairly Far East to Africa, and then back to the East. The legs of the stool were decorated with small projecting bones and teeth, inserted into the woodwork. Above the Detective-Sergeant's head flapped a faded rushwork curtain originally intended, Uncle Stephen had said, to deter the flesh-eating birds and bats from entering one's room during the night.

"So what happened then, madam?"

"I admit that I completely lost my head, and ran in to my uncle, who took steps to defend me. No more than that."

Another voice broke in. "I take full responsibility, officer."

Uncle Stephen had appeared at the top of the stairs. He had changed into his usual sharply-pressed trousers and camel-hair jacket. "The situation was extremely menacing. I was protecting my own flesh and blood against a couple of thugs."

"Yes, sir, they're a nasty enough pair, according to all the evidence. The police are fed to the teeth with them, I can tell you that."

"Very good of you to confirm what I say, officer. I am sorry I had to take the law into my own hands, but you'll agree that I had every justification. I've spent most of my life in places where you have to think quickly the whole time, or you find yourself dead. Worse than dead. May I suggest that we say no more about it? Let me give you a stiff whisky before you go?"

"We're not supposed to drink while we're on duty, sir."

"Of course not," said Uncle Stephen. "I have served with the police myself. In several different parts of the globe."

A little later, when the three of them were sitting amicably together, Millie began to feel intensely sad.

"I cannot help feeling partially responsible," she blurted out. "Do you think, Sergeant, there's anything to be done? Anything, even in theory, that *I* could do? Any possibility?"

At once Uncle Stephen shouted out, "Clap them in irons, I should hope. Use straitjackets, if necessary. Though you'd have to have them specially made big enough. And then you've got to lay hold of the boys first. Eh, officer? They won the first round against *me*, you know."

"We'll manage that all right, sir," replied Detective-Sergeant Meadowsweet. "The police don't fancy having the mickey taken out of them by two overgrown kids. Which is what you and Mr. Morke both said they were, madam."

"But what can be done *then*?" persisted Millie, though somewhat against the grain, as she was perfectly well, although confusedly, aware. "Is there *anything* that I could do?"

"All I am permitted to say is that it will then be a matter for the proper authorities." The Detective-Sergeant thought for a few seconds and, in his characteristic way, he added: "I wish them the best of British luck with it."

Unfortunately, it soon proved that the Detective-Sergeant had been mistaken at the precise point where he had shown most confidence: his conviction that Angus and Rodney would be finally apprehended in virtually no time.

A week passed and there was no hint or rumour of an arrest. On the other hand, Uncle Stephen had no further trouble with the authorities. There were questions at the next two Parish Council meetings, but nothing was permitted to come out of them. As for the two young giants themselves, they appeared to have gone into hiding, difficult though that must have been; or perhaps it was that they were passing unnoticed amidst the freaks and zanies that people urban and suburban areas in the later part of the twentieth century. Millie, however, remembering the pair, found that hard to believe; and shivered when recollection fell for a while into full focus.

None the less, she had begun to go out once more: shopping, visiting the library, even attending a lecture on Criminology by an Austrian refugee. Uncle Stephen was fiercely opposed to all these excursions, and, to please him (as she would have expressed it to a confidante), she gave two undertakings: that she would never be parted from a tiny gun he lent her; and that for any longer journey she would take his car and not lightly step out of it or turn off the engine. Before she was married, Millie had driven all the time. Uncle Stephen's car was a beautiful old Alvis. Millie loved muffling herself up in order to drive it; and it had the advantage that then she was not easily identifiable. The gun went into the pocket of her jeans, where it was no more noticeable than a compact. It fired special tiny bullets which, as Uncle Stephen confided, were, strictly speaking, illegal: a steady stream of them, if necessary; and it fired them almost silently.

Uncle Stephen was at his best when instructing Millie on midweek mornings in the small orchard.

These things were advances, and Millie had no doubt about how much Uncle Stephen loved and needed her; but the whole thing amounted to little more than a half-life, when all was said and done. Millie had no very precise idea of what the other half might consist in, still less of how best to go after it; but she missed it none the less, as people do. In the end, she decided finally that there was no sensible alternative to a further consultation with Thelma Modelle.

She had, of course, been aware of this for some time, and had continued to dream about Thelma quite frequently, but it meant returning to the other suburb, the suburb where she had lived for years with Phineas and the boys; so that she had hesitated and hesitated. Uncle Stephen would have had a fit if he had known what she was proposing.

Then one morning it became unbearable, as things suddenly do. It was a premonition or other compulsion.

She tied up her hair in a dark green scarf, donned heavy-duty garments, and tucked in the ends of her knotted, paler green muffler; all without a word to Uncle Stephen except to the effect that she wanted some different air and would very likely die without it. It was not a very gracious thing to say but it was essential to seem adamant.

"Drive fast," said Uncle Stephen anxiously. "Never slow down unless you absolutely have to. And be ready for anything."

She knew by now what that meant.

"Of course, Uncle Stephen," she said, "I'll be fine."

"I ought by rights to come with you, and look after you, but it's not safe to leave the house on its own. You know how it is, Millie."

"I know."

"Luckily, I went over the car this morning while you were sleeping. She'll go like the wind. See to it that she does. There's a girl."

"That's what I'm going to do." She was tying an *eau-de-Nil* silk scarf round the lower part of her face.

"Goodbye, my sweet."

Through the tight scarf, Uncle Stephen kissed her lips.

She roared away, but really there was a traffic light round the first bend, and always it was red. Uncle Stephen must have known that even better than she knew it.

None the less, she had a perfectly authentic disinclination to linger; and as the other suburb came nearer, one of her hands dropped half-consciously from the wheel and rested for longer and longer periods upon the reassuring object in her pocket.

The Parade, once again; the Lavender Bag; the fish shop! The fish shop was now even more diversified in its wares than when she had seen it last: now there was hardly a fish in sight. Millie felt no nostalgia; nothing but nausea.

She brought the Alvis to rest as unobtrusively as was possible with such a machine; and darted upstairs in her full rig. She had no more made an appointment than on the previous occasion.

But this time the visionary did not greet her upon the landing, and the door of the sanctum, once the rheumatism lady's little sitting room, was shut.

Millie hesitated for some little time. After all, she was presumably hidden from observation, and could give a moment or two to thinking and deciding. Most probably, Thelma's practice had grown since those first days, so that by now a client would have to be specially fitted in. Alternatively, Thelma might have failed and gone. Or gone, anyway. Communities are full of neat or braggart labels referring to vanished enterprises.

Millie timidly tapped.

"What is it?" The voice was Thelma's.

How could Millie explain? It was best to open and enter.

Thelma sat on the floor by the rheumatism lady's miniature gas fire. The black table, with its attendant black chairs, had been pushed into a corner. The zodiacal wall cards hung at madder angles than ever. Thelma herself wore what looked like the same green jeans, though they also looked a year and more older; and a battle-dress tunic, dyed dark blue by the authorities. It could be deduced that business was less than brisk.

"Oh, it's you."

Thelma did not get up, and this time it was Millie who stood.

"Yes, it's me. I want to know what's happening now. Exactly, please. What's happening at this very moment, if possible."

"Well, in that case you'd better shut the door."

Millie complied. She perceived that she should have done it in the first place. At least Thelma had not specifically demurred.

"And you'd better take off your clothes."

"Some of them," said Millie, smiling.

She had unwound the silk scarf from her face before entering. Now she climbed out of the heavy-duty garments and threw them on the floor, where they lay like prehistoric monsters, alive or dead, as the case might be. The rheumatism lady had presumably arranged to take away her carpets since Millie had last been there, because now the boards were bare. They were also mottled, but that happens soon and mysteriously in almost any house.

"Leave that," said Thelma sharply, as Millie was about to unwind the dark green scarf which confined her locks.

Millie desisted. Her brow was moist.

"Take off your sweater if you're too hot," said Thelma.

Millie shook her head.

"This time I shall need your money," said Thelma. "You can't depend entirely on my good will. I might need a new dress. Have you thought of that?"

"How much money?" asked Millie, still on her feet.

"How much have you got with you?"

"Can't you see without asking me?"

"Yes," said Thelma. "Forty pounds in fivers, and ten single pounds. You must want to know badly."

"I do," said Millie calmly. For some reason, Thelma, no matter what her words or deeds, never upset her, as so many people did, even when saying or doing very little. Thelma was like Uncle Stephen in that.

"I'll take forty-nine pounds of it. You may need a pound suddenly when you leave." Millie had noticed before that Thelma was surprisingly well-spoken in her own way.

"Only if you tell me what I've asked you to tell me and tell me the truth and the whole truth."

Thelma shot Millie a confusing glance. Though intense, it was not necessarily hostile.

Then she arose from the floor and drew the curtains across the single window. They were not the rheumatism lady's pretty chintz, but heavy, dun, and unshaped. As they were touched and moved, they smelt. It was as if old clothes were being draped before the fairy windows of a wagon.

Thelma locked the door.

"I'm not locking you in. You can leave any time you like."

And Millie could indeed see that the key was still there.

Thelma lifted the crystal and placed it on the floor. Sure enough, it was much smaller than Millie had always supposed such gadgets to be. Perhaps they came in different sizes, according to the purchaser's needs and resources?

The only light was from under the door and from the small yellow gas fire. The room was odorous as well as stuffy.

Thelma signalized this fact by throwing off her dark-blue tunic. Beneath it she wore a fragile pinkish garment with big rents in it, through which her brown skin could be seen by what light there was. Her mop of hair was uncombed and uneven in length.

"Do what I am doing," directed Thelma; and added, "If you really must go on with this."

When Millie made no answer, Thelma wriggled down on the floor until she lay at full length upon her front with the crystal about two inches before her eyes.

She looked ridiculous; or any other woman in her position would have looked ridiculous. Millie had supposed that crystal-gazing was done seated at a table. Moreover, a very suitable table was in the room with them.

"I advised you to take off your sweater," said Thelma. "Why not be more friendly?"

Millie continued calm. Upon the passage to truth, cross-currents are to be expected.

"I'm all right," she said, and lay down upon her front on the diametrical other side of the small crystal. She rested her chin upon her two hands, as Thelma was doing. At these close quarters, Thelma's lupine aroma was very pungent. Millie tried to concentrate upon gazing into the crystal. She assumed that to be the right thing to do. If only the crystal had been proportioned for a mature woman instead of for a waif!

But that matter began to adjust itself, and before Millie had had time even to begin feeling physically uncomfortable. As she gazed through the crystal at Thelma's rock-pool eyes, the yellow light from the gas fire turned blue; and the circumference of the crystal expanded and expanded, as did Thelma's orbs on the other side of it. Indeed, Millie realized quite clearly that it must always have been impossible for her to have seen Thelma's eyes *through* the actual crystal. All anyone could really have seen *through* it, would have been Thelma's nose and a small distance on either side of it.

Incandescent with darting blue lights, the crystal grew until it filled the room, until it *was* the room, and Thelma's eyes were no longer there, as if her face had split vertically down the middle and her eyes had rolled away round the polished sphere, each in a different direction.

But by now Millie was in a room no longer. Nor was she lying inconveniently upon her front. On the contrary, she was in a small woodland clearing and was observing with perfect ease what therein transpired.

The two boys were sitting, rather absurdly jammed together, on a tree trunk. It was not a whole fallen giant of the forest, but a neatly sawn-off section, awaiting the arrival of the timber float and its tractor, or perhaps left there by intention as a nature seat for wooers, an accessory to picnics. In fact, the boys, ravenous as ever, were at that moment engaged upon a picnic of their own.

Each boy held in his hand a very large, very red bone, from which he was gnawing in the frenzied manner that Millie remembered so well.

On the worn, wintry grass before them lay what was left of a human body.

The boys had already eaten their way through most of it, so that it could not even be described as a skeleton or semi-skeleton. The disjoined bones were everywhere strewn about at random, and only the top part of the frame, the upper ribs, remained in position, together with the half-eaten head.

It was Phineas' head.

Things swam.

Millie felt that her soul was rushing up a shaft at the center of her body. She knew that this is what it was to die.

But she did not die.

She realized that now she was lying on her back in the still darkened room. Thelma must have moved her. The gas fire was as yellow as before, no doubt because there was something wrong with it; and Thelma in her pink rags and dirty jeans was standing before her, even looking down at her.

"You've been out a long time."

"I wish I were still out."

"*You* may, but I don't. I've things to do. You forget that."

Millie hesitated.

"Did you see them too?"

"Of course I saw them. Remember I asked you whether you really had to go on with it."

"What else could I do?"

"I don't know. I'm not your nursemaid."

Millie sat up. "If you pass me my handbag, I'll pay you."

Thelma passed it. It did not seem to have been rifled during Millie's anaesthesia.

"Perhaps we could have a little more light?" suggested Millie.

Thelma threw on her tunic and, without fastening it, began to draw back or take down the window coverings. Millie did not examine which it was.

She rose to her feet. Had Thelma been behaving differently, she, Millie, would have been shaking all over, still prostrate. She seated herself on one of the dusty black chairs. She counted out forty-nine pounds on to the black table in the corner. Then she gazed for a moment straight into Thelma's vatic eyes. At once the sensations of a few moments before (or of what seemed a few moments) faintly recurred. Millie felt dragged out of herself, and turned her face to the dingy wall.

"You can stay if you wish. You know that." Thelma made no attempt to take up the money; though Millie could be in small doubt that the sum would make a big difference for Thelma, at least temporarily.

"You can't expect me to keep open house for you always."

Millie turned a little and, without again looking at Thelma, attempted a smile of some kind.

"I shan't be around much longer," said Thelma. "Surely you can see that?"

Millie stood up. "Where will you go?"

"I shall go back to decent people. I should never have left them."

"What made you?"

"I killed a girl."

"I see."

"I did right."

There was a pause: a need (perhaps on both sides) for inner regrouping. It was a metaphor that Uncle Stephen might have approved.

Millie gathered herself together. "Is that the sort of thing *I* ought to do?"

"How can I tell? Why ask *me*? You must decide for yourself."

Millie gathered herself together a second time. It was difficult to petition. The forty-nine pounds still lay untouched on the hocus-pocus table. "You *can* tell, Thelma, I know you can. They're obscene, monstrous, all those words. You know as well as I do. You're the only one who does. I feel responsible for them. Is it what I ought to do? Tell me."

Thelma seemed actually to reflect for a moment; instead of darting out a reply like the double tongue of a snake, the flick of a boxing second's towel, as she usually did.

"You're not the kind," said Thelma. "It would be beyond you."

"Then what? Help me, Thelma. Please, please help me."

"I told you before. Run away."

Millie stared blankly at the entire, round, empty, world.

"Be more friendly and you can lie up with *me*. I keep saying so. But soon I shan't be here. I have debts."

Millie wondered with what currency Thelma proposed to settle.

"Hurry up and put the money away somewhere," Millie said.

But Thelma again spoke to the point: "I'll place my right hand on your heart and you'll place yours on mine. Then we'll be friends."

Millie glanced at Thelma's ragged pink garment, but all she said was, "It wouldn't be fair." Then she added, "Thank you all the same." What a depraved, common way to express gratitude, she thought.

There was a tapping at the locked door.

"Who's that?" asked Millie, as if she really did live there.

Thelma had leapt upon the money like a cheetah and shoved it hugger-mugger into her jeans.

"It's Agnes Waterfield. She comes every day at this hour."

"God! I don't want to meet *her*," cried Millie.

"Well, you'll have to," said Thelma, and unlocked the door on the instant.

Millie could only snatch her garments and scuttle away like a cat, hoping that Agnes might be too involved in her own troubles and preoccupations to recognize her, though not really believing it.

Outside, it had begun to snow. The big open car was spattered with separate flakes.

Millie sped away. Soon the suburb which had once been home was miles behind.

The straggling and diminishing woodlands touched the road at several places before one reached the main section in which lay Uncle Stephen's house. The ground was hummocky here, and nowadays the road ran through several small cuttings, ten or twelve feet high, in order to maintain a more or less constant level for the big lorries, and to give the tearaway tourists an illusion for a minute or two that they were traversing the Rocky Mountains. There were even bends in the road which had not yet been straightened, and all the trees in sight were conifers.

Thinking only of sanctuary, Millie tore round one of these bends (much too fast, but almost everyone did it, and few with Millie's excellent reason); and there were the two boys blocking the way, tall as Fiona Macleod's lordly ones, muscular as Gogmagog, rising high above the puny banks of earth. It was a busy road and they could only a moment before have dropped down into it. Beneath the snow patches on their clothing, Millie could clearly see the splashes of blood from their previous escapade. The boys were so placed that Millie had to stop.

"Got any grub, Mum?"

Quite truthfully, she could no longer tell one twin from the other.

"That's all we ask, Mum," said the other twin. "We're hungry."

"We don't want to outgrow our strength," said the first twin, just as in the old days.

"Let's search," cried the second twin. Forbearance was extinguished by appetite.

The two boys were now on the same side of the car.

Millie, who had never seen herself as a glamorous mistress of the wheel, managed something that even Uncle Stephen might have been proud of in the old, dead days at Brooklands. She wrenched the car round on to the other side of the highway, somehow evaded the towering French truck charging towards her, swept back to her proper lane, and was fast on her way.

But there was such a scream, perhaps two such screams, that, despite herself, she once more drew up.

She looked back.

The snow was falling faster now; even beginning to lie on the car floor. She was two or three hundred yards from the accident. What accident? She had to find out. It would be better to drive back rather than to walk: even in the modern world, the authorities would not yet have had time to appear and close the road. Again Millie wheeled.

The two vast figures lay crushed on the highway. They had been standing locked together gazing after her, after the car in which there might have been sweets or biscuits; so that in death, as in life, they were not divided. They had been killed by a police vehicle: naturally one of the heavier models. Millie had underestimated the instancy of modernity. The thing stood there, bluely lighted and roaring.

"It was you we were after, miss," remarked the police officer, as soon as Millie came more to a standstill. All the police were ignoring the snow completely. "You were speeding. And now look what's happened."

"If you ask Detective-Sergeant Meadowsweet, he will explain to you why I was going fast." Millie shivered. "I have to go fast."

"We shall make enquiries, but no individual officer is empowered to authorize a breach of the law."

By the time the usual particulars had been given and taken, the ambulance had arrived, screaming and flashing with determination; but it was proving impossible to insert the two huge bodies into it. The men were doing all they could, and the police had surrounded the area with neat little objects, like bright toys; but anyone not immediately involved could see that the task was hopeless.

The snow was falling more heavily every minute, so that by the time Millie was once more left alone among the traffic surging round the frail barrier, the two boys were looking like the last scene in "Babes in the Wood," except that the babes had changed places, and changed roles, with the giants.